W9-CDZ-386

THE LARGER-THAN-LIFE LAVETTES ARE BACK!

Barbara Lavette—Tough, headstrong, torn between love and conscience. She had lost a lover in one war, a husband in another. She would brave the nation's wrath to keep her son from dying in a third.

Carson Devron—Barbara's second husband. He had a god's good looks and a fortune in his pocket. But all that couldn't make him a man —a man who could keep Barbara.

Sam Cohen—Barbara's gentle, tormented son. To find himself, he would follow the footsteps of a father he had never known—into the furnace of war itself.

Tom Lavette—Barbara's brother. He owned a third of California and a piece of the President. He would do anything to get more—even betray his own blood.

Fred Lavette—Tom's son. He hated everything his father stood for. His beliefs would make him a front-line casualty in a war fought in his own country.

Books by Howard Fast

*In Dell Editions

QUANTITY SALES

Most Dell Books are available at special quantity discounts when purchased in bulk by corporations, organizations, and special-interest groups. Custom imprinting or excerpting can also be done to fit special needs. For details write: Dell Publishing Co., Inc., 1 Dag Hammarskjold Plaza, New York, NY 10017, Attn.: Special Sales Dept.,or phone: (212) 605-3319.

INDIVIDUAL SALES

Are there any Dell Books you want but cannot find in your local stores? If so, you can order them directly from us. You can get any Dell book in print. Simply include the book's title, author, and ISBN number, if you have it, along with a check or money order (no cash can be accepted) for the full retail price plus 75¢ per copy to cover shipping and handling. Mail to: Dell Readers Service, Dept. FM, P.O. Box 1000, Pine Brook, NJ 07058.

THE LEGACY

HOWARD FAST

A DELL BOOK

Published by
Dell Publishing Co., Inc.
1 Dag Hammarskjold Plaza
New York, New York 10017

This book is published by special arrangement
    with Eric Lasher and Maureen Lasher.

Copyright © 1981 by Howard Fast

All rights reserved. No part of this book may be reproduced or transmitted
in any form or by any means, electronic or mechanical, including
photocopying, recording, or by any information storage and retrieval
system, without the written permission of the Publisher, except where
permitted by law. For information address: Houghton Mifflin Company,
Boston, Massachusetts.

Dell ® TM 681510, Dell Publishing Co., Inc.

ISBN: 0-440-14720-4

Reprinted by arrangement with Houghton Mifflin Company

Printed in the United States of America

One Previous Dell Edition

February 1987

10 9 8 7 6 5 4 3 2 1

WFH

For Rachel and Jonathan,
my dear friends and advisers in the art of living

ONE

A visitor to San Francisco in the late 'fifties might well have been advised that along with the cable cars, the Coit Tower, and the Golden Gate Bridge, he should look for Big Dan Lavette. While not nearly as well known as the above, except locally, Dan Lavette was nevertheless a sort of civic fixture, and almost any morning, the weather being tolerable, he could be found striding along the Embarcadero with his wife, Jean. Asking for further facts, the visitor would be told to look for a large, heavyset man, somewhat over six feet in height, with a shock of curly snow-white hair and a brown face as lined and creased as a relief map of Northern California. He would most likely be wearing gray flannels and an Irish hand-knit pullover and his arm would be linked with the arm of a handsome, white-haired woman almost as tall as he was. From the Ferry Building to Fisherman's Wharf, they knew every shopkeeper, sidewalk vendor, fisherman, and Embarcadero drifter and walker.

Usually by nine o'clock, the Lavettes had left their home on Russian Hill and were headed down Leavenworth toward the bay, but now and again, in the summertime, when the press of tourists on the

Embarcadero becomes very heavy, they would drive to Golden Gate Park and do their walking between the Japanese Tea Garden and the Pacific Ocean, and back. They were good walkers, and after almost half a century of knowing each other, their silences were as pertinent and as comfortable as their conversation.

On this morning, during the last week of August, they had decided to take their morning stroll in Golden Gate Park. The weather had turned chilly, as it sometimes does in August, and the Pacific mist that enveloped the city showed no sign of dissipating. Once they were in the park, Jean wondered whether this might not be a better day to build a fire in Dan's study and have a cocktail before lunch. Dan was ready to agree, but he pointed out that in the mist, the Japanese garden had a haunting and unusual beauty, and since they were there, why not settle for a walk through the Tea Garden.

"As my master desires," Jean said.

"Right, old lady. That's the way I like to hear it put." Jean was wearing a gray pleated skirt and a white cashmere sweater, and her husband eyed her approvingly as she got out of the car. "You look good today."

"Not every day?"

"I like what you're wearing."

"It's old, and it has no style."

"Well, that puts me in my place."

"No, Danny boy, that makes it all the more delicious flattery, and flattery at age sixty-eight is very special." She took his arm, and they began to walk along the twisting paths of the Tea Garden. They had the place to themselves; not another soul was in sight.

Then, coming around a patch of shrubbery, they faced two men, young men in their middle twenties, wearing jeans, T-shirts and tight leather jackets. One of them had stringy, light, streaked hair that fell to his shoulders; the other was darker, low sideburns, a heavy chin. The one with the light, streaked hair had pale eyes, and he had a long, slender switchblade in his hand. He was nervously alert, on his toes, his body vibrating slightly. The darker one had a set of brass knuckles on his clenched right fist. The light-haired man was tall and well built; the other was smaller and slight.

"O.K., pops," said the one with the knife. "Empty your pockets. And you, lady, just drop your purse."

"Sure," Dan agreed. "Take it easy. No trouble at all." He felt Jean's clutch on his arm tighten, and he whispered to her, "Let go of me, baby." She let go of his arm and dropped her purse to the ground.

"No whispering," the small man said, grinning. "We want to hear it all."

"There's over a hundred dollars," Dan said, taking out his billfold. He held it out, and the man with the brass knuckles took it. "That's a good hit," Dan said. "We don't want any trouble."

"No trouble, pops. I want your watch and also the old tomato's."

As Dan took off his watch, the man with the knife said, "That old lady's stacked like a brick shithouse. You ever had a piece of old ass, Lucky?"

"You got your money," Dan said. "Play it cool and get out of here."

The light-haired man stepped forward and put the edge of his knife against Dan's throat. "You make one move, daddy, and I cut you up like cheesecake." And to the other, "See if the old biddy's real or the tits are phonies."

Jean stood quietly, not moving, not backing away as the smaller man approached her. He reached out to touch her breast, and at that moment, as the light-haired man turned his head to watch, Dan brought up his knee into the tall man's groin. He felt a nick of pain in his neck, and then, as the tall man doubled over in pain, Dan struck him on the side of his face

13

with all his strength. At the same time, he felt the stunning blow of the brass knuckles on his left shoulder. As he leaped away, the small man came at him, and Dan, taking a glancing blow again, managed to grab the little man's arm in both his hands. With all his strength, he swung the man off the ground and threw him across the path into a clump of bushes. The tall man lay on the path, unconscious. The other one crawled out of the bushes, whimpering in pain, his arm dislocated, and stumbled away as fast as he could.

Dan stood trembling, his chest heaving, a trickle of blood running down over his sweater.

"My god, he cut you!" Jean cried.

"It's nothing. Just a scratch."

"Let me look at it. You're bleeding like a pig."

"Thank you," he panted. "Just what I need."

"Give me your handkerchief." His hand shook as he held it out to her. "This will hold it. Thank God for turtleneck sweaters! What a hoodlum you are!"

He nodded, grimacing.

"Are you all right, Danny?"

The pain in his chest eased. "Sure I'm all right." He took several deep breaths. "Wouldn't you know it? Midmorning in the park, and not a cop or a soul in sight. There's civilization for you."

Jean had picked up his wallet and her purse. "I think you killed him, Danny. He hasn't moved."

"Not likely." He bent over and reached into the unconscious man's pocket.

"What are you doing?"

"I want my watch. I paid two hundred dollars for that watch."

The man groaned.

"Danny, let's get out of here," Jean begged him.

"And leave this shithead here to mug someone else? Not likely."

The man was on his hands and knees now, groaning with pain. Dan picked up the knife and handed it to

Jean. Then he pulled the man to his feet by the collar, twisted one arm behind his back, and said to him, "We're going to walk back up there, sonny. You make one move, and I'll break your arm—and believe me, it will give me pleasure."

It was past lunchtime when they finally finished with the police and the depositions. Jean had washed out the cut and put a Band-Aid on it, and Dan had changed his clothes and sat sprawled in a chair in the study, a cigar in one hand, a drink in the other.

"I want you to see Dr. Kellman," Jean said. "Don't think I didn't see you sucking in your breath and feeling your chest."

"It's nothing. I'm fine."

"And the cigar!"

"Woman, for God's sake, I saved you from a fate worse than death."

"I don't know. To be raped at my age—that would be an experience. And what a monster you are! I never would have believed it, that sweet, white-haired old man our Mayor has called a civic treasure."

"Do you know, baby, I haven't been in a real brawl in thirty-five years. I guess, like riding a bicycle, it's something you don't forget. Only I didn't want it. All I wanted was for them to take the money and get out of there."

"It was very brave and noble of you, Danny."

"You're damn right it was! And also stupid—to jump a guy with a knife at my throat."

"Ah, well, it's not every woman who's fought over at my age. Only from now on, we shall walk on the Embarcadero. The world is changing, Danny."

"It certainly is," he agreed.

"The sense of being a woman," Dan's daughter, Barbara Lavette, wrote in her first novel, which was entitled *Driftwood*, "is the sense of being an outsider. There have been other outsiders—slaves, minorities, the

15

Jews, and at one point or another both the Catholics and the Protestants——but through all of remembered history, there has been only one constant outsider, the woman. She is never of the world; she always remains at the edge of it, tolerated, loved occasionally, respected less occasionally, and once in a while given a small gift of power. But even with the power, she is never free to leave the edge of the circle and walk into the center of it."

William Goldberg, who was producing a film based on Barbara's book, singled out that paragraph and said to Barbara, "It seems to me that there's the root of your problem. I'm not arguing with what you put in a book. That's just you. A film is something else. Not that I buy the notion. I don't put my wife in that category, and I've almost got Kelly Jones to play the lead. We're very close, damn close, and if you got any notion of what an arrogant, demanding bitch she is, you wouldn't put her in that category either. Anyway, I'm not sure I understand what in hell you mean. I just smell it all over your screenplay, and that's what's wrong with it."

"I've tried to explain it to you, Bill," Barbara said tiredly. "It's not something I created or invented. It's the essence of the film."

"I never understood why you insisted on writing the screenplay."

"Because it's my story."

"The book is, not the film. Well, sure, it's your story," he added hastily, seeing the expression on her face, "but at the same time it isn't. Anyway, I'm putting another writer on it. I have to."

Jerry Kanter, already assigned as director for the film to be made of *Driftwood,* had with bleak satisfaction informed her that it would happen sooner or later. "It always happens. You got no kick, Barbara. You got paid fifty grand for the first draft, and that's a damn

16

nice price. Anyway, it's a fluke when a book almost twenty years old gets bought for the screen."

"Then why let me do it at all?"

"It's a gesture. This industry's full of gestures, mostly obscene. Anyway, give Bill Goldberg credit. He's the first one with enough guts to break the blacklist out here, and the book's being made into a film. That's what counts."

Barbara was far from sure that it counted or for how much it counted. Now, in December of 1958, she was finishing her third month in Los Angeles. There had been a time when she enjoyed being in Los Angeles, years before, when her father had lived there. Now—well, now she had lived too long in a hotel suite, and now she walked to the window after Goldberg had left her and watched the rain pouring down, sheets of rain falling in an apparently vengeful fury that would make up for all the dry months since last April. From where she stood, through the rain, she could make out a vague outline of the Santa Monica Hills. She wrapped herself in a forlorn yet not too uncomfortable cloak of loneliness, aware that the defeat she had just suffered was a very minor one, but still trapped in the impotence of having her own precious work snatched from her—to be cut up, mauled, and contrived. Nevertheless, the defeat was not overwhelming. Precious was perhaps not the proper word, and she wondered how much she really cared about this story she had set down so long ago. Time is a gentle eraser, and when the telephone rang, she shrugged off the mood and decided that soon, very soon, she would return home to San Francisco and be out of this whole wretched world of film and filmmaking.

The call was from Carson Devron, and Barbara said, "Thank heavens it's you. I needed to hear your voice. Bless you."

"I'll have an explanation for that later. Meanwhile, this rain will be over in about an hour. I'll pick you up

17

before then. We'll drive to the beach and walk in the wet sand. And then I promise you good seafood. Yes?"

"Yes. Absolutely. What shall I wear?"

"Jeans. Heavy sweater, sandals."

"I'll be out front, waiting," Barbara said. "And saved."

"Then I'm happy I saved you," Carson said. "About thirty minutes."

She had met Carson Devron three months before, on the evening of her fourth day in Los Angeles. Goldberg, her producer, had given her a party in his mansion in Beverly Hills. The mansion was a great oversized neoclassic house, vaguely modeled after Southern antebellum plantation houses; and as Goldberg put it, everyone who really mattered was there. Since Barbara was completely unaware of who mattered and who did not matter in what passed as Los Angeles society, she took him at his word but remained unimpressed. Aside from half a dozen film stars whose faces she recognized, she knew no one, and after a number of introductions, both faces and names merged into a confusing and meaningless pattern. Barbara disliked parties, and parties where everyone present was a stranger she disliked intensely. She was not a heavy drinker and not very good at casual conversation. Surrounded by a small cluster of people whom Goldberg had dutifully led to her, she was trying to be agreeable and not too ill at ease when Carson Devron saw her. He saw her first as a woman who caught his interest, not as Barbara Lavette, but simply a tall, large-boned, handsome woman in her mid-forties, her honey-colored hair caught in a bun at her neck and still untouched by gray. Her features were well cut, the brows straight, the eyes slate-blue, the mouth well formed and rather wide—but mostly it was her carriage that caught him, her height, the way she held herself, the set of her head. Carson Devron was talking to Jack Sheldon, a

Los Angeles councilman, at that moment when he noticed Barbara, and he asked Sheldon who she was.

"Which one?"

"The tall woman in the blue dress."

"That, my boy, is Barbara Lavette, the famous or infamous—depending on how you look at it—guest of honor."

"I'd like to meet her," Carson said.

"Go over and introduce yourself. I haven't met her yet. Goldberg was after me, but I haven't made up my mind whether I want to meet her."

"Why?"

"Can't you guess why?"

"You're a horse's ass, Sheldon, if you'll forgive me."

"You can afford it," Sheldon said unhappily.

Barbara had noticed Carson Devron and had taken him for an actor. It was a reasonable assumption. Devron was an inch over six feet tall, blond, handsome enough, hazel eyes, a good face, wide shoulders and the easy stance of an athlete. He had competed in the Olympics and had taken a bronze medal in the decathlon. He had spent summers on the beaches as a surfer; he was a golden California lad, and that was evident enough. It was not that Barbara despised the emblems he wore all over himself; they were simply emblems outside of her world and of no interest to her. So when he pushed through to face her and introduce himself, she nodded and then went on talking. Afterwards, she could not remember to whom she had been talking. What was clear in her mind afterwards and for a long time to come was the way Devron stood in front of her, firmly stationed there, watching her and smiling slightly.

"Miss Lavette," he said for a second time, "my name is Carson Devron, and I very much want to talk to you."

The man to whom she had been speaking slipped away. Devron remained there.

"So you told me. Carson Devron. You're an actor," for want of anything better to say. She was becoming irritated—by the party, by the boring inanity of it, by this man who stood facing her, by his good looks and his blond hair. It made her rejoinder as inane as everything else that passed in that place as conversation.

"Why do you say that?" he wanted to know.

"You're plastic," she was saying to herself. "If I told you that—that you're plastic, that you're ridiculous—how would you react, I wonder? Why don't you go away?"

Instead, she muttered something about his looking like an actor.

"I'm not an actor, Miss Lavette, and I wish you would not decide to dislike me until you can base it on something hideous that you have discovered. I know a great deal about you. You know nothing about me."

"That's true," she admitted. "I'm sorry, I'm not being very pleasant." Now the two of them were alone, or at least as alone as two people can be in a room shared with forty or fifty men and women. "I don't like parties."

"No, I wouldn't think so. But I'm pleased about this one. I mean I'm that delighted to meet you."

"Why?"

"Because I've admired you for years, because I've read your books and because I think you're quite a person."

"Thank you. That's very flattering."

"I don't mean it to be flattering," Devron said. "Yes, I guess I do. I want you to like me."

"I don't dislike you. I don't know you——" She was interrupted by Goldberg, who insisted that Devron meet a film star. "I promised her, Dev," Goldberg said. "Just five minutes, and Barbara can have you again." With that, he drew Devron away, and Jerry Kanter, the director chosen for her film, the one person in the room, aside from Goldberg, whom she had known before the party and during the few days she had been in Los Angeles, came over bearing two glasses.

"You need a drink," he said.

"I don't. Thank you."

Kanter was fortyish, skinny, and a little less than charming. "I see you've met the golden boy," he said to Barbara.

"Who?"

"Devron."

"Who is he?"

"You don't know? Of course, San Francisco is not four hundred miles away, it's another world."

"I'm sorry. When I'm back there, I'll ask them to move it closer to the source."

"Very good. Very good indeed. All right, I'll inform you. The Devrons created Los Angeles—at least from their point of view. They own most of downtown, and they own the *Morning World*. They have more money than God—oh, I forgot. You're a Lavette. The black sheep, but still a Lavette. Perhaps not more money than the Lavettes, but more money than God, anyway."

I don't like you, Barbara was thinking. I do wish I could tell you how much I dislike you. But I'm writing a film, and you'll direct it, and that calls for forbearance.

"As for Devron," Kanter went on, "he's the publisher of the *Morning World*. Got the job last month. Some would say it comes with the family, but what the hell. You don't want this drink?"

"No. I don't want it."

She started away to avoid him if he returned and found herself facing Devron again. "I can't take much more of this place," he said. "Neither can you, from the look on your face. Let's slip out. Have dinner with me, please."

"I can't leave."

"Of course you can. I know you're the guest of

honor, but half the people here don't know that, and the other half don't care. Believe me—I'm an old hand at these stupid parties."

"Then why do you come, Mr. Devron?"

"I came tonight to meet you, and now that I've met you, let's leave, please."

And hardly knowing why she did it, Barbara allowed him to take her arm and lead her through the crowd and out of the house. He asked her whether she had a car, and she told him she had come by cab.

"Good. We'll go in my car. Cars are the nightmare of this place. By the way, why did you come with me?"

"To get out of there, I suppose."

"Then it's not my goddamn good looks," he said, but so ingenuously that it did not sound trite. "There are women who mistrust good-looking men on sight, and I sort of guessed that you are one of them. I'm not supposed to mention that, am I? But it's like being crippled, believe me. You live with it, but you don't get used to it." Before she could comment on that, he said, "I'm thirty-six. You're older than that. How old are you?"

"Good heavens," she said angrily, "what are you— some kind of rich boy idiot? It's none of your damn business how old I am! I barely know you, and I'm not sure that I want to know you any better."

Now one of the red-jacketed parking attendants— hired by Goldberg for the evening—had brought his car around, a 1952 Buick convertible, and stood by the open door, waiting.

"They'll call me a cab," Barbara said. "I don't think I want to have dinner with you."

Her statement demolished him. The face that stared at her uncomprehendingly was the face of a hurt small boy, and he pleaded with her, "What did I say? I'm so sorry. The last thing in the world I wanted is to offend you. Please forgive me."

For a long moment, she stared at him. Then she

nodded, walked around the car, and got in. They started off, driving in silence for about five minutes before he said, "I say things the way I feel them. Can I explain what I mean by that?"

"I'd rather you didn't. Just forget I was angry. It's not your fault. I've been here four days, and I've spent most of them regretting that I ever came. Tonight I felt put upon and degraded, and I don't want to explain that either. It's my fault. I'm not very nice."

"I think I understand how you feel."

"Then we'll leave it that way. Where are you taking me?"

"Downtown. Do you know downtown Los Angeles?"

"Not very well."

"It's as different from Beverly Hills as night from day. I know a good Italian restaurant, near the paper. Do you like Italian food?"

"Very much. I'm half Italian," she said bluntly.

"I know that. Look, I've been working on the paper for twelve years, and you and your father and your family have always been news. So I'd know a good deal about you and Dan Lavette and your family just in the course of things. As a matter of fact, when Dan Lavette faced down those two muggers at the Japanese Tea Garden, this past August, I did a special box on it for the sports page. My word, it was fantastic—for a man of sixty-nine to be that fit and to have that kind of reflexes. Part of me is an old jock, and I just had to tip my hat at the man."

He's trying hard, Barbara thought, and said without enthusiasm, "Daddy's not fit. He had a heart attack ten years ago. He did that crazy thing only because one of the men threatened my mother. You would have to know daddy to understand that."

"I always wanted to meet him—and you too, of course. But I've also read everything you've written. I mean your books. And when you went to prison, I was

23

enraged, if that means anything, and I wrote an editorial about it which they didn't print even though I threatened to resign, which I didn't have enough guts to do, and I know about your husband, who must have been a damned wonderful man——" He broke off and glanced at her. Barbara sat rigid, silent, and for the next few minutes, she said nothing; and then, at last, Devron said almost woefully, "My full name is Kit Carson Devron. You might as well know. I feel ridiculous and I might as well complete the picture."

"I think you're rather nice," Barbara said after a long moment.

That had been three months ago. Now, in a raincoat over blue jeans and a sweater, Barbara stood at the entrance to the Beverly Wilshire Hotel, waiting for Carson Devron. She had been there only a few minutes when he pulled up in his convertible. The car was not an affectation; he was indifferent to what he drove, and one car was as good as another, so long as it moved. Barbara darted ahead of the doorman's umbrella and through the open car door, and then huddled comfortably in the seat as Devron turned westward and then down Wilshire toward the beach.

"How did I save you?" he wanted to know. "And why?"

"I wanted to kill someone. I thought of myself, but I'm not up to suicide yet. Then I considered my producer. That becomes difficult, because the only other Goldberg I ever knew was Sam Goldberg, who was my dear friend and lawyer and we named my son after him. I might kill our director. That would be pleasant. I'm just talking. I can't kill a fly when push comes to shove. Just bloodthirsty thoughts."

"Do you want to talk about it?"

"Yes. I'm not the type who suffers in silence. I've just been informed by my producer that they're scrapping the screenplay that I wrote and rewrote according to the suggestions of every incompetent idiot who read it. They're throwing it out and giving the job to another writer—my book, my life."

"Can they do that?"

"They can. When they buy a book, they own it. They can do what they please. Oh, perhaps I could have had it differently if I had known. But I thought it was so wonderful of them, so brave to do a book by a writer who had been blacklisted, that I never questioned the contract. Anyway, there are some silver linings. I'm through with Los Angeles."

"That's a hell of a silver lining. Look there," Devron said, pointing westward to where the clouds were breaking up, golden shafts of sunlight burning through. "That's the real thing. This place can be very beautiful if you'd forget about the lousy film business. Anyway, it's not for you. It's not for people."

They parked the car and walked along Santa Monica Beach. After the rain, the vast stretch of the beach was empty except for the swooping, screaming gulls. Over the headlands to the north, there was still a black thunderhead, shredding and shot through with fronds of sunlight. The beach sand was wet and firm under their feet.

"What we have here," Devron said, "is too large, too beautiful, and too mucked up for anyone to take it casually. That's why it manages to be hated so fiercely. In New York, they make a religion out of hating the place."

"I've felt that. Even in the north, you feel it."

"I was born here. Doesn't that give it some tiny virtue in your eyes?"

"I don't believe you. Carson, you're a little boy."

"If you see it that way." He nodded. "So my mother's told me on occasion. But old enough to know my own mind. Would you marry me? No, no, let me make it more formal. Will you do me the honor of becoming my wife? I want that more than anything in the world."

Barbara darted a sharp glance at him. Then for a while, she walked along in silence, staring at the wet sand and scuffing it with her toes.

"Some response is called for," he said finally.

She was thinking of the first time they had gone to bed. It was their third date after their meeting. He had taken her to dinner in a little French restaurant on Sunset Boulevard, and afterwards, they had driven up through Laurel Canyon to Mulholand Drive. He had parked his car on an open shoulder of the road, where there was a wide, splendid view of the San Fernando Valley. A full moon lit the valley and the mighty ring of mountains that encircled it. They stood at the edge of the drop, breathing the cold night air, his arm around her, as much of an overt gesture of affection as he had yet made. They had never kissed, never embraced. His attitude toward her had been one of respectful yet affectionate formality. Now, on this night, no words at all passed between them as they stood there. A quality Barbara admired was his reluctance to chatter. He was not afraid of silence.

After about ten minutes, he turned back to the car. She followed him and they drove to her hotel and went up to her room. In the room, she said to him, simply and directly, "I'll use the bathroom. You can undress here."

When she came out of the bathroom, wrapped in a dressing gown, he was sitting on the edge of the bed, naked, his beautifully formed body crouched over as if to hide his erection, the same quality of a small boy caught in wrongdoing that she had noticed before. Barbara opened her dressing gown and let it fall to the floor, standing naked, conscious of the fact that time had not cheated her of her beauty, her stomach still flat, her breasts high and firm, her long legs straight and well formed.

26

"Won't you look at me, Carson?" she asked gently.

He raised his head and stared at her.

She smiled, thinking to herself that she was finally going to bed with a younger man because she wanted it more desperately than she had ever wanted it before, so desperately that she could feel her whole body swollen with desire. When he took her in his arms, she clutched him with a strength that made him wince, pressed her lips to his, sought a passage between his lips with her tongue, and then when he entered her, she exploded with a passion that would not leave her, the waves of her orgasm coming again and again, until finally she lay in his arms, limp and exhausted, light-headed and wantonly happy.

And now, walking on the sand at Santa Monica, he was proposing marriage. The first time in bed with him had not been the last. For almost three months, she had been having an affair with Carson Devron, and aside from her work and her involvement in the making of a film, she had been very happy, happier than she had been in years—or at least a part of her had been happy.

"Are you serious?" she asked him finally.

"More serious than I've ever been."

"You know it's impossible, Carson."

"Why? Why is it impossible?"

"You know why it's impossible. I'm eight years older than you."

"And if I were eight years older, would that make it impossible?"

"You're a man and I'm a woman. That's the way things are. We didn't make it that way, and we can't change it."

"To hell with the way things are!" he said angrily. "The only thing that really counts is whether you love me. For my part, I know what I feel. I love you and I need you."

His anger communicated itself. Barbara felt a

27

growing, racking resentment, at the world, at herself, at the pressures that had brought her here to Los Angeles, at this tall, beautifully formed man walking beside her who for years had been the golden boy of this strange land of oranges, freeways, and wealth. She was not thrilled, not pleased or flattered, but full of a sense of being assaulted.

"Do you love me?" he insisted. "That's the only point at issue."

"My son was born through a Caesarean section," she said flatly. "I'm too old to want children—you know that. You've let drop what your father and mother think of you turning up all over town with the notorious Barbara Lavette who spent six months in a federal prison. Don't tell me you'll do what you want. You're a Devron. You've just been made publisher of the *Morning World,* and for two years you've been engaged to marry another woman."

"That's over. I ended that. I told you I ended that."

"And have you informed the Devron clan that you'd like to marry me?"

"I've informed you."

Barbara stopped walking, turned to face him, grasping him by both arms. They stared at each other, and then she burst into laughter. "Carson, what a dumb quarrel this is. The first real fight we have, all because you ask me to marry you. You're a dear, sweet person. I don't know whether I'm in love with you. I've been through too much to just blithely fall in love like some starry-eyed kid. It's been so good being with you. It made my months here possible and even wonderful. Isn't that enough?"

"No. It's not enough. I can't drop it here and let you go back to San Francisco. I can't forget. I need you. I don't need children. You're the one thing in the world I need and want, and I won't let go of this. You go up north and I'll follow you there. I'll hound you. Don't be deceived by my boyish graces. If you know anything

28

about the Devrons, you know that they get what they want. Now I'm going to put my arms around you. Don't pull away from me."

"I wouldn't pull away from you, Kit Carson Devron. You know that."

In 1847, when Kit Carson, the frontier scout, was thirty-eight years old, he took under his wing an orphan boy of sixteen years whose name was Angus Devron. Devron's parents, immigrants from the town of York in England, had died in a wagon train moving West. Angus continued the journey, arrived finally in the newly conquered village of San Francisco, and there, for want of better employment, joined a raggletaggle group of volunteers who were traveling south to help "liberate" the village of Los Angeles from the Mexicans who lived there. When they arrived in Los Angeles, they found the handful of Americans who had begun the process of "liberation" outnumbered and under siege by the Mexicans. Kit Carson volunteered to go to San Diego, where General Kearny commanded a garrison of American troops, and to return with relief forces. For reasons unknown to posterity, he chose Angus Devron as one of his traveling companions. In due time, the relief column, led by Kit Carson, reached the beleaguered Americans, and the tiny village of Los Angeles was "liberated." In the course of this liberation, young Angus Devron possessed himself of a diamond bracelet. Whether the bracelet was found in one of the empty houses, or was looted from the wife of some Spanish grandee, or was merely a part of spoils unaccounted for was never determined. In any case, the bracelet was sold, and with the proceeds, young Angus acquired eight hundred acres in what would one day be a part of the City of Los Angeles. Angus Devron emerged from this experience with a worship of two things—land and Kit Carson. His land acquisitions increased through his lifetime, and his son, born to him

29

finally at age fifty-eight, was named Christopher Carson Devron. His grandson, born in 1922, the year that Angus died at age ninety-one, carried on the name, the Christopher shortened to Kit. The landholdings, meanwhile, had been added to with rail lines, utilities, office buildings, and finally, by Carson's father, the Los Angeles *Morning World*.

All this, with various embellishments, Carson related to Barbara as they lay in bed that evening. "It was in the army that I dropped the 'Kit,'" he told her. "It's bad enough to go through life with the name of Carson Devron. I had all I could bear of Kit Carson. My mother was the last holdout. Now she's dropped it, thank heavens."

"I might just call you Kit," Barbara said.

"Oh, no. No."

"I like it. I've been Bobby all my life. Kit's no worse."

"All right, if you marry me."

"We were off that subject. Let's sleep. No plans for tomorrow. Perhaps I'll go home, perhaps I won't. We'll see how I feel in the morning."

He began, gently, to stroke her breast. "If you do that, Carson," she whispered, "I'll have to turn you off, cruelly."

"And how will you do that?"

"I'll begin by telling you what a rotten, reactionary newspaper the *Morning World* is. And if I start on that tack, I can't even be pleasant to the man who publishes it, much less make love with him."

"It has a new publisher, namely myself. God Almighty, gave me a chance. I've only been in there a few months."

"Only if you go to sleep."

He continued to stroke her breast, and she sighed and curled up to him.

Sometime during the night, Barbara was awakened by a siren from either a police car or a fire engine. The singsong screaming brought her sharply awake, and then as she listened to it fade into the distance, it made an image in her mind of a tortured cry of agony out of the whole city. She was unable to fall asleep again. She lay quietly beside Carson, trying vainly to rid herself of the memories that were evoked by the wailing cry of the siren. Tired and feeling alone, in spite of the man's warm body beside her, she asked herself why she was there, why she was anywhere, and what possible sense her presence on earth added up to. The fact that Carson had proposed marriage that same day only increased her consciousness of time and age. She felt old, dried up, withered. She would not be deceived by a boy who had conceived a passion for her. She was a fruit squeezed dry of juice, and all the good and beautiful moments were gone forever. The two men whom she had once loved so deeply were both dead—and the lovely, graceful young woman whom they had both loved was also dead. Self-pity was not a common indulgence by Barbara but now she sank into it, and then mercifully dozed off, not really sleeping yet not awake.

The darkness of the bedroom was softening to a pale gray when the telephone rang. Devron started up out of his sleep, but Barbara pushed him back gently. "It's all right, Carson. I'm not sleeping." She picked up the telephone from the table beside the bed, and she heard the voice of her brother Joe:

"Barbara—is that you?"

"Yes. Yes, of course. Joe, it's six in the morning."

"I know. Bobby, I have rotten news. Pop is dead. He died last night."

It had happened at about two o'clock in the morning. Dan Lavette and his wife had been asleep in the bedroom of their house on Russian Hill in San Francisco, the same house he had built for his young bride more than forty years ago.

A low moan awakened Jean. She switched on the

31

light. Dan was sitting up, his face contorted with pain. "It's all right, baby," he managed to say. "I didn't mean to wake you. Go back to sleep."

"I'm going to call the doctor."

He grinned at her. The pain had eased. "What the hell for?" he said. "It's just gas. That's all it is. Nothing."

"Are you sure?" she asked worriedly.

"Sure." He took her hand and lay back. As she reached toward the light, his grip on her hand tightened and then relaxed. She looked at him. He lay on his back, his eyes open.

"Danny!"

He didn't move or respond.

"Oh, my God! Danny! Danny!"

She had heard somewhere of a thing called mouth-to-mouth resuscitation. She pressed her lips to his, trying to breathe life into his half-open mouth. Then, on her knees on the bed, she clawed her way over to the telephone, leafing through the pages of the bedside telephone pad for Dr. Kellman's number. She found the number and dialed it. Kellman answered the phone himself.

"Jean," he said, "pull yourself together. I'll be there in ten minutes."

"What shall I do? I think he's dead."

"I'll be right over."

Her hand had been steady enough when she dialed the doctor's number, but now it shook so that she could hardly get the telephone back in its cradle. On the bed, on her hands and knees, she turned to look at her husband. "Danny," she cried, her voice a shrill wail of agony, "don't do this to me! Don't leave me! You promised me! You promised me you wouldn't leave me! Please, please, Danny!" Then she crawled over to him and kissed his cheek. "It's a game. One of your crazy games. To see what I'd do—to see what I'd do . . ." Her voice trailed away. So quick. His cheek was cold as ice. She put her arms around him, pressing her body close to his, her face against his face. "I'll warm you, Danny, I'll warm you. I could always keep you warm. I can. I can."

She heard the doorbell ring. No servants slept in the house. The doorbell rang again. Jean let go of her husband, got out of the bed, took her robe from where it lay flung over a chair, and went downstairs to let Dr. Kellman in. He glanced at her, and then ran past her, taking the stairs two at a time. Jean followed him slowly. When she entered the bedroom, Dr. Kellman was bending over Dan, his stethoscope on Dan's bare chest. Then he dropped the stethoscope, took a tiny flashlight out of his pocket, and directed the light into Dan's open eyes. Then he closed Dan's eyelids. He was about to draw the sheet up over Dan's face when Jean stopped him.

"Don't cover him. Not yet," Jean said hoarsely.

"It's no use, Jean. He's dead."

"I know. I knew when I called you."

With all his years of practice, Kellman had never discovered what one says at a moment like this. He muttered something about the ten years that had passed since Dan's first heart attack. "I'll give you something for your nerves." That was what a doctor said.

"I don't need anything. I'm all right," Jean replied. She walked over to the bed and stood staring at her husband. She laid one hand against his cheek, held it there for a moment, then drew the sheet up over his face. "I'm all right now. We've had a long run of it, Danny and me. Three years more and it would have been half a century. Could you leave me alone with him for a little while, Milton? I know there are things you have to do. Use the telephone downstairs."

"Of course. I phoned for an ambulance. Be here in a few minutes. I'll send them away. Should I call your son? Or Barbara?"

"Barbara's in Los Angeles. No, there's no use waking her in the middle of the night, or Tom either. I'll call Joe myself—later."

What an extraordinary woman, Kellman thought as he left the room, what a thoroughly extraordinary woman—no tears, no hysteria, just completely contained. Being Jewish, he considered it incredible that a woman as devoted to her husband as Jean Lavette had been to Dan Lavette should show no emotion, or perhaps—as he preferred to think—be capable of concealing what emotion she felt. On the other hand, he knew that in some cases, a death like this was so traumatic that the mind rejected it, which meant that in due time he would have to deal with violent hysteria.

However, neither supposition was correct. Jean Lavette had spent a lifetime in perfecting a mask to conceal her emotions and fears, and for the past ten years, ever since her husband had his first heart attack, she had envisioned the possibility of his death. Being a highly emotional and imaginative woman, she had experienced his death not once but a thousand times. He was the only man she had ever loved, the only man she had opened herself to, the only man who had brought her great happiness and great misery. For almost half a century they had loved, fought, clawed at each other, torn each other's flesh and soul, divorced, married again to others, and then had finally come together because what had been for them at the very beginning still remained. Now Dan was dead and what she had imagined again and again had come to pass. She had known it would come.

After Dr. Kellman had left the room. Jean stood silently and motionless at the foot of the bed, looking at the sheeted object that had been her husband. Then she walked around the bed and uncovered Dan's face. "I'll be long enough without seeing you, Danny," she said aloud, "ever again." His face was burned brown from their long hours on the boat in the bay, the white,

34

curly hair a stark contrast. There was no memory of pain in his face.

"Poor Danny," she whispered, "poor Jean. What a stinking mess life is!"

She caught a glimpse of herself in the dressing-table mirror, and she realized what she had been unconscious of until this moment, that she was weeping. The tears must have begun the moment Kellman left the room. Until then, she had not cried. She was not a woman given to tears, and in her whole life she could count the times when she had wept, and now she could not stop. She dropped down onto the bed, running her hand down the dead man's leg, grasping his calf. Sobbing, "Oh, Danny, Danny, you bastard. What will I do now? What will I do? I can't stick it alone. I simply can't. I don't know how anymore."

Before her marriage to Bernie Cohen, Barbara had written her books and articles under her maiden name, Barbara Lavette. After her husband died, as well as during his lifetime with her, she continued to write under her maiden name, and frequently, simply to avoid confusion, not because the name Cohen bothered her in any way, she used the name of Lavette. Or so she told herself, for it was in the nature of Barbara not to place any great faith in her subjective verities, and in all truth she was never wholly comfortable with the name Cohen, no matter how assiduously she sought for and rejected any trace of anti-Semitism in her character. Her son, Samuel, was reasonably comfortable with the name of Cohen until, almost twelve, he was sent to Roxten Academy in Connecticut.

Until a month before he left, Barbara had never heard of Roxten Academy, nor had she entertained any notion of sending Sam away to an Eastern school. For one thing, a great deal of her life revolved around her son—too much, as Jean frequently pointed out to her. Barbara had raised him herself, indifferent to all

35

urging from her mother and others that she marry again, and, according to Jean, had spoiled him thoroughly. Barbara felt otherwise; to love was not to spoil; and she felt no unhappiness over the sensitivity and gentleness of her son. He was tall and slender, a head of curly sandy hair, a prominent nose, thin and hawklike, pale blue eyes, and a good mouth and a firm chin. If he had no father—dead in the second year of his life—he had a rewarding surrogate in his grandfather, Dan Lavette, whom he adored, and in turn Dan Lavette had taken the child to his heart. Almost as soon as Sam could walk, Dan introduced him to the art of small-boat sailing, and by the time he was eleven, Sam's happiest memories were of the hours he had spent on the San Francisco Bay with his grandfather. Dan at long last had found an apt student for all his lifelong knowledge of fishing and crabbing. It was a mutual joy. Dan has asked no more of life than to be out on the bay with his wife and his grandson, and for Sam it was his own form of earthly paradise.

It was this passion for sailing that had proven the deciding factor in the choice of a school for Sam. When Barbara signed the contracts to turn her first book into a film and realized that she would be spending as long as four or even six months in Los Angeles, she decided that at least a year in an Eastern school might be a rewarding experience for Sam and that there might be some important benefits in removing him for a while from the uncritical affection of his mother and his grandparents. Barbara's grandfather and her brother Tom had both gone to Groton, but she had developed an antipathy toward the place, in part because of a prejudice toward the Eastern establishment, and in part because of the coldness between herself and her brother. It was her lawyer, Harvey Baxter, who had recommended Roxten Academy—having been there as a boy—and the final persuasion was in the brochure, which showed the old ivy-covered buildings fronting on

Long Island Sound, as well as a small marina which belonged to the school. It was only after Sam arrived there that he discovered that the marina was reserved for the upperclassmen and that he would have no chance to set foot on a boat or explore the sound.

He made other discoveries. Roxten was an Episcopalian school and advertised itself as a Christian Preparatory School. In his first interview with the headmaster, Dr. Clement, a rotund, pink-cheeked man with pale hair and gold-rimmed spectacles, Sam was informed that he was more or less an Episcopalian. "Your mother writes," Dr. Clement said, "that you have had no formal religious training. This is not uncommon with the children of mixed marriages, but since your mother was raised as an Episcopalian and is widowed, as I am given to understand, this should present no difficulties in Bible studies and in chapel. I must tell you, Samuel, that your application was given very grave consideration. A child should not be made to suffer for his parent's action; nevertheless, a degree of felicitous behavior will be expected. As you sow, so shall you reap."

He had endured three months of reaping between the time he had arrived at Roxten and this day in mid-December of 1958, when he had been awakened by his uncle Joseph Lavette, calling from San Francisco to tell him that his grandfather was dead. A few hours later, dressed, shivering with an unfamiliar chill called death, he had spoken to his mother, who had asked him to leave that same day for San Francisco instead of waiting a week until the beginning of the Christmas holidays. Now, at eleven o'clock in the morning, he sat on his suitcase in front of one of the ivy-covered red brick buildings, staring dry-eyed and bleakly at glimpses of the sound through the naked branches of oaks and maples, waiting for a cab to pick him up and carry him to the railroad station.

His grief was laced with guilt and tempered with re-

37

lief, which only served to sharpen the guilt, for with the death of his grandfather, he was released from purgatory, from a place he hated and from people he feared and despised. Trying to remember his grandfather, trying to make pictures of the golden days they had spent together, trying to cope with the mysterious finality of death, trying to evoke some memory of his father, whom he did not remember at all, he succeeded only in evoking memories of his days and weeks at Roxten.

Reliving events, he reshaped them in his mind. He imagined heroic responses, as in the first time he was challenged by a group of boys, who demanded that he tell them, once and for all, whether he was Jewish. In his imagining now, he forthrightly told them that he was—something he was uncertain about—and that they could fuck off and take it or leave it. Instead, he had been speechless, and another time when they threatened to pull off his trousers to prove the point that he was circumcised—which he was—he had fought hopelessly while tears of rage and frustration poured down his face, instead of denouncing them with any of the searing epithets he thought of now. He had realized very quickly that he was the first Jew, whether he was a valid Jew or not, ever to be admitted to the sacred precincts of Roxten Academy. His belated decision to fight back provided the ultimate humiliation. He was an unaggressive boy, without any malice in his character, and totally unskilled and incompetent in the art of fighting. He was beaten, bloodied, and bullied—all of which he blamed on his own cowardice and ineptness. Yet he was possessed of sufficient will and pride not to reveal his condition at Roxten to his mother and never to succumb and confess himself defeated.

Now, finally, it was over. He would never return here, and when the taxicab arrived, he dragged his suitcase into it and closed his eyes, determined not to open them again until Roxten Academy was out of sight.

Joseph Lavette, Dan's son by May Ling, his Chinese wife, had been born in 1917, while Dan was still married to Jean, and in time, some of the wounds among the children had healed while others remained raw and livid. Tom Lavette, Dan's son by Jean, and Joe Lavette had never spoken to each other, not even to the extent of exchanging polite greetings; the few occasions when they had come face to face passed in stony silence; but on the other hand, Barbara and Joe, meeting for the first time in 1933, had become very close through the years, each eagerly accepting a sibling out of the other's deep necessity. Barbara and Tom had maintained a formal, polite, but unenthusiastic acquaintance, coldly proper on the occasions when they met, neither seeking the other out. Joe had accepted Barbara's mother uneasily, meeting her for the first time on the day of his wedding to Sally Levy, the granddaughter of Dan's partner, in 1946, but as the years passed, they had come to know and respect each other, if never entirely overcoming the barrier between them.

On this day, the barrier crumbled. It was about three in the morning when Dr. Kellman telephoned Joe to inform him of his father's death. Joe and his wife, Sally, lived in the town of Napa, across the bay and about forty-five miles from San Francisco, in a roomy, wide-verandahed Victorian house on Owen Street. From there, Joe Lavette conducted a family medical practice, which, since it included a good many Mexican families, gave him a decent living but not much more. He had two children, May Ling, named after his mother and now eleven years old, and Daniel, age three and named after his father.

For Joe, to be awakened in the middle of the night by the telephone was not unusual; it came with the practice, and his sleep had adjusted to grabbing the phone on the first ring, in the hope that it might not awaken Sally. It always did, and now she switched on her bed light and turned sleepily to look at her husband. He put down the phone and turned to her, his face full of woe.

"What happened, Joe? What is it?"

"Pop's dead."

"Oh no! No—not Danny. When? What happened?"

"Myocardial infarct—" He swallowed and controlled himself. There were tears in his eyes. Sally had never seen him cry; now it was almost more frightening than the word of death. "Very quick, Kellman said. There was nothing he could do, nothing anyone could do."

Sally put her arms around him. "Poor Joe, poor Danny."

"He woke up and woke Jean. Just a little pain, Kellman said. Then he lay back and died. What in hell good are we anyway? Witch doctors!" He got out of bed. "I'll drive into town and be with Jean. She can't be alone now."

"Let me go with you."

"No, you stay with the kids. You'll have to cancel my appointments for tomorrow. You can come over later." Joe stood by the bed, struggling with the buttons of his pajamas. A big man, he had put on weight lately. Looking at him, Sally could fancy she was seeing his father, big, indestructible Danny Lavette.

Bill Ackerman, who ran the city room of San Francisco's largest newspaper, gave the story to his best feature writer, Clancy Bullock, instructing him to give it the linage and class of a presidential obit, and then added, "No, the hell with that kind of approach. This is different. He's the last of the breed, the last of the old city. The city's gone anyway, shot to hell and up shit's creek with the high-rises and the freeways and the goddamn beatniks all over the place. With Dan

40

Lavette gone—well, the old order passes and now we got the goddamn corporate executives with their briefcases—anyway, give it three thousand words and I'll do a sidebar on one or two items you're too young to remember."

Under his arm, Bullock had a file folder two inches thick. "He certainly made news," he said.

"You can say that again."

"The thing I can't find is where he was born. No birth certificate."

Ackerman grinned. "I'll make that my sidebar. He was born in a boxcar moving out West, 'eighty-eight or 'eighty-nine, I think. Story is, his father was a contract laborer on the old Atchison spur line."

"You don't buy that?"

"Who knows? Anyway, it fits. That would make him sixty-nine or seventy. What does his family say?"

"Sixty-nine."

"His daughter, Barbara, worked for the paper once. That was during the war. Correspondent in Burma or India—you should have it in the file. I remember her, good-looking kid. Go easy on the contempt of Congress thing that she got herself mixed up in. The red menace is going out of style, and anyway, we don't want to kick any shins. Tom Lavette, Dan's son, owns half the city. Keep that in mind. Did you talk to his wife?"

"She won't talk to any press."

"She's a Seldon. Pull the file on old Tom Seldon, the banker. That'll give you some background. Now get to it. I want it by six."

The stout, middle-aged lady sitting next to Sam on the plane that was taking him from Idlewild Airport in New York to San Francisco, waited until an hour into the trip before asking him his name.

"Sam."

"Twelve years old," she decided. "You're big for

41

your age," she informed him, smiling slightly. "All alone, this is a very large trip for you from New York to San Francisco."

He stared at her, puzzled, and she smiled wisely and knowingly. "It's not mysterious. I got a grandson almost your age. Well, almost. He's nine."

Sam remained silent. He was not good at small talk, and practically incapable of it with total strangers. In his mind, the woman next to him was very fat and very old, although she could not have been much past fifty. Her intonation bothered him. Six months ago, he would have been insensitive to it; now it embarrassed him and made him wish that she would not talk to him, that she would leave him alone.

"You got another name?"

"Sam."

"Sam what?"

"Sam Cohen," he muttered.

She cocked her head and looked at him with new interest, and Sam had the feeling that she was taking him apart, probing and judging and examining.

"I'm Mrs. Bernstein," she said. "My daughter lives in Broadmoor. You know where Broadmoor is?"

Sam nodded.

"You don't live there—maybe?"

"No, I live in San Francisco."

"Where?"

"It's no business of yours where I live," he said to himself, thinking, Why can't you leave me alone?

"I mean, I'm not totally a stranger," she explained. "I come twice a year. I stay with my daughter a week. You wouldn't understand, you're young, I mean. But a week is enough, as much as I love her. Then I move to the Palace Hotel for another week. I see her, of course, but I'm not in her house underfoot. You know where the Palace Hotel is?"

Sam nodded.

"It's an old place, but I like it because I'm too old for

the hills. For the hills, you got to be as young as you are. Do you live on the hills?"

"I live on Russian Hill."

"Oh? Tell me something, young man, why do they call it Russian Hill?"

"I don't know," Sam said after a moment.

"You lived there long?"

"I was born there."

"And you never asked anybody why it is called Russian Hill?"

"I never thought of it," he replied defensively. "It's just there. Nobody thinks of asking why it's Russian Hill or Nob Hill or Telegraph Hill."

"Forgive me," Mrs. Bernstein said gently. "I'm too curious. My husband always told me that. He said one day my curiosity would kill me, like it killed the cat. Well, not yet. So don't be annoyed with me."

"I'm not annoyed," Sam said. He was less uneasy now. He was thinking that she was nice, strange but nice. She was Jewish, he knew, and he squirmed with the thought that her being Jewish was what he disliked most. It made him miserable and even more dejected.

"You're going home?"

He nodded.

"From school, yes? How do I know? A young man like you wears a blue broadcloth jacket with a patch on the breast pocket, it's got to be a nice private school. I'll tell you something, Sam, my daughter hears me talking like this, it would embarrass her to death. So she's not listening, you'll forgive me. But to go to a school in the East all the way from San Francisco. It must be wonderful to go to such a place. And now you go home for the holidays?"

"No, I'm going home because my grandfather died."

"Oh? I'm sorry," Mrs. Bernstein said. "I'm so sorry. I didn't know and I sit here talking my head off."

"Why should you be sorry?" Sam muttered. "You didn't even know him."

She stared at him, rebuffed, hurt, and Sam's eyes filled with tears, less for grief at his grandfather's death than for sorrow for himself. He had a sense of being worthless, utterly worthless, and he would have given anything he possessed to be able to say to Mrs. Bernstein, "Please forgive me. I didn't want to hurt your feelings. I really think I like you." But he was unable to say anything, and for the rest of the flight, they sat in silence.

The death of Dan Lavette was front-page news in most newspapers in the Bay Area, even downstate where the story was featured in the Los Angeles *Times* and the Los Angeles *World*. Carson Devron went over the copy for the *World* story himself, partly because of a feeling of obligation toward Barbara and partly because he was intrigued by the personality of Dan Lavette. On the morning when Barbara received the news of her father's death, Carson had begged her to allow him to go with her to San Francisco. Distraught as she was, she nevertheless realized that Carson's presence would be in the nature of a commitment which she was still unwilling to make; and for that reason, she had refused.

Left to himself, Carson went over the *Morning World*'s story with a fiercely remorseless blue pencil. In 1948, when Barbara had appeared before the House Un-American Activities Committee and had refused to supply the names of a group of people who had joined with her to send medical supplies to aid Spanish Republican refugees in the south of France, the editorial writers of the *Morning World* had attacked her unmercifully. They had denounced her as a tool of communism, as a dupe of communism, as a traitor to her class and to the country. Los Angeles journalism of that period was described by some as primitive and by others as right-wing and irresponsible, and indeed all of these descriptions had a firm basis in fact—a situation which Carson Devron was determined to change.

In the midst of the obituary, following a paragraph which described Dan Lavette's achievements as a shipbuilder during the war and his award of merit from President Truman, the writer bemoaned the fact that his daughter had betrayed him: "Unhappily, his life was marred by the trail and imprisonment of his daughter, Barbara, for contempt of Congress when she refused to give the names of her coconspirators in a front organization."

Raging, Carson called the rewrite man into his office. The man's name was Hank Dudly. He was fifty-two years old, twenty-five of them with the *Morning World,* gray, slack-bellied bent and defeated. He cringed helplessly before Devron's anger.

"What in hell do you mean by this?" Carson demanded coldly. " 'Unhappily'—did you ever ask Dan Lavette whether he was happy or unhappy with what his daughter did? It just happens that he supported her, right down the line. Who said his life was marred? And what the devil is this about coconspirators? She was not accused of conspiracy. And how do you know it was a front, as you put it? Three errors of fact as well as interpretation in one lousy paragraph—and you've been with us how long?"

"Since 'thirty-three." He felt hurt, put upon. He could remember when Carson had been led through the newsroom as a small boy. "Now wait a minute, Carson, I was just following policy and presenting the facts——"

"Like hell you were! You wouldn't know a fact if you saw it." Carson ripped the copy. "Tell Joe to put another man on this."

"What?"

"You heard me! If you don't like it, hand in your resignation. I'll shed no tears. Now get out of here!"

The San Francisco papers, on the other hand, carefully omitted all mention of Barbara's prison sentence, merely observing in passing that Dan Lavette was survived by his wife, Jean, his daughter, Barbara, and two sons, Joseph, a physician in the town of Napa, and of course, Thomas Lavette, chairman of the board of GCS, which was possibly the most potent financial empire in Northern California.

All observations that the press made on Dan Lavette's death were tempered by the fact that his son Thomas ruled GCS. It was common knowledge around town that Dan and his son had not spoken to each other for years, but since the bitterness between them was a family matter, made public only by rumor, the newspaper writers trod a fine line, avoiding the unpleasant gossip that had swirled around the Lavettes for so many years. Indeed, the *Chronicle* ran an editorial headed "The Last Giant Passes," in the course of which the writer observed that "with the passing of Dan Lavette, the last of a mighty breed steps into the pages of history. He was one of the giants who made this city unique and splendid, setting a ladder against the sky and daring to climb it . . ." The prose was effusive. Dan Lavette might have read it with more annoyance than appreciation, but on the other hand it was a bestowal of honor and respectability. American forgives its dead, whatever their sins.

Barbara's son, Sam, however, was among the living; and at Roxten Academy, he had been allowed neither forgiveness nor forgetfulness. Since the teachers at Roxten knew all about him, his parents, and their curious past, the knowledge trickled down. Samuel Cohen was a young man whose mother had been in prison, whose father did not exist, whose grandfather had married a Chinese woman after divorcing his wife, only to remarry the woman he had divorced after his Chinese wife's death, and who had a Chinese uncle and a Jewish name. It was understandably irresistible. Sam added to his execrable origins with an essay written for

46

his class in English composition; but in all truth it was less that he betrayed himself than that California had betrayed him.

Mr. Pinchel, the English tutor, taking a lead from the *Reader's Digest,* assigned the class the folllowing topic: "The most interesting character I have known."

"The most interesting character I ever knew," Sam wrote, "is my grandfather, whose name is Mr. Daniel Lavette but everyone calls him Dan except if they love him and then they call him Danny. I call him gramps because he's my grandfather. He taught me to sail a boat. The boat is the Oregon Queen, which is named after gramps' first ship except that this Oregon Queen is a cutter, not a ship. The cutter is a single-mast boat with a heavy keel and maybe three jibs except that we only have two, which my grandfather thinks is better. The happiest times are when the two of us sail in San Francisco Bay, where my grandfather learned to sail with his father who was an Italian fisherman."

Actually, Dan Lavette's father, Joseph Lavette, coming from that part of the Mediterranean coastline where Italy approaches France, was part French; but having been raised in San Francisco, it had never occurred to Sam that the one was ethnically superior to the other, and he went on to describe how, after sailing, they would tie up at Fisherman's Wharf and then walk to Gino's Italian restaurant, where both of them would consume enormous quantities of spaghetti, Sam under a solemn promise not to inform his grandmother of his grandfather's lapse from his diet. And since during the hours Sam and his grandfather spent on the cutter, Dan gave his grandson lessons in bad Italian, Sam was able to engage old Gino in the restaurateur's native tongue. This evidence of an Italian bar sinister in his checkered pattern of national origin was set down by Sam with innocent pride. It was the final brick in the wall of contempt and isolation that the Roxten boys built around him.

From his window seat. Sam watched the landing at San Francisco Airport with the passive indifference of a generation inured to air travel almost from birth. The age of twelve years is still unable to grapple with death; a mystery at every age, to a child it is unthinkable and untenable. It would not remain in his mind, even when his guilt demanded that he retain it, and his mind simply substituted departure for finality. His grandfather had gone away; forever was nothing that he could deal with, and the rebuff he had inflicted upon his fellow passenger, Mrs. Bernstein, had dislocated his concentration on grief. Now he was involved with the tactics he would use to convince his mother that he should not return to Roxten. His planning triggered his guilt once again, reminded him that the person he loved most in the whole world, perhaps even more than he loved his mother, was gone, and as the plane landed and taxied along the runway, he began to cry. Mrs. Bernstein watched him with sympathy and was moved to murmur, "It will be all right."

He replied to himself that it would never be all right again, and then he was pushing along the aisle and off the plane. Barbara was waiting for him, and she folded him into her arms, clinging to him as the ultimate reassurance in the idiocy of life and death. Walking to the car, she asked about the trip. It was the question one asks. She had already wept her tears, and her drawn, pale face was somehow strange to Sam. "O.K.," he said. "It was O.K." And then he began to cry again, but it happened as a dutiful performance.

"Don't cry," Barbara said gently. "Your grandfather had a good life, and there was very little pain in his going away. That's something you'll have to understand now, Sam. We live and we die. It happens to everyone."

They were in Jean's car, the luxurious Cadillac that had been her notion of a modest step downward from a Rolls-Royce, driving along the bay shore, when Sam said bluntly, "I'm not going back."

Barbara's thoughts were elsewhere. "Back?"

"Back to Roxten. I hate the place. Rotten. That's what the kids call it. They're right."

"You don't have to go back, Sammy. Ever. If you don't want to."

"I don't want to."

"All right."

He was silent after that, and Barbara wondered what one says to a child concerning death. What does one say to oneself? She had never thought of her father as an old man. With his great strength, his bulk, his enormous vitality, she had never even contemplated his death. He was her rock, the one male figure in her life who had not deserted her, who had stood by in good-natured acceptance of all the twistings and turnings of her life. Her first reaction to his death had been sheer terror, the terror of a person unmoored, unstable, teetering at the edge of a precipitous cliff. She had first to grapple with that; the grief came later, and then the arrival in San Francisco and facing her mother. Barbara, and indeed many others who knew Jean Lavette, had the feeling that by some witch's magic, she defied age. In her youth, she had readily been accorded the scepter of being the most beautiful woman in San Francisco, and even in her sixties she retained a serene and unlikely beauty. Her face had the kind of sculptured bone structure that resists time, and her tall, long-limbed frame remained youthful through the years. Now, suddenly, she was a wrinkled, shattered old woman, a transformation that tore at Barbara's heart; she had become a helpless, impotent creature, clinging to Barbara. It was the first time. Never, as long as Barbara had known her mother, had she seen her let go, even for a moment, of the image her friends knew, a coldly beautiful, self-reliant, self-contained woman whose shell could not be pierced—certainly not

49

by a stranger and perhaps never entirely even by Barbara.

It was evening now. Staring out over the dark water of the bay, alongside the road, Sam asked plaintively, "What will become of the *Oregon Queen*?"

Lost in her thoughts, Barbara glanced at him, puzzled.

"The cutter," he said. "Danny's cutter."

She had never heard him call his grandfather Danny before, and it took a moment or two for her to sort out her thoughts. "The boat, you mean?"

"Yes."

"Well—it's grandma's."

"She can't sail. That's what Danny always said. No matter how he tried to teach her, she can't sail."

"I guess not. I'm sure she'll let you use the boat."

"I can't sail it alone."

"No, I suppose not," Barbara said, wondering what was behind this questioning about the boat and wondering at the same time what her son felt about his grandfather's death. He had contrived a mask, and Barbara felt she would never know what went on behind that mask. In a moment of utter panic, she experienced the loss of her son as she had lost the other men in her life; and then common sense returned. The reaction to death was always masked.

"I could teach you," he said.

"Oh?"

"I mean I could teach you to sail. It's not a real cutter. I mean if it was—well, there's no way the two of us could handle it. It's something gramps invented."

"You really won't go back to that school?" she said.

"I told you that!" he cried, and then the tears began, and he sat beside her bent and sobbing.

She drove on, relieved that he was crying.

"He didn't have to die," forcing the words through his sobbing.

50

"What did you mean when you said it was a boat that pop invented?" she asked softly.

"You wouldn't understand. You don't know anything about sailing."

"I could try."

"Well," he said grudgingly, "two people can't handle a real cutter. A real cutter has a low mast stepped amidships, and then there's a great big topmast with a gaff. It's a long boat, with all kinds of canvas like flying jibs and a forestaysail and a great big bowsprit and it hangs so deep and heavy in the water it wouldn't be any good in the bay. Don't you think Danny knew that? That's why he had to design the whole thing over and invent a new kind of cutter. But it's a real cutter still, like the old Coast Guard boats."

"I didn't know that," Barbara said lamely.

"I know, mom." He moved across the seat and pressed up against her. "I know. It's the kind of thing gramps talked to me about. He wouldn't talk to you about that kind of thing."

The first time Jean Lavette looked into a mirror after Dan's death, she was repelled and horrified, and the effect was to shake her loose, at least for a moment, from her grief, her self-pity, and her agonizing sense of being totally alone in a meaningless world. She was sixty-eight years old, but the sixty-eight years had passed day by day and hour by hour. She had been young in an age where women were *beauties,* as differentiated from being beautiful or merely pretty. A beauty was of a small, select, and categorized grouping. She was referred to by the term; her genre had been immortalized by Charles Dana Gibson in a hundred paintings; she had been the subject of endless newspaper and magazine articles, and her beauty in itself endowed her with a special and professional social distinction. Just as years later, women began to be referred to as lawyers, physicians, politicians, so in Jean's youth a handful had been referred to as beauties.

She had been one of them, reigning for years in San Francisco as an uncrowned queen and always highly conscious of the distinction bestowed upon her. Now, in her mirror, she saw reflected a haggard, lined countenance, skin gray, eyes bloodshot, hair limp and lifeless. After her initial reaction, she returned to the moment and told herself that she didn't give a damn. Dan was gone. She was beyond vanity and beyond caring. Still, she could not tear herself away from her image. Her eyes filled with tears, and she raised one trembling hand to touch her cheek. Then she stumbled over to a chair, limp and weak. A half hour passed before she was able to make the decision to do her face. It had to be done. She was still in her bedroom. Dan's body had been taken away, and she could hear people entering the house downstairs. Death did away with privacy, and she was still Jean Seldon Lavette, and already too many people had seen her in this condition. Long, long ago, when Dan had pleaded with her for a divorce, she had refused him with the cold statement that Seldons do not divorce; now she specified to herself that they do not make a public display of their grief.

She rose and went into her dressing room, faced the mirror, and began to repair the ravages that Dan's death had imprinted on her face.

Barbara dropped Sam off at her house on Green Street on Russian Hill in San Francisco. He had dozed off in the car on the way in from the airport, and she felt that he had been through enough for one day. She then went on to her mother's house. Her brother Joe was there with his wife, Sally, and Sally's father, Jake Levy, and Jake's wife, Clair. At thirty-two, Sally Lavette was still the long-limbed, flaxen-haired beauty who had once been, albeit briefly, a Hollywood star. She embraced Barbara and wept. She was emotional and she wept without effort. Her father, Jake, a large, heavyset winemaker and farmer, nodded his greeting and sympathy. They were old friends, as close as family. Clair, with the help of her daughter-in-law, Eloise, had been serving food and greeting the people who had been in and out of the house all day. Now she sat on a couch with Sarah Levy, her mother-in-law, trying to persuade the old woman to go home. Sarah Levy was seventy-eight years old, and it was her husband, Mark, dead now a quarter of a century, who had been Dan's partner for many years. As she sat now with Clair, Sarah wept and remembered, her husband dead so many years, her daughter a suicide, her grandson dead in the Pacific during World War Two—and now Danny. She was too old to cope with death anymore, too close to it to regard it as a stranger.

Joe asked Barbara about Sam. "Maybe it was all too sudden, dragging the kid out of school?"

"No, it's all right. I left him at home. He's exhausted. Where's mother?"

"She's at the chapel."

"Alone?"

"No," Sally put in. "Steve Cassala is with her. I'm glad you weren't here before. Old Mrs. Cassala—she must be well past eighty—she became hysterical at Dan being buried in an Episcopal cemetery. She wants us to bring the body down to San Mateo to the Catholic church there——"

"For God's sake, Barbara doesn't have to be bothered with that," Joe interrupted.

"I thought she should know."

"Was mother here?" Barbara asked.

"Thank God, no." Joe said. "Your mother's been at the chapel since four o'clock."

"Alone?"

"No. Jake and Clair were there and Harvey Baxter

53

and Boyd Kimmelman and Steve Cassala. Steve is still there with her."

"He's not talking about a Catholic burial?" Barbara asked worriedly.

"No, no. Steve has more sense than that, and anyway, he doesn't give a damn. He's as much of a failed Catholic as pop was."

"And what happened to Mrs. Cassala?"

"Her grandson, Ralph, took her home."

"I'll go to the chapel," Barbara decided.

It was then that Dan's son Thomas and his wife, Lucy, were let into the house by Mrs. Bendler, Jean's housekeeper. They walked silently past her into the living room, where the others were gathered. When they entered, the conversation stopped, and silence hung heavy as lead. It was years since Tom had been here, in his mother's house, his father's house, years since he had spoken to his sister, Barbara. His half brother, Joe, a tall, heavily muscled man, with a face that might have been Eskimo or American Indian, reminded Tom vaguely of his father. He had heard that this man was a physician. As for the tiny, white-haired old lady who sat weeping on the couch, she was as much a stranger to him as the long-limbed, redheaded woman who sat beside her. The others were strangers, too. God's curse on family deaths! What a bitch it was! And what a fool he had been for coming here! It was Lucy's insistence that had brought him here. "As a simple matter of form," Lucy had said, "Dan Lavette's son cannot be absent. He is now among the honored dead of this somewhat insane city. As with the Romans, we deify our V.I.P. dead and forgive them all their sins." What a cold-blooded bitch his own wife was!

Barbara, on the other hand, was totally unprepared for this sudden appearance of Mr. and Mrs. Thomas Lavette. It was still less than twenty-four hours since her father's death. She was numbed and confused and nervous about being away from her mother. She had

54

left Los Angeles suddenly, violently; and just as suddenly she had parted with the film industry. The palm trees on the streets of Beverly Hills, the beach at Santa Monica, and Carson Devron with his old Buick convertible were all like a dream. Once or twice during this day, she had thought about her brother Tom, but with no clear notion of whether to approach him or how to approach him. She had never been able to hate, to carry a grudge as some precious inner treasure, and now, confronted suddenly, she let go of all the bitter memories and embraced Tom. For him, her reaction was unexpected. He felt limp, and when she stepped back away from him, he nodded, the funereal expression on his face adequately defining his state of mind.

"Is mother all right?" he asked her.

Lucy simply stood next to him, silent, composing in her mind her condolences.

"As all right as she could be under these circumstances," Barbara replied.

It was time for Lucy to express her condolences. Listening to the empty words, Barbara wondered what on earth she could do now. Introduce Joe? "Tom, this is your brother, Joe, whom you have never spoken to before." How does one say that?

Tom solved the problem. "Is mother here now?"

"She's at the chapel."

"I see. Should I go there?"

"That's up to you."

He and Lucy exchanged glances. "It would be better, I think, if we simply came to the funeral. You'll tell mother we were here?"

"I'll tell her," Barbara whispered.

Then they left. There were no introductions to the other people in the room.

At the chapel, Stephan Cassala and Jean Lavette sat in attendance to the coffin and Dan Lavette's body. They made an odd combination. Cassala was sixty-three years old, a tall, thin, gaunt man. A bad stomach wound, a mememto of World War One, had given him a lasting jaundice. His tightly drawn skin, parchment-like, was the color of yellowed ivory, and the discoloration also tinged his eyeballs. He was possessed of an old-world, courtly elegance, and his manner was gentle, almost womanly. Never too close to him, Jean had always trusted him. She was of a time when manners had meaning, and Stephan Cassala's manners were impeccable. He and Dan had been children together, the families close, Stephan the son of a Neapolitan brick-layer who was to become the first important Italian banker in San Francisco, Dan the son of a fisherman. After the death of Mark Levy, Dan's first partner, Dan and Stephan had become business associates, but it was always Dan the mover, Stephan the worshipful follower. This Jean understood, and she was comfortable with him sitting beside her.

Like Dr. Kellman, Cassala was amazed at Jean's apparent lack of emotion. Of course, he told himself, he was Italian; Jean was the other kind; yet he knew better than most the amazing closeness of Dan and Jean Lavette. The white Protestant was not anything he had ever hoped to understand. The meaningful thing was Jean's presence. She had told her son Joe, "I don't want anyone else here. Not tonight. Stephan will stay with me. He wants to, and I have to respect that. But no one else, please."

They sat in silence for the most part. At one point, Cassala recalled the day after the great earthquake. Young Dan, numb with the death of his father and mother, had spent the day ferrying panic-stricken people from San Francisco across the bay to Oakland. They thrust money at him, a hundred dollars, two hundred dollars—anything to get out of the burning city. The following day, he turned up at the Cassalas', his pockets stuffed with over four thousand dollars.

"That money," Stephan mused, "was the beginning of everything, our bank, Dan's fortune——"

"He never told me about that," Jean said. "I wonder why?"

"They were frightened people. Dan felt he shouldn't have taken the money."

"There is so much I didn't know about him. It wasn't long enough."

Cassala nodded. So much that he didn't know about her, or himself, so little that people ever knew about each other in the bit of time allowed them.

It was ten o'clock in the evening when Barbara got to the chapel and joined them as they sat quietly alongside the coffin. Cassala rose and watched the two women as they kissed each other.

"They brought Dan here while you were at the airport." Jean said. "Is Sammy all right?"

"Yes—tired, mother, but just fine."

"I'm glad he's here."

"Tom came to the house. With Lucy," she said.

"Oh? That was dutiful of him."

"It's no easier for him than for us."

"No, I suppose not," Jean said. "Do you want to look at your father? Stephan will open the coffin for you, if you do. I don't enjoy such things. I don't want to remember that stupid travesty undertakers make of a human being."

Barbara shook her head. "No, it's not necessary. I won't forget daddy." She went over to Cassala and kissed him. "You've been more than kind, Steve."

"It's your mother who's been kind enough to let me stay with her. My car's outside, Barbara. Can I drive you home?"

"No, I'll walk with mother to her house, if she feels up to it. Thank you, Steve."

"I'd like to walk," Jean agreed.

Outside on Jones Street, Jean took Barbara's arm. Barbara asked her whether she was all right.

"I'm fine, darling. Just let me cling to you a bit, just to reassure myself that you're here and real. Did Tom stay at the house? Will he be there now?"

"No, he and Lucy left. They'll be at the funeral."

"I've lost my will to hate, or even to resent. Not that I ever hated Tom. You don't hate your son—but what do you feel? He could have stayed at the house, Bobby, he could have waited for me. We're not Kentucky mountaineers to go on with these wretched family feuds."

"He'll come around, mother."

Jean stopped walking, breathed deeply of the damp sea air, and pointed down the hill where fog was already gathering. "Do you know, Bobby, we used to run up these hills. Like what? Gazelles? No, two kids. Strong kids. I was mad about him. Nothing else like Danny ever happened to me—that big, hulking fisherman. Oh, damn him! Damn him! All the rotten things he did, this is the worst—to leave me like this."

"I know, mother," Barbara said. "I know it all so well."

About a year before this night, Jean and Dan had talked about death. It was not a matter that obsessed them, but neither was it a subject which they avoided. Talking about it made Jean somewhat uncomfortable, just as talking about religion made her uncomfortable; for Dan, the subject lacked importance.

"Still and all," Jean said, "you ought to spell out your wishes. I mean write them down."

"I have a will, What else?"

"You know what I mean. Things one wants done afterwards."

"That's on your shoulders," Dan said.

"Oh? And what makes you so sure I'll be here?"

"You will."

"Just don't be so cocksure about it. And if it did

58

happen that way, I might just empty a bottle of sleeping pills and join you."

"Bullshit."

"You always were one for a gentle rejoinder. Now let's face it. My grandfather bought a family plot. Plenty of room there. I just don't know whether you want to lie cheek by jowl with the Seldons."

"I been lying cheek by jowl with one of them for almost half a century. Or should I say laying?"

"You're a nasty, dirty old man."

"You can say that again. Look, Jean, why don't you cut out all this crap. I don't want to be cremated and have my ashes strewn over San Francisco Bay, if that's what you're thinking, and if you're thinking about May Ling, she's buried in Hawaii. I don't want my carcass shipped to Hawaii, and I don't want to go on with this damn-fool discussion. Yeah—" he paused, grinning at her to take the sting out of his words. "One request. No oration, no speeches, no memorial services, no eulogy. I don't want some horse's ass telling the world what a great man Dan Lavette was. To go off with a bundle of lies stinks. So that's it."

Jean arranged it that way. The funeral service in the chapel was not open to the public or the press. The three families who had been intertwined through Dan Lavette's life were there, the Lavettes, the Levys, and the Cassalas, all told about forty people, and with them another forty people who were close to Dan and Jean and Barbara. Dan's son Thomas was there with his wife, Lucy, but they were alone in representing the vast industrial and financial empire that had its beginnings with Dan Lavette and Mark Levy, his partner. Dan Lavette would be remembered as one of the giants who built the city on the hills, but even in death he was not wholly respectable.

The Seldon family plot was in San Mateo, and Barbara drove there in a car with her mother and young Sam. It was a long, silent, and sad trip, which Sam would remember for years to come. His grandmother held his hand much of the way. Once, she said to him, "Dan left the boat to you. That's in his will. Did you know that, Sam?"

"No, I didn't."

"Well, it will be yours now. Perhaps sometimes I could sail with you. Dan taught me—well, I'm not really good. You could teach me more."

"Sure, grandma," Sam said.

In the cemetery, during the burial, Sam stood next to May Ling, his cousin, the daughter of Joe and Sally Lavette. Vaguely, Sam was aware of the strange story of his half-Chinese uncle: how Dan and Jean, his grandfather and grandmother, had been divorced in 1929, after which Dan married his mistress, May Ling, and how this same Chinese woman had been killed in Pearl Harbor during the Japanese attack. He was hard put to comprehend the circumstances that had brought his grandparents together again, and although he had in the past discussed the whole thing with May Ling, neither of them could ever get it straight or make sense out of it. Now they stood side by side, Sam with his light brown hair and very pale blue eyes and May Ling, as tall as Sam, an attenuated Chinese doll, her straight black hair in bangs, her dark eyes filled with tears.

"Do you believe," Sam whispered to her, "that people go to heaven and hell?"

She turned her tear-streaked face to Sam. She had always been enchanted with his eyes. They were his father's eyes, wide-set and so pale as to be almost translucent. "Yes. Don't you?"

Sam was just becoming aware of the delightful protuberances that distinguish a woman's body. His cousin, a year younger, was skinny and flat-chested. He looked at her thoughtfully before replying. "I don't know. Where would gramps go?"

"Heaven," May Ling whispered.

"What would he do there? He couldn't sail and he

couldn't fish and he couldn't smoke cigars and he couldn't eat spaghetti."

"You think you're real smart, don't you?"

"A lot smarter than you."

Standing behind them, May Ling's mother, Sally, whispered, "Be quiet, both of you, and listen to the pastor."

To herself, Barbara said, "All the men I love die. They all lie in the ground." But in another part of her mind, the memory of Carson intruded. It was only a few days ago, not years, only a few days past. He had said he loved her, and now she wanted desperately and with all her heart and soul to love and be loved.

Barbara had no stomach for revenge, nor was hatred anything she could deal with. Her brother Tom had betrayed her miserably, giving aid and comfort to one of the men who had sent her to prison. When she told the story to Carson Devron, a month or so ago, her manner was so calm, indeed indifferent, that he looked at her in amazement.

"You mean to tell me," he said indignantly, "that Tom gave money and support to this detestable sonofabitch congressman on the House Un-American Activities Committee—after he voted to send you to jail."

"Yes."

"And you don't resent it?"

"Of course I resent it. And the worst of it was that daddy never spoke to him again, and I lost a brother."

"From what you tell me, you never had a brother."

"I had a brother, two brothers," Barbara said softly. "I'm not sorry for myself. I'm sorry for Tom. I suppose he did what he had to do. How would you feel if you had to do something like that?"

"What! What do you mean, had to? Like hell he had to!"

Barbara remembered that conversation with Carson. Back at the house after the funeral, Tom and Lucy stood in lonely silence. The house was filled with people strange to them, people who would not meet their eyes, people who knew all the details of the Lavette family, of the relationships, of the hurts and the tragedies.

What a terrible thing, Barbara thought, to be denied a share in grief. She awarded a silent accolade to her mother, for Jean went to Tom and put her arms around him and kissed him.

Then he and Lucy left; it had not been easy for them. Tom said to Jean, "Mother, if there's anything you need . . ."

"I need your father," Jean said gently, "and there's no way around that, is there?"

Barbara didn't hear what they said to each other, but she saw Tom blinking his eyes and she felt he was at the point of tears. More than anything, at that moment, she desired to go to him and say, "It's all right—between you and me, it will be all right." But that would have been a lie. It would never be all right between them again, and if she couldn't hate, she could not pretend to love. She looked at Eloise, Tom's first wife, who had married Adam Levy after her divorce. Someone had quipped then that the Lavette fruit never fell far from the Levy tree. They were all so close and so bitterly entangled. Eloise and Adam had come to the funeral with their two sons, Joshua, who was ten, and Frederick Thomas, who was sixteen and the child of Tom's marriage to Eloise. But Frederick Thomas hated his father, angrily, totally, with the blind, emotional hatred of an adolescent worshipping a mother wronged. Thankfully, he had hidden himself in the library with his brother and his two cousins. He was a tall, headstrong boy, almost six feet already, and the other boys and May Ling always gave in to his will. He would not face Tom or speak to him, nor had he since he was old enough to have his way.

After Tom and Lucy left, Eloise came over to Barbara and said, unhappily, "Poor Tom. It was his father too. Why must it be like this?"

Barbara shook her head. "I don't know, Eloise. It got this way a long time ago, and it just is."

By eleven o'clock on the day of the funeral, the evening fog was rolling in and over San Francisco, and the friends and family had left the big Lavette house on Russian Hill. Only Barbara remained, her son upstairs and sleeping here for the night. Eloise had wanted to stay. In a way, she had become Jean's second daughter. Now, at age forty, she was still very much the fragile, vulnerable woman who had fallen in love with Thomas Lavette's good looks and elegant manners, and thereby had fallen into a continuing nightmare. It was Jean who had taken her under her wing and had given her the courage to divorce Tom, after which Jean and Eloise became very close. But tonight Jean wanted to be alone, and she sent Eloise and her family away with the others. Only Barbara refused to leave.

"Honestly," Jean said to her, "I do want to be alone. I have a great deal to think about."

"And just as honestly," Barbara replied, "I don't want you to be alone. So Sam and I will stay here tonight, and tomorrow you can be as independent as you please."

Mrs. Bendler, who came into the Lavette house each day to clean and prepare dinner, left by eleven thirty. She had made coffee, and Barbara took it to the library, where Jean sat curled on the couch, facing the fireplace. The library had undergone many transmutations since Dan built the house in 1912, but when Dan and Jean decided to remarry, Jean restored the room as closely as she could to its original appearance, and thus it was very much as Barbara remembered it from her childhood. The overstuffed pieces had an old and comfortable look, and above the mantel there was a

63

primitive oil painting of the *Oregon Queen*, Dan's first cargo ship.

Barbara and Jean sat together on the sofa, Jean watching her daughter thoughtfully. "Things go on," Jean said at last. "You drink coffee and it tastes good. You know, I envy the old ladies."

Barbara suppressed a smile. Jean could never connect herself with old ladies, regardless of a chronological age.

"You mean Maria Cassala and Sarah Levy?"

"Yes."

Barbara recalled the scene at the cemetery. Maria Cassala, who was eighty-one, had flung herself on the earth-filled grave, weeping hysterically. Sarah Levy had collapsed by the grave, moaning with grief.

"You envy them," Barbara said, and added silently, "I suppose I do too."

"You know why?"

"I think so."

"I didn't weep," Jean said. "I stood there with my heart as cold as ice, but I couldn't weep. What's wrong with us?"

"I don't know."

"I never talked to you about your father, Bobby. Not really. I suppose there was a reason for that. The good folk of this city discussed our antics over forty years, and I guess that was enough. Neither of us was disposed to add to it. Once, long ago, in a pet of anger, your father said I didn't know the meaning of love. He was wrong. I knew, and I guess I loved him as much as a woman can love a man. Maybe. We tore each other to shreds and then we put it back together, and there aren't many who do that. For the past ten years, we've been inseparable, and oh, God, I was so happy. I think Danny was too. He was the only man in my life who meant one damn thing, and now he's dead, and I don't cry. I'm just cold and numb and without tears, and I'll

64

be this way all the rest of my life, for whatever it's worth."

"No." Barbara shook her head. "Time heals it, mostly."

"I'm too old for time to do any healing. I don't know why I'm drinking coffee. Do you want a drink?"

"Yes."

"Scotch and water and ice?"

"I'll make them," Barbara said, rising.

"All right. I'm tired. Make mine a double. Perhaps I'll sleep."

"Didn't Dr. Kellman give you something?"

"Sleeping pills?" Jean snorted. "Not your precious Kellman. Afraid I'd do myself in or something. Told me to take hot milk. I'll tell you, if I thought it would lead me to Danny, I wouldn't hesitate. Only I don't."

Barbara handed Jean the drink. "Here's to daddy. One last toast."

"You had this kind of grief twice, didn't you?" Jean asked, looking at her daughter strangely.

"Yes, twice."

"Poor kid. Poor Barbara. Poor Jean." She drank, a long gulp that drained half the glass. "You're still young and beautiful. Would you do it again?"

"I've thought of it."

"Oh? Anyone in particular? You're so close-mouthed. You never did tell me about Los Angeles."

"There's not much to tell. Someone once said L.A.'s a great place if you like to eat. Not that the food's good, but there's not much else to do."

"They also say it's a great place if you're an orange. What about the man?"

"His name's Carson Devron. Well—Kit Carson Devron."

"Devron?" Jean looked at her and then looked back into her glass. Then she finished her drink. "Not *the* Devrons?"

Barbara nodded.

"No. Good heavens, no. They're cowboys. They live on beans and jerky and grow oranges."

Barbara leaned over and kissed her. "Mother, you're wonderful. I adore you."

"Kit Carson Devron," Jean whispered. "Does he wear a coonskin cap? I'm a little drunk, darling. Shall I have another?"

"If you wish."

"A short one. I'll get maudlin."

"Your privilege." Barbara mixed the drink and handed it to Jean.

"Tell me about Kit Carson," Jean said.

"Call him Carson—only for my sake. You know, they're quite civilized, mother, and very rich. They own half of downtown Los Angeles——"

"It has a downtown?"

"—not to mention the *Morning World*. I'm not impressed by the wealth, which you might suspect. I met him at one of those dreadful Beverly Hills parties that my producer gave to welcome me into the fold of what they euphemistically call the Industry. He talked me into leaving, and do you know, nobody actually realized that the guest of honor was missing. Well, one thing led to another, and I think he's very much in love with me."

"Are you in love with him?"

Barbara shrugged. "It gets less easy. I'm forty-four. He's thirty-six."

"Well, I suppose you've thought about that?"

"You can be sure."

"I remember reading about him," Jean said. "When they made him publisher of the paper. It's a rotten paper. The *Chronicle*'s nothing to write home about, but compared to the Los Angeles *Morning World,* it's *The New York Times*."

"All Los Angeles papers are awful," Barbara agreed, unruffled. "He's only just become publisher."

"The golden lad, Olympic athlete, Rhodes scholar,

very much the young Greek god. For heaven's sake, Bobby, he's not even real."

"He's very real. I'll admit he's good-looking, but it's not his fault. I'll also admit that he's some sort of throwback, very honorable, which doesn't hurt, and certainly not the kind of man I've ever been interested in." She was thinking of Marcel Duboise, who died in a hospital in Toulouse after being wounded in the Spanish Civil War, her first love, a tall, skinny, wonderfully ugly man, and she was thinking of Bernie Cohen, whom she had married and who had died fighting in Israel, a great bear of a man, Sam's father. "No, not the kind of a man I've taken to."

"But you do take to him?"

"I think I do, mother."

"And the age difference?"

"It worries me," Barbara admitted. "I told him it made things impossible."

"Does it?"

"I don't know. I want you to meet him. He wanted to come with me, but I thought he should meet the Lavettes under happier conditions."

"You know," Jean said, "from all I hear, the Devrons are a tight little clan. Primitives. They'll have something to say about it."

"I'm sure they will."

"Well, what will be, will be. I'm a little drunk, my darling, and I find myself sitting here and thinking that Danny will be upstairs, sound asleep in a room that stinks of cigar smoke. I don't want to cry in front of you, so let's go to bed."

The bed was cold as ice. Jean lay there, looking into the darkness and finding nothing.

Barbara lay awake and brooding. This was her old room, the first sleeping place that she remembered in her life. Whatever her father and mother had done to tear up their life, to dismember it before they patched

67

it together again, the house on Russian Hill had remained. Tom's room, where Sam was sleeping tonight, was next to hers. The furniture upstairs had never been replaced. At least four times, Jean had swept the lower floor clean of its contents, going from period to period, from mood to mood, from Queen Anne to Art Nouveau to Chinese Chippendale, reacting in this manner to loneliness, to dissatisfaction, and to anger, yet her rage against the decor of her living space had always stopped short at the staircase to the bedrooms. For this, Barbara was grateful, yet it made the realization of her father's death only more difficult.

Long ago, while still in college, she had been involved with the great San Francisco longshoremen's strike and the incident remembered as Bloody Thursday. In the course of this, a young longshoreman named Dominick Salone had fallen in love with her, an affection Barbara had been unaware of and indifferent to. In the course of the strike, he had been killed, and after his death Barbara had been full of guilt for her indifference to his feelings. Yet the feeling came and departed, just as the death of Marcel Duboise, the French newspaperman who had been her lover, was a blow she accepted. She survived the grief because she accepted the parting, and that too was the case when her husband had been killed in Israel. She was a strong woman; she had never emptied or destroyed herself by screaming out endlessly against a fate that appeared to militate against any lasting happiness in her life. Her very serenity often made her uneasy and guilt-ridden and caused her to wonder whether she was capable of any truly deep feeling or emotion. As a young woman, she had been easily given to tears; now, like her mother, she lay in the darkness, dry-eyed, trying to grasp the fact that the one man who had never deserted her, who was her strong rock of support and had been for forty-four years of her life, was now gone forever. *For-*

ever was somehow different than it had been with her lover and her husband. Forever was unfathomable.

It was almost dawn when Barbara finally fell asleep, and then she dreamed that she and Sam were out in the boat Dan had designed, not in the bay but out far on the ocean, cloaked with fog and lost beyond rescue.

The Devron mansion, in Hancock Park, was half-timbered in imitation of an English manor house and contained twenty-two rooms. Hancock Park, still an elegant area in 1958, had been even more elegant when Christopher Devron, Carson's father, built his home there. He chose Hancock Park deliberately. For one thing, it was square in the center of Los Angeles, as opposed to the great ranch-estates of his financial contemporaries in Orange County and up the coast toward Malibu. If Los Angeles was his city, he had no intentions of being an absentee landlord. For another, it was on the front wave—forty years before, when it was built—of a city moving westward toward the Pacific shore. It was a Devron instinct to move westward. Now, however, by this year of 1958, Beverly Hills had sprawled out to the west of Hancock Park, and indeed the area was beginning to show wear around the edges—which did not perturb the Devrons at all. The fact that they had chosen Hancock Park made it the place; as simply as that.

Jean Lavette's assessment of the Devrons would have been less scornful had she been less miserable; yet even less scornful, it would have stemmed from two conditions. For one, from the San Francisco consciousness, the knowledge that this tiny city, this jewel of the Pacific, this city of hills and high-rises and cable cars, which claimed to be a miniature New York, a miniature Paris, was in reality a town of less than a million people with very much of a small-town mentality—and out of this troubled knowledge a fierce sense of superiority over Los Angeles, that huge, sprawling, shapeless entity to the south; and for another, the fact that Jean's mother had been an Asquith of Boston. Given those two conditions, her view of the Devrons was understandable, if inaccurate; indeed, as inaccurate and intolerant as the Devrons' assessment of the Lavettes.

In one aspect, however, it was valid. The Devrons were a tight clan, and now, in the Devron dining room, the clan was gathered at dinner. Seven Devrons were seated around the long dining table, Devrons all because whether of male or female gender, whether by blood or marriage, they were nevertheless considered Devrons. At one end of the table, Christopher Devron, seventy-three, a large, rugged man, his face wrinkled like old leather, his thick head of hair snow-white. Facing him, at the other end of the table, Lila Devron, slender to the point of emaciation, dark eyes set in an olive-skinned, aristocratic face. Five years younger than her husband, she permitted no strand of gray to reveal itself in her black hair, and her tightly drawn skin made her appear much younger than her sixty-eight years. Her daughter Willa—Willa Cather Devron—favored her, even as Carson favored his father. Willa and her husband, Drew Anthony, whose Arlington Ranch took up a goodly part of Orange County, were seated on Lila's right, with Carson between Willa and his father. On Lila's left, Christopher Devron's sister, Sophie, and her husband, Jamie Coster, whose legal firm of Coster and Haley had represented, fought for, and sinned for the Devron interests since there had been Devron interests in Southern California. Coster and his wife, the child of grandfather Devron's older years, were both in their early sixties.

In all, it was a family company that dined together at least one night out of every week, and those who knew the Devrons also knew that most decisions regarding their vast interests were decided not at the formal board of directors meetings of their various companies, but at these family affairs. Tonight, they had just finished discussing the acquisition of a thousand-acre tract of land in San Luis Obispo County, debating the pros and cons of its possibilities for development, when Carson decided to make his own announcement, to take the plunge, to mount the barricades.

"I'm thinking of getting married," he said bluntly. "I thought this might be a good occasion to inform you all, after which"—smiling—"we can join battle."

Christopher Devron knew his son. He waited, silent. Lila said, "Join battle? Really, my dear."

"In a general sense?" his sister, Willa, asked. "Or do you have someone in mine?"

"I have someone in mind. I met her three months ago."

"And never saw fit to bring her here?" his mother said.

"I had my reasons, mother."

"I'm sure you did," Christopher Devron acknowledged. "What's her name? Who is she?"

"Her name is Barbara Lavette."

Carson glanced at the assembled faces. They were dealing with the name, running it through their memories. They placed it and waited for Lila to comment.

"Not *the* Barbara Lavette."

"Yes, *the* Barbara Lavette."

"Didn't her father die a few days ago—Dan Lavette?" Christopher asked. "Page three," he added, smiling slightly. "I would have given the old pirate page one." He had founded the *Morning World*.

"Carson, you're not serious," sister Willa said.

The others watched Lila. Their comments had already formed. It was simply a question of what tack Lila Devron chose to take. Few outside this circle knew the power and strength of this slender woman.

She chose an ethnic point of departure. "Dan Lavette was an Italian. His father was a fisherman, if indeed anything is to be known about his parents. It's true he married a Seldon, and I understand that his son, Thomas, is very rich and very powerful. Nevertheless, his life has been threaded through with the most disgusting scandal. If I remember correctly, he had a Chinese mistress who bore him a son out of wedlock."

"Out of wedlock," Carson thought. "How wonderful." And then added aloud, "Since we're talking about wedlock, mother, he also lived with his wife out of wedlock. After which he married her a second time. I think that's quite remarkable."

"I'll be damned," Drew Anthony muttered.

"I don't appreciate flippancy," Lila told her son. "It's not an original thought, but I must remark that the fruit doesn't fall far from the tree. The father was in jail and so was the daughter. Carson, you can't be serious. The woman's a communist."

"She's no more a communist than you are, mother."

"He has a point there, Lila," Jamie Coster said. "I followed the case rather carefully. She was foolish and arrogant and pigheaded, and perhaps she had her fingers in some sticky stuff. But there're no grounds for thinking that she's a communist."

"There are no grounds for thinking she isn't," Willa put in.

"Thank you, sister dear. She isn't. Not that it's to the point; it's just a matter of fact."

"What connection has she with the Seldon Bank?" Christopher asked.

"None. She sold out to her brother."

"I remember," the old man agreed. "Set up some kind of charitable trust. Damn foolish act."

"On the other hand," Jamie Coster reminded his brother-in-law, "the Lavette interests are enormous. Perhaps the second or third largest in Northern California."

"I can offer you no comfort in that." Carson smiled.

72

"She hasn't spoken to her brother in years. As far as he is concerned, she is beyond the pale."

"I'm happy you're not a lawyer, Carson," Jamie Coster said. "You plead a damn poor case."

"How old is she?" Lila asked thinly. "If I remember——"

"Yes, mother."

"If I remember correctly, she must be older than you."

"She's forty-four."

It was entirely the bombshell Carson had been expecting, and it produced a long blast of silence. They looked at each other and then at Carson, and then at Lila and Christopher, who were studying their son as if they had never seen him before. Drew Anthony stifled a giggle when Lila glanced at him coldly.

Willa broke the silence. "Well," she said, leaving that to convey what it would. She was two years older than Carson, a dark, intense woman, not unlike a younger version of her mother.

"Eight years' difference," the old man said at last. "That's a hell of a lot of difference, Carson. She won't be bearing children at that age."

"I think not," Carson agreed.

His mother noticed how gentle and offhand he was, and knowing her son, she concluded that neither arguments nor a show of steel would at this moment swerve him from his decision. She had a few cards to play, but she did not feel that they were worth a great deal. There was no question of cutting him off. Carson's grandfather, Angus Devron, the founder of the dynasty, had provided his grandchildren with trust funds that had prospered mightily, and both Carson and Willa were wealthy in their own right. His father could remove him from the position of publisher of the newspaper, but what then? He had been groomed for the job ever since leaving college; it had to be a family job; and Carson did it well. With this in mind, Lila ended

73

the discussion by saying, unemotionally, "I think, Carson, that we should meet the woman you have chosen before we say anything more on this subject." She had carefully avoided saying "young woman," and now she continued, "I presume you brought this to our attention for what, in a more civilized time, would have been called our blessing. This is appreciated." She rose. "I suggest that we go into the living room and leave the gentlemen to their cigars and their brandy." That was ritual, preserved here if nowhere else in Los Angeles. Asked once by an interviewer how she saw herself and her family, Lila Devron replied without hesitating, "As a civilizing force—which is perhaps the direst need of Southern California."

When the ladies had left the room, Christopher Devron lit his cigar, looked thoughtfully at his son as he puffed on it, and then said, "Carson, you are one curious, stubborn sonofabitch. I want to see this gal. She must have something."

"She has," Carson agreed.

Frederick Thomas Lavette, Tom Lavette's son by his first wife, Eloise, had grown to his sixteen years at a place called Higate, in the Napa Valley of California. Higate consisted of nine hundred acres of rolling foothills, much of the land planted in grapevines, and a thriving winery.

Along with his father, Jake, Adam Levy ran the winery. Not only was it expected of him, he had never desired any other life. He was fortunate in that he could focus his life on two passions, his wife, Eloise, and the making of wine. After eleven years of married life, he remained romantically and totally in love with her. Eloise was possessed of that curious personality that combines innocence and intelligence, a combination found rarely in men and perhaps somewhat more often in women. Eloise was without ambition; her life suited her. She adored her husband, her home, and her children. Big Jake Levy, Adam's father, cherished her. A large, gruff, intermittently angry man, he was reduced by Eloise's smile to the subservience of a lapdog. Jake's wife, Clair, had taken her to her heart at the moment of their meeting, and Adam, long-legged, skinny, long of face and pleasantly ugly, could never quite accept the fact that he of all men should be the husband of Eloise, whose blond ringlets and round face and vulnerable blue eyes matched all his dreams of what a woman should be. Others disagreed with him. Adam's sister, Sally, often thought of Eloise as a doll-like dunce, and Barbara would find herself doubting that good nature as perpetual as Eloise's could be combined with any sort of real intelligence.

It was Barbara's mother, Jean, who was closest to Eloise. She had long ago taken Eloise under her wing, employed her in her art gallery—a brief and abortive venture—and had given her the courage to divorce her first husband, Jean's own son, and the courage to face her family, who thereupon turned their faces from her permanently. Jean knew her best, better perhaps than her own husband. In each crisis Eloise faced, Jean stood firmly behind her—as when Frederick Thomas first refused the visitation rights of his father.

Eloise had two children. Frederick Thomas was born of her marriage to Tom Lavette. At the time of Dan's funeral, he was sixteen. Joshua, her son by Adam Levy, was born in 1948, six years after Fred. For the first five years of Fred's life, his father more or less ignored him. It was only after the divorce from Eloise that he realized that a son was part of the process of becoming a corporate giant. Since it was hardly likely that his second wife, Lucy, already in her forties when he married her, would bear children, Frederick remained his only heir. However, it was too late. Tom's rages at Eloise were a part of Fred's earliest memories; twice he had seen his father strike his mother, and since he knew nothing of Tom's frustration and unhappiness, he conceived a bitter and unyielding hatred of his natural father. The legal visitation periods became a time of horror for Tom and Lucy. A maniacal, destructive child was loosed upon them, and every attempt to discipline or restrain Fred only increased his capacity for overt and concealed destructiveness. He broke crockery, slashed upholstery, scratched precious paintings, lied, stole, and once, aged nine, attempted to burn down the great gray-stone mansion on Pacific Heights that was Thomas Lavette's home.

Throughout this period, five years of Fred's life, Tom exhibited enormous patience. In all truth, he wanted a son desperately, wanted to love and be loved, wanted to dream of a day when his son would join in the management of his growing financial and industrial empire. He had fantasies of doing things together with his son, a kind of comradeship that his own father had never granted him. He endured Fred; he never struck the child; and he even went so far as to plead with Eloise to use her influence. Eloise, in turn, pleaded with Fred, but it was hopeless, and after five years Tom surrendered his visitation rights.

At Higate, Frederick Thomas Lavette was a reasonably happy, imaginative, and headstrong boy. He managed good grades in school without ever trying very hard, became his high school's most valued basketball player, read a good deal—for the most part Jack London and Edgar Rice Burroughs—and became the acknowledged leader of what he named "the wolf pack." The wolf pack consisted of Fred's younger brother Joshua, his cousin Sam, and his other cousin, May Ling. She was included by sufferance. In addition to these four, there were the two children of Cándido Truaz, the Mexican foreman at Higate, Rubio, who was thirteen, and his sister, Carla, two years older, a lovely, round-faced quiet child. Like May Ling, she was there both by sufferance and by Sam's argument that there were female as well as male wolves.

76

Sam, who worshipped Fred, spent his summers at Higate, and it was during the summer months that the wolf pack ranged through the hills of the Napa Valley.

The Christmas recess had just begun, and Barbara, still staying with Jean, had given in to Sam's pleading that he spend the next two weeks at Higate. It was a cold December day, and high up on the ridge above the winery, the boys had built a fire. The flame was well protected by a stone fireplace that Adam Levy had built when he was a boy, and the four boys and two girls huddled around it, roasting and devouring the unlikely combination of frankfurters and marshmallows. Sam and May Ling picked up on their conversation which had begun at the cemetery, and once again May Ling was comforting herself with the thought that her grandfather had arrived safely in heaven.

"How?" Sam challenged her. "You saw what they did with gramps. They put him in a coffin and buried him. How would he get out?"

"Not his body. His soul," May Ling countered.

"Ha!" Sam snorted. "You think his soul is up there with wings, playing on a harp? I bet I know gramps better than any of you. He couldn't even play a kazoo. And you know something—he was supposed to stop smoking cigars. Dr. Kellman said that if he kept on smoking cigars it would kill him. Grandma would throw away his cigars when she found them in the house. But you know what, he kept them hidden in the boat. Then when we'd be out on the bay, he'd hand me the tiller and stretch out and open a can of beer and smoke a cigar. Then he'd say to me, 'Sammy, a woman is just a woman, but a good cigar is a smoke——'"

"What?" Fred interrupted.

"That's what he'd say."

"Well, it doesn't make any sense."

"Anyway," Sam said to May Ling, "where is he going to get cigars in heaven?"

77

"From God," May Ling answered.

"You're crazy."

"You kids are both crazy," Fred said with authority. "You're dumb enough to believe that stuff they feed you in Sunday school," he told May Ling, "and Sammy's dumb enough to argue with you. Anyway, nobody believes that anymore. Didn't you ever hear of evolution?"

"I heard about it," his brother, Joshua, said.

"We were not created, we evolved—from monkeys, to make it simple. All a natural process."

"What an awful thing to say!" Carla whispered.

At that moment, May Ling's dog, a big German shepherd called Casper, joined the group.

"And we no more have souls than Casper there," Fred stated.

"Casper has a soul!" May Ling cried out.

"And he goes to dog heaven when he dies?" Sam grinned.

"He does, he does!" May Ling leaped to her feet. "I hate all of you!" And then she raced off down the hill, followed by Casper. Carla ran after her.

The boys looked at each other and then were silent for a little while; and then Sam said, "I wish there *was* a place you go to after you die. It's scary. Aren't you ever scared when you think about it?" he asked Fred.

"Father Garvey says you go to heaven if you don't sin," Rubio said uncertainly.

Fred shrugged. "Hand me another frank," he said lightly. But inside him, a cold knot of fear began to build, growing like a lump of ice next to his heart. He had never really faced it before, the fact that he too would one day die.

The day after the funeral, Maria Cassala went to the Catholic church in San Mateo and spoke to Father Michaelson. Tentatively, pleadingly, she asked for a mass to be said for Dan Lavette's soul. It was difficult for her to convey the exact circumstances to Father Michaelson. She was a timid woman, and although she had lived in America for well over half a century, her English was not good. Most of her life had been confined to her home, and there for the most part she spoke to the members of her family in Italian. At first, the priest thought that she meant her son, which puzzled him, since he knew the family and had never heard of a son called Daniel. But then, gradually, he was able to unravel the facts of the Cassala family's relationship to Dan.

"Yes, of course. Why not?" the priest asked the old woman.

She wept as she explained that he had married out of the faith, that he had divorced, had been married again to a Chinese woman who was not even a Christian, and had died in a state of sin, without remorse or the presence of a priest. Father Michaelson, who was in his mid-thirties and had few Italians in his parish, was both intrigued and touched by the depths of the old woman's belief. She was pleading with him to ease the suffering of someone beloved to her who was condemned, by the fervency of her own faith, to burn in hell for all eternity. The situation unsettled him, and he could only think to ask, "Was he a good man?"

"Believe me, I tell you the truth. Would I lie? Would I lie to a priest?"

"Of course not," Father Michaelson assured her.

"Would I lie to God?"

The priest shook his head.

"He was a good man—" She sought for words and lapsed into Italian: "*Compassionevole, generoso, gentile—molto gentile.*"

"Then God will forgive him," the priest said.

"You pray for him—please?"

"I'll pray for him," the priest agreed, strangely touched.

* * *

Maria's son, Stephan Cassala, had remained in San Francisco, and for three days following the funeral, he came each day to the Lavette house on Russian Hill. Whenever he appeared, his arms were filled with food— cake, candy, delicacies, once a smoked turkey, another time a baked ham. He was gentle, soft-spoken and unobtrusive, and Jean had the feeling that he could not let go of the dead man. How was it, she asked herself during those days, that Dan had made a connection with so many people who remembered him and valued him? How was it she knew so few of them, and who would reach out to her family after her death? To a degree she resented Cassala's presence; he was connected to a part of her husband that was still strange to her; but in another way, she welcomed him. He was content to remain downstairs while she took refuge in her bedroom, and he spared her and Barbara the necessity of formal and uneasy words spoken to people they did not know.

Thus he was there, leaving to return to San Mateo, on the evening of the third day after the funeral, and on his way out opening the door for Carson Devron. Stephan smiled and nodded. He didn't recognize the face, and he asked whether Carson was a friend of the family.

"A friend of Barbara's," Carson replied.

"Yes, of course. I'm an old friend of Dan Lavette's," Stephan said. They shook hands. "Barbara went out for a breath of air. You can wait for her. Mrs. Lavette is in the library."

"How is she? I mean, how is she taking it?"

"As well as can be expected. Do you know her?"

Carson shook his head. "No, we've never met. I don't know whether I should intrude. I thought—I can come back."

Stephan shrugged. "Half of San Francisco has intruded these past few days. Danny was almost as recognizable around town as the Coit Tower. Let me take you to Mrs. Lavette. Then I have to leave."

He brought Carson into the library. There was a fire in the grate, and Jean sat facing it, half dozing. She rose as they entered, and in the muted light of the room, the tall, white-haired woman was quite different from what Carson had expected. Through the years, her slender figure had not changed a great deal. She still carried herself erectly, and the single lamp and the firelight were kind to her haggard face.

"I'm Carson Devron," he said, holding out his hand to her. "Barbara may have mentioned me to you. We're friends. I felt I had to come."

She took his hand firmly, peering at him, "Stephan," she said, "please put on a light." And to Carson, "Self-pity—you sit in the dark. There," as Cassala switched on another lamp. "Of course Barbara spoke about you, and I'm glad you came. Dear Stephan here clucks over me like a mother hen—not a very good simile." She went to Cassala and kissed his cheek. "I couldn't have survived without you, truly, But now, go home. Barbara will be back in a few minutes."

Cassala left, and Jean turned to Carson and said, "Please, do sit down. Can I give you something? A drink? Have you had your dinner? There's enough food in the refrigerator to feed an army."

"Nothing, thank you. I had a bite to eat before I came here. I stopped by at Barbara's house first. I suppose I should have called."

Jean smiled. "But knowing Barbara, you were afraid she'd tell you not to come."

"Yes."

"Well, I have a strange daughter, as I'm sure you know. The man who let you in, Stephan Cassala, was as close to a brother as Danny ever had. He and I share a peculiar grief; there's just not much of either of us left with Dan gone. He's been very kind, but he has a wife and a family in San Mateo, and it's time he left me to struggle on. Forgive me for chattering like this." She sat facing Carson. "But I do feel I know you. Barbara has talked about you a great deal."

Carson nodded. "I thought she might. I know that a time like this——"

"A time like this," Jean said, "is very naked. I don't know why people must be so damned apologetic about death. It's the only certainty we face, and perhaps the only time we are decently honest with ourselves. Barbara tells me you want to marry her."

"Yes, I do."

"You're eight years younger than she is. Do you think you can live with that?"

"I didn't ask her lightly, Mrs. Lavette. I'm thirty-six, but I grew up a while ago. I had four years of the army. I was married once, ten years ago. It lasted six months."

"I'm sorry," Jean said. "I plunged right in, didn't I? But Barbara will be back any moment, and I wanted a few direct words before she arrived."

"And you don't mince them, do you? All right, Mrs. Lavette. What I started to say is that I'm not a casual repeat offender. I waited a long time before I decided to marry again, and I don't want to lose the best woman I've found because we happen to have been born not according to social schedule. I came here to offer my condolences, and instead . . ." His words trailed off.

"Thank goodness. Condolences are meaningless. You didn't know my husband and you do know my daughter. I prefer we talk about her and about yourself. My daughter is an interesting and remarkable woman. The Girl Scout image is deceptive. She has lived through many kinds of hell, and she has come out of it with her head up, which doesn't mean that she's ready to accept the world as it is. She has too many rules. I, for one, could not live up to them. Do you think you could?"

Carson laughed. "That's a wonderful description of Barbara. I could try."

They heard the outside door slam, and then Barbara's voice: "Mother—where are you?"

"In the library."

Barbara came into the room. She was wearing an old, heavy sweater, her hair blown and her cheeks flushed with the night wind. She saw Carson, paused, and then said, "Hello, old friend. So you did come after all." She bent to kiss Jean. Carson had stood up, and now he waited. She went over to him and kissed him.

"You've both had a bad time of it, haven't you?" he said.

"As such things go."

"Whatever I can do——"

"Being here is nice," Barbara assured him. "Have you and mother had time to talk?"

"Some. Yes, we talked."

Jean watched the two of them with interest and said nothing.

"I was thinking of you, Kit Carson," Barbara told him. "I walked all the way down to Market Street and then rode the cable back. It was good, first time out of the house since the funeral. I was thinking that I never want to go back. It's not that I hate Beverly Hills. It's simply a place that fills me with sadness and despair, and if I were only one of those clever and cynical writers, I could write a book about it and turn it to good use. This way——" She shrugged.

"I have to live in Los Angeles," Carson said.

"I know. That's what I was thinking about."

"Do you want to give it a try?"

"Perhaps. I was thinking about that, too. I'm going to make some tea, and then we can talk about it or not, just as you wish." With that, Barbara left the room.

"Well, Carson," Jean said, "this is what my husband

83

used to call a moment of truth. Do you think you can hack it?"

"I think so."

Jean nodded and leaned back on the couch, staring into the fire. If Barbara left to live in Los Angeles, she would be alone, more alone than she had ever been.

TWO

Barbara and Carson Devron were married in June of 1959. Since it was a second marriage for each of them, the ceremony was held in the small chapel at Grace Cathedral, after which there was a very modest reception in Jean's house on Russian Hill. Barbara would have preferred a simple civil marriage in the chambers of her father's old friend Judge Fremont, but Carson explained to her that such procedure was out of the question. Carson's mother, Lila Devron, felt that since ten years had passed since his first unfortunate marriage, this one should be celebrated in a manner compatible with the Devrons' position in Los Angeles. But it was only six months since Dan had died, and Jean was firm on where and how the marriage should take place. In the end, there were present at the reception Carson's mother and father, his Aunt Sophie and her husband, Jamie, and his sister, Willa, accompanied by her husband, Drew Anthony.

On the Lavette side, the ranks were equally thin. Barbara's son and her two brothers were present, Tom and his wife, Lucy, and Joe Lavette and his wife, Sally—which did not add comfort or warmth to the evening, since Joe and Tom barely knew each other, and Barbara and Tom had not spoken to each other for years before her father's death. Nevertheless, Jean felt that some effort had to be made to confront the Devrons with a family situation and make them understand that the Lavettes of San Francisco—Seldons on the distaff side—were the equals if not the superiors of the Devrons of Los Angeles in wealth, appearance, and breeding. All of which Barbara found annoying and rather ridiculous; yet it was an arrangement which she was able to accept by placing herself in her mother's position and thereby viewing it as a part of Jean's valiant effort to survive her husband's death.

All things considered, it did not come off too badly. The Lavettes were polite and even gracious, to each other as well as to the Devrons, and the four Lavette women, Barbara, Jean, Sally, and Lucy, were well groomed and attractive.

Above all, they were on their own turf. The Devrons had come up from the south, and howsoever they saw themselves, no native of Los Angeles can wholly escape a feeling of inferiority in regard to San Francisco. Whatever they may have felt about the woman their son had married, the fact remained that she was a Lavette, and that the Lavettes were one of the few California families the Devrons could meet on equal terms.

In matters social as well as financial, the Devrons took their cue from Lila, and when Lila embraced Jean, the remaining icy edges were melted. Carson standing with Barbara, remarked that his mother was a most remarkable woman.

"They both are," Barbara said.

"But different, quite different, I imagine." He was thinking of an evening a week past when Lila had told him, flatly, that the wedding would not take place. They were in Lila's small sitting room, adjoining her bedroom in the house in Hancock Park. Lila had commanded his appearance, before dinner, just the two of them, herself and her son. Lila had opened the conversation by reminding Carson that he had never overtly disobeyed her.

"We've had our differences, we've argued," Lila said, "but you've never done anything directly contrary to my wishes."

Knowing what was coming, Carson nodded and waited.

"You're not making it easy for me."

"No, mother, I'm not."

"Very well, I'll come directly to the point. The wedding will not take place."

"Just like that, mother? Why didn't you issue your ultimatum a week ago or a month ago?"

"I admit to being a fool about it, but not enough of a fool to let you destroy yourself."

"You realize that I don't see it your way?"

"Of course."

"You can take me off the paper," Carson said softly, "but there's not much else in the way of inflicting punishment—except to make it impossible for us to be friends. I think I love you, but that's not enough, is it?"

"I have no intention of inflicting punishment. I simply forbid it. I don't want you to marry that woman."

Carson shook his head.

"Nothing more?"

"I'm going to marry her, mother. That's it."

And now, watching Lila embrace Jean Lavette, Carson admitted to himself that he knew his mother hardly at all.

When Barbara informed her son that she intended to marry Carson Devron, his reaction consisted of a blank, stony silence, an inner withdrawal such as only a twelve-year-old son can achieve. He did not take to Carson. Carson tried mightily, with charm, gifts, and even to the extent of inviting himself onto the cutter. He was a good sailor and he bowed cheerfully to Sam as the captain of the craft—all to no good effect. Sam remained locked in himself.

"It's nothing he does," Carson said to Barbara afterwards. "It's what he doesn't do. I thought the boat might make a difference, but it only made it worse. There's no way I can reach him."

"Give it time, please," Barbara begged him. "He's never had a father. His grandfather was someone he worshipped. If you had asked me, I would have said stay away from the boat. That was his and Dan Lavette's domain."

When the wedding was finally scheduled, Sam announced that he would not come. "It has nothing to do with me," he said flatly. Then they talked. It was the first time Barbara had ever talked openly and seriously with her son, holding nothing back, revealing her own fears and doubts.

"I'm no good at living alone," she said. "I'm forty-five years old and I'm frightened. I've always had you. But that comes to an end, and sooner than you might imagine."

"Why does it come to an end?"

"Let me try to tell you. It's not something that's easy to spell out. For your own good, your own health, and your own life, you and I must each of us stand on our own feet. I've always tried to have it that way. In a few years, you'll be going to college, and after that—well, whatever you decide to do with you life. We can love each other, but heaven help us if we cling to each other."

"You mean you don't want me around?"

"Sammy, Sammy darling, that's the last thing in the world that I mean. I do want you around. I want to look at you and embrace you and feed you. But I want you to be free, and in the same way, I must be free. Carson is not like your father, but no one can be like him and I can't go back and become a young woman again. I found a good, decent man who loves me, and

I'm lucky, very lucky, and that's something I want you to understand."

"I'm trying to," Sam said. "I'm trying."

"And you do understand that after the wedding, we'll be going away for a few weeks, Carson and I. School will be over then. If you wish, you can spend the time at Higate."

Sam nodded.

"Don't be provoked with me, please, darling," Barbara begged him.

She told Carson about it afterward. "There's nothing as closed, as unreachable as a boy his age. So it's your decision. I won't send him away to school again. I can't. It was just too awful for him."

"We'll give it time. I'm not an ogre."

"Hardly. You're right. We'll give it time."

"And the honeymoon?"

"He'll stay at Higate. It's the place he loves best, and we'll only be gone for a month."

Adam Levy was president of Higate Winery. His father, Jake Levy, sixty years old now, still ran the sprawling farm in the Napa Valley and supervised the work at the winery; but in the years since Prohibition, when Jake and Clair Levy had bought a ruined winery and nine hundred acres of good land for a few thousand dollars, the Higate Winery had become the fourth largest in the state of California. They had offices on Sacramento Street in San Francisco and a warehouse in Los Angeles, and while every tillable acre at Higate was in vines, their production was such that they rented almost a thousand acres in the Sonoma Valley and had begun buying additional grapes in the San Joaquin Valley.

This meant that Adam Levy was away from the Napa Valley place a good deal, a condition that his wife, Eloise, accepted without complaint. Barbara envied her the ability to live what appeared to be a totally contented life within so circumscribed a world. In her forty-first year, Eloise was almost unchanged from the very pretty and vulnerable young girl Barbara's brother Tom had married and then divorced. But her prettiness, almost a cliché—a round face, blue eyes and blond hair—masked a woman whose life was filled with pain, anxiety, and fear. The pain came from a vicious form of migraine which she suffered from chronically, and the anxiety was equally constant.

She lived with named fears and nameless fears. The onset of her migraine attacks—known to medicine as cluster headache—was usually without warning, and the pain was utterly devastating, and no hour of her life was without the anticipation of pain. The nameless fears were many and had their origin years ago in the belief that her divorced husband, Thomas Lavette, would take away her son. As this fear faded, after the birth of Joshua, her second son, it was replaced by an amorphous anxiety that had no hold on reality and increased her vulnerability; and since she had few defenses, she tended to fall into an attitude of doll-like imperturbability that was frequently taken for stupidity. Mrs. Johnson, who was Frederick's grade adviser at the local high school, made this mistake. She had felt it worthwhile to visit Frederick's mother at home, and now she wondered whether all she had said did not fall on deaf ears or, more likely, totally uncomprehending ears. Eloise simply sat and listened, her face betraying no emotion at all.

"But it's not that he's bad. He's not rowdy or disruptive?"

"Disruptive?" Mrs. Johnson asked. "Yes, of course disruptive. He makes fools of his teachers. That is disruptive."

"But how? I don't understand how."

"I have been trying to explain how. Miss Catell is his English teacher. She had given the class an assignment, and the following day, she asked for their input

92

concerning the assignment. Your son proceeded to inform Miss Catell that input means something that is put in, not something given out, and then he went on to advise her that her knowledge of the English language was primitive at best. You can imagine the effect on the class. You can imagine the effect on Miss Catell."

"But was he right?" Eloise asked desperately.

"It is not a question of right or wrong, nor is it the first time he has done this, and not only in Miss Catell's class, but in the class of Mr. Pikwick, our science teacher, whom he corrects constantly, and in his social studies class—and need I go on? If I can't make you understand what his effect is on the school, then really——"

"I think I do understand," Eloise whispered. "I will talk to him——"

"That won't be enough. I think I must ask you to take him out of school."

"It's only a few weeks until the term ends," Eloise pleaded.

"I would like to talk to his father."

"My husband's in San Francisco. But tomorrow, I promise you."

The following day, Adam went to the school and spoke to Mrs. Johnson, and that evening he spoke to his son. He had never thought of Fred as anyone but his son. Like Eloise, he was soft-spoken, a very gentle human being, and with both his mother and father, Fred reversed the roles, as if they were his children, never indulging his bitter, caustic wit where they were concerned. He listened to his father now, and shook his head hopelessly.

"I'm not an idiot. I can't sit there day after day and supposedly be enlightened by idiots."

"They're not idiots, Fred. They're qualified teachers."

"Who qualifies them?"

"I'm not denying your intelligence," Adam said patiently. "You're a lot brighter than most people your age. That ought to give you enough forbearance to work this thing out. You have to finish the semester, and then another year and you'll be in college."

Fred nodded. "I'll try."

Grimly silent, Fred sat through the next two weeks, and then the summer vacation began. He was waiting eagerly when Barbara arrived with Sam, and then with scarcely more than a nod to Barbara, he led Sam in a race up the hillside, not pausing until both boys collapsed breathless at the old stone fireplace.

"Oh, God, this place is real!" Sam said. "Everything else stinks. This is real, and for a month I don't have to look at that phony creep my mother married."

"From which I gather you don't care for Kit Carson."

"You can say that again. Suppose I ask old Jake for a job? Do you think he'd give me one? I could stay the whole summer maybe, if I had a job here."

"How old are you now?" Fred asked him.

"Almost thirteen."

"Well, you could try. You're almost as tall as I am. No more wolf pack this summer, because I'm working in the bottling plant. Except on weekends. I loused up at school, and they almost dumped me. I wish they had. I was just too smart-ass with the idiots they call teachers, but I did have them going ape."

"Oh, Jesus, I wish you were at Roxten with me. I needed you, Freddie. They ran my ass ragged." He turned to his cousin and asked curiously, "But why would they want to dump you? Mom says you walked off with all the honors, and you're on the basketball team."

"It's my nasty nature. Example. This guy Burns, he teaches social studies. Talks about pedestal people. He means people you put on a pedestal. I hate that *Time* magazine talk, and anyway, he's not saying pedestal

94

but pederast. So I stand up and say, 'Mr. Burns, you don't mean pederast, surely.' So he snaps at me, 'What the devil *is* pederast?' So help me, he doesn't know what the word means. I feel called upon to explain. Could I do otherwise, Sammy?"

"Absolutely not," Sam agreed, as ignorant as Mr. Burns of the meaning of the word.

Carrying Sam's suitcase, Barbara followed Eloise up the staircase into the room which Sam would share with Joshua, Fred's eleven-year-old brother. It was a pleasant, sunny room, and Barbara expressed her delight in it. "I don't know how to thank you," Barbara said.

"Barbara, I love you, and we love Sam, and the boys are crazy about him, and anyway we're family, and whatever I did, I could never repay you and your mother for all your kindness."

There's no payment or repayment, Barbara thought. This place in the Napa Valley, with its sprawling stone buildings, its children and dogs and endless rows of vines, like a gigantic knitted carpet, had given her a family. Without the people who live here—Jake Levy and his wife, Clair; the old lady, his mother; and Adam and Eloise; and Barbara's brother Joe and his wife, Sally—without them, there was only herself and her mother and Sam. In other places, a family might be taken for granted, but California was still a land of exile.

Eloise was asking about Jean.

"I don't know," Barbara said. "There are days when she appears to be her old self, and then the depression begins again."

"I've begged her to come and stay with me."

"No. Even Oakland is an uncivilized hinterland as far as mother is concerned. She won't leave San Francisco, and mostly she doesn't set foot out of the house. I hate to ask it with all the kids here, but if you could

95

only spend a day or two with her. She does love you, Eloise."

"I'll manage. I will. I have enough help to keep the house going, and Adam will understand. When do you and Carson leave?"

"Tomorrow. We fly to New York, and then we take the *Cristoforo Colombo* to Genoa. We'll spend a week in Florence and Rome, and then two weeks at a hotel on Ischia in the Bay of Naples."

"How wonderful! How I envy you!"

"I don't know—well, I hope it works. We'll be away five weeks."

"Of course it will. I never had a real honeymoon. The first time, with Tom, was just miserable, and then when I married Adam, I couldn't bring myself to leave Freddie."

"I know," Barbara agreed. "I have my own guilts, but Carson needs a break from the paper. Only, it's odd. It sounds so damn romantic, and I feel so old. You know, I'm forty-five."

"You never looked better. You don't look a bit different from the first time we met."

Barbara burst out laughing. "What nonsense!"

"Truth. Only if I could plan a honeymoon, it would have to begin in Paris."

"Yes. That's what Carson said."

It was as close as they had come to their first real quarrel. Carson proposed that they begin their honeymoon with a week in Paris. "I told you I was with the Second Armored when we entered Paris, and I've never been back there. I always planned to, and somehow I never got around to it. And now to go there with you, the way you handle French, well, that would be something, wouldn't it?"

Barbara shook her head. "No, I don't think so, Carson."

"Why?"

96

"I can't go there on a honeymoon. Try to understand."

"What am I to understand? Is it Marcel? He's been dead twenty years. Or Bernie? He's been dead over ten years. Do you never let go of anything?"

"They're both dead. I don't want to talk about them."

"But that's it, isn't it? And if it is that, then there's all the more reason to go to Paris and rid both of us of the ghosts."

"There are no ghosts," Barbara said gently. "I want this trip to be something good and wonderful. I've never in all my life been on a vacation trip where I was relaxed and happy. I can't be relaxed and happy in France."

"Which means that we never set foot in France."

"No, no, Carson. It doesn't mean that. We'll go to France—anywhere you want to go. But please, not on our honeymoon."

His reaction revealed a part of his character she had not seen before. He sulked. He pulled away from her. He became a small boy thwarted. The saving grace was that it lasted only an hour or so, and then he said to her, "I'm being an idiot about the whole thing. Of course I understand."

She was not sure she herself understood, and by no means sure that Carson understood, and she said it to Eloise now, "I don't know why I'm telling you all this, only I'm so damned frightened."

"Of what?" Their roles were reversed. It had always been Eloise, terrified of everything, who came to Barbara for sustenance.

"Of what I've done," she confessed. "Of this marriage. It was just that the whole world went to pieces with pop's death—and there I was."

"But, Bobby, he loves you and you love him." The expression on Eloise's face was so woebegone that Barbara burst out laughing.

97

"Absolutely. And we shall both live happily ever after."

When Dr. Kellman informed Jean that he would be willing to give her sleeping pills, but only four at a time, she stared at him in astonishment and then burst out laughing. It was the first time Kellman had seen her laugh since Dan's death. "Milton, you are a dear," she said to him. "You're a sweet, worried darling. But I am not going to take my own life."

"It never crossed my mind."

"Oh? Then why four at a time—and do you know silly that is, dear Milton? I could simply put them aside for a few weeks, and then *finis*. Have no fears. I sleep poorly, but I am told that is one of the afflictions of age. I am sixty-nine, you know, and that makes for an old woman. By the way, is this a professional call?"

He had dropped in unexpectedly, and now, standing awkwardly in her living room, he assured her it was not. He was a slender, bald man in his fifties who peered through heavy glasses at the tall, white-haired woman who faced him. "By no means an old woman," he said to her. "You're in good health. What you need is fresh air and exercise."

"Ah, a message Barbara left with you. And if this is not a professional call, let's sit down and have something—a drink? No, I think it's early for both of us, and I am not becoming a sorrowing lush, if that has occurred to you."

"Never."

"Then tea?"

"Tea will be fine. I have twenty minutes. Stole ten from my patients and ten from the hospital."

"I envy you. I have nothing—day's end to day's end. And I don't pity myself. I simply state a fact."

"Then the fact must be changed."

They sat in the tiny breakfast room at the back of the house, where the window overlooked the bay and the bridge, where she and Dan had faced each other so often, and Kellman admired the view. "I always dreamed of a view of the bay and the bridge. Never managed it."

"The bay was here when Dan and I built the place," Jean reflected. "Not the bridge. But you know, Milton, you reach a point where you don't see things out of one pair of eyes. There has to be another, otherwise it's meaningless. You don't care. Times when Danny and I used to watch television, not too often, but now and then. I can't watch it alone. It's just a bore."

"Because you lock yourself up in his house. The bay is out there and the bridge is out there. Get out. Walk. Ride the cable cars. Go into the shops."

Smiling, Jean nodded. "Doctors are wonderful."

"Shall I give you a prescription for the pills? A long walk would do you more good."

"No, forget the pills. You'd worry too much."

Jean let him out, closed the door behind him, and then faced the mirror in the foyer. She peered closely at the wrinkles around her eyes and lips, straightened a bit of hair, drew her shoulders back. "What would you say, Danny?" she whispered. "A fine figure of a woman? Well, not really, and you'd choose your words more carefully, wouldn't you? Still a touch of piss and vinegar in the old broad—yes, that's more like it. Suppose we give it a try."

She went upstairs and changed into a suit of brown tweed, the jacket over a cashmere sweater, combed her hair, toyed with the thought of dyeing it, and tied it at the back of her neck in a manner she decided was at least thirty years too young for her.

The hell with it, she thought. I like it that way, and there's more points from old Dan. And calling out to her housekeeper, "Mrs. Bendler, I'm going out!"

"Shall I have them bring the car around?"

"No. No car."

"Will you be back for dinner?"

"I don't know. You can go home. I'll probably have a bite somewhere and go to the movies."

Outside, the sun was shining and the wind was blowing. "It's seven months," she said to herself as she started down the hill, "seven long, rotten months. Time to stop weeping."

The reason Barbara almost missed the hotel ferry from Ischia to the mainland was that she had stopped in the village to buy a silk scarf. The street of smart shops that lifted up from the harbor of Ischia always made her uncomfortable; it had a most unlikely resemblance to Rodeo Drive in Beverly Hills, and the prices were equally outrageous. She mulled over the scarves too long, glanced at her watch, paid for the one in her hand, pale blue, and then raced down to the pier. The handsome, yacht-like ferry had just parted company with the dock, and at the stern, a tall, gray-haired man grinned at her and shouted, "You can make it if you're a jumper."

The space was four feet and widening, and without pausing to think or slacken her pace, Barbara jumped. The man reached out and caught her arm as she teetered on the edge, and once she had regained her balance and her breath, she thanked him and told him he had saved her from an unwanted bath.

"You do swim?"

"Very well."

"Then I haven't saved your life, have I?" He had an Italian accent, and he was studying her with amusement and interest. He was quite tall, well over six feet, perhaps in his middle fifties, sparely built, pale blue eyes under shaggy brows. He had a pleasant, lined face, a reserved yet ingratiating manner.

He was vaguely familiar, and Barbara had a feeling she had seen him at the hotel. "Not my life—not even my scarf," she said, pointing to where the blue scarf floated, receding. "But I do thank you—we haven't met, I don't think."

"I'm at the hotel. No, we haven't met. I saw you with that handsome young man—your husband?"

"Yes, I'm Barbara Devron."

"And I am enchanted. My name is Umberto Leone, and since I saved neither your life nor your scarf, perhaps I can make up for my ineptness with a cappuccino or a brandy."

Barbara saw no reason to refuse. The trip from Ischia to Naples took over an hour, and it was more pleasant to sit on the upper deck sipping coffee and talking to a charming Italian than to be alone and stare at the gulls; and aside from Umberto Leone, the only other passengers were four stout German ladies whom Barbara was happy to avoid.

And Leone was charming. He had that Italian gift of making a woman feel very important without assaulting her in any way. He informed Barbara that he was married, that he had four children, and that he was president of a small automobile manufacturing company in Milan. "But once a year," he said, "I have my two weeks at Ischia. It is still the most wonderful place I know of—for the moment. In a few years, conceivably, it will be another Capri, but not yet. And with this lovely ship, one has Naples across the bay. I adore Naples. It is true Italy. Yes, it has poverty and thieves and beggars, but it also has the Neapolitans."

"I've felt that," Barbara agreed. "I find it more exciting than Rome, and more colorful. My husband doesn't agree with me. The poverty repels him."

"Understandably, since you are from California."

"Oh? I don't follow you."

"I have been there only twice, but I always think of it as a place that has no knowledge of poverty."

"I don't know whether that's a compliment or not." Barbara laughed. "But you are wrong, Mr. Leone. We

101

have our poverty—too much of it, from our point of view."

"Perhaps. A tourist sees what he is supposed to see. But tell me—why this trip to Naples alone? For most Americans, the shops on Ischia are preferable."

"I'm not off to shop. I'm going back to Pompeii. I was there with my husband last week, but only for a few hours. The place fascinated me, so I decided to go back alone and spend a whole day there."

"Your husband did not enjoy it?"

"He did. He feels that once is enough. He's going fishing, and I'm not enamored of fishing, and we both felt that a day apart from each other would be beneficial."

"It can be. Have you been married long?"

"A few weeks. We're on our honeymoon." He was regarding her curiously, and Barbara added, "It's the second marriage for both of us, if you were wondering."

"I would not be so impolite as to wonder. You make a very handsome couple, so naturally people notice you and things are said. Your husband is a newspaper publisher?"

"Yes, the Los Angeles *World*. Your English is excellent. Did you live in England or America?"

"I travel a good deal. And during the war, I was with your forces. I was not an automobile manufacturer then. I despised Mussolini."

"But since I am a rich American, you think I might have admired him?"

He spread his hands. "Possibly. But I doubt it."

"I didn't admire him, not in the slightest. And since we're into personal matters, doesn't your wife object to your vacationing alone?"

"Why should she? She's a sensible woman, and this is a safety valve. You see, we are happily married, but I am also a man. I am not a prisoner. Neither is she."

"That's very enlightened," Barbara said, smiling slightly, "for——"

"You were going to say, for an Italian."

"Was I? Then forgive me."

"No need. Why should you know more about Italians than I know about Americans?"

"Because I'm half Italian, for one thing."

"No? Truly?"

"Truly. Two grandparents were Italian. I never knew them. They died before I was born. The other two were dyed-in-the-wool white Protestant Americans. So you see, I should have a rounded knowledge. But I'm afraid I don't."

"You're an interesting woman, Mrs. Devron. How were you planning to go to Pompeii?"

"There are cabs at the dock. I'll hire one for the day."

"I have my car at the dock. I don't want to press you or give you the feeling that I am making advances. I have no motives except to look forward to a pleasant few hours. But I will be absolutely delighted to drive you to Pompeii."

"No—no, really, it's not necessary. It's very kind of you——"

"It's not kind of me. Instead of spending the day alone, I would have delightful company. I am reasonably civilized, so I am sure you would have no—well, how would I say it in English?—no uncomfortable moments. Also, being Italian, I speak Italian. But perhaps you do?"

"No, I don't."

"Ah, then I would be useful? Please accept my invitation. And if it would embarrass you to tell your husband that you rode to Pompeii with a man you knew only slightly, then my lips will be sealed."

"No, if we should drive down together, there's no reason to make a secret of it. I'm married. I am not enslaved."

103

"Bravo! Then you accept?"

"No. It's very kind of you, but I don't think I should."

Yet by the time the ferry docked at Naples, Barbara had accepted Leone's offer. The truth was that she was bored, that while she wanted to see Pompeii again, she did not relish the thought of a day alone; yet she could not face the knowledge that possibly she had been bored on other days of this honeymoon, that something inside of her had been turned off or turned around or changed, that she had entered into a marriage with a thread of misgiving stitched through her mind. She loved Carson; when she asked herself whether she truly loved him, she always replied in an affirmative, uncomplicated way; she loved her husband.

Leone's car, parked at the pier, was a low-slung, sleek sports model, black and beautifully crafted. "It's a Carlotta—my wife's name—my own. I mean, this is what I make," he explained, but diffidently, almost as an apology. "We are a small company—between two and three hundred cars a year, but each is a work of art. I don't mean to be boastful. Truly, I dislike people who make a fetish of automobiles. But building them is my way of life . . ." His voice trailed off. He was embarrassed. Barbara found herself liking him, his openness, his treatment of her as an intelligent equal.

"It's a beautiful car," she said. "And I come from a place where cars are an ideology and a fetish, so please don't apologize. Anyone who builds something so graceful should not apologize."

"But you yourself are indifferent, indifferent to cars, indifferent to clothes——"

"Is that a charming way to say I dress wretchedly?"

"You dress wonderfully but indifferently. You look good enough in what you wear not to care? Am I not correct? You shop for a scarf in Ischia and then when you lose it jumping, you never mention it again."

"The arrogance of a rich woman."

"Perhaps not."

They drove through Naples. On the road south, Leone said, "Have you ever been to Vesuvius?"

"The volcano? No."

"Then should you go to Pompeii without seeing the monster that caused it to be embalmed in ashes? I think not. It will only take an hour to look into Vesuvius, and it's something you will never forget."

The way the black sports car roared up the twisting road to Vesuvius made Barbara think that Leone had once been a racing driver, but since he had not mentioned it, she did not bring it up. She was full of guilts and mental reservations, yet she was enjoying herself immensely. Leone had taken down the top of the car, and the wind in her face and her hair made Barbara feel more alive, more aware than she had felt in all the months since her father's death. The whole tight world of the Devrons and the Lavettes was for the moment forgotten. They parked and rode the cable car almost to the lip of the great volcano, and then they climbed to the lip itself. When Barbara leaned far over, the better to see the smoking interior, Leone caught her around the waist and then quickly begged her pardon. "It's dangerous," he explained. "Don't you ever think of danger?"

"No, not very often."

"I noticed. Better to be a little afraid. Then I would drive more carefully." Then he went on to speak about racing cars when he was younger, but with distaste. "To throw a life away for that—it is stupid!"

"Yet you build cars that go a hundred and twenty miles an hour."

"Because people want them. No, that's a foolish excuse. Because the machine itself is beautiful."

They lunched at the tourist restaurant at Pompeii on excellent red wine and poor pasta. "The spaghetti in the south is not the best, except perhaps in one place on Capri," he apologized.

"I know the place."

"Do you?"

"Have you ever heard of Richard Halliburton?" He shook his head. "No, you wouldn't. He was an American writer who went all over the world looking for adventure, old-fashioned adventure like swimming the Bosporus and climbing the Alps, and anyway, he was a girlhood hero of mine and a million other girls, and one of the things he did was to swim in the Blue Lagoon. Well, I told Carson about it, and nothing would do but for him to rent a rowboat and go into the Blue Lagoon and swim. I sort of spoiled it for him because I swam there too, and then we saw this iron stairway, and there at the top of the cliff was this little restaurant, with the tables outside and overlooking the bay."

"I know the place, yes." Leone smiled.

"We had spaghetti with sweet butter sauce and red wine. It was the food of the gods."

"And your Carson—did he enjoy it as much as you did?"

"More."

They went on into Pompeii. Leone watched Barbara as she stood in the forum, her chin lifted, shoulders thrown back, as if by some spell she could cast time away and make the city live again.

"I have resisted telling you how beautiful you are. I am sure you heard it too many times."

"I am forty-five years old, Mr. Leone," she answered dryly.

"Does that cancel it? I will call you Barbara if you will call me Bert. We've not been properly introduced, but we've been together five hours."

Barbara studied him thoughtfully before she replied. "If you wish."

"I do wish. I am ten years older than you, Barbara. Mrs. Devron. Mr. Leone. Ridiculous. I have not even taken your arm. We are friends—I trust. Why do all

American women consider Italians to be unnaturally amorous?" His manner robbed his words of any sting.

"I would hope they are naturally amorous."

"Ah. Touché. I find it hard to believe that you are half Italian. You are too American, which I find delightful."

"The way silly children are delightful? But I don't want to stand here and chatter. There's half the city I haven't seen, and I won't get back here a third time."

They set off down the Strada dell' Abbondanza, Barbara overcome with a curiosity that was insatiable. She was in and out of the houses, wandering through the gardens, fascinated by the ancient bakery, the frescos, the workshops.

Leone followed her dutifully, watching her with interest and saying little. She turned to him once, wondering whether he was bored.

"No, no, not at all."

"But you've been here before."

"Many times. But never with you."

"That's very kind. But I could find a taxi back to Naples."

"Nonsense. I am enjoying myself. But tell me, Barbara, what do you find so enchanting about this place?"

"I'm not sure—" They were approaching the amphitheater now. "May we go inside?"

"If you wish," Leone agreed.

They went through the gate, onto the grassy floor of the great amphitheater, standing at the bottom with the tiers of seats rising all about them.

"You were saying?"

"I think it's the sense of a city where people had some purpose, where their community made sense. They lived in a place where their fathers and their grandfathers lived. It was a city, yet it was a place where they knew one another. We have something of that in San Francisco, but our city is so much bigger——" She was staring at the rows of seats. "This amphitheater is so big—I mean for so small a town."

Leone nodded. "Big enough for the whole city—for all the grown ones and the children too. You see, this was their obsession, to sit here and see men slaughter each other."

"Oh, no, not truly," Barbara protested. "Shaw says it was all a charade, that gladiators did not kill each other."

"I know what your George Bernard Shaw says, and he is a very clever man but he is wrong. They did kill each other. In the year fifty-nine, a pair of gladiators from the town of Nuceria were fighting two local gladiators in this very arena. There were about seven hundred Nucerians in the crowd who had come to see their gladiators fight. The rest of the seats, some twelve thousand of them, were filled with the citizens of Pompeii. Well, the crowd went crazy, as crowds do sometimes, and they set upon the Nucerians and slaughtered them, every last one of them. It was a terrible bloodbath. So you see, the life they lived cannot be defined this bucolic, peaceful ruin."

"Is that true, what you're telling me?" Barbara whispered.

"Absolutely. When we get back to the hotel, you'll find a history of Pompeii in the library there. You can check my facts."

"But how could people create a city as beautiful as this and behave like animals?"

"Animals? No, animals do not do such things. People. Remember, I lived through the war."

"So did I," Barbara said softly. "I was in Germany. You're right, Umberto, animals don't do such things."

Driving back to Naples, Leone said to her, "You love your husband——"

"Yes, I do."

"Selfishly, I wish you hated him."

"Do you hate your wife?"

108

"I neither love her nor do I hate her. She is my wife."

Carson was dressing for dinner when Barbara came into their hotel suite. He kissed her and then remarked that she didn't look too happy with her second venture into antiquity.

"The arena down there threw me off, and I've been a bit blue ever since. I'll get over it. Just the thought of people enjoying the spectacle of men cutting each other to pieces."

"They still enjoy football. I do."

"It's not the same thing, hardly."

"I suppose not, although future generations may not agree with you. Anyway, you got the archaeological bug out of your system. Did you take a cab? I'm rather nervous about you running all over southern Italy alone in a cab."

"No, not this time. I met a lovely gentleman on the ferry, and he drove me down there."

Carson paused in knotting his tie and turned to look at her. "Oh? Someone we know?"

She shook her head. "An Italian automaker, name of Umberto Leone."

"Yes, I've seen him," Carson said slowly. "Makes the Carlotta. How did it happen? Did he pick you up?"

"That's a nasty thing to say."

"I'm sorry. I didn't mean it that way."

Barbara dropped into a chair and stared at Carson. "How did you mean it?"

"I was just wondering how you happen to meet a strange man who drives you down to Pompeii. It doesn't matter. Let's forget it."

"It matters. I ran for the ferry this morning and jumped. He caught my arm and saved me a bath in the Bay of Naples. I thanked him. I'm not a child, Carson."

"You're in a beautiful mood."

"Right. I am in a rotten mood, and you're not helping. I don't want to make something out of this, because it's nothing. I met a charming man. He drove me down to Pompeii and he drove me back, and I love you and I married you, and I don't leap into bed with strangers."

"Then you spent the day with him at Pompeii?"

"Yes!" she snapped, rising and going into the bathroom and locking the door behind her. A few minutes passed before she heard Carson's voice through the door.

"Barbara, how abject must my apology be?"

"Reasonably so."

"I behaved like a horse's ass."

"More or less."

"Am I forgiven?"

"Yes, I'm hungry. You're forgiven."

"Ischia," Fred informed Sam, "is an island at the northern tip of the Bay of Naples. Capri is at the southern tip, and that's the one they sing about in songs, but it doesn't have the class of Ischia."

"How do you know?"

"I read the guidebooks."

"I been to Catalina," Sam said.

"Son, you are a peasant. Catalina is for peasants. You know something, my lad, if I were one year older, we could both be heading for Ischia, lying in the sun, poolside at a classy hotel, picking up the exquisite little babes—what am I talking about? I bet you never laid a hand on a girl."

"I tried with May Ling. She got sore."

"May Ling," Fred said with contempt. "May Ling is a stick. She doesn't have tits. That's child molesting, and anyway you don't crap on your own doorstep. How old are you—thirteen?"

"That's right," Sam agreed sadly.

"Oh well, give it time."

"How come you could be heading for Ischia if you were a year older?"

"Well, by then I'll have about five hundred dollars saved up, and certainly my eighteenth birthday has to call for a small bundle from Grandma Jean, and what's more uplifting for a poor farm boy than a trip to Europe?"

"Have you spoken to your mother about it?"

"Oh, I'll talk her into it."

"That'll be the day."

They were sitting in Fred's room, which like Fred himself, commanded Sam's fervent admiration. Unlike Fred's brother's room, which was neat and clean—Joshua being a very sober and neat eleven-year-old—Fred's room was piled with books, fishing rods, snowshoes, bats, gloves, three basketballs, a huge medicine ball, and an assortment of Fred's clothes. Eloise never set foot in the room. Just to observe it through the open door set her to trembling. Once a week, a Chicana woman fought unsuccessfully to clean it. Sam had been given a job in the bottling plant, sorting corks, a position he took seriously and worked at with a will. He had never worked at any job before, and at the end of each week, he was given five dollars, his own money earned with his own hands. The hours were not long, and he was at Higate with people he loved.

"Anyway," Fred said, "this Ischia is a great place, and there's no reason why your old lady shouldn't have some fun. You can't ask her to live alone for the rest of her life."

"Why not? Anyway, she's not alone. I live with her."

May Ling, age twelve, five feet and eight inches already, her black shoulder-cut hair and black bangs framing a face of near perfection, asked her mother why boys liked to touch girls. Sally, whose mind raced

111

over a dozen rejoinders that fitted the question appropriately, found that none of them were adequate for this situation, and simply stared at her daughter for a very long moment. Twelve had no right to be that innocent, not in this enlightened or benighted—depending on how you looked at it—year of 1959. A few weeks later, telling Barbara about it, she confessed that she was baffled.

"If you were really speechless," Barbara said, "then that was a first, wasn't it, Sally?"

"Now you're putting me on. I don't chatter anymore. What would you have said?"

"I'm trying to remember what I knew about sex when I was twelve. Of course, that was another age. But I do think that at twelve I had been pawed considerably, if clumsily. Why don't you tell her how the whole thing works?"

They were in the living room of Barbara's house on Green Street in San Francisco, Sally in from Napa for a day in town. Sally was kinetic; only total exhaustion could keep her motionless. Now as she spoke, she moved constantly about the little room, catlike in her avoidance of the overstuffed Victorian pieces that had once belonged to Sam Goldberg, Dan Lavette's lawyer, and which Barbara preserved and treasured when she bought the old house. Barbara watched her movement enviously. She changed positions like a dancer, and in Sally's presence, Barbara always felt oversized and clodlike, although they were the same height.

"Tell her?" Sally exclaimed. "You have to be kidding. I couldn't face it—not with May Ling. Just looking at her makes me feel impure. Well, I am. I mean reasonably impure."

Barbara began to laugh. "Impure. Sally, you are incredible."

"I often think so. I've been writing poetry again— after years of avoiding it. I'm waiting for her to start

112

menstruating. That's a good way to explain. I think she's late. Do Chinese menstruate late?"

"Will you please sit down," Barbara begged her. "Sally, May Ling is one quarter Chinese."

Sally dropped onto the couch.

"Do you want another drink?"

"Of course I do. I couldn't touch the stuff while I was carrying Danny or nursing him without Joe having a fit. A slight case of inebriation is absolutely necessary to living with your brother Joe. Don't look at me like that, Bobby. Have you ever tried living with a saint?"

"No, I guess not." She filled Sally's glass from a pitcher of martinis. Sally was testing the couch.

"You're not selling this wonderful old sofa. If you are, I want it."

"I'm not selling anything in the house. It's remaining just as it is. I'm giving you and Eloise keys, and you can use it whenever you're in town."

"And how does Carson take your hanging on to this place? Doesn't it give him a tentative feeling?"

"You don't mince words, do you?"

"I'm sorry, Bobby. I get carried away."

"Well, it's a lovely old house, and available houses in this neighborhood are as rare as hen's teeth. And better than a hotel room. We will be coming here a good deal. I don't know how much of Beverly Hills I can take. You lived there."

"If you call it that. It wasn't the best time in my life." But it was not until she was on her way out that Sally thought to ask Barbara about the honeymoon.

"It was good. It had its high moments."

"And low ones, I suppose. That's the nature of honeymoons."

The next morning, Barbara locked up the house to leave for Los Angeles. She had already loaded her car with all the luggage the trunk and the back seat could hold, and Sam was in the car, waiting impatiently. Barbara paused to look at the place. It was a small, narrow house, sitting on the slope of the hill, one of those marvelously decorated old wooden houses that had survived the 1906 earthquake undamaged. It was wonderfully ugly. There were two bay windows, triptych style, one above the other and dominating the front of the house. Two wooden Medusa heads, unexpectedly benign, crowned each window, and there were six steps up to the entranceway, which was framed by wooden columns, pseudo-Moorish. Over the doorway and the windows, every bit of wood was carved, and this improbable carving was repeated in the rows of dentils upon which the roof rested. The house was clapboard, painted white.

Barbara had first seen the house in 1934, when she had become involved in the great longshoremen's strike, using her station wagon as a first aid depot for injured strikers. She had come to Sam Goldberg, who was her father's lawyer, for advice and sustenance. Seven years later, in 1941, after Sam Goldberg's death, she had bought the house from the estate. It was the place she returned to after her stint as a war correspondent. It was the place where she had lived with her husband until his death, and it had been home to Sam for thirteen years of his life. When Carson suggested that she sell it, she was dumbfounded. "You can't be serious," she said.

"I am. You're my wife. Does it make sense to have a home of your own in San Francisco when you're living in Los Angeles?"

"It's not a home of my own," Barbara argued. "It's a place for both of us. We don't need the money, and the taxes are inconsequential. It means so much to me——"

"That's it. You have to cut loose from the past sometime, Bobby."

"Don't press it, please, darling," Barbara begged

114

him. "I can't sell that house. Try to understand. I did a lot of understanding about the Beverly Hills house."

While they were on their honeymoon, Carson's real estate agents had been looking for a proper house. Carson had decided against Hancock Park. For one thing, it was too close to his parents; for another, it belonged to the past. In 1959, Beverly Hills was still elegant, as Los Angeles considered elegance; it was conveniently located in the vast sprawl of the city; and Carson considered it a very decent place for them to take up residence. Barbara's antipathy toward Beverly Hills, he felt, concerned the film crowd, and he argued that one could spend years in Beverly Hills without consorting with film people. Barbara doubted this. She felt that if she had to settle for Los Angeles, it should be toward the ocean, either in Santa Monica or in Pacific Palisades. Both places, Carson felt, were too far from the downtown center, and when finally Barbara saw the enormous stucco-covered mansion that Carson felt would constitute a proper home, she threw up her hands in despair.

Carson was gentle and persuasive. "Of course I'd want a small house. I know there are only the two of us and the boy. But the fact remains that I am the publisher of the paper. Hell, I could dump that too, and maybe in time I will, and then we could fall into a beach house at Malibu where we'd both be a damn sight happier. I know that, Bobby. But right now, I am what I am. I am what you married. I have to entertain—no, not the kind of people you find so distasteful. But I am a sort of pivot factor out here, people from Washington, people from Sacramento, from Europe, from Japan and Hong Kong—they flood in and there's no way in the world I can avoid it. You just might enjoy it."

"Being a hostess?" Barbara said dubiously.

"Have you ever tried it?"

"I seem to have avoided it."

115

"You might like it. It's not easy, not if it's done properly. It wants diplomacy and intelligence. I don't mean that it has to interfere with your writing . . ."

In the end, Barbara gave in. She had made a commitment, and this came with it, the house came with it, and Carson came with it, and she loved him, and perhaps she loved him most when he was like this, like a small boy pleading for a new toy.

And now she had loaded her car, locked up the house on Green Street—she was to keep it and accept the house in Beverly Hills—and was off to Los Angeles with Sam sitting beside her, glum and wishing that he was still at Higate, sorting wine corks.

In the East, at least until the recent generation, families proliferated and extended themselves. Some families had been in America three centuries, some two centuries, far more a century or less. When the first immigrants left Europe or Africa or Asia, the cut in the umbilical cord was savage and final, and in so many cases those left behind never again saw or spoke to those who had departed. In Ireland, where deep poverty made a return trip unthinkable, the going-off was frequently accompanied by what came to be known as "the American wake," except that there were more tears for the living who departed than there would have been for the dead in a real wake. But once in America, the families reconstituted themselves, and as generations passed in the new land, there were fathers and mothers and grandparents and great-grandparents and multitudes of uncles, aunts, and cousins. But with the transition to California, the process repeated itself. To California came the odds and ends of families, he and she often with no other kin, with a cord clipped from the past, and thus the new family, beginning its slow growth once again on the West Coast, possessed a tight, almost precious sense of itself. It went beyond

116

blood ties. Friends were often treasured, and friend and family frequently merged.

In that manner, in the somewhat more than half a century since the great earthquake, the Lavettes, the Levys, and the Cassalas had taken on certain aspects of a single family, even though they had mixed blood with the Seldons, the Whittiers, the Harveys, and the Clawsons. It took a while in California for the fine lines among Catholic, Protestant, and Jew to be drawn, and when they were drawn, the texture was uneven and easily parted. Thomas Lavette, Barbara's older brother, had originally married Eloise Clawson. Fred was their son. When Tom and Eloise were divorced, Tom married Lucy Sommers, who was the granddaughter of an Irish gold miner and the daughter of a partner in the Seldon Bank. Threads can be severed; in good time they come together. Thomas Lavette, at this time, in 1959, had the reputation of being the third wealthiest and the third most powerful man on the Coast. Perhaps not. Possibly the fourth or fifth. Whatever the case, his wealth and influence were enough for him to be known as one of the kingmakers. The king who was in the process of being made was Norman Drake, the onetime congressman who, as a member of the House Un-American Activities Committee, had been active in citing Barbara for contempt of Congress for refusing to reveal the names of people who had joined her in sending medical aid to survivors of the Spanish Republican army. And because at least a part of Drake's unenviable body belonged to Thomas Lavette, Dan Lavette had not spoken to his son for years before his death.

In the old East, this might have rent the family asunder. In California, responding to different forces, Tom still felt himself part of the family. His wife, Lucy, shared his feeling. They both felt that for Tom to present Norman Drake to Carson Devron not only would be tactless but would come as an action re-

117

flecting, from Carson's point of view, upon the whole family. Do what he might, Tom could not live and act as Thomas Lavette in proud isolation; he had to function as Thomas Lavette of the Lavettes. The difference was subtle but important.

"Why they tossed this in your lap," his wife, Lucy, said to him, "I don't know. I sometimes doubt that they're as clever as you say."

The "they" whom she referred to were a group of very wealthy and powerful men who controlled most of the industry in California and a substantial part of it in the rest of the country. They had no name for themselves and they were loosely organized, but they knew who they were. It was almost ten years since Tom had become a part of their circle, and somewhat less than ten years since he had introduced Norman Drake to their tutelage and in a large measure ownership.

On this day, Tom and Lucy were having breakfast, as they did each morning they were in town, in the solarium of their gray-stone mansion on Pacific Heights. Tom endured the plant-filled room. Lucy loved it. The huge old house had been built by Lucy's father shortly after the earthquake, and Lucy treasured it as she treasured the memory of her father.

"And if they are as clever as you seem to think," Lucy went on, "then their choice of Norman Drake is, to say the least, incongruous. To think of that wretched, sniveling little man as President of the United States—well, it boggles the mind."

"The point is that he is ours. He's our wretched, sniveling little man."

"And how on earth do you propose to get him elected?"

"The same way he got elected to the Congress and the Senate."

"And what is that? Does your voter recognize his own deplorable self? Is it the lowest common denominator? Or is he everyman? If so, heaven help us."

118

In recent years, Tom had come to face the fact that he disliked his wife. She was aggressive, very competent, and brighter than he was. For the first years of their marriage, he had accepted this condition with gratitude; few people knew how many of the most successful moves of GCS were inspired by Lucy; and while this had pleased Tom at first, now it only irritated him and deepened his frustration. There was little love between them in the beginning, but there was dependence and necessity; when the dependence and necessity evidenced itself of late Tom responded with outer irritation and inner rage. He now said coldly, "The point is not his vote-getting ability, but how do I sell him to Carson Devron? And I have to. He's mine. I brought him to the others. I brought him to my tailor. I even got him to stop picking his nose in public. And that miserable damn sister of mine had to marry Devron."

"You don't bring him to Carson," Lucy said. "You bring him to Christopher and Lila. Momma and daddy. They understand these things. They will sell him to Carson."

"Christopher Devron," Tom said thoughtfully. "The old man still runs things, doesn't he?"

"I would presume so," Lucy said.

The old man, Christopher Devron, reminded Tom of his father, Dan Lavette. He had the same air of command, the same poise, the same large, erect stature that defied time. He was seventy-four, and his face was as wrinkled as the desert mountains, seen from thirty thousand feet, but his eyes were pale blue and direct and coldly judgmental. The eyes had examined Tom carefully and calculatingly before he nodded and said, "So you're Dan Lavette's boy. I never met your father, but from all I know, he was one uncommon and singular man. And I know a hell of a lot, sonny, so you don't have to explain. We're a newspaper family, and a

119

knowledge of our own peculiar state history goes with the territory. So your little club wants to foist Norman Drake on the American people?"

"That's one way of putting it——"

"I know your associates," Devron interrupted. "Dined with them a few times, but I'm not a joiner. I also know Norman Drake."

"Then I think you might agree with me——"

"What makes you think so?" Devron interrupted. "Don't presume, boy. There's damn little chance I'd agree with you on anything, particularly on qualities possessed by Norman Drake. Unless you're going to tell me he's a vote-getter."

"He is," Tom said gently.

"And what else are you going to tell me about him?"

Tom grinned. "Nothing. Not one damn word more."

The old man accepted his smile and returned it. He opened a bottle of brandy and poured two glasses, handing one to Tom and setting the decanter down almost with reverence. "Like it?" he asked as Tom drank.

"Wonderful brandy."

"California brandy. Don't ever forget that, sonny. Our brandy's as good as any in the world and our climate's a damn sight better. Now, about Norman Drake—he ain't without quality, not by any means. He doesn't bite the hand that feeds him, he loves money, and he was born right here in Southern California. Those are qualities. Could he become President? Well, sonny, it's high time we had our own boy in there, and you're not the first one to bring up Norman Drake. As far as my own taste is concerned—well, if you're going to dabble in politics, you'd better turn off taste and smell. If you're going to seek out virtue, you go to a church, not to a cathouse."

"Would your paper support him?" Tom asked flatly.

"Right to the point, huh? I kind of like you, Thomas. My son publishes the paper, and my son is married to your sister. I don't imagine you and your sister have a great deal in common."

"We talk to each other."

"That's something. Not a hell of a lot, but something. I don't expect family to love each other, but they should stay connected. You're not a Catholic, are you?"

"I was raised an Episcopalian."

"Of course you were. Your grandfather owned a piece of Grace Cathedral, didn't he?"

"He willed them some property—yes."

"I liked old Tom Seldon. He was a good man, for a banker. Now it looks like the Democrats are going to play with that young snotnose from Boston, the Kennedy kid. Norman Drake. He might do it. I don't think America's ready for the Pope yet, and that kid from Boston might just give Drake the edge he needs."

"Can you convince your son of that?" Tom asked warily.

"I think so. His daddy still owns the paper, and if I can't convince him, his mother can. How certain are your people that Drake can have the nomination?"

"They appear to be certain."

"All right, sonny. I'm not saying yes, and I'm not saying no. But I sure as hell will think about it. It's interesting—Norman Drake as President. My God, how low we have sunk."

The butler picked up the telephone, and then told Barbara the call was for her. Or perhaps he was not a butler. Carson preferred to call him the houseboy. In Beverly Hills, they had things like houseboys. The sprawling stucco-coated mansion on Rexford Drive that Carson had bought for himself and his bride required three persons as full-time help simply to keep it operative: a cook, a housemaid, and a houseboy. The gardener came in twice a week, and for large dinners and parties, caterers joined the cook. The servants

121

were quartered in a cottage behind the pool. The house had an enormous living room, a library, large dining room, kitchen, pantry, and seven bedrooms. Carson bought it furnished, but he assured Barbara that she had a free hand to replace any or all of the furniture. Given that privilege, gift, assurance, promise, Barbara had been overcome by a sort of paralysis, a larger token of the kind of paralysis that overtook her now with the phone ringing, indeed whenever the phone rang. She had answered telephones all her life, yet in this house her ordinary response was constantly frozen. It was not simply that she hated the huge pseudo-Spanish Colonial mansion; it dwarfed her and diminished her. At first, she had confronted it. She had answered the phone; she had made notes; she had studied the oversized chairs and couches and tables—and then, bit by bit, she began to surrender. The surrender began in her search through the house for a room in which to work. She chose a room, but it was dark. In the burning sunlight of Southern California, all the rooms of the house were dark. An electrician came and rigged lights, and she sat under the lights and the words that were the tools of her trade would not come. Carson called it "writer's block." "Every writer experiences it," he assured her. Then, when she had sat by a ringing telephone three times without touching it, Carson talked to her, was offered no explanation, and then instructed Robin, the houseboy, to answer the phone. He decided that Barbara was depressed, but when he brought up the question, she refused to discuss it. She remembered the depth and terror of the depression she had suffered in prison. She now told herself that there was a qualitative difference between depression and being depressed.

And now the butler, houseboy, or whatever, a Korean named Robin Park, answered the telephone and then went to Barbara's workroom, where she sat staring at her typewriter, to tell her that the Santa Monica chief of police was on the phone and wished to talk to Mrs. Devron.

"You said the chief of police?"

"Yes, missy, chief of police."

"Doesn't he want Mr. Devron?"

"He say missy not mister."

She picked up the telephone, and the voice at the other end asked her whether she was Mrs. Devron.

"Yes. What is this all about?"

"We have your son here, mixed up in malicious mischief. I been talking to him, and seeing who his father and mother are and him being a juvenile, well, I'd rather talk to you before we charge him with anything."

"Is he all right?" Barbara cried out. "Is he hurt?"

"No, ma'am, he is not hurt."

"Please, I'll be there as soon as I can."

Afterwards, recalling her mood and her thoughts during the drive from Beverly Hills to Santa Monica, a few miles along Wilshire Boulevard, Barbara could only remember a miasma of disaster. She, whose life had always been a thing of purpose and decision, was now rudderless and purposeless. She felt that since she had first come here a year before, to write a screenplay based upon her book, every turn of her life had been without volition or mind. She had let go; she was married to a man who was a stranger; she lived in a house she hated, surrounded by objects that had belonged to someone else; and a wall had grown up between herself and her son. Once, long ago, she had been easily given to tears, but now the tears had dried up along with everything else, and she drove on between the rows of used-car lots and junk-food emporiums in stony-faced silence.

Once in the police station at Santa Monica, Barbara demanded to see her son. The police chief, a heavyset, harassed man, assured her that her son was all right. "You'll see him, Mrs. Devron."

"I want to see him now. Where is he? In a cell?"

"He's not in a cell, Mrs. Devron. Will you please calm yourself? He's in a room down the hall, and he's not hurt, and you can see him in a few minutes."

"What has he done?"

The police chief looked at her bleakly. He had a glass of water and a package of Tums on his desk, and he picked off two of the Tums and swallowed them with a gulp of water. "My stomach," he apologized. "Kids—why on God's earth do kids do what they do? Will you tell me that?"

"Please, what did he do?"

"He was up on the bluff over the Pacific Coast Highway. Three of them. The two other kids got away. They were tossing rocks down in front of the cars."

"Oh, my God," Barbara whispered.

"They hit a car. Smashed the windshield. The driver was hurt."

"How badly hurt?"

"They took four stitches in his cheek. He was lucky. He managed to control the car, and there was a lot of flying glass but none of it in his eyes. He could have been blinded and he could have been killed. There's enough real crime without kids doing a thing like this."

"You're sure my son—that he was the one."

"We're sure. He talked. There was a police car right behind, and one of our officers got up on the bluff before the kids took off. I'm not saying your son threw the particular rock. They were all throwing rocks."

"What will you do with him?" Barbara asked wanly.

"I don't know." He took another Tums and chewed it. "I got a kid his age. I hate it when it happens to kids. We book him, and this man who was hurt—his name is Westcott—he prefers charges—" He shook his head angrily. "The kid's thirteen years old. Well, Westcott's here. You want to talk to him? Maybe you can settle this thing with him or maybe he wants to sue you. I don't know. No, I'm not going to charge the kid, Mrs. Devron. He's scared to death, and maybe he's been punished enough. If he was my kid, I'd take him home and whack the hide off him."

Westcott was a small, skinny man, sitting on a bench in the police station, still shivering from his experience, a taped bandage on the side of his face. He kept shaking his head and muttering that he didn't know. "It was a terrible thing, a terrible thing, Mrs. Devron. How do kids do something like that?"

"I don't know. I'm so sorry."

"The boy ought to be punished. It's a terrible thing."

"I can't wipe out the experience," Barbara said. "I agree with you. It's a terrible thing, and it shouldn't have happened. He's not a bad boy or a cruel boy. I don't know why it happened. I haven't seen him yet. But I can pay for the damage to the car and for—well, whatever . . ."

"I'm going to talk to my lawyer," he said.

"Yes, of course." Trying to keep her hand from shaking, Barbara wrote out a check for a thousand dollars.

"The car's insured," he said, staring at the check.

"I'd rather pay for it."

"This don't mean I'm not talking to my lawyer."

"I know," Barbara whispered.

He took the check finally, and then Barbara followed an officer down a hallway. The officer opened a door. "There he is. You can take him home."

Sam sat behind a small wooden table on a kitchen chair. It occurred to Barbara that this was an interrogation room, and she had to wage an inner struggle to keep back the tears, to keep from embracing her son, to keep her face from revealing emotion. Sam stared at her. The officer left the two of them alone. Sam tried to speak, gulped wordlessly, and managed at last, "What are they going to do to me?"

"Nothing," Barbara said. "We're going home."

They walked out of the police station and got into the car. "Are they just letting me go?" Sam asked hoarsely.

"That's right."

"You hate me, don't you?"

"No!"

"You think I did it on purpose."

"I don't know what I think. The way I feel, it's hard enough for me just to drive. So you try to work out what you think, and I'll try to work out what I think. I don't want to discuss it until we're at home."

Then they drove on in silence, with Sam huddled in the front seat, as far from his mother as the seat permitted. When they reached the big house on Rexford Drive, Barbara told Sam to go to his room and wait for her, which he did without even glancing at her. Barbara went into her bathroom and splashed cold water on her face and then rubbed her face dry. She wore no makeup during the day, and looking into her mirror, she saw a pale, drawn countenance. All her life, Barbara had lived with the security of being a beautiful woman. It was nothing she had earned or accomplished, but it was there, comforting her, sustaining her, regardless of a pretended and frequently studied indifference. As she often reflected, it was her luck; others were less lucky. She might at times resent it intellectually, but emotionally it was always there, like an enveloping and comforting security blanket. Now, for the first time, she saw nothing beautiful in the face that stared from the mirror, and then anger at herself, at Sam, horror at the whole incident drained away into a kind of sick fear.

"What are we doing to ourselves?" she whispered. "What has happened to us?"

She was forty-five years old, and tired and

126

frightened, and her son had almost killed a man, a stranger, and almost killed him out of some mindless act of violence, and now she would have to deal with it, and deal with her husband, who would know about it because the newspapers knew about these things, and who was her husband? The last thought raced through her mind. Who was her husband? Who was this man she was married to? Who was this boy? She was a middle-aged woman married to a boy made out of plastic. Wasn't that her initial thought? Plastic.

"Oh, no, no, no," she said aloud. "I am being so rotten unfair to one of the best men I've ever known. What has happened to me?"

She took several deep breaths, and then she stood absolutely silent for a long moment, and then she went into Sam's room. He was sprawled on the bed, and he lay there, his face turned away from the door, not moving. Strangely, since he was sprawled out, she realized for the first time how very tall he was for his age, an inch or two under six feet, his frame long and slender. She could have melted then, telling herself that her son was the one thing in the world that she loved above all else, her link with life and reality, with the past and the future; and she had the feeling that here and now, before her eyes, the boy was turning into a man. Don't lose him, she pleaded with herself. Try to understand.

"Sam, get up!" she said sharply, and when he didn't move, repeated, "Get up! Now!"

He turned and sat up.

"Over there. In that chair. We're going to talk."

He pulled himself off the bed and slumped into the chair. "What's the use? I did it."

"What you did," Barbara said evenly, "has to do with what I did, and either we make some sense out of where we are or there's no damn hope for either of us."

"I don't know what you mean," he muttered.

x

127

"I think you do. How did you get out there to Pacific Palisades? That's miles from here."

"I cut school. We hitched."

"Why? Why did you cut school?"

"I hate it. I hate Beverly Hills. I hate the kids."

"That's a lot of hate. Is that why you threw the rocks? Because you hate school?"

"I don't know why I threw the rocks," Sam said. "I just did it."

"You're bright. You're so bright that sometimes it frightens me. Yet you go out to the Palisades and throw rocks at people you don't know. Why?"

"I don't know why. I didn't know we'd hurt anyone. It was just something to do. I didn't want to hurt anyone." He began to cry, and through his tears, he blurted out, "I didn't want to come here. You made me come here. I hate it here. Why can't I go home? First you sent me to that rotten school in Connecticut, and now you make me come here. I hate it here."

"Stand up," Barbara said softly.

He stood up, and Barbara put her arms around him and held him to her. "I love you very much," she said softly. "This has been a bad day for both of us. Now I want you take a shower and change your clothes. We'll talk about this later."

"I didn't want to hurt anyone," he pleaded.

"I know you didn't," Barbara said.

Strange, she thought, something like this happens, and it's awful and frightening, yet I feel a crazy exhilaration, as if this proves something—only I don't know what it proves, unless it proves that we're alive, both of us, and it takes something as desperate as this to make us alive. And then she asked herself what she was thinking. "I hate this place," she said aloud. "I hate it as much as he does, this house, Beverly Hills—no, I don't hate it," as an afterthought. "I don't know where it is or where I am." She enumerated what she didn't know; she didn't know herself, her son, or her husband. If she was in love with her husband, why had everything been chilled and dead inside of her until now, and what was happening to her now? Her thoughts went back to Italy and to the day she spent with Umberto Leone, but the recollection was nothing new. The memory of that day had been racing through her mind for weeks, and always with the question of why she had not permitted him to make love to her, and always answered with an equivocation of one sort or another. Now, for the first time she allowed the fantasy to play out, filled as she was with emptiness and hunger. Possessed of the certainty that she would never see him again, she could allow herself the desperate need to be with such a man, without comprehending why she had the need.

If Carson knew about the incident at Santa Monica, he made no mention of it. Barbara felt that he did not know, and she had decided not to tell him. Carson, on the other hand, was pleased with the change in his wife. Her mood of depression had passed. At a dinner party given by Phil Baker, the executive editor of the *Morning World,* Barbara appeared to be entirely at ease, gracious and charming. She enthralled the gathering with the story of how she had gone into Nazi Germany in 1939 and had been arrested by the Gestapo.

"But weren't you absolutely terrified?" Cecil Baker asked her. Ceil Baker was a golden California girl, much younger than her husband. It had to be explained to her who the Gestapo were. Barbara felt relaxed and expansive, and in no mood to condemn ignorance—or, as Carson defined it later—idiocy.

"I was very young and very romantic," Barbara said. "My friends in Paris wanted desperately to make some contact with the underground in Germany, if there was one, which I doubt, and since I was without any politics and without even a modicum of common sense, and

129

since I was a journalist, I volunteered. Oh, my editor back in New York loved the notion."

"Which caused you to hate editors ever since," Baker put in.

"Oh, no, not at all. But I went and tried stupidly to find a man who was already dead and then tried to interfere with the brutalization of some old Jews by Nazi thugs—and, well, I survived."

"To Carson's good fortune."

"Indeed. I'll drink to that," Carson said.

Then the talk turned to politics, and someone mentioned the fact that Norman Drake had announced his candidacy.

"What every red-blooded American boy wants. Why not Norman Drake?"

"Why not indeed?"

"The little bugger's a vote-getter. He plays for keeps."

Baker said nothing; he was aware of Barbara's history. Carson glanced at her uneasily.

"Will you fellers support him?" The question was put to Carson and Baker.

Baker shrugged. Carson said, "We haven't come to that."

"You must be thinking about it."

"We're thinking about it," Carson agreed.

Back in their bedroom, in the house in Beverly Hills, Barbara sat in a chair and watched Carson unbutton his shirt. She had hardly spoken at all since leaving the Bakers', and now Carson wanted to know whether something was troubling her.

"You can't guess?"

"I thought you were having a good time."

"I was."

"Norman Drake?"

"What does it mean—you're thinking about it?" she asked coldly.

"You lost me somewhere."

"Did I? Maybe. You said you were thinking about the paper supporting Norman Drake."

"Yes."

"That's all?"

"Bobby, what should I say? We're thinking about it. We're discussing it. People who know say he'll get the party's designation. We have to think about it."

"Which means you could support him."

He walked over and bent to kiss her. She drew away. "Don't! I'm talking about a damn serious matter. I'm not a little girl."

Carson pulled back and crossed the room, and then turned, provoked. "No, you're not. All right, look, Bobby, you hate the man's guts. With reason, I'll grant. That was years ago. It's over and done with. McCarthyism's over. The blacklist is over. It was your Harry Truman, the darling of the liberals, who presided over the blacklisting and the terror. We ended it. We run a decent, honest newspaper, but we're not a Democrat paper and we're not a liberal paper. You know that! You've always known that! And as far as the Democrats and the liberals are concerned, where the hell were they when you were sent to prison?"

"You're shouting."

"I'm sorry." He dropped onto the bed, facing her. "Come on, Bobby, we've scrapped over a lot of things, but politics isn't one of them. We've both tried to make this marriage work, and God knows, it hasn't been easy. Maybe no marriage is easy. But I try."

"That's just it."

He shook his head.

"You try," Barbara said. "I try. Good God, Carson, what's wrong with us?"

"Nothing."

"Nothing. But your paper will support Norman Drake."

"That's the paper."

"And my husband's the publisher."

"Oh, no," Carson said, standing and striding across the room again. "That won't wash. You are not married to the paper. It's an entity with its own responsibilities."

"And Norman Drake is one of them."

"If he's the candidate, yes."

"All right," Barbara said, taking a deep breath. "Leaving me out of it. I don't prate about patriotism. I agree that too often it's the last resort of a scoundrel. Nevertheless, this is our place. We were born here and we speak our native language, and we brought something to the place. If I desired to be wretchedly sentimental, I might say that San Francisco is my mother. I don't know how you feel about Beverly Hills—" She began to laugh at the whole ridiculous image.

"Now you're being offensive," Carson said.

"Nobody's mother. I take it back."

Carson was grinning. "Northern Californians are as insufferable as New Yorkers. Just say your piece, girl. Kill the adjectives."

"Thank you. I was just wondering whether you feel anything about this country. Do you love it? Do you hate it?"

"I'm not that dense, Bobby."

"I didn't think so. What has America done to have Norman Drake inflicted upon it?"

"We have our sins."

"Don't do it, Carson."

"All I said is that we're discussing it. Can we go to bed now?"

The telephone call, a few days later, was from a man who introduced himself as George Merkounian. He wanted to know whether he was speaking to Mrs. Devron, and Barbara assured him that he was.

"This is very private," he said. "Are there extensions on this line?"

"Either tell me what you want, Mr. Merkounian, or I shall hang up."

"Yes, yes, of course. I simply want our discussion to be confidential. I am Mr. Westcott's lawyer."

Barbara had put the incident to rest, and for a long moment she was unable to relate to the name Westcott. Sam had been going to school properly, doing his homework, day after day of quiet remorse. Under other circumstances, such behavior would have worried Barbara; now she had accepted it as a reaction on the boy's part from guilt and fear; and now, as she put the name Westcott into perspective, Mr. Merkounian went on, "I think we should meet and talk, Mrs. Devron. My office is not far from your home, just north of Wilshire on Canon. My client, Mr. Westcott, has some just grievances, but there is no reason for us to engage in public exposure. I always prefer to settle these matters out of court."

"I gave a thousand dollars to Mr. Westcott," Barbara reminded him. "He appeared to agree that it was adequate to cover the damages to his car and whatever his medical bills were."

"He also tells me that he assured you he would take legal action. So hadn't we better talk before this goes further?"

"Very well," Barbara agreed, and then he gave her the address and they made an appointment for the following afternoon.

She walked to the office on Canon Drive, reflecting, as she had so many times, that almost no one walked for more than a block or two in Beverly Hills. She tried desperately to overcome the feeling of depression that was overtaking her again, to regain the mood she remembered when walking on the Embarcadero in San Francisco, but here there was no wind-blown bay, no smell of the salt air, no stands selling fresh-caught crab and sourdough bread, only the funereal, empty sidewalks, devoid of humankind other than herself, the close-cropped lawns, the palm trees, and the enormous stucco-covered mansions. In the business section, south of Santa Monica Boulevard, there was a stir of life, the men and women plastically homogenized, the women blonde, tip-tiled on high heels, the men suntanned, their shirts open to the third button. She felt awkward, oversized, out of place. In the office building on Canon Drive, she felt a sudden headlong rush of fear. Why hadn't she told Carson about the incident? Was there still a possibility that Sam could be punished for what he had done? Could he be taken away from her and sent to one of those dreadful youth correctional institutions that she had read about? What defense did she have against Westcott and his lawyer?

The law firm, on the third floor of the building, was labeled Merkounian and Abbott. Merkounian was tall, slender, affable, and good-looking, his dark eyes admiring, his manner ingratiating. "I always wanted to meet you, Mrs. Devron. A pity it should be from an adversary position." He tapped a finger on a copy of the *Hollywood Reporter* that lay on his desk. "I read here that your picture will open in a few weeks. I have often wondered how it feels to have a book turned into a motion picture film. It must be very exciting."

"I didn't come here to talk about that," Barbara said.

"Please sit down, and please don't think of me as your enemy."

"I can't very well think of you as my friend—to call me and threaten me on the phone. My son did something that was thoughtless and hurtful——"

"I did not threaten you," he interrupted. "Please sit down."

Barbara dropped into a chair. Her hands were trembling. She clasped them together over her purse and waited.

"My client, Mr. Westcott," Merkounian said, "suffered severe pain and anguish. The law provides recourse for such things. You know that. It's true that if this were an incident in which some Chicano kid were involved, that would be the end of it. But in this case, we have the son of a very wealthy and socially prominent couple."

"My son," Barbara said. "Mr. Devron has not adopted him yet."

"I know that. Now look, Mrs. Devron, I'm not going to beat around the bush. We could go to court and sue you for a million dollars. Your negligence leading to your son's action. I'm not saying we could win for a million dollars, but there could be a very substantial award. Mr. Westcott doesn't want to go to court. Neither do I." He paused and watched her thoughtfully. "Your husband doesn't know about this, does he?"

Barbara hesitated. Then, "No, he doesn't."

"We are willing to keep it that way, and for a reasonable sum, enough to pay for my client's physical and mental anguish, we will be glad to end this matter."

"How much is your reasonable sum?" Barbara asked coldly.

"Fifty thousand dollars."

"Your client was not badly hurt," Barbara said slowly, controlling herself. "Only the windshield of his car was damaged, and he had a cut on his cheek. I grant that it was a frightening incident, but I have had rocks hit my car as a natural occurrence."

"This was not a natural occurrence. It was an act of malice."

"I don't have fifty thousand dollars."

Merkounian smiled. "Come, come, Mrs. Devron. You are married to one of the wealthiest men in Southern California. You are a Lavette. Shall I read you some history of the Lavette family? You have sold your book to films—no, I won't argue this. We are willing to settle all claims and release you and your son from all responsibility and charges of negligence for

135

fifty thousand dollars. We will grant you two weeks to comply. Otherwise, we will serve you."

Boyd Kimmelman had come into Sam Goldberg's law firm in 1945, after his discharge from the army's Judge Advocate section. Goldberg had died some years before, and Harvey Baxter had taken over the practice. The history of the firm, which bore the name Goldberg, Benchly, Baxter and Kimmelman, encapsulated the history of Northern California. Goldberg's father had come to California in '52 to dig for gold. He never struck gold and ended up with a fruit stand in Sacramento—yet managed to put his son through law school. Adam Benchly's father, a British sailor, had jumped ship in San Francisco in 1850, found work in a saloon which eventually he owned, and had produced three sons. Adam Benchly and Sam Goldberg had become partners and opened their law practice together in 1891, after Benchly had run for mayor and had been defeated by three hundred and twenty-two votes, most of which had come from citizens safely dead. In time, Barbara's father, Dan Lavette, had become their most valued and wealthiest client. Benchly and Goldberg were both dead these many years, but Harvey Baxter and the younger member of the firm, Boyd Kimmelman, continued as Barbara's lawyers, supervising the legal affairs of the Lavette Foundation, which Barbara had set up when she came into her inheritance. They had defended her during her trial for contempt of Congress, and they handled the matter of Dan's will and Jean's affairs after Dan's death. It was to Boyd Kimmelman that Barbara turned now, putting off Carson's questions with the excuse that she felt obligated to spend a day or two with her mother.

Barbara had a curious relationship with Boyd. He was a small, feisty man, about Barbara's height, solidly built, with a thatch of sandy hair that he wore in a close-cut brush. His bright blue eyes were perpetually eager and excited, and they were set in a round, innocent face that belied his aggressiveness. He was a good, imaginative attorney and was utterly devoted to Barbara. In the firm, he was the needed counterbalance to the staid, conservative Harvey Baxter, who was some ten years his senior. Kimmelman was forty-four, a year younger than Barbara.

Now, facing her in his office, he listened to her story, asked a few questions, and then said, "Just give me a minute or so to think about it, Barbara." He leaned back in his chair and closed his eyes. Barbara walked to the window, which overlooked Market Street, and watched the hurrying throngs of people, the cars, the color, and the excitement. Always, when she returned, there was that same sense of comfort, of security. For all of her wandering and experience, it was only here that she felt a valid sense of being. The months in Beverly Hills were dreamlike, and already the pressing despair that had brought her here had begun to lighten. Kimmelman's voice brought her out of her reverie.

"He can sue you," Kimmelman said. Now he was watching her thoughtfully. "You haven't told your husband about this?"

"No."

"None of it? Not the incident?"

"No, none of it."

"I won't ask you why."

Barbara turned from the window, walked over to Kimmelman, bent and kissed his cheek. "You're a dear man, Boyd."

"So much for Boyd. Did you hear me, Barbara? I said I think he could sue you—for negligence. He can't sue Sam, and I don't imagine he could initiate any criminal proceedings against Sam, and if he brings suit against you—well, who can say? I've never heard of a case exactly like this, but I'm sure I could dig one up. Good chance you'd beat him if you didn't get a jury that wants to soak the rich."

137

"I'm not rich, Boyd."

"You know that and I do. Who else? Your husband's rich. Please sit down, Barbara. You came in here a totally depressed victim, and now you're standing there and smiling at me."

"I don't know why. I just feel that a great weight had lifted, and I don't know why."

"Will you sit down, please."

Barbara sat facing him. "You're going to tell me to pay up, aren't you? You're still traumatized from our last session in court. That was ten years ago, Boyd, but I'm sure you've sworn an oath to yourself never to let me set foot in a courtroom again."

"More or less."

"I don't have fifty thousand dollars," Barbara complained.

"You're not seriously thinking of inviting a lawsuit, because if you are, it's going to cost just as much and you could lose. Not to mention your husband."

"But it's blackmail," Barbara protested.

"Of course it's blackmail, legalized. I'd say a great big chunk of non-criminal law is legalized blackmail, and it goes on every day. Now how much cash can you get up?"

"I have something over twenty thousand in savings, which is what remains from my flirtation with the film business. I own the house on Green Street outright, so I guess I could mortgage it——"

Boyd shook his head hopelessly. "All your life you've tried to think poor. This is crazy, Barbara. Will you come down to earth for one moment. You will not mortgage the damn house! Your mother is one of the richest widows in town. She'll give it to you! I'll give it to you!"

"Boyd, you're shouting at me."

He closed his eyes and nodded. "Yes, I guess I am. Please forgive me."

"You're a dear. I'll forgive you anything."

"Thank you. Now, will you promise to ask your mother for the money? Ask her for the whole thing as a loan. She'll be happy to help, believe me. I'll put together some papers, and we'll go down to Los Angeles tomorrow and end this stupid business. And if it were my son, I'd put him over my knee and let him know what for."

"I wish I could."

"Meanwhile, where will you be staying? At your house?"

"I'm having lunch with mother, but I'll stay at the house."

"All right. I'll talk this over with Harvey, and unless there's some change in plans, I'll meet you at the airport. I'll call you at about nine in the morning, and we'll make arrangements."

She had been away from the house on Green Street for months, and she approached it tentatively, but the moment she entered the small, shadowed vestibule, her heart lightened and she felt a sense of great relief and tranquillity. She prowled through the house, thinking what a pleasant, nice little house it was. Indeed, it was very neat and clean, and if Eloise and Sally had used it, no trace of their presence remained. It was only twelve o'clock, and only a ten-minute walk to her mother's house on Russian Hill, and she felt that she could savor this place awhile longer. She dropped into the old leather chair in the living room, where her husband, Sam's father, would sit and doze as he listened to his Bach recordings. So long ago, eleven years since he had died, slain somewhere in Israel. Poor Bernie. But the thought was without tears, without grief. Time erases things, yet time also deceives, and right now she could feel that it was not eleven years but only yesterday. What a strange, beguiling place the old house was! It was almost as old as the city itself, built by Sam Goldberg for his bride, and then a place where he lived alone after her death and then bought by Barbara, and now standing unlived in but ready for her and waiting. She didn't want to think, to analyze herself and her marriage. Sitting here, she felt good. For all the grief and agony that had befallen her during her life in this house, the memories were comforting. Here she had brought her son from the hospital, and here together they had faced the first twelve years of his life. Barbara sat with her eyes half closed, remembering many things and trying not to remember that the following day she would go back to Beverly Hills.

"You have told me everything, and you have told me absolutely nothing," Jean said to Barbara, after she had poured the coffee and set out a plate of bakery cookies. She apologized for the cookies, just as she had apologized for the failed soufflé. It was Mrs. Bendler's day off, and since Barbara had suggested that they eat in her mother's home, Jean had prepared lunch herself. "I'm a rotten cook, and baking remains a mystery."

"You look wonderful," Barbara said. "I'm glad."

"I look and feel like an old woman. Of course you shall have the fifty thousand dollars. I'll write a check before you leave, and don't argue with me and don't tell me you'll use your own money. I'm as rich as God, indecently rich, and I will not talk about money; and as far as Sam is concerned, I can understand why he did what he did, and if you don't understand it, that, my dear, is a problem to work out yourself. I say again, you've told me nothing."

"I don't know what you mean."

"You, my darling, are absolutely impossible. Do you intend to live your entire life as some ridiculous Girl Scout?"

"I never joined the Girl Scouts, mother."

"Oh, clever! I would have expected better from you."

"You're really provoked with me, aren't you?" Barbara said, puzzled.

"Of course I am. Why didn't you go to Carson? The Devrons stink with wealth."

"I couldn't."

"You couldn't. Oh, great! You couldn't. What does that mean?"

"It means that Sam is my son, not Carson's."

"That's a pity, isn't it? Not that it means anything. If Carson is your husband, he's Sam's father. Does he want to adopt him?"

"We never discussed it."

"Does Sam like him?" Jean asked.

"Mother, it's my life and my son." Barbara was silent for a moment, staring at her coffee cup. "No, Sam doesn't like him, and Carson is very much aware of it. Mother, I'm a big girl. Marriages are not made in heaven when you're twenty. I don't know where they're made at my age."

"Do you want to talk about it?"

"No, I don't think so."

"No, it's not something you discuss with your mother, is it? Still, I think you should talk about it—to someone."

"Perhaps. How about you?"

"Well, I'm a widow. America's filled with them. I was reading the other day that widows own seventy-five percent of the wealth of the country. I try not to feel sorry for myself."

"You look wonderful. You're still the best-dressed woman in town—it's rotten lonely, isn't it?"

"Lonely?" Jean shrugged. "I have seven charities at the last count. I have the Civic Art Committee. I'm on the museum board, and the governor has just appointed me to the new state advisory council on the arts. I'd give it all for ten minutes with Danny. I pass someone on the street smoking one of those wretched cigars, and my heart stops and I'm ready to dissolve.

141

Sammy would say that I'm dumping on you, and I suppose I am, but I have no desire for pity. There are good days and bad days. Steve Cassala's in town tonight. He's taking me to dinner. Poor, dear man. I think he's been quietly infatuated with me for the past thirty years or so, and never a word passed his honorable lips, and his own marriage has been a loveless, hopeless disaster, pious Catholics, so no divorce ever. It's a lovely world, Bobby dear, and now his wife's here in the hospital, dying of cancer, and Steve is being as gentle and dutiful as a man could be. So we'll have dinner after he visits her. Why don't you join us?"

"Oh, no. Better with you alone. But I didn't know that about Joanna. Poor woman."

"Yes, and Steve tearing his heart out with guilt. Do you know Joanna well?"

"Not really, weddings and funerals. I've seen her two or three times—last at daddy's funeral."

"You can stay here, you know. I won't be late."

"I'll stay at Green Street—unless you feel strongly about my staying here."

Jean shook her head and smiled. "I think you need a night alone."

But back in her house on Green Street, Barbara came to the conclusion that the last thing in the world she needed this day was a night alone. She dialed a call to Carson at his office at the paper, and then put down the telephone before the call went through. Then she called the house in Beverly Hills and spoke to Sam. It was four o'clock now, and he was home from school. She asked him what he was doing.

In a strangely mature manner, he said, "Mom, are you checking up on me?"

"Absolutely not. I just wanted to talk to someone I love," and then wondering why she had said that, thinking that it was a very odd thing for her to say.

A long pause before Sam answered, and then he said, "Where are you—at grandma's?"

"No, in the old house. At Green Street."

"I wish I was there with you. If you stay there, can I come up for the weekend?"

"I'm coming back tomorrow."

Again a long pause. "Sure. Don't worry about me. I'm just hanging out here. I'm reading *The Three Musketeers*. It's great."

"Is it? I never read it."

"You should. It's great."

Barbara put down the telephone, stared at it for a moment or two, then dialed her lawyers' number and asked for Boyd Kimmelman. "I was wondering," she said to him, "whether you're free for dinner tonight?"

"Tonight, tomorrow night, the next night."

"Would you mind taking me to dinner?"

"I'd love it."

"About eight? Here at my house."

"I'll be there."

Then Barbara called a cab, and took it to St. Mary's Hospital. Walking with the sister who led her to Joanna Cassala's room, she had a strange, almost unbearable sensation of *déjà vu*. It was the first time she had been in a Catholic hospital since Marcel's death. That was in 1938, twenty-one years ago. Was it possible—twenty-one years? She was twenty-four then, living in Paris, writing for a New York magazine. He was a journalist. The memory of him, of her first love that was like no other love, of his leaving her to go to Spain to write about the civil war there, his being wounded, and then his death of gangrene in the Hospital of the Sacred Heart in Toulouse—all of it flooded over her mind and body; and the nun walking with her asked, "Are you all right, miss?"

"Yes, I'm all right."

"I know. These things are so sad."

"Is there no hope for Mrs. Cassala?"

"I'm afraid not."

Stephan was in the room, sitting by the bed. Joanna,

143

dark-eyed, emaciated, smiled tremulously when she saw Barbara. "How good of you, how thoughtful, to come all the way from Los Angeles."

Barbara kissed her. Stephan, blinking his eyes, rose to give Barbara his seat. "Raise the bed a little, please," Joanna said to her husband, "so I can look at Barbara. Don't look at me," she said to Barbara. "I'm a sight, no makeup, nothing." Then she began to chatter about Beverly Hills, the film people, the Devrons. In her mind, Barbara had always been a wonderful, glamorous figure. Now Barbara answered her questions, attempted to be amusing and entertaining; but after a few minutes Joanna closed her eyes and became silent.

"She tires easily," Stephan said. A while later, he stepped out into the corridor with Barbara, who wiped away her tears, hardly knowing whether she was crying for Joanna, herself, or her memories.

"It was so good of you to come," Stephan said.

"I was here. Mother told me. I didn't know."

Stephan shook his head hopelessly.

Sitting in the restaurant that evening with Boyd Kimmelman, sipping her second martini, Barbara said, "When we were kids, we used to argue that God was a woman. What nonsense! Only a man could screw up things so remorselessly. That poor woman! What a rotten mess this whole thing is!"

"It has its moments, as for example right now. You're talking to a man who is very much at peace with the world."

"Good. You're talking to a woman who is suffused with guilts. It's a common notion among Jews that you have a corner on the practice of guilt. Believe me, a good, standard white Protestant woman, especially one from what they used to call a good family, could show you depths of guilt you never dreamed of."

"That's very interesting," Boyd said. "Go on."

144

"I shall. Two martinis make me slightly drunk and very articulate. There's a theory that writers are articulate. Nothing to it. They talk silently to a sheet of paper. Lawyers are something else entirely. Why did you get divorced, Boyd?"

"That's out of left field, isn't it?"

"Out of John Barleycorn."

"It was during the war. I was in Germany. I got a Dear John letter, and when I got home, I never saw her again. Harvey Baxter took care of it, bless his soul. She was living in Hollywood with a film editor."

"Weren't you terribly angry?"

"No. To tell you the truth, I was relieved."

"But that was almost fifteen years ago. Why didn't you marry again?"

"Ah." He was grinning now.

"You're laughing at me."

"No, dear Barbara. I couldn't laugh at you. I think I'll have another drink. The first thing a good attorney learns is not to say too much. That's why all lawyers are bores."

"You're not a bore."

"Give me time. Now in answer to your forthright question, I lived with a lady for five years or so, and then it just washed out. I don't know how better to explain. I don't find the institution of marriage so enticing. When I think of poor Steve Cassala, of two miserable wasted lives—do you know any happy marriages?"

"Some. My father and mother, for instance. Well," Barbara said, "that one had some blood, sweat, and tears, but they worked it out. I know of a few others——"

"Yours?"

"Well, I had lunch with mother, and she said I should talk to someone. I think she regards me as a prim, virginal oversized Girl Scout. Do I give you that impression?"

"Not quite."

"I think she meant a shrink, not a lawyer. Most of my friends are in what they call therapy, a middle-class word for seeing a priest. I don't think I could stick it. You were asking me about my marriage. It stinks."

"Oh? I think we should order some food."

"If you wish. Boyd, what's wrong with me? I loved two men, and one of them died in the Spanish war and the other in Israel. And now I've married a good, decent man I'm not in love with and who wants children I can't give him, and who hasn't slept with me since a week after our honeymoon ended. Oh, he's tried, poor soul—what in God's name am I doing? I think I'm quite drunk, and please order me a large plate of spaghetti and another martini."

It was a little after seven o'clock in the morning when Barbara awakened. Boyd still slept, lying on his stomach, one arm flung out over the side of the bed. Barbara turned on her side to look at him, and then she ran her hand gently over his thatch of sandy hair. He stirred without waking. Curiously, she felt no regrets, no guilts, only a strange, comfortable calm and satisfaction, as if she had been away for a long time and had finally returned to herself. It had been good, easy lovemaking between two people who were not in love with each other but who nevertheless cared for each other a great deal. They had known each other a long time. Boyd had defended her when she was on trial for contempt of Congress; he had fought for her and pleaded for her. He had said to her last night, "I never permitted myself to fall in love with you, Barbara. A man who doesn't set some limits on himself is either a maniac or a fool or both. I'm neither." It was nicely said, as she thought of it now, but there were all too many men in the past who had decided they were in love with her. The word was wearing thin. She was pleased that Boyd hadn't used it, and it was enough

146

that he made love with tenderness and sincerity and gave her something she had longed for so desperately. She knew that there were women who appeared to manage a life of completeness without men. She was not one of them, and the thought of existence without love in the physical sense was bleak indeed. Whatever hangups, blocks, and various neuroses might have possessed her, any inhibition against the joy of a body of the opposite sex was not one of them. She had argued it out with Eloise, who was shocked to find Fred and Sam immersed in a copy of *Playboy*. "But why not?" Barbara asked. "Why shouldn't they see how lovely a body can be?" She stretched lazily now, letting the covers slide away; her own body was still tight and supple.

Boyd awakened, yawned, stretched, and then propped himself up on an elbow and stared at her. "You're a beautiful woman, Barbara," he said.

"I've been told that before, sonny."

"At seven-thirty in the morning?"

"It's happened."

"Any regrets—now?"

"No. Of course, I haven't thought anything through. It's too early, and I feel languorous. There's a word for you. You can use Sam's bathroom, down the hall. I'll be languorous a few more minutes, and then a shower. There isn't a damn thing to eat in the house, but I can give you coffee, black, if it helps."

"You go back to Los Angeles today?"

"Yes."

"I couldn't persuade you to stay a few days?"

"And turn a friendly one-night stand into an affair? Is that what you were thinking, Boyd?"

"I don't know what I was thinking. I'm naked under these covers, and thought requires a modicum of clothing, if that makes sense. If I tell you what I'm thinking, we'll both be very confused."

"Then we'll get dressed and talk about it."

But over coffee in the kitchen, they didn't talk about it. Boyd said he would go back to his apartment, change his clothes and shave, pick up some papers at the office, and then stop by with a cab to drive them to the airport. "After which, we'll see Mr. Merkounian and take care of this thing."

"Fifty thousand dollars," Barbara said. "When I was just a kid, back from college after my second year, I got involved with the big longshoremen's strike of 1934. Mother and daddy were divorced, and mother had married John Whittier, the shipping magnate. I worked in the union soup kitchen, and whatever money I had I spent on food——"

"I know," Boyd said softly. "We were neck-deep in that at the trial. I remember that you sold everything, including your car, to buy food for the strikers."

"One of my good conduct medals? It's a crazy, crazy world, Boyd. And now Merkounian collects fifty thousand dollars for his client that I've taken from my mother. I don't feel a shred of guilt for what happened last night, but this thing fills me with such guilt and sadness——"

"You don't have to pay it, Barbara. You could face your husband with it and let them take us to court. I'm not sure we wouldn't win."

"Famous last words? No, I'll pay."

"All right. In any case, I want you to cash the check before I pick you up, say about eleven. I intend to bargain a bit with Mr. Merkounian. I think he'll take a lot less."

"That's a curious name, isn't it, Merkounian."

"Armenian. Good, hardworking folk and very shrewd. I think we'll be able to deal."

"And speaking of names, how did it happen to be Boyd Kimmelman?"

"Ah, so after all these years, we've come to that. Sooner or later, it happens. Did you know that your father's name was Daniel because he was born in a box-

148

car on the Santa Fe Railroad, and your grandfather decided that he was delivered in a lion's den?"

"No, I never knew that," Barbara said in amazement. "How on earth do you know? Or are you inventing the whole thing?"

"I got it from Harvey Baxter, who got it from Sam Goldberg. My own name is less romantic. A fellow named Frank Boyd saved my father's life during the earthquake. Result, Boyd Kimmelman. Now you cash the check, and I'll pick you up at eleven or so."

Cándido Truaz had worked for Jake Levy for almost thirty years. He knew as much about the blending and maturing of wine as any man in the Napa Valley, and Jake, just past sixty now, leaned heavily on his skill and knowledge. He would tell Clair that if anything happened to Truaz, he'd turn the whole kit and kaboodle, as he put it, over to Adam and wash his hands of the wine business forever. Not that he had too much faith in Adam. Adam was interested in a variety of things, and Jake's philosophy was that if a man made wine, nothing else in the world should intrigue him. But now Truaz, a big, heavyset Chicano, with a brown, lined, and perpetually worried face, came to Jake and told him that he had something to say but he didn't know how to say it.

"I don't give a damn how you say it," Jake told him. "If you got something to say, say it straight out. We never talked to each other any different, did we?"

"No, Jake, we didn't."

"All right. What's eating you?"

"My daughter's in trouble."

He had three daughters. "Who? Which one?"

"Carla."

Carla was sixteen, round-limbed, dark-eyed, already full-breasted. The Truazes lived in a small cottage on the edge of the Higate property. Carla was in high school.

Jake never minced words. "What is it, Candy? Is she knocked up?"

"We don't know yet."

"Well, why the hell don't you? Take her down to Napa to see Joe, and he'll give her that rabbit test or whatever the hell they do. Then we'll know what to do with the sonofabitch who took advantage of the kid."

"Oh, Jesus," Truaz sighed. "That's it, Jake. It's your grandson Freddie."

"No! I'll be damned. Are you sure?"

"That's what she says. I beat it out of her."

Jake shook his head unhappily. "What a mess! No use beating up on the kids—except that I'll break that little bastard's ass. Aah—I can't. That's Adam's job. That horny little sonofabitch!"

"What do we do?" Truaz asked miserably. "If Freddie was a Chicano kid, I'd know what to do. He'd marry her or he'd never walk again. But with Freddie——"

"Ah, wait a minute," Jake said, putting his arm around Truaz's shoulder. "Come on, old friend, they're kids. I love Carla. She's a fine girl and a lot too good for Freddie. You think I'd stand in the way if they wanted to get married? No sir. But Freddie's not eighteen yet and Carla's sixteen—or fifteen, which is it?"

"Sixteen."

"Well, you know what comes of that kind of marriage. Nothing but grief. Let's first find out whether she's pregnant, and then we'll work it out. Meanwhile, leave Freddie to me."

It turned out that Carla was not pregnant. She sat crouched over and sobbing in Joe Lavette's examining room, listening to Sally, Joe's wife. "This time you're clear," Sally told her, "and you might as well learn, Carla, that if you go to bed with a man, it doesn't necessarily mean that you'll become pregnant. On the other hand, don't play that game. It's Russian roulette.

150

This time you are lucky. Next time, you may find your-self pregnant——"

"There won't be a next time," Carla wailed.

"Oh, don't give me that crap. It would be nice if you could stay clean until you're married, but life doesn't always work out that way. I'm going to give you a little book, and you sit in the waiting room and read it and learn something about the way a body functions. And for heaven's sake, don't go running to your mother if you fall into bed with a boy again. Come here to me. Now how did you get those bruises on your arms?"

"Papa. He was right. He should have killed me."

"Oh, beautiful! You have the sense of a rabbit, which is why you fell into bed with Freddie in the first place. Think a little. What do you want to do with your life?"

"I want to be a movie star like you."

Sally burst out laughing, and Carla's tear-stained face contorted with hurt. "Oh, no, I'm not laughing at you," Sally said quickly. "You're pretty enough to be a movie star. It's just that all those years have gone by, and I'm married to Joe and being his nurse and raising kids—I guess you couldn't understand. But let me tell you this, honey, if you want to be a movie star or any-thing else that takes brains or talent, don't louse up your life by having to marry some jerk you don't give a damn about. That way lies only misery."

Misery was something Adam Levy was experiencing in full measure, and he begged his father, "Please, let me handle this. I don't want Eloise to know."

"How are you going to handle it?" Jake demanded. "If he was my kid, I'd bend him over and put his ass in a condition that wouldn't let him sit down for a week."

"Pop, you don't whip a boy his age. Just let me handle it."

But as Eloise told Jean, when she drove into San Francisco to see her a few days later, it had by no means been kept from her. "I was in the kitchen downstairs," Eloise said, "but the way Adam was shouting, I heard every word. Josh was outside somewhere, thank heavens. I never saw Adam really angry at Freddie before—or really angry at anything. He was shouting that Freddie had betrayed him, that Freddie had acted stupidly and ridiculously—and I didn't have the slightest notion of what it all meant. I didn't know what had happened. And then he shouted that with all the girls in the Napa Valley, he had to—he had to"—Eloise could not bring herself to mouth the word *shit*—"defecate on his own doorstep."

Jean embraced her. "Eloise, you are wonderful. You are absolutely wonderful."

"I am not at all wonderful, Jean dear, because at that point I was at the edge of getting one of those dreadful headaches of mine, and I marched upstairs and told them that it had to stop. Freddie was standing, looking out of the window, and Adam was shouting that Freddie had better turn around and face him or else, and then just as I entered the room, Freddie cried out that Adam had always hated him, which breaks my heart because Adam adores him, and then I burst into tears and that ended it."

"And Adam told you the whole story."

"Yes, but, Jean, I don't understand any of it. Freddie hasn't spoken to Adam or me for two days. He's always worshipped Adam, and now I'm so frightened——"

"Of what?"

"Of losing Freddie."

"You're not going to lose him, Eloise. Why do you go on thinking the world is a rose garden? You've suffered enough pain and misery to know different."

"I've never suffered, that's the trouble. I'm so afraid."

Boyd Kimmelman decided finally that he would see Mr. Merkounian alone, and he settled the matter for twenty-five thousand dollars in cash. As he told Barbara later that day, before he left for San Francisco, "It was a dubious undertaking—the lawsuit, I mean—from the beginning, and Merkounian was worried about what might happen if Carson found out about it. So it was harrassment and blackmail. Now it's nailed down. You can bet your life that neither Merkounian nor Westcott will declare that money. There's nothing that stimulates the greed of any red-blooded American like a little tax-free cash. You can buy nearly anything and anybody with cash, and they will button their lips, Barbara, believe me, and here's the other twenty-five thousand to give back to your mother. So it's over."

They had met at the Polo Lounge in the Beverly Hills Hotel, Barbara guiltless and undisturbed by the fact that she was sitting here having a drink with a man she had gone to bed with the night before; more disturbed, indeed, by Boyd's easy cynicism.

"Is there any nook or cranny where a little honor is left?" she wondered. "You're an officer of the court, Boyd. Aren't we aiding and abetting?"

"Are we? I settled a case out of court for a cash payment. It's perfectly legal. Your mother lent you the money. You will pay her back, I'm sure. No aiding and abetting at all. Funny thing, Merkounian is a decent guy. Grew up on a little farm in the San Joaquin Valley, and the family broke their backs to put him through school. Now he's a Beverly Hills lawyer. The Armenians were massacred by the Turks, the Jews by the Nazis, but neither of us smell any burning flesh. Now how the devil did I get into that?"

"I think I know," Barbara told him, smiling wanly.

"I'm going back tonight. Will you be all right?"

"I suppose so." Barbara took a check out of her purse and put it in the envelope with the twenty-five thousand dollars that Boyd had handed to her. "It's my check for twenty thousand, and I want you to give the whole thing to my mother. She'll be very indignant and

153

persuasive, but don't let her beat you down. Make her take it."

"Where did you get twenty thousand dollars?"

"My worldly wealth. Don't let it worry you, Boyd. I'm all right."

"I hope so. We never actually talked about your marriage. Do you want to?"

"No."

"O.K. Will you be coming up to San Francisco soon again?"

"Dear Boyd," Barbara said, taking his hand, "I'm a rotten candidate for an affair. Thank God neither of us is in love. I don't know when I'll be back home. I don't know much about anything except that this wretched business is over, for which I am very grateful to you."

But it was not over. Two weeks later Sam told her that he knew all about the settlement with Mr. Westcott. He approached her with this at a moment when she had just finished reading an editorial in the Los Angeles *Morning World*. The subject of the editorial was Norman Drake:

"Mr. Drake," the editorial said, "has announced that he will be a candidate for the presidency. Mr. Drake comes to this point in his career with years of experience in the House of Representatives and in the United States Senate. Better equipped than most candidates with an intimate and working knowledge of government, he has proven himself to be a thoughtful and energetic legislator as well as a brilliant campaigner. A native Californian, he is well acquainted with the special and particular needs of the West Coast states, an area all too long neglected by the Federal Government in Washington. While this newspaper has in the past disagreed on occasion with some of the views of Norman Drake, on an overall basis we support both his position and his program. We welcome him into the race."

Carson had departed for downtown a half hour before, making no mention of the editorial. Barbara was sitting at the table in the breakfast room, drinking her coffee, reading the editorial, when Sam joined her. Robin Park, the Korean houseboy, set down a plate of bacon and eggs in front of him.

"I'm not hungry," Sam announced.

"I want you to eat a proper breakfast," Barbara said mechanically, not looking up from the paper.

"I can't. I'm not hungry."

"Yes—" She had finished the editorial. The meaning was sinking in. She looked at it again, picking out sentences, snatches.

"I have to ask you something," Sam said.

Barbara looked around her. The breakfast room was floored with tile, and one side of it was sliding glass doors that opened on the terrace, the pool, and beyond that the tennis court. Her tennis was adequate at best, and she had little love for the game. Carson was a brilliant player. The court had been the deciding factor in his insistence on buying the house.

"Can I ask you something—please?"

Barbara put down the newspaper and looked at her son, the thought occurring to her that he never spoke about his boat, his beautiful boat that his grandfather had willed to him, lying tied up at the marina in San Francisco. Why had she thought of that right now? The editorial she had just read was still hammering at her mind. Her world was bending and swaying. There were no props; it was like a silent earthquake, felt by her alone, and across the table her son was watching her, this tall, slender boy who, she felt so frequently now, was the only reason for her existence. What else? She had stopped writing. The meals were planned for and cooked by their cook. Sometimes she did the shopping, but for the most part food was ordered by telephone from a specialty shop on Rodeo Drive. She had looked at the prices once and they sickened her, but when she complained to Carson about it, he waved her

155

complaint aside. "Your time is worth more," he said, and she wondered what he thought she did with her time. The long, wonderful walks that were so necessary to her creativity as a writer were impossible in Beverly Hills. San Francisco was a place where one walked. To walk in Beverly Hills was to recoil, to encounter culture shock, to become the prisoner of something alien and beyond her, an alienation she had never experienced in Paris or London or New York.

"Mom!"

"What is it, Sam?" she said gently. "What do you want to ask me?"

"Am I Jewish?"

It was the last thing in the world she had expected him to say, and her immediate thought was to tell him that it was time for him to leave for school; and then she said to herself, "The hell with school. There's something important here, and, God help me, I've forgotten what's important and what isn't."

"Well, that depends," Barbara said seriously. "I've never been absolutely sure about what makes a person Jewish except having a Jewish father and mother and a different religion, I suppose. But most of the Jews and Christians too, whom I know, appear to have no religion at all. I've been told that according to Jewish law, in a mixed marriage, if the mother isn't Jewish, the child isn't. But I'm not sure that really counts for much."

"My name is Jewish. Cohen is a Jewish name. When I went to Sunday school at Grace Cathedral, as soon as the kids heard my name they knew I was Jewish. That's why I hated to go there. I look Jewish."

"You what?"

"I look Jewish." He glanced at his wristwatch. "It's late. I have to get to school."

"Never mind school. You can be late today, and I'll give you a note. We're going to talk. You think you look Jewish. Steve Cassala is Italian. He has dark eyes and dark hair and a long, sharp nose. Does he look Jewish?"

"He's Italian, like you said."

"Does Jake Levy look Jewish?"

"He's not Jewish."

"No? Did it ever occur to you that Levy is also a Jewish name? Isn't Grandma Levy Jewish?"

"I don't know. I never thought about it."

"Why are you thinking about it now? Did something happen in school?"

"No." Sam hesitated. "Westcott," he said.

"That is over and done with and in the past."

"No, it isn't!" Sam said shrilly. "You paid him twenty-five thousand dollars. Someday I'll pay it back to you. I swear I will."

For a long moment, Barbara simply stared at him, speechless. Then she said evenly, "Very well, suppose you tell me how you know about the twenty-five thousand dollars."

"I went to see Mr. Westcott. He told me."

"You went to see him? But why?"

"I wanted to apologize for what I did. I have almost eight hundred dollars in my savings account. That's the money that gramps used to give me. I offered to give it to Mr. Westcott."

"Did he take it?" Barbara asked, anger welling up inside her.

"No. He told me—" Sam shook his head. "He used a lot of dirty language."

"Tell me what he said."

"You're sure you want me to?"

"Yes, I want you to. I've heard dirty language before. It won't shock me."

Sam took a deep breath. "Well, he told me to take my money and shove it up my ass. Then he called me a dirty little Jew bastard. He said that the Jews were taking over California, but that he and others would soon put a stop to that. He called you names."

"What names?"

Sam shook his head. "Then he told me about the money you paid his lawyer—" Sam had tears in his eyes now. "Did you do that so I wouldn't have to go to jail?"

Barbara went to him and put her arms around him.

"Is that why you did it?"

"No, darling, no. There was no question of your going to jail. He threatened a negligence lawsuit, and Boyd Kimmelman felt that the best thing I could do would be to settle the matter, and now it's over. I don't want you to think about it or mention it again, not to anyone. It's over and the money means nothing to me."

"I'll pay you back someday—I promise."

"We'll see. Meanwhile, it's over. I'll get you some warm breakfast, and then I'll drive you to school and explain your tardiness."

When Barbara returned from driving Sam to school, she telephoned her mother in San Francisco. "I wanted to hear your voice," she said to Jean. "You're an understanding person, and I've been thinking about that and I wanted to speak to you. Do you know that I've been married six months and it's almost Christmas again?"

"Are you all right?" Jean asked anxiously.

"I'm quite happy and very sad."

"What happened?"

"Too much to tell you on the phone."

"You have me totally confused."

"I suppose so," Barbara agreed.

Then she drove out to the beach, parked in the lot that faces the beginning of Sunset Boulevard, and sat on the sand facing the ocean. She sat there for almost an hour, watching the great breakers rolling in and soothing her soul with the sound of the ocean. It was a warm day, but at this time of the year there was only a scattering of people on the beach, some children with their mothers, a few young couples, and off to her left a group of muscle-builders tossing a medicine ball. She was close to her menstrual period, and already she could sense the change that came over her body at such times, a kind of effusion, a kind of swelling warmth, a physical sadness and need. Without thinking about the future, she knew what would happen.

It was late afternoon when she returned to the house in Beverly Hills. Carson was on the tennis court, playing a furious game with Kirk Alman, a very important star, whose new film had just been released. Two pretty, young, and exceedingly blonde girls sat on the sidelines, watching. With only an hour or so of fading daylight remaining, Carson was playing relentlessly, desperately, as if he were contesting the setting sun as well as his opponent across the net. As Barbara stood there watching, Sam came out of the house and joined her. "No one ever beats Carson," Sam said. "He's too good. He could be a pro if he wanted to." Barbara started to speak. Sam turned and walked back into the house.

The game finished. Carson vaulted the net and shook hands with Kirk Alman. The two pretty girls clapped hands, squealed with delight, and ran to the players, one to embrace Alman, the other to plant a kiss on Carson's cheek. Carson walked over to Barbara and kissed her. "What a good game!" he said. "I'm soaked. Let me shower and then we'll have a drink."

"Alone. I want to talk."

"No problem. I'll chase them away." Carson introduced the girls. Barbara had met Alman several times before. The two blonde young ladies were actresses. Barbara nodded and smiled. While Carson was showering and dressing, Barbara went up to Sam's room. He was bent over his desk, working on a model airplane, carefully cutting the thin slices of balsa wood with a single-edged razor blade.

"How was today?" she asked him.

"O.K."

"Did you ever play tennis with Carson?" she wondered.

"Once. He let me win."

"Well, you can understand that, can't you?"

Sam nodded without replying. Barbara left the room, closing the door gently behind her. Downstairs, she mixed a pitcher of martinis. Carson walked into the library as she was pouring them.

"Cheers," he said as he took his first sip. "That was a good game. Kirk hates to lose. He gets surly, so it's just as well you didn't want them to stay. You know, Bobby, Southern California spoils you for anywhere else. Tennis in December."

Barbara listened and watched him. What a lovely man, she thought. Sweet, kind, decent. She wanted to cry. Years ago, she would have wept. Old habits die hard, but they do die.

"I suppose you saw the paper," Carson said.

She nodded.

"Shall I talk—or you?" Carson asked her.

"You," Barbara said, dropping into a chair.

He leaned on the bar, studying her. "You're quite a woman," he said. "Times when it scares me."

She shook her head. There was no reply to that.

"You saw the paper?"

Barbara nodded. "You asked me that. I read the editorial."

"Angry?"

"No."

"I want to explain."

"All right."

"I'm not squirming off the hook. Phil Baker wrote the editorial, but that's not the point. It was a family decision, and on top of that it was a decision of the board. Would you like to hear some of the thinking behind it?"

"Yes, I would."

"In any case, Bobby, a presidential candidate is not a normal, usual type of human being. The drive, the ego, the compulsion required to take on such a campaign and see it through is rather unique, and regardless of the energy, the talent, or the brilliance of the candidate, the deciding factor is money. This is the age of television, and television is damned expensive. All right. We specify Norman Drake. He has the drive and he has the ego, and the whole compulsion of his existence is to be liked, to be voted for. Whatever you and I may think of him, he touches something in a hell of a lot of people. They see themselves in him. He's a vote-getter. He works for the party. He's born and bred in California, and we've never had one of our own down there in Washington, and there's money behind him. Unlimited money. Personally, I despise him, but candidates are not chosen on moral or social grounds. I know he was a member of the House Un-American Activities Committee, but good heavens, if we are to hold a measuring rod up against everyone who played a role in the McCarthy era, we'd have no one to turn to. I'm the publisher of the *Morning World*, but I don't own the paper and I don't make the decisions for it."

Barbara rose and poured herself a second drink. She had never been a drinker, a glass of wine, a cocktail now and then for a special occasion. Recently, in Beverly Hills, the occasions were more numerous.

"When the board made its decision, how did you vote?" she asked Carson.

"I abstained. They understood that."

"I suppose," Barbara said, "that I could be caustic, nasty, clever. The occasion calls for it. Only I don't feel clever, only sad. So damn sad."

"Aren't you making too much of it?"

"Perhaps." She dropped into a chair again, staring at the drink. The drink was a pretense. She had never solved anything by getting drunk. The few times she

161

had been drunk were mostly happy times. Words were a pretense too. They floated around without ever touching the crux of it. And what was the crux of it? She was in a strange place in a strange house with a strange man. Dreams had the same quality of strangeness. In a dream, you reached out to touch something and it dissolved.

"I wonder," she said, "just to satisfy my curiosity, whether you'd tell me something. In the course of things, as this presidential campaign develops, would you be expected to entertain Norman Drake here in this house?"

"That's an odd question. It's conceivable, either in my father's house or here."

"Here, which means in my house. I don't exactly think of it as my house. But I live here."

"That's anger!" Carson said. "You're sore as hell at me, and you sit there calm as a damn Buddha. If we're going to talk, let's talk. Don't just sit there and have me make a fool of myself. You're a lovely woman, Barbara, a very gifted woman, but you're not the only person on earth who ever had a principle and lived by it. I'm not a monk and I'm not some damn saint, but I am not a bastard. If you don't know where the Devron money came from, you sure as hell know where the Lavette money came from. I try to run an honest paper——"

"What is honest?" Barbara exclaimed. "To sell out your country and your people?"

"Bullshit! God damn it, no! I won't stand here and accept that. I've sold out nothing—and if you want to run a contest in honesty, let's start at the beginning. I haven't looked at another woman since we married, since I met you. Were you honest about that day with that Italian gigolo or whatever the hell he was?"

"I was, if you call that honesty. But I don't think I'm so honest. I'm as frightened as you are to look at myself and find out what I really am. But I'm a woman

162

and you're a man. You're the mover, and I'm the one who's moved. Since I've been here, my soul has shriveled. It's not your fault. It's the way things are. It's not that our marriage has failed; it's just that I don't know how to make any marriage work. My whole life, I've been a stranger who kept looking for some place where she belonged. And now this city, this house—oh, my God, Carson, it's all tangled up and I don't know how to untangle it. We're married, but we haven't any marriage. Two weeks ago, when I was in San Francisco, I had dinner with an old friend and then we slept together."

Carson put his drink down and stared at her. Barbara waited. Finally, she demanded, "Say something!"

"What?"

"Ask me why," she said, almost frantically.

"No. Like hell I will!"

"I'm sorry," Barbara whispered. "I'm so sorry. I've hurt you so much. But it would have hurt, no matter what I said, no matter what you said. When a thing like this is over, it hurts." Then she got up and walked out of the room, knowing that her tears would help nothing.

THREE

At the age of seventeen, Samuel Thomas Cohen had reached his full height of six feet and one inch. He was a slender young man, long-limbed and effortlessly graceful in his movements. He had his father's pale blue eyes and prominent hawklike nose, sandy hair, and the long, well-shaped head of the Seldons. His mouth, like his mother's, was wide and full. He had few friends in San Francisco, indeed made no effort to cultivate friends apart from the time he spent at Higate in the Napa Valley; and he was so insistently a loner that it troubled Barbara. She often thought of him as drifting into himself, yet the same process was at work with her. He was gifted with ability, yet it took no specific direction. He read a great deal, and often enough he and Barbara would have long discussions about books they both read—yet he never read even one of the five books his mother had written and published. His marks at school were high, but his work was effortless. A year before, he had tried out for the track team at school, had broken the school record for the 440-yard run, and then had lost interest. Alone and on foot—and at times on his bicycle—he had explored every street and roadway in San Francisco, yet he once said to Barbara, abruptly and apropos of nothing that she could relate his remark to, "This isn't my place. I'm a stranger here." Yet once, in his room and on his desk, she had picked up a sheet of paper, caught in spite of her respect for his privacy by the first few words:

"Don't destroy the cable cars. Try to understand what they mean. My great-grandfather, Thomas Seldon, told my mother about the horses, beaten and lashed as they struggled up the hills. Another man, who was an engineer, saw the same thing. His name was Andrew Smith Hallidie, and he invented the cable cars to stop the suffering of dumb animals. Nothing that stops suffering should be done away with. It's a way to remember. Now, since nobody knows how the cars work, let me try to explain it. One continuous cable supplies the power for all the cars, and this cable runs through a slot eighteen inches under the street. Anyone who lives in San Francisco knows the sound of this cable. I call it the song of the cable. This cable travels at a constant nine miles an hour, passes over wheels twelve foot in diameter at the cable house. One electric motor drives the wheel which pulls all the cars and that is explained by the theory of inertia, and this is the cheapest and best transportation system in the world and all other systems are stupid and wasteful. Eighty years ago, we had over a hundred miles of track in the cable system; now we have only seventeen miles. The good things are always destroyed. The stupid things remain. That's why I want to remind people how the horses suffered and how they were whipped to drag the wagons up the hills. I know the horses are gone and dead, but we have to remember. Now I will explain how the cars work and what the gripman does."

It broke off abruptly there. Barbara read it a second time, telling herself, "Try to understand him. Try to reach him."

* * *

Dr. Judith Albright, at the age of sixty, preferred to call herself a therapist rather than a psychoanalyst, even though she had her degree in medicine and had practiced medicine for twenty-five years before turning to therapy. As an oncologist, she had witnessed death for too long; not only was the shock of each additional cancer patient an unending emotional drain, but she began to look upon her own body as a grim stranger to herself. When she abandoned oncology for psychoanalysis, she felt well prepared for her new discipline, considering that nothing reveals the soul so cruelly and clearly as the imminence of death.

She was a stout, pleasant-looking woman who had mothered three children, a widow these past four years, gray-haired, with warm dark eyes. Since she had spent her working life in San Francisco, she was no stranger to the history of the Lavette family, and when Dr. Milton Kellman suggested that she might be able to help Barbara Lavette, her face lit up with interest.

"Dan's daughter, that lovely woman who married Carson Devron? I thought she had abandoned us for the pleasures of the southland."

"She divorced Devron three years ago. You don't really read the newspapers, do you, Judith?"

"At times. A newspaper consumes an hour a day. I don't really have an hour a day to spare for the *Chronicle*. Do you, Milton?"

"Occasionally. In any case, she's a very depressed and unhappy woman. I've known her many years, and I'm close to the family. Her mother suggested that I might find someone to help her. Odd thing. Some years ago, when Dan Lavette died, I tried to get the mother to accept some therapy. She wouldn't hear of it. A pox on all of your tribe. But she came out of it very well. Barbara, on the other hand, has gone downhill—slowly but constantly increasing depression. I saw her two weeks ago when she had a slight case of the flu, and I brought up the subject. She wouldn't hear of it. And then yesterday she called me and asked me whether I knew someone who might help. A very curious and sudden change."

"Not so curious as you might imagine." Dr. Albright consulted her appointment book. "Suppose we say next Wednesday at ten A.M. The morning hour will be all right, won't it?"

"I imagine so. I'll tell her, and I'll call you if there's any change."

On the morning of the Wednesday in question, Dr. Albright awaited her patient with not a little curiosity. San Francisco has always been a very small city, both geographically and in terms of its population, deceptively put together as a great metropolis. In both its history and its local gossip, its inhabitants share a sort of tribal intimacy; yet for all that she had known of the Lavettes for almost half a century, Dr. Albright had never met one of them. The card Dr. Kellman had given her informed her that Barbara Lavette was forty-nine years old, that she had one child at the age of thirty-two, by Caesarean section, that her depression was intermittent but apparently less so of late, that there were no pathological indications to account for it, and that her health was reasonably good. All of which did not prepare her for the strikingly handsome woman who entered her office precisely at ten o'clock. She was tall, five feet and eight inches in height, her light brown hair only slightly streaked with gray, worn off her brow at shoulder length. She wore no makeup, but her color was good, and her brown gabardine suit was well cut if not particularly stylish. Her erect carriage was rather singular in a depressed person, but Dr. Albright realized that might simply be the continuation of a lifelong habit. She was not a pretty woman; her mouth was a trifle too wide, her lips too full, the chin straight and firm, the planes of her face flat and long. "A very handsome woman," Dr. Albright thought, "and she would be quite beautiful if she put her mind to it."

170

Barbara, on the other hand, saw a stout, motherly woman, who looked for all the world like a comfortable housewife turned grandmother. Dr. Albright welcomed Barbara with an easy smile, asked her to sit down, and mentioned that Barbara appeared to be surprised.

"I didn't know what to expect," Barbara said. "My images come from film and television."

"Where so many of our images come from these days, unfortunately. I'd like you to be comfortable and to forget, if you can, all the clichés of the psychiatrist. And then if you decide to remain in treatment with me, perhaps we will both learn something. You see, for years I practiced oncology—until my own depression set in. I turned to psychiatry only eight years ago, so I am still learning. I tell you this because, above all else, I want us to be at ease with each other."

As she spoke, Barbara had been glancing around the room. The outer office had been plain and without much character, a young woman in a nurse's outfit, seated behind a desk, some wooden files, a carpeted floor, and four chairs. Dr. Albright's office, in contrast, had a colorful Chinese rug, an antique Adam desk, two tapestry-covered easy chairs, as well as a formal—or what Barbara imagined to be formal—psychiatrist's couch, leather-covered, with a raised headrest and no arms. On the walls were five framed diplomas and a group of fashion prints in antique frames. The desk itself was crowded with framed pictures of children in various stages of growth. The room was bright and sunny, and through one window, Barbara could catch just a glimpse of the bay.

"You were thinking," Dr. Albright said, "do you have to lie down on the couch?"

"Yes, something of that sort. It wouldn't be easy for me. Frankly, I don't like the idea."

"I don't like it very much either, Barbara—I'll call you Barbara, and I'd like you to call me Judith. I don't know how much you've read or known about psychiatry or therapy, as I prefer to call my own treatment, but I'm not a Freudian. I've studied him and I honor him, but I'm a stubborn woman and I take only what I believe from the old man." She rose from behind her desk and seated herself in the easy chair facing Barbara. "This is the best way, I think, for someone like you. We face each other and we're comfortable. We talk for a few minutes less than an hour. Or you talk and I listen. Or I ask you questions, and you can answer them or not, just as you wish. No compulsions. Sometimes we'll talk about dreams. Or perhaps you'll leave here today and decide not to come back."

"I thought about that," Barbara said. "First I thought about not coming here at all, but I felt that would be a kind of nasty trick on Milton after I came to him and asked for someone. Then I said to myself, I'll come once and see what it's all about."

"Well, that makes sense."

"Does it? We talk for an hour. I don't know that any of it will make any more sense then."

"Perhaps not. But you must have felt very unhappy, to have asked Dr. Kellman to refer you to someone."

"Yes. It was a low point."

"I can understand that," Dr. Albright nodded. "I sometimes think that a profound depression is the most awful thing a human being can experience. Do you want to talk about it?"

Barbara shook her head. Dr. Albright waited. Barbara stared past Dr. Albright at the framed fashion prints.

"My daughter found them in an old copy of *Godey's Lady's Book* that she picked up somewhere. Then she found the antique frames. She was only fifteen. They're very nice and I sort of treasure them."

"Yes," Barbara said. "This makes no damn sense unless I talk about it. I'll tell you how I feel. I feel empty. I feel as if everything inside of me has been drained out and I'm totally empty. I have absolutely no interest in anything. I pretend. I love my son and I don't want him to know how I feel, so I pretend with him. I pretend interest where there isn't any interest. I'm a writer and I can't write, because I don't care enough about anything to write about it. I don't want to go anywhere or do anything. I read and I don't care about what I'm reading. I feel lousy rotten!" she blurted out. "I feel fucking lousy rotten, and it's all so damn hopeless—" And then she burst into tears, her whole body racked with sobbing.

Dr. Albright sat silent, watching Barbara and waiting. When the paroxysm had spent itself and Barbara was able to halt her sobs, the doctor handed her a box of tissues. Barbara wiped her eyes and blew her nose and then said, "I'm so sorry, I'm so ashamed."

"Why?"

"I haven't done this in years."

"I did it last month, when a dear friend of mine died. Thank God we're women and we can weep with grief."

"I used to cry so easily, years ago when I was very young," Barbara said woefully. "I was always ashamed when I cried."

"But now you feel better—I know, ashamed, but better."

"Yes." She managed a smile, wiping her eyes again. "I'm depleting your tissues."

"Please. You know, when I practiced oncology, the drug companies sent me an unending supply of drugs. Now that I practice psychiatry, I receive an unending supply of tissues."

"You're kidding."

"Oh, no. It's true. Tell me, Barbara, did you ever experience this kind of depression before?"

"No—I don't think so." She closed her eyes for a moment. "Yes—once."

"Would you tell me about it?"

173

"It was when I was in prison for contempt of Congress." She hesitated. "Do you know about that?"

"Yes, I remember it. That was about ten years ago, wasn't it?"

"Yes."

"Of course. Dr. Kellman was involved in that. One of a group of people who gave you money to buy drugs for a hospital in the south of France. And then you refused to divulge their names to the committee. How long were you in prison?"

"Six months."

"And the depression? How long did it last?"

"About a week."

"Would you tell me about it?" Dr. Albright asked. "What led up to it, if you remember."

"I remember very well indeed. It was the first visiting day, and my father came down to the prison—it was on Terminal Island down in San Pedro—and just before he came I had this feeling that I didn't want him to come, I didn't want anyone to come, and then after he left—well, it happened."

"And how did it end? Did something else happen?"

Barbara found herself smiling at the memory. "Yes. One of the officers—that's a euphemism for prison guards, women, you know—well, one of them, a particularly nasty one, came into my room one morning and accused me of shamming, of goldbricking, and well—well, I just exploded with anger and called her every filthy name I could think of. The girls out in the corridor, prisoners, applauded, and I got two weeks of what we called shit patrol, cleaning the toilets. But no more depression. That won't work again, I'm afraid. There are only two toilets in my house here and I clean them regularly. It doesn't help. Of course, there's a qualitative difference between those and prison toilets."

Dr. Albright said, "In case you're wondering what's wrong with me, I'm suppressing laughter. We had an instructor at the Psychoanalytic Institute to whom laughter was anathema. He had a lovely Viennese accent, but he was an idiot. Laughter is marvelous, and I'm suppressing it because I'm deficient in independence. Tell me, Barbara, when did your father die?"

"In December of nineteen fifty-eight."

"Dan Lavette. It's hard to think of a man like Dan Lavette dying. He was a part of it, like the bridge or Nob Hill."

"Yes, he was part of it," Barbara agreed.

"Coming back to the prison incident," Dr. Albright said. "After your outburst, your punishment was the toilet detail. How did you react to it?"

"I think I loved it," Barbara said unexpectedly.

"Oh? Go on, tell me why?"

"I'm not sure I know exactly why. Believe me, I have no proclivity toward toilets—but I guess as crazy as it sounds, it was a challenge. It gave me something to vent my anger on, and I was angry. To my way of thinking, I had done nothing wrong. I had raised money to buy medicine for sick people, and I had refused to be turned into an informer. I didn't realize at the time how angry I was; I guess I couldn't face the rage and indignation inside of me, because it was so hard to hold myself together and to overcome my fear."

"Your fear of prison?"

"Prison, all the things I had heard and read. I remember thinking again and again that I could die there and I would never see my son again. My husband was dead and I was in prison—" The tears began again, and as she reached for the tissues, Barbara mumbled, "Must we talk about this? I'm making an utter fool of myself."

"Just a little more. I want to hear a little more about your attitude toward the punishment. By the way, did you think of it as punishment?"

Barbara was silent for a while, and Dr. Albright waited, not pressing her to speak.

"I think not," Barbara said finally. "I'm not exactly sure that I can explain the way I felt. All my life, I've brooded over this question of rich and poor. I suppose I was the ultimate little rich girl. I grew up in my mother's house on Russian Hill. Eight bathrooms. I never knew how many there were until one night in prison when I couldn't sleep, and I passed the time counting bathrooms. Eight. I tried to remember how many there were in my grandfather's house. He was Thomas Seldon, and when I was a little girl, he lived in a great, baronial brownstone mansion on Nob Hill. They tore it down in nineteen thirty. But all through my childhood, I was never rid of the fact that I was the only granddaughter of Thomas Seldon."

Lost in her thoughts now, memories racing down an endless corridor of time, the huge brown mansion on Nob Hill, the half-moon driveway in front of it, the high black gates, the dim, cavernous rooms, the jungle of plants in the solarium—and then into the present where she sat facing a stout, gray-haired woman, and talking; she had not talked as much in years.

"What did you ask me?" Barbara wondered.

"Whether you reacted to the toilet detail as punishment?"

"Yes, of course. There was one bathroom that hadn't been used for years. The water had been turned off. The pipes were rusted and the bowls and sink were black with filth and stain. I cleaned it. When I finished with it, the pipes were shining, the bowls pristine white. I had a feeling of triumph that makes no sense, but it was like no other feeling I ever had."

Dr. Albright glanced at her watch. "Would you believe it, Barbara? Our fifty-minute hour is gone." She stood up. "If you want to continue, I'll keep ten o'clock on Friday open for you."

"Can I think about it?"

"Of course. Why don't you call me tomorrow afternoon and let me know what you've decided."

After Barbara had departed, Dr. Albright called Milton Kellman.

"How did it go?" Kellman asked her.

"Very well indeed. Your Barbara is quite a lady."

"Will she continue?"

"I hope so. But I can tell you this, Milton. The depression is not endogenous. I don't believe there's any physiological basis. If we can work for a while, she'll overcome it."

There are those in the East who insist that there is no proper springtime in California, but that is only because their antennae are tuned otherwise. To those born and bred in California, there is a subtle and wonderful harbinger of spring. When the whole land is awash and one feels the rain will never cease, there is a sudden end to the winter precipitation. The air clears and the sky dissolves into pale, pale blue. There are new sweet scents in the air, a wakening and movement in the intense green of the hillsides. There never was such green, all the more wonderful for its transience, for no sooner is it in full flush than it begins to pale and wither, beginning the transition to the dull brown of summer's end. But while spring lasts, it bestows its gifts lavishly, perhaps nowhere more so than in the Napa Valley.

All this was felt if left unsaid by the three young men and the young woman who sprawled around the fireplace on the hillside above Higate. Below them, they could see the gently contoured vine-covered fields and the stone houses of the winery, and in the distance the wide sky, flecked here and there with cottonball clouds. Since it was a warm afternoon, they had built no fire in the old fireplace, and the childhood practice of burned marshmallows and blackened frankfurters was in the distant past, as were such gaucheries as terming themselves "the wolf pack." Instead, they lazily passed a joint of marijuana from mouth to mouth, less affected by the smoke than by the fact that they were here together for the spring recess, all except May Ling's brother, young Daniel, who was only eight years old—all of them the "lineage," as Fred put it, of the "royal order" of Lavette and Levy. He stated the fact sardonically. Twenty-one years old, a junior at Princeton, long-limbed, fair-haired, he was almost the image of his father at that age, although he would have bridled at the suggestion.

"Here we are, children," he told his companions, "the descendants of the empire-builders, the heirs, the reapers of what others have sown, celebrating our royal lineage with a joint. Thank God it's the last toke. If there's one place in America you can't buy pot, it's at Higate."

"Don't be too sure," his brother, Joshua, informed him. Joshua was almost sixteen, solid, heavy, built like a young bull, his hair pale orange, his skin dappled with freckles. "I don't buy, but if I wanted the stuff, the Chicanos on the place could supply."

"You can buy in Napa," May Ling said. A few months older than Joshua, she had the long Lavette limbs, her grandmother's ivory skin and tiny Oriental features. Her every movement was unconsciously graceful. "You can buy at my high school. I don't, but there's nothing to it if you want the stuff."

"If you did, Sally would take your head off," Fred told her.

"Not to mention what Aunt Sally would do to you, Freddie love," Sam said, "if she ever knew you were feeding her darling daughter dope."

"It's a celebration stick. No more. We stay pristine pure until we go back to school."

"Can you buy at Princeton?" May Ling asked curiously.

"It's a marketplace. In Woodrow Wilson, the townies come in and sell on the premises."

"He's exaggerating," Joshua said.

178

"Like hell I am."

"Just don't let it get to mom. She'd take a fit."

"What's Woodrow Wilson?" May Ling wanted to know.

"Who, not what," Sam informed her. "The last dreamer. He actually believed he could stop war."

"Don't be such a smart-ass. I know about the President. Freddie's talking about a where, a place."

"It's an eating association of sorts," Fred explained. "At Princeton, your social standing and your belly are one. Instead of fraternity houses, they have eating clubs. I spent two years at Ivy, which is top-drawer establishment, proper place for a Lavette of San Francisco, and then neither my liver nor my immortal soul—considering that I have one—could stand any more of it. Grubby stupidity combined with alcoholic ecstasy. So for my third year, I switched to Woodrow Wilson, grubby intelligence combined with the sweet smell of pot. It's a house they put up for folk like myself who can't bear to rub elbows with the jocks or the moronic rich, and it has its advantages."

"Such as?" Sam asked.

"Pool, for one thing. You grow up as a peasant on this wine farm, and you never hear the sweet clicking of pool balls. At this point, my fame is fantastic. If they ever chuck me out of the wine business, I might just make it as a poolroom hustler. And then, to elucidate further on old Woodrow, we have a place on the premises where your date can stay the night. A glorious convenience. Not to mention the fact that some of my fellow inhabitants there have real, valid minds. They think, they probe, they are not satisfied with didactic shit."

"Is that what you want?" Sam asked. "The wine business?"

Fred stretched, yawned lazily, and ground out the last tiny end of the marijuana cigarette. "Not really, although pop has been needling me about a master's in viticulture at Berkeley. That's Josh's end of the stick. He really digs it."

"Not without you, big brother," Joshua said comfortably.

"Still and all," Sam said, "you're the only heir to the big money. Your father owns the Lavette enterprises and practically everything else in California."

"I don't like the term real father," Fred said coldly.

"Biological father. Better?"

"You know something, Sammy, I've given a lot of thought to changing my name to Levy. That would mean a legal adoption by pop, and they've held off because they want me to maintain my position as a Lavette. Bullshit! I haven't seen or spoken to Thomas Lavette, my biological father, as you put it, in five years. I would love to go back to the ivy-clad halls of learning as Frederick Levy. Tell them all I'm Jewish. As a matter of fact, I'm half Jewish."

"You are not," May Ling told him. "Aunt Eloise isn't Jewish, and Uncle Adam is not your biological father, as you insist on putting it. I'm half Jewish—you are not."

"First Chinese Jew," Joshua said.

"Oh, you are bright, Joshua Levy! Like a five-watt bulb in the sunshine."

"The fact is," Sam said, "that we're a hopelessly mixed-up lot. You can joke about it, Freddie, and decide you're going to be a Jew. I've been living with the name of Cohen all my life. At Roxten, they made my life miserable because I was Jewish. What do I tell them—that I'm one quarter Italian, one quarter WASP, and one half Jewish? Mother says that if your mother isn't Jewish, according to Jewish law you're not Jewish. That didn't mean a damn thing to Adolf Hitler. There's a gang of Irish kids down at North Beach, and when I was just a kid they beat the hell out of me because they decided I was a Jew bastard. Josh is just

180

one quarter Jewish, but his name is Levy, and the way I look at it, that makes him a Jew."

"And what about me?" Mag Ling said. "My mother is half Jewish."

"And your father is half Italian and half Chinese."

"This is the craziest discussion I ever heard," Fred said. "You know something, Sammy, the Knesset—that's the Israeli parliament—well they had to decide what was the definition of a Jew, and I'm told that anyone who says he's Jewish is Jewish. So there you are."

"I'm going there," Sam said.

"Where?"

"Israel."

"You got to be kidding."

"You mean to live?" May Ling asked incredulously. "You mean you and your mother?"

"I don't know—maybe I'll live there. Maybe not. Not mom. Just me."

"Come on," Fred said. "You're old enough to stop dreaming. You're going to Princeton next year, where all good Lavettes go."

"I doubt that. I don't think mom could afford to send me to Princeton."

"Come on, Grandma Jean is loaded. She wouldn't think of you going anywhere else. She twisted my arm until I said uncle, and you're her prime heir, not me. I'm being reserved for the Thomas Lavette millions. You know what I'm going to do? I'm going to take his money and shove it."

"That'll be the day," Joshua said.

"If you come into all that bread," Sam said, "you can't just walk away from it. No one walks away from a hundred million or whatever it is. The trouble with you, Freddie, is that you've always been a rich kid, and it just never occurred to you how it feels not to have money."

"Rich kid my ass. Pop isn't rich. You know he

181

doesn't own Higate. Grandpa Jake owns it, and nobody tells him what for. And I'll tell you something else, Sammy boy, you grow up at Higate, and you're a peasant, no matter how much bread you have. And as for walking away from it, your mother did it, didn't she? I hear she came into fifteen million after old Tom Seldon died, and she gave the whole damn thing away. You ask me—that, sonny, is class. Real class. Jesus God, what a gesture!"

At the invitation of Tom Lavette to join him at a small dinner party, Carson Devron made the trip from Los Angeles to San Francisco. Carson's father, a man who never minced words, had told him bluntly that to sever connections with the Lavettes because of a divorce would be both immature and damaging. "A decent alliance between us," he told Carson, "would give us the whole state, the north and the south. And don't ever become bemused by my use of the word state. California is not a state. Connecticut, Rhode Island, Vermont—those are states. California is an empire, the richest damned empire on the face of this earth. We'll have a man in the White House one day, mark my word, and meanwhile, you husband your connections. You don't sulk and let them wither and die."

On Carson's part there was no deep animus toward Tom Lavette. He knew the story of Norman Drake, onetime member of the House Un-American Activities Committee, in regard to Barbara, and one could take the position that Tom Lavette had behaved very badly toward his sister. On the other hand, from Tom's point of view, his sister had betrayed him. Carson had never discussed the matter with Lavette, and since the divorce, he had nurtured a romantic, agonizing memory of Barbara. The memory soured him for other women. His sexual affairs were brief and unsatisfying, and he measured each woman he met against Barbara. Tom Lavette provided at the very least a connection with the family, and Carson reacted to this in an adolescent manner. Tom was her brother. He looked like her, the same high cheekbones and straight brow, the same tall, well-knit figure, the same light brown hair and gray eyes. It was at least a connection, some small bulwark to Carson's resistance to his family's urging that he marry and produce children.

Tonight, at the dinner party, Lucy Lavette had provided a pretty young woman, Alice Kimble, as Carson's dinner partner. She was a blue-eyed blonde, recently divorced, who practiced the dubious virtue of saying practically nothing. The other guests were a man called Mark Fowler and his wife, Marian. Fowler was short, stocky, with heavy sloping shoulders and a shambling walk, a soft-spoken ape-like man with flat, heavy features, in contrast to his tall, slender, good-looking wife. Carson had met him casually at various publishing affairs and conventions. He owned a string of eighteen mostly small-town newspapers in Northern California and in Oregon, as well as five television stations. His enterprises were family-owned, and as with many nonpublic corporations, rumors of his wealth varied widely. Carson had heard it said that his properties were worth half a billion dollars, but no firm figure was available.

At dinner, the conversation turned to politics, and Carson listened with some bitterness to Fowler's offhand dismissal of Norman Drake. "We should have known from the beginning," he said. "The man's a fool, and limited. Grossly limited. That's no reflection on you," he said to Tom. "We were all taken in. I dislike the term kingmaker, but it defines us, and a kingmaker ought to be damn sure he selects the right material. Hell, it never was any different. There hasn't been a President since Lincoln who wasn't made, chosen, cut, and shaped by a few men who knew what they wanted."

"What about F.D.R.?" Carson asked coldly.

"If we had Jim Farley here, he could give us a fine lecture on that point. Yes, Roosevelt was a vote-getter once he made his mark, but who put him in a place where he could make his mark? The same was true of Harry Truman."

"Who do you have in mind?" Tom asked him.

"Dick Nixon."

"Nixon!" Carson exclaimed. "After what Kennedy did to him? I'd say that Nixon is finished, and I might add good riddance to bad rubbish. The man is a disaster."

"Yet when Norman Drake washed out at the convention, you supported Nixon."

"We had no choice. I think we've heard the last of Mr. Nixon, and believe me, that doesn't make me unhappy."

"You're wrong, Carson. Understandably so, but wrong. There's a strange charisma about Mr. Nixon. Like Norman Drake, he appeals to a level of mediocrity that most of us possess, to a nugget of meanness that we like to pretend we are free of, but unlike Drake, he has brains and a consuming, raging ambition."

"He's a loser," Carson argued. "A whimpering, whining loser."

"Yes, but a very unusual one. He thrives on it—because people who don't understand him underestimate him. He's down but not out, believe me."

"What is your thinking, Fowler?" Tom asked him. "You really believe that Nixon has the stamina to come back?"

"We have five years. Kennedy will be reelected—no way in the world you can stop that, even if this business in Vietnam heats up into a real war, as I suspect it will. That gives us five years, time to plan, to gather our resources"—Carson's face was cold and unsympathetic—"and to meet the man. I appreciate your reaction, Carson. It's the honest reaction of a decent human being. All I ask is that you keep an open mind until we can have an informal, off-the-record evening with Dick Nixon. I assure you, you'll be surprised. I'll arrange the meeting if you agree to come, just you, myself, Tom, one or two others. How about it?" For all of his homeliness, his mashed-in face, his overmuscled, hunched shoulders, he was an ingratiating man, a persuasive man.

"I'll come," Carson agreed after a long moment of silence, "but I promise nothing. If you can accept an adversary opinion."

"We need one. It brings out the best in Dick."

"You look tired this morning," Dr. Albright said to Barbara.

"Two hours of sleep will do it every time."

"You couldn't sleep?"

"Carson called me at two o'clock in the morning. He had been in town for dinner at my brother's house, and then pacing in his room at the Mark Hopkins. I imagine he had a few drinks, and at two o'clock he decided to call me—pleading with me to let him come over. He had to talk to me."

"When did you last speak to him?" Dr. Albright asked curiously.

"Over a year ago. And before that, not since the divorce."

"And you let him come?"

"I can't refuse Carson when he pleads. He's like a child. And Sam is up at Higate. Do you think I shouldn't have?"

"What do you think, Barbara? I don't know what happened."

"We talked," Barbara said.

She had dragged herself out of bed, tired and chilled; combed her hair and brushed her teeth; and then Carson was at the door, apologizing.

"Please forgive me, Bobby. I've never done anything like this before. I feel like an idiot——"

"Stop it, Carson. You're here."

He looked around him curiously. He had been in the little house on Green Street only once before, years ago.

"Sit down," Barbara told him, leading him into the living room. "I'm going to put on some coffee. Are you hungry? Do you want something to eat?"

"No. Thank you."

"You'll have coffee?"

He nodded. She left him there and waited in the kitchen while the water boiled, trying to recollect how he had his coffee. Black, yes, black. Why did it all seem so very long ago? He had changed; he had lost weight and his face was drawn; he was no longer the beautiful golden boy but a man approaching middle age. When she returned to the living room with a tray, coffee, toast, and a pot of jam, he was sitting rigidly, his hands clenched.

"Carson, will you please relax," she said to him. "You were in trouble and you called me. That's all right. We're not enemies or strangers. We're good old friends." She handed him the cup of coffee. "Toast and jam? It's that dark Seville marmalade that you always liked so much."

He managed a tired smile.

"Now, what happened?"

"I don't know. It's just that my world has been creaking, and suddenly it came apart. The whole damn thing came apart. I feel like I'm standing on a precipice, and I'm not alone. The whole damn world pushing behind me. I want to run away. I swear to God, I want to chuck the whole thing and run away, and I know I haven't got the guts to do it."

"We've all felt that way, and none of us have the guts to do it. Tell me what happened. You had dinner with Tom."

"With Tom and a man called Mark Fowler, newspaper publisher and television. He owns five stations, which is right up to the legal limit. Very powerful, very rich. He's one of a group of men who, along with your brother, calls the tune west of the Rockies. The whole purpose of the dinner, as I see it, was to enlist me, meaning the Devron interests, in a scheme to groom Richard Nixon for the presidency five years from now."

Barbara was not impressed. It didn't appear to add up to a crisis worth dragging her out of bed at two o'clock in the morning, and she observed that after his defeat by Kennedy, it was unlikely that Nixon could be groomed for anything. "And even if he were to be inflicted on us again, you were not very, disturbed about putting Norman Drake through the same process. Is Nixon any worse?" And when Carson stared at her without replying, she said unhappily, "I didn't want to bring that up, Carson, but it is the same kettle of fish, isn't it?"

"Yes."

"Then I just don't understand."

"I suppose it adds up. You take something for granted, and then you don't take it for granted anymore. I don't know. You see it from another angle. You touch it and it's rotten—and then you begin to look at other things, and it's all rotten. It's not a question of illusions. I don't have that many illusions. It's like a sickness that's all around you, and suddenly you realize that you're as sick as the rest."

"Did you go along with them?"

"Fowler pointed out that this is how Presidents are made. I couldn't argue that. Yes, I agreed to meet with Nixon and talk to him. Then, afterwards, back at the hotel, my world went to pieces. Can you understand me? Does it make any sense—what I'm saying?"

"Yes, it makes sense."

"And then the fear began. I've never been afraid

187

like this before, Bobby. You know that. Not during the war—never. My God, I was so frightened. I called you. I'm sorry——"

He was sitting on the couch. Barbara went to him and sat beside him. "It's all right," she said. "You'll work it out, Carson."

"We talked for another hour," Barbara told Dr. Albright. "Then he went back to his hotel. He talked about other women in his life since our divorce. There's one now who is in love with him. He may marry her. He said he still loves me."

"Barbara, when did it begin? His impotence? His inability to make love to you?"

"On our honeymoon."

"After your day with the auto manufacturer?"

"Before that. I don't know how he is with other women. He was wonderful with me before we were married. I wish I could understand this thing he's going through now. Do you?"

"He's not my patient. You are."

"I felt like his mother."

"Yes."

"No, if that's what you're suggesting. He didn't marry his mother."

"I suggested nothing, Barbara."

"I did."

"Perhaps. Do you understand why you divorced him? That's the important thing."

"It wasn't the Norman Drake business. Last night, when he was talking about how his world had been shattered, I wondered why mine had never been shattered. Not that way. I've been through so much— growing up in that golden cage up there on Russian Hill, and then the longshoremen's strike, and then Paris and the Spanish war, and Marcel's death, and Germany and the war, and Bernie's death. Carson never even touched the edge of my world. Yes, I was depressed.

That's why I came to you—my world was shattered, wasn't it?"

"By now you know what depression means, Barbara. It's turning your bitterness, your resentment, your frustration against yourself—all your suppressed rage building up through your life and turned in."

"I was thinking," Barbara said slowly, "while you were talking, of my first day in the studio when they hired me to do the screenplay of my first book. I was given an office, a desk, a typewriter, and a ream of cheap yellow paper. I've never used yellow paper. It's a silly economy. The white bond costs five dollars a ream and the yellow paper is a dollar or two less. So I told one of the secretaries to order me a ream of white paper through studio supply. Two days later she came to me in tears. She was being fired because she had ordered the white paper. This happened in a place where they throw around money as if it were going out of style, where they charge all their wretched twenty-dollar lunches and limousines and parties and travel expenses and anything else they can think of against the picture, and this poor kid was being fired because she ordered white paper instead of yellow. At first, I couldn't believe it, and then I was so angry I could have killed the producer——"

"Did you?" Dr. Albright asked gently. "Did you kill the producer?"

"Of course not," Barbara replied impatiently. "But I stopped the firing. I told them that if they fired the girl, I'd walk out of there. Later, they might have welcomed that. But then they still needed me."

"Politely? Restrainedly?"

"Yes. I simply made it clear to them how I felt."

"Barbara, when I asked you before whether you killed the producer, I was not being literal. We both understand that. You don't go around killing people."

"Of course——"

"Wait. Let me go on a moment. You had witnessed

an obscene piece of business. Wouldn't it have been quite appropriate for you to explode in anger, to tell them precisely what you thought of that kind of behavior?"

"I don't do things that way," Barbara said, after a moment.

"You did in prison—the incident with the guard."

"Yes. I guess I was provoked to a point—" She shook her head tiredly.

"And that other incident you told me about, that time in Germany before the war, when you saw the old Jews struck and kicked by the SS men?"

"I lost my head completely."

"But you saw nothing very wrong in your brother's cold-blooded scheme to foist a man like Richard Nixon on the American public——"

"Of course I did!" Barbara exclaimed. "It stinks!" She leaped to her feet, pacing across the room, turning on Dr. Albright. "What was I supposed to do? Tell Carson that these were bad boys and that he was fine and human to be shocked by their behavior! I have lived in this lousy male world for almost half a century. The shock was worn off. I'm a woman! You fight it up to a point, and then you throw up your arms and you accept it and you admit to yourself that you're no damn different from any other woman and that you've all been stepped on and walked over and defecated on since time began. You know, I could have finished that screenplay. I'm sure you wonder why I keep talking about it, because how important is it in that stupid industry where they ruin everything they touch. But it was important to me. It was my first book and maybe my best and I tore it out of my guts, and that was a time when women didn't write about what they really felt. Yes, my first draft needed work. I knew that. And this man, the director, Jerry Kanter, came to me and told me that if I went to bed with him, he'd see to it that no other writer was put on the job. Oh, he was a doll!

190

Barbara, he said to me, you are absolutely the first writer I ever asked to join me in the sack. Actresses, that's something else, but lady writers look like shit. It comes with the trade. But you, baby, are something to write home about, and all you have to do is bend that WASP backbone of yours a little and I'll see that you stay on the job at four thousand a week, which ain't hay, believe me——"

She stopped and stood facing Dr. Albright, her breast heaving, her fists clenched. Then she dropped back into her chair. Dr. Albright pushed the box of tissues toward her.

"Stop it, damn you! I'm not going to cry."

"What did you say?"

Barbara shook her head angrily.

"What did you say to Jerry Kanter?"

"I told him to go to hell."

"Just that?"

"It was enough."

"What would you have said to him if he weren't Jewish?"

"What? Why, it never even occurred to me that he was Jewish."

"No? That's strange, Barbara. It occurred to me the moment you mentioned his name. And I never met him."

"Really, I don't know what you're getting at," Barbara said, her annoyance increasing.

"And your producer, Mr. Goldberg, he was Jewish, too."

"Yes, doctor, it's very much a Jewish industry. Jews began it."

"Can you accept the idea that a Jew can be a bastard? You know, they're not that different from other people."

"I don't know what you're getting at," Barbara said stubbornly. "I don't see what this has to do with anything."

"You're also very provoked with me."

"Yes."

"Well, that comes with the territory. I'm no orthodox shrink, as you have discovered by now. Your first husband's name was Cohen, and after his death, you changed your name to Barbara Lavette."

"Years later. And it just happens that my name was Lavette. I write under that name. Carson's name is Devron. I am still Barbara Lavette." And when Dr. Albright made no rejoinder, she added, "Yes, Judith, you've touched a nerve. I don't like anti-Semitism, not the taste or sound or smell of it."

"I didn't think you did. Still and all, it's a complex matter, isn't it?"

"What is?"

"Anti-Semitism," Dr. Albright said. "It's very complicated in America. My husband was a brilliant surgeon. He died three years ago. His name was Wurtman and he was Jewish. Would I have kept the name of Wurtman if the situation were reversed, or would I have taken his name if his name were Albright? I'm not sure."

"And you suggest that I changed my name from Cohen because I did not want people to think I was Jewish."

"Am I suggesting that?"

"It happens that I'm not Jewish. My father's partner was Jewish. He was the best friend my father ever had. My lawyer, Sam Goldberg, was Jewish. I named my son after him. I live in a house I bought from his estate. And I married a Jew. So for you to even suggest that I am an anti-Semite is—"

"Go on. Say it."

"Obscene."

"Good. We're at a point now where we can talk to each other, and I don't think we have much further to go. It seems to me, Barbara, that the essence of anti-Semitism is the notion that the Jew is basically differ-

192

ent. We've threaded him through our lives, and still when he turns out to be a complete swine, like that director of yours, we're shocked and horrified. And then a nasty little worm of anger and frustration begins to build up." She glanced at her watch. "I'm afraid our time is up."

Still angry when she left Dr. Albright's office, Barbara realized that she was stimulated and by no means depressed. She had not been depressed for weeks now.

Love came to May Ling on her sixteenth birthday, sweetly, gently, in the gloaming, as she thought of it. She had her mother's love of words, odd words, different words, and particularly those words that tugged and prodded nostalgically. When twilight, the quick beneficent California twilight, fell upon the Napa Valley, it was for her the gloaming. She loved the song— in the gloaming, oh, my darling. She was hopelessly romantic, yet gravely wise. If anything, she lacked exuberance, preferring refuge in her vivid fantasies. Only one quarter Chinese, she was totally Oriental in appearance, with her grandmother's skin, straight black hair and tiny uptilted nose. Curiously enough, her young brother, Daniel, eight years old, took after their mother, with Sally's pale skin, straw-colored hair and blue eyes. Nothing could convince May Ling that she was not hopelessly unattractive, certainly not her mother's assertion that she was very beautiful. She was five feet and eight inches tall, quite slender, and in a culture that worshipped oversized breasts, hers were tiny. In the face of fervent pleas, Sally refused to allow her daughter to curl or dye her hair, and in this she was wise, for May Ling was indeed a beautiful young woman, wonderfully graceful and soft-spoken and gentle. She wore her black hair banged and bobbed short and endured it with resentment, but it enhanced her delicate beauty, as Sally well knew. Yet bit by bit,

May Ling was becoming aware of herself, resenting her difference less and less. She discovered in her father's library a book of Chinese philosophy called *The Natural Way of Lao-tzu*, translated from the Chinese by her great-grandfather. This led to the further discovery that her father, Joseph Lavette, could actually speak Mandarin Chinese. She read Lao-tzu, delighted with its directness and simplicity, and from this went on to other explorations in old Chinese philosophy, and then bedeviled her father to teach her Chinese. The truth is that Joe Lavette remembered very little of the Mandarin that his grandfather had taught him when he was a child, but he could still read the ideographs, and one day he returned from the hospital in San Francisco, where he did his surgery, with a stack of Chinese books and newspapers. After that, there were evenings when Joe and May Ling sat together, struggling with the Chinese characters, triumphantly unlocking a word here, a sentence there.

And then, for that evening when love came to May Ling, which was November 22, 1963, Sally brought out, from a bed of tissue paper in an old chest of drawers, a gown which had belonged to Joe's mother. Today was May Ling's birthday, and the gown was a gift that Sally had treasured ever since she first married Joe. It was of heavy black silk, decorated with royal dragons worked in gold thread, and when May Ling first saw it, she was speechless, staring at it with dark, delighted eyes. It fitted her perfectly except for its length, but since it came to above her ankles, that was not a problem. From the same bed of tissue paper, Sally revealed a pair of black silk slippers, embroidered in the same gold thread, but alas, May Ling's feet were at least two sizes larger than her grandmother's, and plain Mary Janes were substituted. Nevertheless, May Ling was impressive enough in the gown to make both her parents stare at her in wonder and delight.

The birthday party, to which family and friends

were invited, was Jake Levy's gift to his granddaughter, and it was scheduled to take place in Higate in the old bottling plant, now converted into a reception and tasting room. A four-piece band had been hired to provide the music, and aside from May Ling's friends in Napa, Levys and Lavettes and Cassalas swelled out the list of invited guests. Fred had been sent a round-trip ticket from Princeton for the Thanksgiving holidays, and Barbara and Sam drove over for the evening.

Joe, Sally, and May Ling were on their way to Higate, Joe driving with May Ling in the place of honor beside him, and Sally and Daniel in back of the car, when they heard the news over the radio of the assassination of President Kennedy.

They reacted variously. May Ling burst into tears; young Daniel was not certain he knew what it meant; Joe muttered softly about the hopeless barbarism of the human race; and Sally, after the first shock, realized that this would put a damper on what she had hoped would be a delightful and enchanting evening—an evening that May Ling had been looking forward to for months.

"How can we have a party now?" May Ling asked woefully.

"We will have the party," Sally told her. "This is a dreadful, terrible thing, but we'll help no one by canceling the party. Life goes on. President Johnson has already been sworn in. He didn't throw up his arms and call it quits. So just wipe away those tears. Terrible things happen every day, but we don't stop living."

"Can we, daddy?" she asked Joe. "Can we still have a party? Wouldn't that be cruel and heartless?"

"No, it wouldn't be cruel and it wouldn't be heartless either. We wouldn't plan a party now, but your grandfather has decorated the room and hired a band, and there's probably enough food to feed an army, not to mention the fact that Freddie has flown in a day early and people are on their way from San

195

Francisco and Oakland and San Mateo. I know how you feel, but we'll try to enjoy the party just as much as we would have if this hadn't happened."

May Ling tried, as did the others at the party. For Barbara, the lovely child in the incredible Chinese gown was like a re-creation of the woman after whom she had been named, Joe's mother, the Chinese librarian who had been Dan Lavette's mistress and then his wife; and Barbara was relieved that Jean had pleaded a cold, and thereby was absent.

"It's just wonderful," Barbara said to Joe. "It makes me believe in something—I'm not very sure what—but she is May Ling. She moves the same way, her voice is the same."

"Yes, genetics works most strangely."

"Oh, for heaven's sake, stop being a damned scientist. How a clod like you ever produced such a child, I'll never know."

"Thank you, sister."

"Nevertheless, I'm glad mother isn't here. It's too far along for her to see the other May Ling again."

"It's only the dress," Joe said.

"Of course it's only the dress."

The party took place, but try as they might, dancing, eating, drinking, the guests could not erase the shadow of something grotesque and hideous. The fact that it had happened two thousand miles away did not help to lessen its impact, and May Ling, who was imaginative and very sensitive, could not drive the images of violence from her mind. She was receptive to the attentions being paid her, in particular the interesting new attitudes of her three cousins, Fred and Sam and Joshua; she embraced her great-grandmother, Sarah Levy, now eighty-three years old, who was thoroughly bewildered by the transformation of what she had always considered a proper Jewish girl into this exotic Oriental creature; and she responded with a grave

196

thank you to Fred's declaration: "You, cousin, are one dynamite lady."

But it was with Rubio Truaz, the son of Cándido Truaz, that May Ling found her first love; and that too was due in part to the strang miasma that the news of President Kennedy's assassination had cast over the party.

It began—although there may have been roots going further back—when May Ling cut the cake, handing a piece to each person with a smile and a few words, something that surprised Sally, who had always considered her daughter to be the epitome of shyness. There were three families of Chicanos at the party, and May Ling tried to say something specially nice to each of the group. She managed this until it was the turn of Rubio Truaz, and then her voice dried up. They stood for a long moment, staring at each other, and then he smiled and nodded and took the piece of cake.

Rubio Truaz was eighteen, in his first year at Berkeley. Jake had persuaded his father to send him to Berkeley, where he could take a number of courses in viticulture, rather than to put him to work at the winery. Like his father, he was tall, over six feet in height, heavily muscled in the shoulders, a pleasant, well-formed head, small features, widely set brown eyes and curly black hair. He was bright, read a great deal, came out of high school with a straight A average, and possessed a mind of his own. He had no intention of spending his life at Higate. In his own romantic fantasies, he saw himself as a lawyer, a committed defender of the rights of the sorely oppressed Mexican-Americans who constitute a community of such numbers in California. His father, Cándido, was subject to no such illusions. Cándido had begun life in America as the child of poor Mexican farm workers; he had labored in the lettuce fields from the time he was five years old and had come finally to Higate as a grape picker. Now, thirty-three years later, he had his

197

own home, a washing machine and a television, and children who never went hungry. If the winery was good enough for him, it was good enough for his children; but on the other hand, he did not check Rubio's curriculum at Berkeley, and Rubio had no doubt that when the time came, he would have his own way.

May Ling had known him since they were children and his sister, Carla, and he had been accepted as members of the wolf pack—ill-at-ease members, perhaps, for even at a place like Higate the barrier between the Chicanos and the Anglos, as the Mexicans called them, was never completely broken.

It was about ten o'clock that evening, the food and the cake eaten, the four-piece band playing slow, old-fashioned music, that May Ling told Sally that she was going outside for just a while.

"Alone?" Sally asked her. "Why don't you take Sam or Freddie?"

"I'd rather be alone. I want to walk and think."

"All right. But don't be too long. We'll be leaving in an hour or so, and I think you ought to open your presents."

"Must I? It embarrasses me."

"I think you should."

May Ling slipped outside at a moment when no one appeared to be watching her. She wanted very much to be alone, to taste the bittersweet of the evening, to contrast her own saddened happiness with a world where a President could be shot down in cold blood. The evening was cool, but not cold, and a bright moon cast a silvery radiance over the fields and vine-shrouded buildings. She walked up the hillside to the old fireplace where they had spent so many hours as children, and there, sitting with his hands clasped around his knees, she found Rubio Truaz. The meeting was unexpected. He scrambled to his feet.

"I didn't think anyone would be here," he said lamely.

"Neither did I."

"When I saw you—"

"When I saw you—"

"I mean," he said, "that when I saw you, I thought for a moment that I was dreaming, because I was sitting here thinking about you, and then I looked up and there you were."

"I only wanted to be alone and breathe some fresh air."

"I'll go down if you want to be alone."

"No. Oh, no. You were here first."

"That doesn't matter."

"No. We can both stay here for a little while. I have to be back in a few minutes. They want me to open the presents. I hate to do that."

"Why?"

"Because someone whose present isn't as nice or expensive as someone else's feels bad. I don't want anyone to feel bad at my birthday."

"I know. If I had the money, I would have given you a diamond necklace."

"Why? And what on earth would I do with a diamond necklace?"

"Wear it. Not that it would make you any more beautiful than you are."

May Ling thought about it for a moment before she answered. "No one ever said anything like that to me before."

"I said it a hundred times, but very quietly."

"Thank you," she whispered.

"Can you sit on the ground in that dress, or will it spoil it?"

"I'll be careful," May Ling said, dropping down to the ground. Rubio sat beside her. They sat silently for several minutes, looking at the buildings below them and listening to the faint sound of the music. At last, May Ling said, "I feel so guilty because I'm so happy tonight, and such a terrible thing happened."

"It is terrible, and terrible, cruel things happen all the time. That doesn't mean we can't be happy."

"Are you?" she asked him.

"I guess I've never been really happy before, because I never felt this way before."

"What way?"

"Like I want this to go on forever, just the two of us sitting here. But I guess you don't feel that way."

"But I do. Sort of. Yes."

Then she heard Sally's voice calling her. The moment was over, but in May Ling's mind the moment would remain forever.

There is no doubt that in the earlier periods of man, the sense of time was very different. People lived in a world that was not obsessed with schedules and surrounded with clocks and watches. Time was an easier thing; its flow was gentler; and there was less necessity to mark the beginning and the end. Barbara sometimes brooded about this, remembering the day of Kennedy's assassination as the beginning of a period, a new phase of her existence. On the other hand, an inner clock was also working. Menopause had overtaken her, and although she had known what would happen and had expected it to happen, she was nevertheless deeply shaken. She had discussed it at great length with Dr. Albright, wondering how much it contributed to the long months of depression.

"Of course it's a factor," Dr. Albright said, "a very important factor. A source of life inside of you dries up, and that's a gigantic psychological blow. Flushes, weariness, fear, and it's the lot of all women, and in your case, you cope with the quality of being a romantic. So many women have that beaten out of them and crushed before they ever reach your age."

Was being a romantic a blessing or a curse? Barbara wondered. It was her only kinship to Kennedy, whom she had never seen nor met, but he too was a romantic, the last romantic, and now he had died in a hospital in Texas, his head blown open.

Barbara drove home alone from May Ling's party, leaving Sam to spend the night at Higate, and driving through the darkness, she could not pull her mind out of the drama and tragedy that had happened in Dallas. She had been to Dallas once, years ago, autographing copies of her book at the big Cokesbury bookstore, and she remembered the people she had met that day, mostly women, their timid smiles and soft, slurred speech. In her memory, they were self-effacing, gently apologetic for putting her to the trouble of autographing a book. A truck came by, swerving toward her and almost driving her off the road. It broke the chain of her thoughts. She turned on her car radio, listened to the flow of mechanical chatter about what had happened that day, and then switched it off. A hot flush was beginning, taking over her body, her face tight and uncomfortable, her arms wet with sweat.

"Oh, Christ," she said, "now. Why now?"

It was almost one in the morning when she got home. She took a bath, and after that, she couldn't sleep. She prowled through the empty house, tried to read and discovered that the words made no sense, and then decided to pay neglected bills. Once her father's estate had been settled, a trust fund provided her with enough money to live comfortably if not opulently. She smiled at the thought now; Dan Lavette had been much too wise to leave his daughter a sum of money outright; again the romantic whose guilt would drive her to dispense with it, to give it away.

She wrote out a few checks and then paused. "The devil with this," she said aloud. "I've written nothing in three years. It's time I put an end to that." She closed the checkbook, took the cover off her typewriter, inserted a sheet of paper, and typed out a title: "The President's Wife." Dawn came, and she was still at the typewriter, pounding away.

When she finally stopped working, it was well past seven o'clock. She was exhilarated and excited, not sleepy, not tired, but alive and filled with a sense of herself. She went into the kitchen and made a pot of strong coffee, and drinking it, she leafed through the pages she had written, lingering over one part:

"So it had come finally, at long last, that thing she had dreaded so, that thing that would surely happen to every other woman on earth, but not to her, that thing which they called the menopause, the change of life. She tried to remember all she knew about it, the stuff of her biology class in college. The ovaries stop producing eggs, but there was another part, something to do with the female hormones. She searched through the bookshelves for her old textbook. Had she kept it? Then she found it. Estrogen and progesterone—the two hormones produced in smaller and smaller quantities. She read on in increasing panic: changes in the skin tone, wrinkles, a different distribution of the body fat, fat deposits at the back of the neck, that curse called the 'dowager hump'; and as she read, she felt a cold sweat break through the hot flush that had overtaken her."

"Not bad," Barbara said as she put down the page. "Not bad at all. You've got a hook into something, old girl, and let's see where it takes you."

She felt a personal sense of triumph. She was able to put it down in sharp, clear typewritten words and look at it coldly and objectively. That was the beginning of something, not simply a book, something else that she would have to think about very deeply. She had a second cup of coffee, layered two slices of toast thickly with peanut butter and jam, a dispensation to herself since Sam was not present, and then went upstairs and showered and dressed—after which she called Boyd Kimmelman and asked him to take her to lunch. They made a date for one o'clock. She then called Eloise in Higate, and was told that Sam had been invited to stay for Thanksgiving, which meant missing only a couple of days of school, which he had assured Eloise he could comfortably miss. Could he stay? Barbara agreed reluctantly, convinced that Sam had invited himself. She then went back to the typewriter, felt suddenly sleepy, and decided to stretch out on the couch for just a minute or two. She awakened in panic, discovered that it was five minutes to one, dashed some cold water on her face, ran a comb through her hair, and arrived at Gino's Italian restaurant twenty minutes later.

She kissed Boyd and apologized breathlessly. "You should be raging at me," she said, "but you're a dear man and you sit there smiling. I'll try to make up for it. I'll never be late for lunch with you again."

"What happened?"

"I fell asleep. I was up all night writing. I wrote for six hours straight—six hours. Can you believe that, Boyd? God, I'm so excited! I've started a book. Where have I been these past few years? I suppose I'm heartless, because the whole notion leaped into my mind after I heard the terrible news about Kennedy. I'm calling it *The President's Wife,* and I want to tell the woman's point of view, the story of a woman married to this power-compelled man who has finally made it to the ultimate top, all the power and all the glory, and what happens to the woman? That's what I want to write. What happens to the woman? Oh, I know, I'll have to go back to that hateful city of Washington and prowl around, and I swore I never would, but this is something, believe me——"

"I do believe you, but do you suppose you could pause for just a minute or two while we order lunch. I'm starved."

"Of course. I'm thoughtless, and you've been such an angel."

"You're right." They ordered lunch, and when that had been done, he said to Barbara, "It sounds great, and I'm damn pleased that you've pulled out of that slump, but where do I come into it?"

"Two ways. But first, the legalities."

"What legalities? If you're writing fiction, there aren't any legalities. I presume your President's wife will be a fictional person?"

"Absolutely."

"And your supporting characters, will they all be fictional?"

"No, they can't be. I have to anchor it in history, and there will have to be at least some real people."

"All right," Boyd told her, "we'll take them as they come. Let me pour you some wine. The point is, it's almost impossible to libel a public figure the way our laws are set up. In England, it's another matter, but our laws are very liberal on that point." He poured the wine. "Now what else?"

"I want you to find me a President's wife I can talk to."

"Just like that?"

"I have faith in you, Boyd."

"Bobby, darling, faith has no place here. The field is too limited. Mrs. Roosevelt might have succumbed to your charm and beauty, but she died last year. What kind of questions do you want to ask this lady?"

"Very intimate questions."

"Honey, you are a notorious woman, an ex-jailbird, a divorcée. You are absolutely asking the impossible."

"As I said, I have faith in you. You have all sorts of connections. I have faith in you."

"You said that twice. You really think I could set this up."

"Absolutely."

"Then if you have all this admiration for my qualities, why won't you marry me?"

"You never asked me."

"Suppose I asked you now."

"That's not asking," Barbara said. "You were hungry. Why don't you eat?"

"I'm asking you."

"You're not serious?"

"Completely so."

"Boyd darling, I've married enough. It doesn't work."

"You always married the wrong man."

"True. That's why I must stop."

"I'm too short—right?"

"How tall are you?"

"Five eight."

"So am I. You're tall enough."

"If you go barefoot."

"Boyd, I'm trying to be sensible. That's new for me."

"You don't love me."

"Sure I do. You're darling. I go to bed with you, don't I? I wouldn't do that if I didn't love you."

"Tell me something," Boyd said. "If Marcel had lived, would that have worked?"

"You do have a way of asking questions. I don't know, Boyd. I sometimes think that sort of love comes only once, only when you're very young. That was twenty-five years ago." She shook her head. "No more of this. We'll talk about Presidents' wives."

Since the death of his wife, Joanna, in 1959, Stephan Cassala had become an increasingly frequent visitor to the house on Russian Hill. His mother, Maria Cassala, had died a year after his wife, at the age of eighty-three, a gentle death, passing away in her sleep. His son, Ralph, a professor at Stanford working experimentally in the field of subatomic particles, had married and lived in a small house on the edge of the campus. This left Stephan Cassala alone in the great house at San Mateo that his father had built half a century before, a monumental pile of stone and wood, created as the realization of the dream of a semiliterate Sicilian immigrant. At sixty-eight, Stephan was retired. A ten-percent interest in the Lavette shipping company, sold by Dan more than ten years ago, had given Stephan all the money he would ever require, more than sufficient to keep the house at San Mateo functioning. But after his mother's death, the house became a hollow, echoing morgue, and he put it up for sale and took an apartment in San Francisco.

He fell into the habit of dropping in at Jean's house at cocktail time two or three days a week. They would have a drink, and then they would go to dinner and occasionally to the theater or a film. Other times they would meet for lunch and then stroll together along the Embarcadero or in Lincoln Park. Even at seventy-three, Jean cut a handsome figure, erect and slender, her blue eyes still clear, her hair white and thick. All of his adult life, Jean had occupied a place in Stephan's fantasies, but in his mind, she was unapproachable and properly so, the wife not only of his best friend but of a man he literally worshipped. Now the fires had quieted, and he was grateful for the fact that she regarded him as a dear friend, someone to be with and to lean on.

Jean, on the other hand, was even more grateful. Stephan never approached her as an old woman; in his eyes, she was still the queenly woman, the *beauty* of a time long past, when that in itself was a title and an accolade, and his manner toward her was of an old-world courtliness. Tall, darkly handsome, his skin sallow, his white mustache rather grand, he was as unlike Dan as anyone could be; yet they made a handsome couple, and Stephan never presumed beyond a rigidly established formal relationship.

Still, Jean had guilts about the whole thing. "I don't know what I would do without him," she told Barbara. "We live in a society that has no place for the old."

"You're not old, mother."

206

"Am I not? Don't speak nonsense, my dear. I'll soon be seventy-four, and that is old. Every man I ever knew is either dead or has become one of those doddering old fools in the clubhouse on California Street. As for the women, they've surrendered their minds, those that are still alive."

"Which means nothing. You're very much alive."

"I like to think so, but what will I do, Bobby? The poor man's in love with me."

"That's wonderful. He's had a rotten life."

"I am not in love with him. I'm an old lady, and I am not in love with anyone except my grandsons. I'm one of those unfortunate creatures who was only able to love one man, your father."

"I don't know too much about sex at your age," Barbara said, "but has he ever made a pass? I mean——"

"What on earth are you talking about!" Jean exclaimed.

"Then the whole thing's academic, isn't it? He's a dear friend. He interests you. He escorts you——"

"You will never grow up, will you?"

"Perhaps not. But I'm working at it. I've started a new book, and I've sent off a hundred pages to Harris Fielding. You do remember him?"

"Is he still alive?"

"Mother, all sorts of people are still alive, and he's still a literary agent, and in his letter he wanted to know whether the remarkable Jean Lavette is still as beautiful as ever."

"No, I don't believe that."

"It's the truth. I'll show you the letter. I told him absolutely, even more so."

They were sitting in Barbara's living room, and Jean could not resist glancing at a mirror, across the room and obliquely reflecting her.

Telling Dr. Albright about it a few days later, Barbara said, "Sure as God, my mother is going to seduce

207

him. Stephan Cassala will be making love to Jean, and he'll be guilt-ridden and absolutely certain it was his idea."

"And the notion of a seventy-three-year-old woman going to bed with a man doesn't bother you?"

"Should it?"

"I asked you."

"I think it's rather great," Barbara said.

"When are you going to New York?"

"When school ends. I'll ship Sam off to Higate. I'm still a bit wary of the weather in the East, and anyway I hate to leave Sam alone in the house. It's years since I've been East. My agent loves what I've done, and Boyd has come up with a President's wife who will talk to me."

"Good." Dr. Albright consulted her appointment book. "Suppose I see you once more, Barbara, a week from now. After that, we'll call it quits."

"You mean I'm finished?"

"For the time being. If you want to talk, I'm always here."

Barbara was silent for a while. Then she said, "May I ask you a rather foolish question?"

"There aren't any. Go on."

"What we've been doing—that's certainly not psychoanalysis, Freudian or otherwise?"

"Absolutely not."

"Then what have we been doing all these months?"

"Just talking to each other. You felt rotten then and you couldn't work. You feel better now, and you're working. It's a kind of therapy, and it helps some people, not all by any means. Are you upset because it's not something more complex and mysterious?"

"Oh, no. No. I'm delighted to know that I'm only moderately crazy."

"As we all are, Barbara. It's the human affliction."

* * *

Sitting in the lounge at the Woodrow Wilson Society at Princeton, reading and trying to understand a book that had been circulating as a sort of cult object among his associates, Fred Lavette looked up and became aware that he was being confronted. He marked the page and closed Hermann Hesse's *Siddhartha,* and then nodded at the four young men who stood facing him. One of them, Herb Katz, a senior, said, "What do you think?"

"Of this?" tapping the book.

"Read it twice."

"I'm not looking for salvation. I only want to be able to discuss Hesse with the bright chicks. I'm addicted to bright chicks."

"I'm addicted to large tits," Phil Strong said, pulling up a chair. He was an anomaly, an intellectual jock who lived at Ivy and hung out in Woodrow Wilson. He was six foot two, a lineman, whose big body hung easily and loosely under a pleasant, good-looking face and a crop of stiff, sandy hair. Katz was smaller, wiry, intense. The third in the group, Alan Greenberg, was pudgy, middle height, with a remarkable resemblance to Bob Hope; wherefore he was called Hopeful. The fourth young man was black, tall, long-limbed, an excellent basketball player whose color relegated him to Woodrow Wilson, a fact that did not disturb him. Bert Jones had made friends at Woodrow Wilson, and it was a good deal less likely that he would have made them anywhere else on the Princeton campus.

The other three pulled up chairs to face Fred, who inquired with some impatience, "What is it? Do we discuss Hermann Hesse or tits—or is this a deputation?"

"A deputation," Hopeful told him. "The Siddhartha speaks of repose. The quiet mind attains clarity. We approach you at a moment of Lavette clarity."

"Knock that off," Strong said. "Just feed it to him straight."

"A little delicacy is called for," Katz said.

"How do you feel about civil rights?" Bert Jones asked Fred.

"That's a dumb question. In fact, that's a provocative question. I've signed every petition you've shoved in front of me. How should I feel about civil rights? I'm no bloody fascist."

"That's a positive reaction," Katz said. "Very good."

"Look, Freddie," Jones explained, "we're very serious about this. There's a big drive coming up to register black voters in Mississippi—a national thing. Every college is sending people down to work on it, and we want to see Princeton in on it."

"Just to show the colors," Strong put in. "So they won't point a finger at the old alma mater and say we head up the shit list."

"Nothing very big. You wouldn't expect any kind of mass movement out of Princeton, but the four of us are committed, and we need you."

"We really need you, Freddie."

"Now wait a minute, just hold on," Fred told them. "You have the wrong place, the wrong time, and the wrong guy. As they say, my mind to me a treasure is. I'll sign your petitions and I'll put my ten or twenty bucks into the kitty. Intellectually, I'm all for you, but I am not made for the barricades."

"In other words, when the chips are down you point to the next guy."

"Exactly."

"Take it easy," Bert Jones said. "Just take it easy. All of you laying it on Freddie at once. That's too heavy, and let's not feed him the crap about guts. That's stupid. The point is that we need Freddie, and we got to convince him."

"Very true," Strong agreed. "Just look at it another way, Freddie, the camaraderie, the five of us together, free, like one long picnic——"

"Why do you need me?" Fred asked suspiciously.

"Let's cut out the crap," Katz said. "You're the only

one of us that has a car, a big, proper five-passenger car."

"Will you hold it down!" Fred hissed. "That's all I need, for one of those lousy proctors to hear that I've got a car. This place crawls with them. Man, do you want to destroy me?"

"Freddie, we don't want to destroy you. We cherish you. We only want to enlighten you."

"The way I hear it," Strong said, "there are at least two profs who've had their asses burned by one Freddie Lavette, who insists upon correcting their speech and impugning their thinking. Oh, they would love to know that he keeps a car, that sin of sins, that violation of violations——"

"You wouldn't!"

"Of course we wouldn't. We'd die before we'd leak it."

"You bastards," Fred said. "You miserable bastards."

"You'll enjoy it," Katz said.

After dinner one evening, a few weeks before Barbara was scheduled to leave for New York, Sam said to her, "Mom, let's talk."

"Oh? Don't we?"

"I mean seriously. I've been a long time getting up the courage to say what I want to say, so I think we ought to sit down and be very serious about it."

"That sounds alarming."

"I don't know—maybe."

She wanted to take it lightly, the manner of his approach so grave and quiet, but her heart fell. He was too much like his father, six feet and one inch now, his slender form filled out, his eyes pale blue, very pale blue. Barbara remembered an evening in Karachi in 1944, when she had been a war correspondent, and that evening she had gone to a British officers' dance and had met an old friend, Mike Kendell, an American correspondent. He said he had been in North Africa during the fighting there, and she asked him, as she had asked so many people, about the man she would one day marry and who would become Sam's father. Not so strangely—for war is filled with strange coincidences—he had met him, and in describing him, Kendell mentioned the eyes several times, very pale, icy blue. Her son had those same eyes, and now, turning eighteen, the same hawklike face. A sudden feeling of panic washed over her. She had raised him alone, fed him, cared for him, shared his griefs and frustrations, invented stories to amuse him, washed his dirty clothes, sat terrified in his grandfather's boat while he guided it through a stormy bay, given him books to read, books she loved which he would love, talked to him for hours about every subject under the sun—all of this, and now he was like a stranger, a mysterious shell. How could this be? How was it possible?

She led the way into the living room and poured herself a glass of sherry. It was a rich, heavy sherry, a new product at Higate.

"Will you have a glass?" she asked Sam.

"No, thank you." Very formal, very precise.

She grimaced. "I don't care for it. Too sweet."

He seated himself in the old leather chair that had been his father's favorite, and Barbara couldn't help thinking how alike they were, in their movements, in their slow, easy manner of speech. She sat facing him.

"All right, Sammy," she said. "We're here, and we've filled our bellies. Let's talk."

He sat in silence for a few long moments, and Barbara waited. Then he said abruptly, "I love you. I think you're one of the finest persons I ever knew—not just because you're my mother."

"Thank you, darling," thinking, God help me, what occasioned that?

"I had to say that, because were going to argue."

"It's nice, even if you had to say it."

"I meant it."

"I know you did."

"Mom, I'm not going to Princeton."

"Oh?" Not so terrible after all. What had she been afraid of? "It's a little late in the game, isn't it? I mean, you've been admitted, and that's a pretty decent achievement, even with the family background. Well, it's not the end of the world. I've never been a great Princeton buff. I think Stanford is every bit as good a school, and even though it's late, we could pull a few strings. Stephan Cassala is on the board down there, and it would be wonderful to have you so close."

"Mom," he said slowly, uneasily, "I don't mean Stanford."

"What do you mean?"

"I mean—" He shook his head. "I don't want to go to college right now."

She was silent for a while, and Sam waited. She was asking herself, "What do I say now? How do I handle this? How do I get inside him and guess what goes on there?"

"Sam," she finally said, very quietly, "there has to be a time when a young man decides what he's going to do with his life. If the world were different, we could just live our lives. In this world, we can't. We're a part of a very wealthy family, but we're not rich. My father left a trust fund that provides enough to cover our needs, and it will continue for the rest of my life and then the money will go to you. As you know, I took nothing from Carson. I'm writing again, and I think I have a piece of what may be a good book. I'll earn some money that way, possibly a good deal. I would see you through college, of course, but if you were to throw away the opportunity for a college education, I would not support you. As much as I love you—and you're the most important thing in my existence—I would insist that you stand on your own two feet."

"I know that," he said unexpectedly. "I respect you for saying that. I wouldn't have it any other way."

He had knocked the props from under her. What do I do now? she wondered. "And what do you expect to do if you don't go to college?" she asked him. "Get a job? What kind of a job would it be? You're only eighteen. You're not trained for anything."

"You're right. I'm not much good at anything right now. Oh, I guess I know something about raising grapes and making wine. I did work three summers at Higate, but that wouldn't count for much." He paused and looked at her, and then blurted out, "I want to spend a year in Israel."

There it was. She had a dreadful, sinking feeling—as if all sensation had stopped and her body had turned into a cold lump. No way, she told herself. You take this calmly and rationally.

"Why?"

"What?"

"I asked you why," she said, unable to control the chill in her voice. "Why do you want to spend a year in Israel?"

Then they weighed each other in silence, Sam staring at the floor. It was very quiet in the room. A clock ticking sounded explosive. She was determined not to break the silence. Let him speak.

"Because I don't know who I am," he said at last, looking at her now. "I don't know what I am or who I am. You're Barbara Lavette. I'm Sam Cohen. All my life I fought it inside of me, because I never wanted to be Sam Cohen, and it would have been so easy for me to be Sam Lavette. But I had to be Sam Cohen. I had to be. Do you understand me, mom?"

The question came like a plea for help, for succor. Fighting to remain calm, to keep back the tears, Barbara nodded. "I think I do."

"I would find myself hating Jews." The words came pouring out now. "You can't even imagine how I felt.

214

You never felt that way. And then I'd feel sick, and I'd hate myself, and then I'd be with Jews and sometimes I'd pretend I wasn't Jewish and other times I'd say I was, but I never called myself Lavette, I never lied about what my name was—and then you told me that story about how my father took that flight of old army planes from Barstow across the country to Panama and then to the Azores and Czechoslovakia and got the arms and the stuff that helped save the Jews there and how he was killed by the Arabs and buried there, someone I never even saw or if I saw him I was too little to remember, and I'd try to understand what made him do what he did, and maybe I'm not Jewish because my mother isn't, but I have to know. I have to know what I am, and I have to see a place where a Jew isn't a freak——"

"And isn't this the place?" she cried out, unable to contain herself. "How can you say that? Did I marry a freak? You live in San Francisco. The Jews built this city. They were here in 'forty-nine, when it began. You're named after a man whose father was here two generations before the Lavettes, and he was Jewish. I loved Sam Goldberg, just as I love Jake Levy. How can you think of them as freaks?"

"You don't understand," he said hopelessly. "You just don't understand."

"I'm trying to. I'm trying to understand why you can't see yourself as an American. Your uncle Joe is half Chinese. Does this make him less American?"

"I don't know what an American is, I don't know what a Jew is, and most of all, I don't know what I am."

"And you think you'll find the answer in Israel?"

"You found something there, didn't you?"

"I found your father's grave," Barbara said bitterly. "I found a place where people have to fight and kill just to exist. Is that what you want, to kill or be killed?"

"No. I don't want to kill anyone or be killed." He went over to Barbara, squeezed onto the edge of her chair, and put his arms around her. "Mom, I love you so much, I don't want to hurt you, I don't want to cause you any pain. Do you remember something you said to me? I was just a kid, but I never forgot it. You said we can love each other, but heaven help us if we cling to each other. Do you remember?"

"I remember," she whispered.

He got up and stood facing her. "Do you think it's easy for me to leave you alone here? I know you have grandma and lots of friends. Don't you think I thought about it and thought about it and told myself that I belong here with you, taking care of you——"

"What?" Barbara exclaimed.

"Well, that's what I thought."

"Then just unthink it," she said with annoyance. "The last thing in the world I want is a son who thinks he has to take care of me. I'm perfectly capable of taking care of myself, and I intend to go on doing so. Oh, I'm not angry with you, Sammy," she said more gently. "I'm provoked at myself. I should have raised you as something, either an Episcopalian or a Jew, something definite. Trouble is, I can't stand to set foot in Grace Cathedral. As soon as I smell that musty odor, I want to turn and run, and as for being Jewish, I don't know one blessed thing about it. Your father was willing to die in Israel, but he never set foot in a synagogue, and all the time we were married, he never did or suggested one single thing that I could hang on to and say, that's Jewish. And then when you were thirteen, I knew there was something that Jewish children have——"

"It's called a bar mitzvah," Sam said coldly.

"Well, I forgot. But I did speak to Boyd Kimmelman at the time, and he said I should forget about it and that it didn't matter. Oh, Sam, why are we talking like this? You can take off this summer, if you want to, and go to the Continent. You've never been to France

216

or England, and if you want to make a few weeks in Israel a part of it, I'm not averse to that. Freddie might go with you, and you two get along so well together, and I would feel more relaxed about the whole thing. But I won't permit you to give up your education—I simply can't. I can't agree to that."

Sam sat down again, facing his mother and measuring her. Finally, Barbara said, quietly and deliberately, "I hate war. I hate it with unmitigated loathing. Joe's mother, May Ling, was killed in World War Two. Josh Levy was killed in the Pacific. Two men I loved, one of them your father, died in wars. As long as I have breath and strength, I will fight and oppose war, any war. You will have to register for the draft. I want you to be in college, where you will be exempted—at least for the next four years, and God willing, by then this new slaughter in Vietnam will be over. I am your mother, and as your mother I have some rights. I think you will agree to that."

Sam nodded.

"You have been accepted at Princeton. I must go to New York and Washington. I'll be gone a little more than a week. Will you agree at least to think about what I've said and make no decision until I return?"

"All right, mom. I can promise that."

"You are," Jean said to Barbara the following day, "a most curious child. There are times——"

"I'm hardly a child. I am fifty years old, mother, and I resent——"

"Don't. I am aware of your chronological age, but on the other hand you haven't changed very much since you were eighteen."

"Thank you."

"You told me what Sam said and asked my opinion. I think he's right, and I think I understand him."

"You've never been to Israel. I have."

"True. By the way, I do hope to go next year, and if

217

Sam is there, that will be pleasant. Stephan is going with me. It's always better for a woman to travel with a man than alone. Does that shock you?"

"Nothing you do shocks me anymore, mother."

"Don't be so damn prissy. Shall I tell you what I think or would you prefer to go away and sulk?"

Barbara burst out laughing.

"Am I that amusing?"

"You're wonderful," Barbara said.

"I'm an old lady who has seen a great deal. Now listen to me, my dear. You've gone through life playing your own role of being a sort of a cross between Joan of Arc and Florence Nightingale——"

"That's not fair!"

"No, probably not, and I'm not trying to be fair, only to knock some sense into your head. And I must admit, you've taken a very considerable beating in the process. The thought that you could be guilty of anti-Semitism horrifies you. As far as you were concerned, Jews were no different from anyone else, except that they were discriminated against and slandered and abused by people like myself. No, no, don't interrupt me. Just let me finish, and then you can have your say, because, my dear, you are sitting here facing a practicing anti-Semite. Yes, precisely"—smiling at Barbara, who sat rigid—"and if you wish me to specify, when I met your father, something more than half a century ago, I considered Jews to be on a level with Chinese, and as for the general opinion of Chinese then—well, you've grown up in San Francisco. On our first date, he introduced me to Feng Wo, who was then his bookkeeper in the little shack Danny had down on Fisherman's Wharf. And I was sick, literally sick to my stomach at the thought of being introduced to a Chinese—Chinks, we called them, yellow filth—and being invited to take his hand. Yes, Bobby, and I don't exaggerate. Your father's best friend and his partner for years, was Mark Levy, Jake Levy's father, and in

218

all those early years I never had Mark Levy to my home, to this house. It was something that was not done. I was a Seldon. I knew that Jews were wretched and unacceptable creatures. Feng Wo was not only May Ling's father, he was a cultured and brilliant man. He did the first translation of the writings of Lao-tzu ever done in this country, and Mark Levy was a gentle, good man and his wife, Sarah, was lovely. None of that mattered. You see, I am not simply exercising a private confessional here or trying to convince you of what an awful creature your mother was. I am trying to explain something about anti-Semitism, what a deep-seated and disgusting affliction it is. I changed, but I had to be torn to shreds in the process. I had to learn to look at myself, and that is not easy, believe me. Oh, it's still there; it's in all of us; but I have learned to look at it and snarl at it and tell it to keep its ugly head down. But you, my dear, with your penchant for curing the lunacies of this idiotic world we inhabit—you cannot face the thought that there's even a shred of anti-Semitism in your makeup."

"And you think there is?" Barbara whispered.

"It's in the air we breathe. Do you remember when you kept the horse Danny gave you at the riding place down in Menlo?"

"Yes."

"Did you know that no Jews were allowed there?"

"No. I never thought of it."

"And when you lunch with Harvey Baxter at his club—do you know they still don't admit Jews to membership?"

"I'll never set foot in there again."

"And Sam, walking around with that name of Cohen, and wearing it like some kind of yellow star—don't you realize what goes on in his mind? Let go of him, Bobby. Let him go to Israel. Let him find out who he is. That's the only way to have him, to let go of

219

him, the way I had to let go of you when you went to France. That wasn't easy."

"I know." She stared at her mother thoughtfully, newly. "There's so much we don't know about each other, isn't there?"

"Too much."

"Tell me," Barbara said, "feeling the way you did at that time, how did you ever come to marry daddy?"

Jean smiled, closed her eyes for a moment, the years unrolling. "Yes, that's a good question. He was Italian and at least a Catholic by birth. As far as my mother and father were concerned, Catholics were one rung higher than Jews, but a narrow rung. Danny's father came from a tiny fishing village near France, so I could pretend that he was half French. Not really. No, Bobby, it was the man, this huge, strapping, beautiful curly-haired kid who had the whole world by the tail. He was a man. I was surrounded by boys and I met a man."

Sally Lavette organized her life and the lives of the people around her, or, as her husband sometimes felt, contrived it. From the age of thirteen she had plotted and contrived to marry Joseph Lavette. A war had intervened, with Joe away in the South Pacific, learning the art of surgery by trying to put back together what Japanese shells and bullets tore apart, but when the war was over, Sally had her way. She published two books of poetry, and through a series of charming letters, contrived to have the critic and poet Louis Untermeyer specify her as one of the most talented young poets of the postwar era. When her husband put his medical experience to use in a clinic in a Los Angeles *barrio,* she contrived a separation from him and clawed her way to stardom in Hollywood. She had brains as well as beauty, a steel trap of a mind, long legs, a narrow waist, and a strange pantherlike face. When stardom palled, when the stupidity and vulgarity of

220

studio and Beverly Hills life became intolerable, she contrived a reunion with Joe, persuaded him to become a small-town doctor in Napa, gave birth to a second child, and published a third book of poetry called *The Family*. Sally was a natural and instinctive actress, in that she was wholly capable of becoming the person she played. She was neither heartless nor unloving; she loved Joe Lavette as much as she had ever loved any man, and her two children were a constant source of wonder and repayment—wonder because of the unlikely fact that she, Sally, had created these two human creatures, and repayment for the injustice of life in making her a woman.

Nevertheless, she was a good mother. It was a role she had created, in the same manner that she created the home, the examining room, the kitchen, the living room, and whatever else was required—to the point where the local paper, interviewing their local celebrity, gushed, "If one were to seek for the ideal American housewife in the ideal American home, Sally Lavette would have to be cast for the part."

Joe Lavette, a large, shambling, overweight, and compassionate man of forty-seven years, accepted all this with gratitude. He worshipped his wife, nine years younger, and still beautiful as well as competent. She doubled as his nurse in his house-office; she cooked; she cared for the children and cleaned the house and still found time to write poetry. Whatever nuggets of discontent she nurtured were reasonably well hidden. She was determined to have a family that was a family. Each morning, they had breakfast together; each evening, they sat down to dinner together, unless Joe was away on an emergency call. All these, Sally felt, were very important props for any real family.

It was at dinner this evening that Sally's so carefully contrived picture began to disintegrate. It came about because for the second night in a row, May Ling barely touched her food.

"I'm just not hungry," she protested to her mother.

"At this point," Sally said, "I am less concerned with your inner needs than with mine. You will eat your dinner. You have had good, tasty food set in front of you, and you will eat it. The world is filled with children who go hungry," she continued, indulging in the ancient non sequitur, "and I will not see that food wasted."

The exchange was watched silently and anxiously by Joe. He left all matters of family discipline to Sally.

"I can't eat."

"She's in love," Daniel said, pausing in the process of shoveling food into his mouth. He was nine years old and untroubled.

Joe reached across and touched his daughter's brow.

"I'm not sick, daddy."

"Please eat. You're thin enough."

May Ling was on the edge of tears, and when Sally snapped at her, "We've discussed this enough. Now eat your dinner!" she began to sob, pushed back her chair, and ran upstairs to her room.

Joe looked at his wife in amazement. "Now what was that all about?"

"She's in love," Daniel repeated.

"That's all. Enough out of you!"

"Should I go up and talk to her?" Joe wondered.

"I think not. I'll take a tray up to her later."

"And what's all this about being in love?"

"We'll talk about that later."

Joe had a small emergency after dinner, a lady who had sliced deep into her hand with a carving knife. He cleaned the wound and took three stitches. He had finished setting the surgery to rights and was washing his hands when Sally entered. The absence of Sally for any length of time, even for an hour, caused Joe to look at her newly. There was always the slight shock of surprise that this woman could remain so unchangingly

222

young and lovely while he, as he felt, turned old and gray and fat.

"Did you get her to eat?" he asked Sally.

"A glass of milk and some cake. It will hold her."

"I don't think she's ill," Joe said.

Now, as so often, Sally despaired of him. "She's not ill. She's in love. She's been in love. At that age, love is a very serious business."

"You mean Ruby Truaz?"

"Yes."

"Well, she'll work it out."

"Joe, it's not that simple. Ruby's been drafted. He's been ordered to report for induction." She was watching how carefully and thoroughly he dried his hands. Why did his small habits irritate her so?

"Oh, come on. That makes no sense. He's a college student. They're not drafting college students."

"He's also a Chicano."

"I still don't see it. They're far from the bottom of the barrel."

"Joe, you never read a newspaper———"

"I don't have time."

"The point is, there have been two bad stabbings over in Angwin, and they're accusing what they call a Chicano gang, and there's a lot of bad feeling in the country. Ruby just happened to be in the wrong place at the wrong time."

"It's a rotten break for old Cándido, but it's not the end of the world. Even if this thing of May Ling's is serious, which I doubt———"

"It's damned serious. Your daughter is very gentle and shy, but she has a mind of her own."

"A few years in the army won't kill him."

"It's killed other people, your mother and my brother among them, and May Ling is terrified that they're going to send him to Vietnam, and she's read all sorts of horrible things about what's going on over there."

"That's nonsense. There isn't a chance in the world that we'll get involved in a war over Vietnam. Why should we? It makes no damned sense."

"Of course not, because everything this stupid government does makes sense. Is that what you're telling me?"

"Come on, Sally," he said, "let's not get into one of our dumb political arguments. I'm a small-town doctor, and I don't know beans about politics, and I'm not sure you know much more than I do. May Ling's seventeen years old. This is her first love. There'll probably be a dozen more to follow."

"She wants to marry him."

"Sure. Don't tell me you take that seriously?"

"You don't know one damn thing about your daughter, do you? This has been going on for six months. They've been sleeping together——" His face fell, and Sally added quickly, "Don't worry about that. May Ling is no fool. She's not pregnant. Try to remember the way I was when I was a kid, wild and brash, and every thought I had popped right out of my mouth. May Ling is different. It's all inside, and they're the kind that you can't reach. She is absolutely determined to marry this boy."

"How can she? You mean behind our backs? She's underage. How old is he?"

"Nineteen or twenty."

"Well, they're both too young. I'll talk to her. I can get through to her. God Almighty, how do you know they're sleeping together?"

"She told me."

"You mean she'd tell you something like that?"

"The world changes, doesn't it, Joe?"

"I barely know the boy. Have you spoken to him? What is he like?"

"I grew up with the Truazes. They've always been at Higate—as long as I can remember. He's bright and decent and good-looking. I don't know how great it would be for her to marry a Chicano, but you and I are such a pair of mongrels that I don't think we have a leg to stand on in that direction."

"I don't want her sneaking off," Joe said. "If those kids can't be reasoned with, let her get married properly."

When Barbara's plane lifted off the runway at San Francisco Airport, she felt a sense of release and freedom that was both new and exciting. The flight to New York was her first journey outside of California in five years, and it was years before then that she had last experienced this kind of exhilaration. She was a schoolgirl on vacation, an errant adolescent released, a woman free, single, and attractive, without a care in the world. The cares were there, bundled up, tightly packaged, but thrust out of sight for the next two weeks. She was fifty years old, and she weighed only four pounds more than she had weighed at age twenty. She wore a gray flannel suit, thin, lightweight wool, a bright, pale blue kerchief that set off the color of her eyes, and a white silk blouse, and she carried a pearl-colored cashmere topcoat. She had gone on what was for her a wild splurge of spending, being assured of a large advance on her new book, two hundred and fifty dollars for the suit, almost four hundred dollars for the topcoat, a hundred dollars more for two dresses, and sixty dollars for a pair of high-heeled brown shoes that raised her almost to six feet. They were exceedingly uncomfortable for her to walk on—since she rarely wore high heels—but were irresistible. The shoes produced the deepest guilt, but the admiring looks from a variety of men made these and other guilts quite bearable. It was a clear, bracing May day, and the pilot enthusiastically informed his passengers that there was not a cloud in the sky between San Francisco and New York. San Francisco temperature, seventy degrees

Fahrenheit; New York temperature, seventy-two degrees.

It was all quite wonderful, the smoothness of the flight, the country unrolling so unbelievably far beneath them, even the tasteless plastic-like food. She ordered a vodka, and after that, two glasses of wine, and when she walked off the plane in New York, she was just the slightest bit, but deliciously, high.

Harris Fielding, her literary agent, was waiting at the incoming gate. He was close to seventy now, but he had aged well in the twenty-five years since she had last seen him. They had been brought together via Jean's introduction, and Barbara had the vague impression that sometime during Jean's divorce from Dan, Jean and Harris Fielding had had an affair of some sort, carnal or otherwise. Now he greeted Barbara as if only days had passed since their last meeting, asking immediately after her mother's health.

"She's well, thank you."

"And as beautiful as ever?"

"Yes—I suppose so." Time was an illusion. She understood why he never came to San Francisco. Young, beautiful Jean Seldon would remain in his memory as long as he had a memory.

"I wrote after Mr. Lavette passed away. It must have been an awful blow to both of you."

The words had to be said. It was more than five years since her father had died. The wind blew memories away. If she clung to them, the memories would devour her. God help people who couldn't let go of the living or the dead, yet Barbara wondered whether mastering a way to let go was not the prop that sustained her. Sometimes, late at night, when she thought of all the departures that threaded through her life, she would go into a cold sweat and begin a sickening passage of fear. But not this day. On leaving San Francisco, she had made her symbolic separation from her son. His departure for Israel, if he went there, was

226

still in the future, and for these few days away from California she was determined to be free from both the present and the future.

Driving into New York, Fielding remarked on her silence.

"I've been thinking," Barbara said. "Is there a space shock as well as a culture shock? It's a long time since I've been flung across the continent. Basically, I'm a product of another age, when we traveled by train."

"No, I just can't think of you as the product of another age, my dear. You're as young and as vital as when we first met. It's like seeing your mother again, unchanged by time."

"That's sweet of you. I've had my fiftieth birthday."

"I've had seventy. I don't advertise it in this age of arrogant youth. But enough of this. I find chronology boring. How long will you be in New York?"

"I have five days here, and then I must go to Washington. I loathe the thought. To me it's a hateful city, but I have an appointment there with a President's wife, and there I must go."

"Well, that is something. The incumbent's spouse?"

"My lips are sealed. My lawyer worked a miracle getting me this meeting with a lady who has agreed to talk to me and answer my questions, but only on the condition that I never reveal her name. I am to have no tapes and take no notes. She laid down a whole set of rules, and I wrote to her, giving her my word of honor that I would respect them. She knows all about me, my past, my sins, and all the rest. You see, she very much wants the book to be written."

"I don't understand why you can't take notes."

"I do, and I don't need them."

"And the pages you have already written?"

"They lead in, as you know. I may have to make some changes, but not too many."

"Thank goodness, because our publisher loves what

he has read. You'll meet him tomorrow. Shall I arrange anything else, parties, TV, radio?"

"Oh, no. No. Absolutely not. I want to be here as a tourist. I've never had that experience in New York. Each time I was here. I have been led around by the nose. Now I want to do it alone."

It was new, this kind of being alone. She had been alone so often during her life, but never this way, not looking for anything, not searching, not on an assignment, not waiting for something to happen, but simply alone with the city around her, free to go where she wished and do as she wished. She had a room at the Plaza, in the corner on 58th Street. The weather was perfect, the sky clear blue, the air was as sweet and clean as ever in San Francisco. With skirt and sweater and comfortable shoes, she walked for miles, ate hungrily in restaurants chosen at random, and each night fell into bed utterly exhausted. She saw only one play, Peter Weiss's *Marat-Sade,* which thrilled her and troubled her, and one film, *Zorba the Greek,* which she enjoyed immensely. She wandered everywhere in Central Park, indifferent to newspaper stories about crime and mugging, fascinated by the opening of the foliage, by the smell and color of a spring that has no duplicate anywhere in California. She walked on Fifth Avenue all the way up to Mt. Morris Park, climbing this strange stone hill in the midst of a black world, and then spent the rest of that afternoon wandering through the streets of Harlem, having her dinner of pork ribs, grits, and collard greens in a restaurant where hers was the only white face. When she mentioned it to Harris Fielding the following day, he said, "Barbara, you did a very dangerous thing."

"Why?"

"Because you could have been mugged or killed."

"But who would want to kill me? There were thousands of people on the streets there, and no one bothered them."

228

The city filled her with delight. People saw her with pleasure. She walked the length of upper Madison Avenue, something she had never done before, as excited as a child by the window displays, the galleries, the antique shops, the parade of the treasures of the world, brought here from every corner of the earth, a price tag on everything. At 96th Street, she walked through the transverse of the park and downtown on Broadway, here in another world entirely, just as she found other worlds on other days in Greenwich Village and on the lower East Side and in the sunless caverns of the financial district. She was unfettered, childlike in her wandering, going out to the Statue of Liberty and climbing inside it, and then eagerly taking the boat ride around Manhattan Island. The five days went all too quickly. Why had she waited half a century to discover this place, to feel it instead of always passing through?

Her mood impelled her to take a Greyhound bus to Washington, something she had never done before, and she was seated next to a white-haired old lady from Tulsa, Oklahoma, a widow seventy-nine years old, who was touring the whole country by bus. They talked all the way to Washington, although most of the talking was done by Mrs. Seever, who was one-eighth Osage Indian and who had eleven grandchildren and four great-grandchildren. She informed Barbara that while she had met all sorts of interesting people on her trip, which began five weeks ago, she had never met a real, actual writer, which made her certain that her store of biographical and family information would be well received. In all truth, Barbara was quite content to listen, and the hours passed pleasantly.

"Well, Miss Lavette," said the President's wife, "you're not what I expected. You're much too young and attractive to be a communist out of the nineteen thirties."

"I never have been a communist, and lately I seem to be revealing my age over and over. I'm fifty."

"Not forty-nine. I like that. I don't like peope who remain forty-nine forever, and I, certainly, should not believe everything I read, in particular about politics. Do you?"

"When I can, I prefer fiction. So I don't have to believe it."

"Yes there's much more truth in it than in what they call nonfiction. The novelist can tell the truth. The biographer can't."

"That's an interesting observation," Barbara agreed, "and probably true."

"You're here for the truth," the President's wife said with satisfaction. "Will you have tea or some sherry?"

"Sherry, if you don't mind."

She poured the sherry. "Dry. I don't like sweet sherry. Now suppose we begin. I have the whole afternoon set aside for you."

"I would like to begin by thanking you for agreeing to talk to me."

"Not at all. I'm as eager to hear your questions as you are to have my answers. I'm curious about the answers, too. I suppose I've been interviewed dozens of times, but never quite like this. By the way, are you Jewish? Don't be shocked. I expect your questions to be just as direct. You don't look Jewish, but one never knows."

"No," Barbara said, struggling for composure. "I suppose if I am anything in that way, I'm an Episcopalian."

"Now why did I think you might be Jewish? Something I read. No, I must stop asking the questions. That's your job."

"Very well. I shall be very blunt and direct. To begin, knowing what you know now, if you could go back to your wedding day, would you go through with it?"

"My dear Barbara, what woman would? You don't mind if I call you Barbara? Answer—no."

"At this point, do you love your husband?"

"You are direct and blunt. Well, I shall abide by our agreement. The answer is no."

"Do you think he loves you?"

The President's wife poured another glass of sherry. "For you, my dear?" Barbara nodded. "No, he doesn't," said the President's wife. "He endures me."

"Yet there must have been moments of happiness?"

"May I tell you why a man enters politics, Barbara? It's not a goal, it's not the consummation of any dream. Did you ever hear a child say, I want to grow up and be a politician? Usually, he's a lawyer—not always but most of the time. He hangs around the organization as a young man, business, favors, and then he gets his taste of some small office, just a lick of power. It's enough. A psychiatrist friend of mine once speculated that paranoia is the illness of mankind, but while it may be a slight rash on most of us, it's the disease of politics. Two sides of a coin—fear and power—and a need to belong to the club. No noble motives, my dear, no wish to make the lot of man better, no urge to right wrongs, just get elected and move up. Do you suggest moments of happiness with such a man? Nonsense."

"Did you ever love him?"

"I tried."

"Why didn't you leave him?"

"Well, that is complicated. One broods over that too long, and it takes a certain kind of courage. We were not like the children of today. And there are pressures."

"Yet in the public view, you were always the loyal and faithful wife, supportive and loving."

"Such things are orchestrated. You either play your role or leave the cast. I never had the courage to leave the cast."

"Was he kind to you?"

"No. Of course, a point came where I didn't give a hoot whether he was or not."

"Did he ever turn to you, lean on you, ask for your guidance?"

"Really, my dear!"

"But the role of First Lady—that must have meant something?"

"Whoever invented the term ought to be horse-whipped. When himself walks into that White House, he is the most powerful man on the face of the earth, and if you don't think that power extends over his wife—well, dear Barbara, you're just whistling Dixie. Do you remember Fannie Brice's song, 'Sometimes I like to dream of a cottage by a stream'? No, that's maudlin. There's no way I can explain this to you, and I certainly never tried to explain to anyone else."

"I think I understand," Barbara said. "I'm trying to put myself in your place. I have to if I'm ever to write about this intelligently."

"Then have some more sherry."

"Thank you." Barbara then said uncertainly, "May we talk about sex?"

"Why not? Nothing else has been sacred to you."

"I'm sorry. I know I'm intruding and pressing, and my only excuse is that I'm very much excited by this project and very much compelled by what I'm doing, and please believe me that it's as hard for me to ask these things as it is for you to answer them."

"I think I'm answering very easily. It's a relief, Barbara. No one has ever interviewed me this way. What about sex? Do you want the most powerful man on earth to be loving and tender in bed? When I was a child, Barbara, I used to speculate on how the Queen of England went about moving her bowels. Did she use toilet paper, like ordinary mortals? No, my husband and I have not slept together for many years. Is that what you wanted to know?"

"I feel foolish." Barbara said unhappily.

"If you would stop being so damned respectful and see me as an ordinary and wretchedly unhappy woman, we could get on with this. You wrote that you wanted to talk to me in terms of my being a woman. You wanted to see the President's wife as a woman. I'm trying to be helpful."

"But surely the power and the glory must have meant something?"

"Of course it did. When people kowtow to you and anticipate your every need, and it's always the presidential suite and Air Force One, and those silly fools on the television ask their silly questions, as if you were the Delphic Oracle, it has to have an effect, but then you sit alone because himself is off and running—and you're alone, as alone as any woman has ever been."

"Could it be different?"

"Then what you're asking, Barbara, is whether the presidency could be different. If we had a system where a decent, good-hearted, and honorable man, equipped with common sense and wisdom, could be elevated to the presidency, that would be another matter. But what do we have? A man must be demoniacally possessed to want that job. It must become an obsession. He must claw and fight and deal and compromise and sell his very soul to the devil. You're not reading a history book or an election commercial. You're talking to his wife. We read of emperors and kings and tyrants, but since the world began no man has ever had this kind of power in his hands. He can press a button and wipe out half of mankind, he can launch armies, airplanes, battleships. And because of custom or morality or what you will, he has to be married to what is euphemistically called the First Lady. Come, have some more sherry."

They went on talking until the light faded, and when it was time to leave, the President's wife kissed Barbara on her cheek and said to her, "I like you, dear, and I'm very pleased that we had this talk. Of course, if you ever mention my name or if your fictional character bears the slightest resemblance to me, I shall deny ever having seen you. But you are a dear and very innocent. That's why I talked so much. If you were one of those sharp-nosed lady journalists one sees around Washington these days, I would have had you out of here in ten minutes."

"I don't know how to thank you. You've been so kind and helpful." Barbara was just a bit tight. "I couldn't have imagined what you are like. You're so wise about so many things."

"I was trained in a hard school. Remember, I have been a President's wife. Your cab is waiting, so you'd better run."

When Barbara returned to her hotel, she discovered that there had been three telephone calls that afternoon from Eloise. Barbara called Higate immediately. Adam answered the phone.

"You're still in Washington? You're calling from there?"

"Yes. What's wrong?"

"We don't know. Your mother told us where we could reach you. I don't know what you can do there, Barbara, but Eloise thinks you can help us. She's frantic. Freddie and four other kids left Princeton to get into this civil rights thing, down in Mississippi. That was three days ago. He promised to call, because truthfully we were against it, and so he promised faithfully. He never called, and Eloise is frantic and thinks you can get some information. I really don't know what you can do, but there might be some kind of national organization there in Washington that would tell you something. Anything."

"Let me try," Barbara said. "Do you know where they were going, what their destination was?"

"Only somewhere in Mississippi. That's all we know."

"Let me try," Barbara said, "and I'll call you tomorrow."

* * *

It was an odd time, a strange time, but perhaps no stranger than any other time. The Sioux Indians staked a claim to Alcatraz Island in San Francisco Bay, and thousands of San Francisco citizens who hardly ever thought about the prison sitting out there in the bay, now stood on the Embarcadero and on the hills, staring at it. King Hussein of Jordan came to San Francisco, and one of the first things he wanted to see was Alcatraz. Possibly the Sioux reminded him of the Israelis. It was a time when death made strange bedfellows. General Douglas MacArthur died, and so did Ben Hecht, who once wrote a book about miracles. Pandit Nehru died, and so did Ian Fleming, who created James Bond, who had a license to kill. Bond survived his maker and the license to kill took on plague proportions in various parts of the earth. Herbert Hoover, who had once been President of the United States, died, and the younger citizens were sure that they had heard the name somewhere, and our nation responded to the trouble in Laos by stating that Laos had to be saved even if it had to be destroyed. Mwami Mwambusta IV, who was the black king of Burundi, came to San Francisco, and his robes created a stylistic explosion among local dressmakers, and another black man, Martin Luther King, spoke out for equality, and people listened because it was the kind of voice the country had not heard in a long, long time. In response to that voice, hundreds of young, idealistic college students went to Mississippi, to convince blacks that they had the right to register to vote.

Fred had never been South before, not from the East, and south in California is not really South. He had been to Tijuana and he had been to Vancouver. In terms set down by Princeton circles, he was not a very traveled person. Herb Katz had spent a summer in Paris, and Phil Strong had done a semester at Cam-

235

bridge. Greenberg had been to Spain on a student tour. Only Bert Jones shared Fred's insularity.

"When you get born black," Jones said, "you don't travel—unless the man gets you and inducts you. Travel is not for the poor."

"Freddie is not poor," Katz said. "The Lavettes are to California what the Rockefellers and the Lamonts are to New York. The trouble with Freddie is that he's a peasant. He grew up on a farm in some bleak place out there in the desert."

"That," Fred told him, "is a perfect illustration of the insularity, the ignorance, and the blind prejudice of the New Yorker. A winery is not a farm, and the Napa Valley is not in the desert. But how would you know that? You poor, shrunken, provincial inhabitants of that cruddy city do not have the vaguest notion of what this country is all about."

"You ever been to Mississippi before, Freddie?" Jones asked him.

"Thank God, no."

"Then, sonny, *you* do not have the vaguest notion of what this country is all about. Take my word for it."

They drove to Washington on the first leg of the journey, where they would be briefed at the headquarters of the movement. Fred's car was a 1960 two-door Ford, which he had bought with five hundred dollars of birthday money from his grandmother. His original inclination had been for an MG, but the word was around that sports cars were a disaster, since it was impossible to make out with a girl in bucket seats. Now that he had accepted the Southern trip, he was excited and pleased with himself, facing the fact that his liberalism had been wholly intellectual, and he had the warm if nervous feeling that comes of embarking on an adventure of virtue. He liked the other boys; they were old friends and they were upstanding characters, neither grinds nor jocks, and while objectively big Phil Strong was as much a jock as anyone on the football squad, he had a brain and he had deserted the eating clubs for Woodrow Wilson. And while Fred had passed the time of day with Bert Jones and had eaten at the same table, he had never really made a close relationship with him or indeed with any other black man. Katz and Greenberg challenged him intellectually, a provocation he welcomed and enjoyed. He didn't have to play second fiddle to their knowledge and mental antics; he could keep pace with them.

The briefing in Washington, given by a tall, thin black woman whose name was Claudia Kendrick, was sober and without frills. They were told that, in a certain sense, they were going into enemy country, and that their safety would depend upon restraint, caution, and common sense. "You will have to learn what every Negro in the South knows, that when you are given a choice between staying alive and the exercise of your manhood or pride, you choose life." She warned them against complex intellectual persuasion. "The Negroes you will be talking to are poor people, most of them poorly educated, many of them illiterate. They are not used to whites who want to help them. They will look at you with suspicion and mistrust. You must win their confidence. Use simple words and avoid an approach that is superior. When they ask you, as they will, why you are doing this, try to make them understand that you need their help as much as they need yours, that you need their votes to make the whole country a better place. But the central fact is that with the vote, they can win their freedom, and if they don't register, they can't vote. And have patience. Try to understand their circumstances and their fears."

They spent that night at a motel outside of Fredericksburg, Virginia, spreading a road map on the floor of Fred's room and sprawling around it to plan their journey. There had been a brief argument over getting Jones into the place, but since they were so close to Washington, they felt it was safe to assert their strength, and they bullied the room clerk into allowing Jones to share a room with Strong and Katz. From here on in, they decided that they would put up at black lodgings or camp out. They decided that they would take Interstate 85 as far as it was completed, then Route 78 to Birmingham, and then continue on Route 11 and Interstate 20 into Mississippi. Without pushing too hard, they would reach Greenville, South Carolina, the following day, Birmingham a day later, and then push on early in the morning into Mississippi. It was well past midnight when they got into bed, and Fred was drifting into sleep when he recalled that he had forgotten to call his mother. Well, it could wait. She knew how he was about telephone calls, and anyway, nothing was going to happen. Even getting Jones into the motel had been a lead-pipe cinch.

"You know," Fred said to Jones the following day, "I would have come anyway. You didn't have to blackmail me. This is good stuff."

"It's a turning point in history," Katz said. "You don't want to tell your grandchildren you just sat on your ass when history turned."

"We are now in enemy territory," Jones told them, "so you white boys just watch your step."

When they stopped for gas outside of Durham in North Carolina, the cold, hard look of the man at the pump underlined Jones's words. Pulled over by a police car in Charlotte, Fred showed his driver's license, and the cop, studying it, and then looking from the license to Bert Jones, remarked that Fred was a long way from home. "He is, I ain't, officer," Phil Strong drawled. "School closed and we're spending two weeks with my aunt in Mobile." The officer was still staring at Bert Jones. "This colored boy here," Strong said, "we picked him up back a ways, and we're riding him to Greenville. We had some carburetor trouble and he fixed it, so it just don't seem fair we should leave the boy standing there on the road."

"O.K., move it," the cop said, and when they pulled away, Jones snorted, "Colored boy indeed!"

The others burst into laughter.

"Phil, where'd you find that accent?"

"Beautiful."

"Next stop Hollywood. Man, you're an actor."

"That was heavy stuff coming down there," Strong said. "Maybe we ought to just dump old Jones onto the roadside. One thing they don't cotton to down here is a dark boy riding with light boys."

"The next one of you calls me a boy, I am going to bust his head. Do you read me?"

Just before darkness, they pulled off the road and made camp in a clump of woods. The land dropped down to a beautiful lake in the distance, the setting sun beyond it, red-gold on the lake, all of it visible through a scrim of great oaks and dripping Spanish moss.

"So damned beautiful," Greenberg said.

Katz and Jones built a fire. They had two pounds of frankfurters, cans of beans, and a six-pack of beer. With Phil Strong, Fred pored over the road map, trying to determine precisely where they were, certainly not far from Atlanta. "I think we ought to shift to 29, right down to Montgomery."

"Any reason?"

"It just looks like a better road. It's about the same distance. If we cut out of here like at dawn, we should be there by one or two in the afternoon."

"Where?"

"In Mississippi. I'd like to make Jackson before dark."

"That would be nice and cool, to see some friendly faces and be told what we're supposed to do."

They sat around the fire, eating frankfurters and beans, drinking beer, and talking in curiously muted tones. Perhaps more than the others, Fred had the feeling of being in another world and another time, an eternity away from the gentle, sun-drenched Napa Valley, where there was a tribal affinity with friends and relatives. Enemy country. No he didn't buy that. It was still the United States. He put himself in the position of relating his adventures to May Ling and Joshua and Sam. He could really make something of Phil Strong's performance with the cop.

"How about a song," Greenberg suggested.

But it was a lame effort, and they let it go with a single attempt. The darkness closed in. They spread their blankets around the fire, but sleep came slowly. It was a warm evening, and no one made any attempt to keep the fire burning, as if they were together in their desire to have the darkness enclose them and protect them.

A hand gently shaking him awakened Fred, still in the darkness, and Jones's voice: "Time to rise and shine, California boy, if we want to make Jackson by dark."

It was four o'clock. Four hours later, when they stopped for breakfast, they were almost to Montgomery, and Jones said to them, "I am sitting right here with a very low profile. Just bring me an egg sandwich."

"He's right," Strong said. "We have snotty middle-class kids written all over us."

"Speak for yourself," Katz said. "My father runs a candy store in Brooklyn."

"Stop boasting. I just don't like these roadside places. We'll stop at a grocery store and load up with bread and cheese and Coke. It's just one more day, and maybe we can stay out of trouble."

"My God," Fred said, "I think we're all getting spooked over nothing."

"Maybe yes, maybe no," Jones said. "I grew up in Boston, so I'm no expert on the South. But this is an angry place. I can smell it."

They didn't find a grocery that suited their needs until they were on the outskirts of Montgomery, and even then, people passing looked at them with suspicion and hostility. They drove on, munching on the bread and cheese.

"Maybe it's dumb the way we did it," Katz said. "We don't look like anyone around here, except maybe for Freddie and Phil. Freddie looks like a valid, slightly decadent character out of Faulkner——"

"I always fancied F. Scott Fitzgerald," Fred said.

"—and Phil sort of looks like a redneck. But everything else is wrong, the California plates, the jeans. I always figured folks around here would wear Levi's. Most of them don't. They wear old, beat-up khakis."

"It's always smart too late."

"Relax. We've just about made it," Strong said.

"Look at it like this," Katz said, "because like you, all I know is what I read, and the way I've been reading it they never liked us since the Civil War and maybe before then, but just look at it this way. Here there are maybe three, four, maybe five thousand guys like us, with school over, convinced we know how to straighten out something that's been going on for a hundred years. They have to hate us."

"Well, what in hell do you want to do? Turn around and go back?"

"Who said anything about going back?"

"You can't saw sawdust."

"Meaning what?"

"It's done. Here we are."

"Before you go jumping on Herb," Bert Jones said, "you got to admit he's right. None of us are heroes. This is a spooky place. So I say Freddie keeps this old can rolling steadily until we get to Jackson, and we can sit down with some local talent."

"You know, Bert," Fred said, "I never thought to ask before, but what's your major?"

"English lit, which I will one day teach, God willing."

"And God willing, I'll call my mother. I muffed it

again. You know, twelve days from now we graduate from the ivy halls, and they're coming in and they're sore as hell with me taking off like this."

"You told them?"

"He told them."

"I couldn't just disappear."

"Invent something," Greenberg said. "Can you see me telling my mother I'm off to Mississippi with the ghost of old John Brown?"

"I like the way you put that."

"I think we're coming to the state line."

"What makes you think so?"

"We passed through Demopolis back a while. That's about fifty miles from the state line."

It muted their voices. Suddenly, they were talking in whispers. Katz said with annoyance, "What the devil has gotten into us? We've sailed through the Carolinas and Georgia and Alabama, and now you're all spooked crazy over Mississippi."

"Man, because that's where it is at."

Fred was thinking of a song they played back at the winery. The kids would be crowded into his room, May Ling and Sam and Joshua and sometimes Rubio Truaz and his sister Carla—Carla, oh, I sure did fuck up things with Carla—and he'd put the record on. Was it the Weavers? Or was it Peter, Paul, and Mary? One or the other. "Old John Brown, he said to me, the Negro people must be free. He went from Harpers Ferry to Torrington, and he saw a lot of slaves and he told them, Run."

"God damn it, Freddie," Jones said, "you're pushing seventy miles an hour!"

"Cool it, Freddie," Strong added. "What we don't need is to be picked up by the local cops."

Fred dropped his speed to fifty.

"Forty-five would be even better," Strong said.

"You want to get to Jackson before dark, don't you?"

"We have all the time in the world. The day is young. You remember what they told us back in Washington. The local cops would just as soon dump us into the cooler as not."

"Never been in jail," Greenberg said.

"We'll arrange it, sonny. All in good time. Meanwhile, everything cool and easy."

It was about two o'clock when they stopped for gas at Meridian, satisfying their hunger with chocolate bars and Cokes. The man at the pump, heavyset, cold-eyed, served them in silence.

"A nice, friendly place," Katz said.

"Where you boys headed for?" the garageman asked them.

"Going to my uncle's place," Strong said, his imitation of a Southern accent somewhat sour.

"Is that your nigger?" the garageman asked, pointing to Jones.

There was a long silence, and then Jones said. "I'm nobody's nigger, you fat sonofabitch."

The garageman started toward Jones, thought better of it, turned on his heel and strode toward his shack. Fred had paid for the gas, and now he raced around the car into the driver's seat. "Get in, get in," Strong snapped. They piled into the car, and Fred ripped the car away like a contender in a drag race and sent it screaming down the highway. Twisting around, Katz said, "You won't believe it, but that crazy bastard's standing there with a shotgun."

"That was one dumb crack," Strong told Jones.

The gas station was out of sight; Fred had cut his speed. "I don't believe it," he said softly. "I just don't believe it."

"Did you hear what he said?" Jones protested.

"You and your fuckin' pride."

"God damn it, Strong, what in hell do you expect! You want me to knuckle down and say, Yowsa, mistah gas jockey, I is sho 'nuf mistah Strong's nigger boy."

243

"No," Katz said, "you could have told him we all have shares."

"Oh, funny, funny! You're all such hotshot liberals, but when push comes to shove, it's Jones, do your minstrel act."

"That's not fair," Fred protested. "That crazy bastard went for a gun."

"I'm sorry," Strong said. "We're all shook up. I had no business lacing you down. No one appointed me the captain of this contingent. And Katz's sense of humor stinks."

"It stinks," Katz agreed.

"How do you think I feel?" Jones demanded. "This place is as crazy to me as it is to you. The fact that I'm black gives me no insight into lunatics. We're packed into this car, four white kids and one black kid, with California plates and a Princeton sticker on the windshield—we're just as plain as the time of day."

"Let's cool it," Greenberg said. "We're all sorry, Bert, and we're all insensitive and we're all scared."

"Maybe. Or maybe you don't even know what scared is. I know."

Then they were silent, and Fred drove on, more slowly now, very carefully. Somewhere between Meridian and Jackson, he saw the barrier across the highway, two wooden sawhorses, two workmen and a third man in boots, whipcord breeches, brown shirt, and a Western hat. He wore a deputy's star, and as Fred pulled to a stop in front of the barrier, the deputy walked up to the car and studied its occupants. After thirty seconds or so, he said, "Princeton College," and nodded. The boys waited in silence. The deputy was silent another thirty seconds, and then he said, "Road's out ahead. Take the detour."

"What detour?" Fred asked him.

"Right there, sonny." He pointed a few feet down the road, behind them, to where a dirt track led into the jack pines.

"It doesn't look like much of a road," Fred said slowly.

"What's wrong with the main road?" Strong asked.

"Washed out. The cutoff's all right. Just drive slow." He smiled. The two workmen smiled. "Lead you back to the main road two miles up ahead."

"I don't like it," Strong whispered to Fred.

"What else can we do?"

Strong shrugged. The deputy pointed to the side road again. Fred hesitated, praying for another car to come along from either direction; but except for their car and the deputy's squad car, parked on the shoulder beyond the barrier, the road remained deserted.

"Better get going, sonny," the deputy said.

"Anything to get out of here," Katz whispered.

Fred nodded, put the car into reverse, and then turned onto the side road. He drove slowly into the thickness of the tall, gaunt jack pines, the car lurching over the ruts in the road. After seven or eight minutes, during which the others sat in uncertain silence, Fred stopped the car.

"How far have we come?" Strong asked him.

"More than two miles."

"Those clowns back there were putting us on," Katz said. "Grinning at us. We should have known. I say we turn around and go back and if they don't let us through, we try some other road to Jackson."

Jones, poring over a road map, told them, "There is no other road into Jackson."

"You see this road?"

"This isn't a road. No. The only road is Route 80."

Through the jack pines ahead of them, Fred was able to make out a clearing of some sort and what appeared to be an old shack. In any case, it could be a place where they might turn around.

"I'll try it," he said to them, and then drove ahead. It looked like an abandoned farm, a rotting shack and barn, atangle of corroded metal that might once have been a still. It was all very quiet, forlorn and poor, filled with the afternoon sunshine. To Fred it was a place out of another world, outside of his experience, a film set, used and forgotten. As he edged the car off the road, carefully, to make his turn, six men came out of the barn. Their faces were hidden by white hoods that fell to their shoulders, old pillowcases with eyeholes cut out, and each of them carried a shotgun. One of them carried a heavy, coiled bullwhip, and another a coil of rope slung over his shoulder. Fred braked to a stop as two of the men stepped in front of the car. Another put his gun through the open window, pressing the muzzle to Fred's neck, and said, "Now, sonny, you and your friends just get out of that old car nice and easy, nice and easy." Then he stepped back. The other men took their places around the car. "Outside! Get your hands up against the car!"

The boys got out of the car, their hands shaking as they placed them, palms down, on the roof. Fred didn't know what the others were feeling; for himself, it was like a sickness, that pervaded every inch of his body. He felt his heart swelling, as if it would burst out of his chest; his mouth was dry, his lips quivering.

"Check them out, Artie."

Fred felt the hands run over his body, in his pockets, emptying them.

"This here one's from California. Eighty-one bucks. Princeton College. You ever heard tell of Princeton College, Matt?"

"Shit, you are one ignorant bastard."

"The nigger's got twelve bucks on him."

"That is big money for a spade."

"Hey, Matt, get this! This here good old boy is Mister Philip Strong and he is a bona fide member of the National Association for the Advancement of Colored People. He also has fifty-two dollars in United States bills."

"He is one big sonofabitch."

246

"You figure he is advancing this here nigger? Bertram Jones. That is a pleasant name for a nigger."

When Fred turned to see what was going on, a fist caught him on the cheek, slamming his head against the car. Then his hands were tied behind him.

"You got our money," Strong was protesting "You don't have to tie us up."

"Mister, you are going to bear witness to Southern justice. Nobody invited you motherfuckers down here. Once and for all, we are going to make it plain that Mississippi is off limits."

Fred's nose was bleeding from the impact of his face against the car. "Oh, God," he thought, "how did all this happen? How did we ever get into this?"

Because Barbara could think of no other place that might provide information as to the whereabouts of her nephew Fred, she took a cab to the local NAACP office on U Street, where a harassed and overworked black woman informed her that she was only one of many worried aunts or mothers. Putting down the telephone, she told Barbara, "That won't stop—not for a minute. Everyone wants to know where their kids are and everyone's worried sick. But we are not directly involved. These are civil rights activist groups from the campuses."

"I don't know where to turn," Barbara said. "I'm from California. I don't know Washington." She didn't add that she loathed the place.

"I'll make a couple of calls and see what I can find out. A friend of mine, Claudy Kendrick, runs the clearing center for the registration volunteers, and if they was going down there to push registration then she might know something." She dialed a number. "Claudy," she said into the telephone, "this is Millie. I got a lady here from California who's worried sick about her nephew. He was with a group from Princeton who went down to Jackson, I guess, for the registration push." She listened. "Yes, they drove." She listened again, and minutes went by while Barbara became increasingly tense. "Yes—sure, I understand."

She put down the telephone and turned a woeful face to Barbara. "Now don't go getting upset with what I got to say, Miss Lavette. God knows, I am upset enough right now, and I don't even know if your nephew was involved here."

"Please tell me," Barbara said.

"Yes. A terrible thing happen yesterday. They just got word. A Negro boy was lynched down there, not far from Jackson. Don't know who did it, maybe the Klan, and Claudy don't know his name or where he's from. But she says this. Four white boys was with him, and they was whipped——"

"Whipped?" What do you mean?"

"They got lashed, bad lashing, and they is in the Charity Hospital in Jackson. I don't know the details or what their names are, but they had a car that was burned and the car had California plates——"

"But the boys are alive?"

"The white boys, yes, seems so from what Claudy says. She don't know too much. You can go over and see her." Her phone was ringing again. She ignored it.

"It's all right. Please, answer it," Barbara said.

"Do you want Claudy's address?"

Barbara shook her head. "No, thank you." She almost raced out of there, found a cab finally, and back at her hotel, put through a call to the hospital at Jackson. Half an hour passed before she could break through the busy signals, and then a woman's voice asked impatiently whether she was a reporter.

"I'm the aunt of one of the boys, one of the white boys."

"Which one?"

"Frederick Lavette."

"Yes. Well, his condition is good."

248

"May I speak to him?"

"I'm sorry. We don't have telephones in the wards."

"And the other boys?"

"I'm not authorized to release information."

Then Barbara put through a call to Higate. Adam answered. "He's all right," Barbara told him. "Freddie's all right."

"Thank God. We just heard about this godawful thing in Mississippi, and Eloise was sure that it was Freddie and his friends."

"Adam, it was," Barbara said. "Don't get upset. I've just spoken to the hospital at Jackson, and Freddie is all right."

"You're sure? How can you be sure?"

"Adam, I'm here in Washington, I'll catch the first available plane for Jackson and I'll be there in a few hours, and I'll call you the moment I've spoken to Freddie."

"No. I'll come."

"Adam, be sensible. You'll have to tell Eloise, and you know what this will do to her. She won't be able to travel and you can't leave her. I would suggest you call the hospital in Jackson, the Charity Hospital. Meanwhile, I'll leave immediately, and I'll be in touch with you the moment I know anything. If Freddie can travel, I'll take him with me, and conceivably we can be at Higate tonight or tomorrow morning."

The afternoon was dark and sultry, the rain pouring down when Barbara got out of the cab in front of the hospital in Jackson. No one helped her with her suitcase. She left it at the door and pushed through a crowd of reporters, cameramen, and local police, literally fighting her way to an information desk, where a beleaguered woman was attempting to answer her telephone and a machine-gun flow of questions simultaneously. No hope there; Barbara squirmed out of the crowd, surveyed the four uniformed policemen, selected the most sympathetic in appearance, and went to him and pleaded, "Please, my son is here, and I don't know if he's alive or dead. Please help me."

"What's your name, lady?"

"Barbara Lavette."

"You got some ID on you?"

Barbara found her driver's license and a credit card. The officer studied them for a moment. "I don't know. We got orders to let nobody talk to them."

"For God's sake, it's my son." The tears came easily. She had been on the edge of tears all day.

"Don't cry, lady. Hold on." He called to another officer, "Lieutenant, you got one up there name of Lavette?"

The lieutenant joined them. Reporters began drifting over. "The tall, skinny kid with the blond hair."

"Is he alive?" Barbara begged him.

The questions came from the reporters now: Who are you, lady? You a mother? Give me that name again? Come on, lieutenant, give us a break.

The lieutenant drew her away down a corridor, and the other officer blocked the press and barred their way. "Just keep walking, ma'am, down this way," the lieutenant said. "You got to understand that we're in one awful spot with this. Nobody wanted a thing like this to happen."

"It happened. Can I see my son, please?"

"It happened. Sure it happened. It could happen anywhere. People are pushed, and they go crazy. But until we get a line on what really happened, we got to keep those kids and the reporters apart."

"Will you tell me whether my boy is alive!"

"I'm taking you there, ma'am. He's alive. He's hurt but he's alive. So just ease off, please, ma'am."

They went up a flight of stairs. Nurses, men in white, the flurry and motion of a hospital, and then the doors to the ward, with another officer stationed in front. The lieutenant opened the door for her, and she entered the ward, six beds but only three of them occupied. One of the boys lay on his stomach; the other two were sitting up, both of them covered with bandages and dressings from neck to waist. Freddie had a dressing and strips of plaster on his face. A doctor was changing a dressing on the boy who lay on his stomach. The other boy sitting was large, round-faced, and he managed a smile at Barbara. Freddie just stared at her. She went to him, bent and kissed him, whispering, "I got in as your mother, Freddie. Go along with it."

Still, he stared, unable to speak.

"Are you Freddie's mother?" the other boy asked. "I'm Phil Strong. Freddie's all right. He's just had a hard time. We had such a hard time. Just a hard time. That's Al Greenberg, over there on his stomach." Then he began to cry, not emotionally, his face unchanged, the tears rolling down his cheeks. Barbara would remember it as one of the most unsettling things she had ever seen, the big, oversized young man, sitting there in bed, his trunk swathed in bandages, crying so quietly.

"It's not the pain," Fred said unexpectedly. "It doesn't hurt so much now. It's Herbie and Bert. They hanged Bert Jones and they whipped Herbie Katz to death. That's why Strong is crying."

"You can sit down, ma'am," the lieutenant said, pulling up a chair alongside Fred's bed. "I guess you can stay as long as you want to." He left the ward then. The doctor who had been working on Greenberg said to him, "That's it, kid. You can sit up, if you want to." He helped him into a sitting position. "Best if you lie on your stomach to rest."

As he started for the door, Barbara intercepted him and asked him, "How are they? How serious is it?"

The doctor, a very young man, an intern in his twenties, looked at Barbara and then nodded at Fred. "That's your son?"

"Yes."

"Step outside a minute, please, ma'am."

In the hall, he explained; "Not that there's anything that I have to keep from them, but they're upset, damned upset. With reason. I never treated anyone who had been whipped before. Animals—those bastards. I'm sorry. I get carried away. I'm from Pennsylvania, and I just can't hack it with these idiots. The boys are all right. I mean, they'll heal all right. No torn muscles, no nerve injuries, just a lot of very bad abrasions and bruises. Painful as the devil. Your son has a cut cheek, result of a blow, but just a cut. No stitches. It's mostly shock, both physical and psychological, that they're suffering from. I guess they're lucky, if you can call it that. The other white boy, Katz—do you know him or his parents?"

Barbara shook her head.

"He died. They whipped him to death. I don't know why I'm telling you this———"

"I want to know, please. He was their friend."

"Well, the story I get from the boys is that first they hanged the Negro boy. Made them watch. Then they whipped Katz until he lost consciousness. Then they whipped the others, but not as severely. Funny thing, Mrs.———?"

"Lavette."

"Yes, of course. Thing is, they say some sort of deputy cop steered them into the situation. Then he must have called the ambulance, which is another thing I'll never understand about these people. We worked like hell to save Katz, but his heart just gave out."

"When can I take him home?" Barbara asked.

"Tomorrow. No reason why he can't travel tomorrow. Then you can have a doctor look at him when you get him home."

252

Barbara went back into the ward and sat down next to Fred and took his hand.

"Please stay here, Aunt Barbara," he whispered.

"I'll be back, Freddie. I have to call your folks. They're worried sick. Then I'll be back. And remember, I'm your mother. I want to get you out of here with as little fuss as possible." She turned to the other boys. "Can I help? Can I call your folks?"

"They know," Strong said.

"They ought to be here pretty soon," Greenberg told her.

"We sure screwed up," Strong said. "Poor Katz, poor Jones. We sure messed things up."

Wandering through the great cathedral in Milan, Jean Lavette said to Stephan Cassala, "I do love being a tourist." He could concur in that. They had already seen the *Last Supper,* worn, faded, a shadow of what Leonardo had painted, perishing slowly in the Santa Maria delle Grazie; the altar paintings at San Lorenzo and Santa Maria della Passione; four palazzos, La Corte, Marino, Ciani, and di Brera; and now, finally, the great cathedral. "It's really very snobbish," Jean went on, "but I manage to enjoy my shortcomings. Otherwise, life would be utterly impossible. I mean, one sets oneself apart. Here is all of human history, and one simply observes it, as if one were a visitor from Mars. Yet this place touches me. Saint Peter's leaves me cold, reminds me of Grand Central Station in New York—or of Grace Cathedral back home. I grew up almost across the street from Grace Cathedral, always felt it was a sort of large annex to daddy's mansion. But this place—I think I could believe in something if I remained here long enough. Do you feel it?"

"I don't know, Jean. *Duomo,*" he said thoughtfully, thinking that it sounded more reasonable in Italian. "It's a strange place, I grant you. Do you know, they

253

began to build it in thirteen eighty-seven, and it's not finished yet. I look at it, and I wonder how many good Catholics were murdered by war or otherwise since they put down the foundation stones. Ah well, you must not expect too much emotion from a failed Catholic."

"I suppose we're all lost souls, more or less. Danny dropped his Catholicism the day we were married. When did you lose yours, Steve, or shouldn't I ask?"

"Ah, yes, why not? I'm quite tired, Jean. Suppose we make our way across the square and have a coffee?"

They made an impressive couple, walking slowly across the wide plaza, the tall, slender old man and the white-haired old lady, both of them so very straight and proper. When they took their places at a table on the sidewalk in front of one of the cafés and Stephan ordered for them, Jean reflected on the pleasure of traveling in Italy with someone whose Italian was so fluent.

"When I left the Church," Stephan said, stirring his coffee. "Well, that was a long time ago."

"You don't have to. When I'm too inquisitive, Stephan, you must learn to ignore me."

"You're never too inquisitive, Jean."

"Bless you."

"In nineteen eighteen, in a trench in France, we were ordered to attack. The first platoon never got out of the trench. They were cut down on the lip. I was in the second wave, and fifteen minutes later the war was over for me, and I was lying there with a hole in my belly big enough to put my fist in. That was when I left the Church."

Jean nodded. "Try to understand, dear Stephan, that when I am very supercilious, I am simply evading something in myself."

"As you said before, we are tourists."

"How far can you stretch that? I keep thinking of

Freddie. When it's your grandson, your own flesh and blood, it's very hard to be a tourist."

"But you said he was all right, back on his feet, even playing ball again."

"But inside—I don't know. I shall have to reserve judgment until I see him and speak to him. I pray that he will forget, but how does one forget such a thing?"

"We don't forget. We manage to live with it."

"And once your fellow man has turned barbarian, how do you look at other people?"

"As a tourist, I suppose. It becomes a foreign country wherever you are, a kind of exile. Only—" He hesitated; his dark eyes clouded, turned inward. "Only, there's no place to go home to."

Friends of Barbara Lavette sometimes remarked on the fact that through the years she had managed to maintain a polite if not effusive relationship with her brother Thomas. Those who idealized Barbara felt that she was incapable of hating anyone, but in this they were wrong. She had experienced a good deal of hatred, of burning fury, of lasting and deep-seated anger. Others, more cynical, commented that it was hard to break relations with a thousand million dollars, regardless of the character of the owner, and still others accepted the theory that rich families remain united because they are rich. In truth, Barbara pitied her brother, and since it is said that one never pities those one respects or loves, but uses pity as a substitute for guilt, it may well be that there was a deep-seated guilt in Barbara. "Because," as she once told Dr. Albright, "I've had so much and he's had so little. I've been able to love and to feel and to weep when I had to, and he hasn't been able to do any of that, and I have a son who loves me and he has a son who hates him."

Thus when Tom called and asked Barbara to lunch with him, explaining that he had something of great

255

importance to discuss, she readily agreed. They met at the Mark Hopkins, after Barbara had demurred over his invitation to his private corporate dining room. Barbara was willing to maintain a social relationship, but for reasons she did not wholly understand, she was unwilling to set foot in the towering high-rise that was the international headquarters of the far-flung Lavette enterprises.

At fifty-two, Tom still had a fine head of hair, the blond locks turning silver at the edges. He had put on weight, but he was not fat, and his face remained unwrinkled. Handsome, beautifully tailored, his eyes clear gray, he displayed no trace of his dark, curly-haired, heavily muscled father. The genes had opted for what Barbara thought of as the ultimate WASP, the quintessential establishment figure, the new corporate lord whose power and influence reached to every corner of the earth. That was her own projection; in actuality, she sat facing a very troubled and unhappy man whose stomach gave him little peace. He pecked at his food without enthusiasm. "No, they don't think it's an ulcer. Nerves. If I knew as little about my business as they do about theirs, I'd retire. But I didn't bring you here to bore you with my digestive problems."

"It's a family prerogative," Barbara acknowledged. He was being human and rather humble.

"You don't have such problems?"

"I'm disgustingly healthy. Do you get any exercise, Tom?"

"Enough of that. I want to talk about Frederick. Have you seen him?"

"I had dinner there last week."

"How did you find him?"

"Very well—physically, I mean. In good health. But different. If you remember the way he was——"

"I don't remember," Tom interrupted. "I haven't seen him for seven years."

"I'm sorry. Well, he's a brilliant boy. A average, Phi Beta Kappa, all sorts of honors, not easy at Princeton, as you well know. He used to be a bit flip about it—not insolent, yet not given to hiding his light under a bushel. He'd hold forth on just about any subject under the sun, and not superficially either. It could be a very distinct pain in the neck; I remember once, at dinner, his delivering himself of a lecture on the ancient Sumerians. Of course, Eloise worships the ground he walks on, and no one wants to hurt her by saying, Oh, Freddie, please shut up."

"Sounds damned spoiled to me."

"Oh, no. That was years ago. But since that wretched business in the South, he's changed a great deal. Very quiet and very little to say. You must understand, Tom, that aside from that awful thing that was done to him, he had to witness two boys whom he loved put to death in the most horrible and bestial manner."

"Why in God's name did he go down there?"

"Because he had to, I suppose. I can understand that. You do things that you have to do—when you're young and when you're like Freddie."

"Well, I'm damned if I understand it. What did those kids die for? What did they change?"

"Tom," she said gently, "no one sets out to die. It happens. Perhaps it changes something. We can only say thank God he's all right."

"Well—yes. Of course." He was silent for a minute or so, toying with his food, tasting the wine. Then he said suddenly, explosively, "Damn it, Bobby, I haven't seen him for seven years! That's not right! He's my only child. Here I've built this damned empire with a net worth of over a billion dollars—I am fifty-two years old. A man thinks about that. What happens to it?"

"I don't know, Tom. I've not given much thought to that."

257

"What does he want to do with himself, now that he's out of school?"

"Tom, you know the situation out there at Higate."

"I'm afraid I don't. I've never been there. I've never considered the Levys as part of my family," he said coldly.

"Come on, Tom. They were part of the family before either of us was born. It was Levy and Lavette that we inherited. No, I'm sorry. We must not squabble. Anyway, when Jake Levy bought Higate, back in nineteen eighteen, it was a kind of ruined, worthless place. Today, it's one of the great wineries of California. It's what they call a very serious and highly respected label, and up there in Napa, wine is not a business, it's a religion. I've listened to the kids, Freddie and his brother, Joshua, and my son, Sam, sit around and talk endlessly about wine. You wouldn't believe it. So when you ask what Freddie intends to do with himself, I don't think he's ever seriously considered anything apart from Higate. Jake Levy is sixty-five and he still supervises the place, but Adam actually runs the business. Freddie, they tell me, has worked out an entirely new approach, using stainless steel vats——"

"Bobby, he can't waste his life out in the boondocks, making wine! He's a Lavette. He's my son."

"Tom, he's lived there. It's his life."

"I want to see him, talk to him."

"I think you should."

"He wouldn't come. He's washed me out of his life. I don't exist for him."

"Have you tried?"

"No." He shook his head unhappily. "I can't do it, I can't face that kind of rejection. Bobby, I don't even know what he looks like."

"He looks much the way you did thirty years ago. If I were you, Tom, I'd try. I don't know how the boy would react. I don't think he knows himself. I'd do it gently. I wouldn't throw any challenges at him."

Back in his office, Tom dictated a letter, made changes, dictated it a second time, and then tore that copy up and wrote a third letter by hand. "My dear son," he wrote. "It's been many years since we have seen each other. When I heard of that terrible occurrence in Mississippi I realized how strong my feelings for you were. I want very much to see you again. If it is possible for you to spend an hour or two with me, either here or over lunch, I would be most grateful. You can call me at the above number or drop me a note or stop by any time that is convenient for you. I will welcome a meeting with affection and gratitude." He signed it, "Thomas Lavette." He would have liked to have put, "Your loving father," but there his courage failed him. He addressed the envelope himself, that no one else might read it, and he went out to the corridor and dropped it into the mail chute himself.

The reply came three days later. "I'll be in San Francisco on August 12th," Fred wrote. "I can stop by at your office at four o'clock." It was signed simply, "Frederick Lavette."

On the twelfth, Thomas Lavette sat in his office waiting. He had cleared the afternoon, no appointments, no calls, no interruptions. He was nervous, apprehensive, a bit frightened. Suddenly, he had become aware of the size and fittings of his office. He felt that the huge nonobjective paintings on the walls were too large, too garish, the furniture tasteless, the immense mahogany spread of his desk pretentious and ridiculous. Even the magnificent view from the windows, a view of the whole shimmering surface of San Francisco Bay and the hills beyond, troubled him, and he would have exchanged it gladly for a shadowed wall of buildings. Yet, knowing nothing about his son, why was he presuming what he would like or dislike? Or was he simply concluding that Fred would adopt an adversary position to everything he chose or liked or favored?

At four o'clock, almost to the minute, his secretary buzzed him and informed him that Mr. Lavette was here.

"Well, bring him in. I told you that. I told you not to keep him waiting."

He got up immediately and walked around the desk. He'd be damned if he'd greet him from behind that enormous desk. There would be barriers enough. He stood motionless as the door opened and Fred entered. Barbara had mentioned an image of himself thirty years ago, but in truth, he had no image of himself thirty years ago. This was a stranger, this slender, tall, light-haired young man, blue blazer, gray flannel trousers, white shirt, Princeton tie, orange and black—did that portend a suggestion of a connection—a reaching out?—the handsome face gravely noncommittal.

Tom offered his hand and his son took it, the grip firm but not lingering.

"Thank you for coming," Tom said. Fred nodded. "Can I offer you something, coffee, a cocktail?"

"No thank you, sir."

"Will you sit down?" Tom asked, nodding at one of the easy chairs.

"I'd like to look at the view for a moment—if you don't mind?"

"Of course."

Fred walked over to the huge window. "It's overwhelming—almost as good as the Top of the Mark. I don't think I could get anything done in a room like this. I'd just stand here and stare out of the window."

"That's why I sit with my back to it."

"Yes, that figures." He turned and studied his father. His memory was of a man, whereas Tom's memory was of a boy. The boy was gone; the man was still there. "I can understand why you wanted to see me," Fred said, "and in your place, I would want to. The childish anger I had, the feeling that you had used my mother badly and hurt her—well, I can handle that. But there's nevertheless a tremendous gulf between us, and I'm not sure I can ever lessen the width of that gulf."

Tom nodded.

"I had to say this."

"I understand. I would like to hope that in time it might be otherwise, but I understand your feelings and I can respect them. I meant what I said before. I am grateful to you for agreeing to come here. Please sit down." Tom picked up a cigarette box. "Do you smoke?"

"Only pot, and I've rather put that aside since coming of age."

Tom smiled, thinking that all things considered, he liked the boy. At least he was straightforward and blunt. You didn't have to wonder what he was thinking.

"I'm sure," Tom said, "that you know something about this monster which we have created and which we euphemistically call GCS. We spread into a dozen different industries, and we're very large, wealthy, and successful, for whatever that is worth. I don't think I have to stress the fact that I had a very deep desire to see my son. You may not think of yourself in those terms, but I do. You're my only issue, as they say, and whatever your feelings about me are, GCS is a fact apart. I mean it exists as an entity, apart from both of us. Well—" He paused, struggling to find appropriate words. Fred watched him silently, impassive, waiting. "Let me put it this way. You've finished school and you're stepping into the world. You face a choice of careers. I think that puts you in a fortunate position." Tom shook his head, provoked at himself. "Let me try to be as straightforward as you have been with me. I want you here. I want you in the business. I want an opportunity to work with you and train you to take it over some day. It's no small thing. We are the most powerful conglomerate in California, and with the Fortune Five Hundred, we rank in the top twenty-five."

"A sort of toad-into-prince thing," Fred said, and then added hastily, "No, I'm not being snide. Please believe me, I'm not unaware of the immensity of this offer, or the importance. But you must admit it has the elements of bad drama, the poor country boy discovering his Daddy Warbucks and being offered an empire."

"I spoke in all good faith," Tom said, a kernel of anger beginning to form. "I offer something real. We're not dealing with cheap drama."

"I know. Please forgive me. But try to see it from my point of view. I'm not capable of running a small business, much less a giant like this. The only thing in the world I know anything about, in a practical sense, is wine. The only thing I want to do is make wine. Higate is a very small enterprise compared to GCS, but it's ample for my needs. As I said before, the gulf is too wide. I think we can both be decently polite to each other and decently civilized, but if I said I could go any further than that, I would only be lying."

Tom controlled himself. Inside, anger had begun to burn. He was asking himself, "Who the hell does this snotty kid think he is? I offer him the world, and he's sitting there, laughing at me. Fucking me—plainly and simply fucking me." His wife, Lucy, had warned him. "Offer him nothing," she had advised. "If he wants it, he'll ask for it. But if you offer and he rejects you, it will hurt too much. He's hurt you enough." Still, he managed to control himself and say to Fred, "All right, that's your decision. But the door isn't closed. If we can meet occasionally, perhaps we'll get to know each other a little better, perhaps we'll get to like each other."

"Perhaps," Fred said.

*　　*　　*

On a Saturday afternoon, late in August of 1964, the wolf pack gathered on the hillside overlooking Higate. They were all of an age where the very suggestion of the name "wolf pack" would have embarrassed them; nevertheless, it lingered in their minds, even as childhood lingered. They were all present, Sam and May Ling and Fred and his brother, Joshua, and Rubio and Carla Truaz. It was three days before Sam was scheduled to leave for Israel and the last day of Rubio's leave. Rubio was in uniform, and each time May Ling looked at him, her eyes became moist. Since there was a chill in the air, the boys had built a fire, and Joshua was roasting marshmallows, his contribution to the leave-taking. He had squeezed four marshmallows onto the end of a pointed stick, allowed them to become a flaming torch, and had then blown out the flame and offered the blackened candy to his mates.

"That," Fred said, "is absolutely disgusting. How can you eat anything like that?"

"Mostly by mouth," Sam replied, pulling off a sticky marshmallow. "I like them."

"Me too," Carla said.

"A difference of opinion," Joshua said calmly, "is always intriguing. To your generation, marshmallows are disgusting. To mine they are funky."

"Listen to him." May Ling laughed, the melted candy all over her fingers. "Your generation indeed!"

Rubio stared at her with what Sam thought of as the longing expression of a lovesick calf. Carla, more opulently lush and beautiful than ever, had switched her affection from Fred to Sam. His impending departure made the situation quite wonderful and romantic.

"It just doesn't seem possible," she said, "that in three days you'll be leaving for Israel. Will I ever see you again?"

"Now isn't that silly? Of course you will."

"For a year—a whole year. It's not even a real

263

place. It's something you learn about in Sunday school."

"It's a real place, all right, and it's nothing compared to Fred's fancy travels."

"Freddie, you're going away?" May Ling cried. "Oh, no. When did you cook this up?"

"We've been talking about it," Fred said, "and last night mom and pop gave it their final O.K. We had talked about my taking some PG courses in viticulture at Berkeley, but pop doesn't think much of them, and he feels they don't compare with what you can get at the Viticultural Institute in Paris and in Colmar. He's also making arrangements for me to travel in the Gironde area and study the Médocs. We're really working to develop a superb Cabernet Sauvignon, something that will identify the Higate label with real class everywhere in America, and that means I'll be spending a good deal of time in Bordeaux. I'll be gone about a year, and I'm not sure I'll learn much, but I will drink some very beautiful wine."

"Lucky stiff! You get all the breaks."

"Like Mississippi," Rubio said. "You can live without that kind of luck."

"I would have died—right there," May Ling whispered.

"I did, sort of," Fred said uncertainly. "I think a part of me died there. I mean that part of me is gone forever. Maybe that's what happens to someone in a war. I still dream about it. I see poor Jones hanging from the beam over the barn door, and I see Katz lying there with his back all torn to shreds. It's not real. If it were real, it wouldn't be as bad, but it's like one of those ghastly nightmares you have as a kid, and it stays with you all your life."

After that, they fell silent for a while. As the sun moved toward the west, the shadow of the hillside above enveloped them. They were in their own dimmed world, looking down at the sun-kissed, vine-covered fields and the sprawling buildings of the winery. All of them shared in the sad, sweet sense of childhood's end.

FOUR

The death of Sergeant Rubio Truaz, born in the Napa Valley of Northern California, twenty-one years old, a Chicano—which term indicates a Mexican of California birth—was witnessed by millions of people. Such is the miraculous nature of our time and the wonder of television. Sergeant Truaz was on patrol. Or perhaps not yet on patrol, because the TV cameras don't move out on patrol. Or possibly the patrol was starting, or finishing. That point was never really clarified, but what was very clear was that the camera, loaded with color film, was on Sergeant Truaz when the bullet struck him. The bullet struck a grenade that was attached to Sergeant Truaz's belt, and the grenade exploded, sheathing Sergeant Truaz from head to foot in burning chemicals. The incendiary grenade covered him with green fire, and the microphone of the TV crew picked up his wild screams of pain as he leaped around in his agony and then rolled over and over on the ground until at least two of his comrades managed to fling a body bag over him and thus put out the flames. Afterwards it was said that his screaming was a wild track, put into the film by the TV people to heighten the effect, but this was not the case. The screams belonged to Sergeant Truaz; they were his very own, and they went on for seven minutes before a medic reached him and gave him a shot of morphine, which probably did little to alleviate the pain. A few minutes later he lapsed into unconsciousness, and about an hour after that he died.

They ran the film on network television without identifying the soldier in question, and that was followed by anger from many quarters, accusations and counteraccusations, but it was not the first and would not be the last time this was done in the course of the Vietnam war. Cameramen risked their lives to get shots of men in action, and thereby bring the war directly into every American living room, and what better perception of front-line action than to see a man take a bullet or a shell fragment.

And since such photography was done under nerve-racking conditions, it was impossible to pause to get the name and rank and whatever of every miserable, filthy grunt the camera rested on—not to mention the red tape one would be enmeshed in if one tried to clear each name with the army or the marines.

So it happened that the death of Sergeant Truaz, an extraordinary glimpse of what war can be like, an incredible piece of photography, was witnessed by millions. Among these millions was May Ling.

Barbara was at a cocktail party that evening, so she was spared the tiny, unimportant incident in a very large war that titillated or shocked or horrified or stunned or sickened or entertained so many millions of others. She had come to New York during this spring of 1966 for the publication of her new book, *The President's Wife*. The book was published on the eleventh of May, the day that the government of the United States made known its formal reply to the mainland government of China, concerning the use of atomic weapons. The government of China had proposed to the government of the United States that each country pledge never to use atomic weapons against the other. Very easy for the Chinese to propose such a thing; the statisticians had worked out a schematic, using the latest calculators, which proved that such was the numbers of the Chinese that if one were to fight them with nonatomic weapons, one could not kill them fast enough to counteract the birthrate. Give up the use of atomic weapons indeed! The government of the United States indignantly refused, and this refusal was condemned by a good many people, including Senator Robert F. Kennedy. One reveiwer of Barbara's book wondered if Miss Lavette was not "leaping onto the anti-government bandwagon, which has become a hallmark of the 'sixties. Ostensibly," the reviewer went on, "Miss Lavette is writing a book about a woman; but in fact, her novel is a crushing indictment of the Presidency and of the method whereby Americans choose their Chief Executive. If the Presidency is, as Miss Lavette claims, encased in a procedural process that demands such characteristics as a malignant lust for power, an indifference to the needs of others, and the inability to manifest normal qualities of affection, then we are indeed in a most unhappy situation. But Miss Lavette comes with dubious credentials. Who is this President's wife she writes of?"

Who indeed? The critics received her book with restrained annoyance. Was the President Lyndon Baines Johnson? Was she not echoing, with the privileges of fiction, the shrill scream of a million voices crying out, "Hey, hey, L.B.J., how many kinds have you killed today?"

Her publisher, Holden Greenway, a round, overweight Balzacian man of explosive and colorful emotions, was not disturbed. "The book is selling like fried catfish at a Carolina picnic. Oh, I love you, Barbara Lavette, and I'll tell you something about critics. The critic is the eunuch in the harem. He watches the trick

271

being done day in and day out, and the poor, miserable bastard knows he'll never do it himself. Still and all," he said, "you want to meet them. They're a mixed lot, and there are some damned good ones mixed in with the whiners. Also, they don't actually believe in anything west of the Hudson River. So we'll have us one large bash of an old-fashioned literary cocktail party, and when they see this beautiful woman I've snagged for my list, they'll sing a different tune. Ours is a cosmetic society."

"In which case, you'd better look twice," Barbara replied. "A middle-aged housewife, and not very cosmetic."

The party was held in Greenway's apartment on Sutton Place, Barbara's first literary cocktail party in more than twenty years. It was called for five o'clock, but by six o'clock, the only people present aside from Barbara were Greenway and his two sisters, Kate, who was fifty, and Sylvia, who was fifty-three. They were both overweight, and they wore long brown satin skirts and hair piled high on their respective heads.

"They are good girls and very literary," Greenway whispered to Barbara. "Very romantic, full of tragedy. They were betrothed to two young fellows who joined the Canadian air force, flew in the same bomber, and were shot down in flames over Germany. Tragedy is as idiotic as love and honor, and frequently just as ridiculous. They cherish their loss. It's much more rewarding than being married to some brainless stockbroker." He whispered all this with a cheerful smile. "Of course, I'm lying. They *are* married to brainless stockbrokers, who will come later. They always come first, because they remember everyone's name. Don't be nervous, my dear Barbara, because in a half hour, there will be a hundred people here. No one would be gauche enough to be less than an hour late."

He was right. The room filled up, and one after another, the string of celebrities was introduced to Barbara. The two Greenway sisters remembered every name. Greenway himself retreated to a corner and got systematically drunk.

"Those who know him avoid him," Kate told Barbara. "He becomes insulting, rude, and unbearable. But he is a great publisher. He will do wonders for your book, my dear."

"My own impression," said the symphony conductor, using Barbara's other ear," is that you're writing about Mrs. Johnson."

Trying to deny that, Barbara's words were muffled by a comparison between President Johnson and the Emperor Tiberius. A small writer with a high-pitched voice complained that they were maligning the best man ever to sit in the White House. Barbara relinquished any attempt at an opinion. The enormous living room had filled with people.

"He wrote *In Cold Blood*," someone said to her. "Of course you've read it."

"*Cactus Flower*."

"No, it's not original—a translation of some sort."

"That is Jacqueline Susann," Sylvia said to her. "I did just introduce you to Jacqueline Susann. Or didn't I? I don't make those mistakes."

The tall blonde facing Barbara said, "Don't look at me as if I'm a stranger. I'm your damned alter ego. I played you in the film."

And Barbara thought, panic-stricken, She is the one, and I never saw the wretched thing.

And from his corner, Greenway plowed to her rescue, wheeling the blonde away, booming, "Come on, gorgeous, when you're drunk and horny as I am, a print will serve as well as the original."

A bearded man who had written a book about the Kennedy assassination breathed on her, close and hotly, "Because, Miss Lavette, it's the theme of today, assassination, murder, the new government, the new path to power."

Barbara was rescued by a full-breasted, hawk-nosed woman who wore a long, loose shift of India cotton. She steered Barbara out of the crowd into a reasonably unpopulated corner of the room, explaining, "Rescue is the key element in these local tribal rites, otherwise known as the literary cocktail party. If your publisher weren't sodden drunk, he might remember that."

"He did. He rescued me once. I was about to be shafted by the Hollywood star who played me in the film of my book—which I never saw—" Barbara began to laugh. "I've never really been to one of these before—oh, once perhaps, but that was so long ago and not like this. It's wonderful."

"Awful wonderful."

"Exactly."

"Let me introduce myself. We met half an hour ago, but you don't remember. How could you? My name is Netty Leedan, and I'm the author of *The Feminine Enigma,* and you're one person I've wanted to meet for years, and here we are, and I'm not going to let the opportunity slip away."

"Of course," Barbara exclaimed. "Oh, this is good, truly. I've read your book and parts of it over again. It's quite wonderful."

"And you agree with me?"

"You don't want me to agree, do you? I mean, it's made me think and probe and examine myself, but do you know, you're setting out to turn the world over on its head. I've tried that. It doesn't work."

"It will, believe me, Barbara. May I call you that? Call me Netty. I've been reading you and about you for years. It's an old saw to say that when the time of an idea has come, it's irresistible, but it's true, and this is the time of the women's revolution. It's here. It's in the air. The feminist movement is going to be the great movement of our century."

"Do you really believe that? But why?"

"Perhaps because everything else has failed, because we've reached rock bottom—no, that's not the reason. But some of it. Perhaps it's this filthy, unspeakable war we've gotten ourselves into. There's a world of women watching it. It's in their living rooms, on their TV screens—a living testimony to how the men have failed. We may fail too, but we've never had a chance to try."

"No," Barbara said, "we've never had a chance to try. We couldn't do worse, could we?"

"Hardly."

"This is no place to talk. Why don't we have lunch?"

"How long will you be in New York?"

"A few days."

"Tomorrow, then. You're free? Good." She scribbled an address on a bit of paper. "Here, at twelve-thirty."

Afterwards, Greenway said to Barbara, "I see that Netty Leedan cornered you. Being drunk, I can characterize her as a nut. Hell, you don't need that, Barbara—a gaggle of sex-starved biddies."

"Perhaps I do," Barbara said. She doubted that he was as drunk as he made out to be. "Yes, I think I do." She was reasonably tight herself, taller than Greenway by three inches, deliberately looking down at a man who held a good part of her creative life in his power, wondering whether her feeling, her reaction, was of contempt or simply indifference.

The address Netty Leedan had given her was on 54th Street at Madison Avenue, a place called The Women's Exchange. It was a large, pleasant restaurant, quite full, mostly women, although here and there a man shared a table with a woman. Netty waved to her, and Barbara joined her.

"The food's not bad," Netty said, after they had ordered. "As a matter of fact, it's quite good. But it's not the food. I think I'd come here no matter what they

275

served. The organization that runs the place came into being years ago, time when a woman with a child and no man, married or unmarried, had absolutely nowhere to turn. No welfare, no relief, and damn little charity. This place taught such women to do work at home—sewing, embroidery—and it sold the stuff they made. Oh, it didn't mean much except that sometimes it meant the difference between life and death. Not much place for it in our world of today, but I like to eat here and be reminded."

"It never occurred to me," Barbara said slowly, "that at home there was nothing like this. It's very interesting how many things never occurred to me."

"But a lot of things did occur to you, and you wrote about them. I'm a Johnny-come-lately compared to you. You've done it; you're a woman, but you fought it out in their world."

"You don't fight it out in their world, Netty. You scrabble at the edges. It's always in spite of and never because of. Whatever you do, it's considering that you're a woman. And don't think for a moment that the ass and the tits don't help. I don't make a practice of talking dirty; I hate that kind of talk, and it always makes my skin crawl; but how do you put it? Lady, I'd like to fuck you—oh, that adds up to points, and it takes you in and out of places you'd never squeeze through if you were a size forty with acne. I am fifty-two years old, and one small advantage of my age is that from here on, I'll make it with other virtues, or not make it at all."

"You're still damned attractive. Do you mean to tell me that Greenway hasn't made a pass?"

"No. I don't like him, and I think he knows it. And the book is selling."

"It is. You're a celebrity. Hell, you have been for years. Look, I want you to stay in town a few extra days. We're having a meeting in Carnegie Hall, the first big thing we've ever attempted. If it works, it will be the real beginning and we'll finally have a women's movement that matters. I just feel in my bones that this is the moment, the time, and we need you. I want to be able to spread the word that Barbara Lavette will be our keynote speaker——"

"Oh, no! I'm a rotten speaker. You don't want me. I've done it only once in my whole life, years ago at Sarah Lawrence, and my vocal cords froze——"

"You can do it."

"Please."

"No. Believe me, you can do it."

In the end, Barbara allowed herself to be persuaded, and for the next two days, she wrote and rewrote her ten-minute address, spoke it into her mirror, reread it with disgust, lay awake dreading the situation that faced her, and then called Netty Leedan and pleaded for escape, only to be told that it was too late, that the announcement had been made on radio and television and in the press. Then, in the late afternoon on the day of the meeting, Sally telephoned from Napa and told Barbara about the death in Vietnam of Rubio Truaz.

After that, for the next hour, Barbara sat in her hotel room, alone and doing nothing, not reading, almost without thought, just sitting. Then she changed her clothes for the evening and walked the few blocks from her hotel to Carnegie Hall. She left her speech at the hotel.

How strange, she thought, how very strange indeed to be doing this. She was not at all sure how she came to be there, sitting on the platform, one of a row of women, facing a packed hall, mostly women but with a good sprinkling of men, nor did she know why she was so deeply moved. The pressure of emotion welled up inside her, and she felt that she was at the point of tears. That would not do; it would not do at all, and she fought to step away from herself, to see the time and the place and the moment and to see it all apart from herself. She had never been in Carnegie

Hall before. What an immense place it was! And how, she wondered, did one go about filling it with all these women? Or was there indeed some new and mysterious current at this moment of human history? She tried to marshal her thoughts, to sort out what she intended to say, to arrange a proper sequence of events in her mind; but it was no use. Some witch's spell had cast her into memories of her youth, the sundrenched streets of pre—World War Two Paris, the trees in blossom, the broad stretches of the boulevards. Her own name tore her out of the reverie. Netty Leedan was introducing her. Barbara stood up, and there was a storm of applause as she walked to the podium and stood facing the microphone and beyond it the audience.

"I did have a speech written out," she said to them, once the applause had died down. "I spent two days writing it and rewriting it, and I tell you this because I don't want you to feel that I am totally irresponsible, standing here without a scrap of paper. I also don't want to give the impression that I am so practiced a speaker that I can do this. I'm not. This is the second public address I've made in my entire life and the other was more than twenty-five years ago. But something happened a few hours ago, and it made me realize that I couldn't come here and read what I had written about the inequities women suffer. I can only talk about what has happened, so I beg you to bear with me."

She paused. The audience was watching her. Her eyes moved from face to face. Strangers—or sisters? Netty Leedan had called them sisters. The thought occurred to Barbara that the only women she had felt were sisters, bound to her by ties stronger than blood, were the women she had known in prison. She cast that away. Just talk to them and tell them how it happened.

"My father," she said, "Dan Lavette, was the son of Italian immigrants. He was a fisherman. In San Francisco, where I live, there is a place called Nob Hill, a place but also a symbol of success and power. My father fell in love with a beautiful woman who lived on Nob Hill. Her name was Jean Seldon, the daughter of a very wealthy and powerful banking family. Jean Seldon, my mother, is a remarkable woman, but then, so many years ago, she was a product of her time and a victim of her time—as my father was. My father clawed his way to wealth and power, and in the process, my mother lost him. The gulf between them was wide to begin with, and time widened it. My father took a mistress—a Chinese woman whose name was May Ling. I say Chinese, but actually she was the second generation born in America. But you would have to know San Francisco at that time to realize how little that mattered. May Ling was a lovely, intelligent woman, well educated, and she gave my father a great deal. My father divorced my mother in 1929, and a few years later, he and May Ling were married.

"I tell you all this not because of any compulsion to reveal the tangled family history of the Lavettes, but because it must be a preface to what happened to me today. My father and May Ling were in the Hawaiian Islands when the attack on Pearl Harbor took place, and May Ling was killed there. Her death was as senseless, as meaningless, and as tragic as any death in any war. No, perhaps not as meaningless, for when war kills a woman or a child, the particular murder is robbed of all the euphemistic rationalization and patriotic hyperbole with which men justify the mass slaughter they periodically inflict upon the human race.

"My father and May Ling had one child, my half brother, Joseph Lavette, who is a physician practicing in the town of Napa, in Northern California. Joe married the daughter of the family who own the Higate Winery in the Napa Valley, and their first child, a daughter, was named May Ling after Joe's mother. Again, I ask you to bear with me if I appear to wan-

279

der, but I must tell this in the only way I can. In Higate, as in most of the California wineries, many of the workers are Mexicans. I call them Mexicans only to identify them, for many of these families have lived in California for generations, some before any Yankees came there. The foreman at Higate is a man called Cándido Truaz, a Chicano, as these American-born Mexicans call themselves, and his son was a young man whose name was Rubio Truaz. Rubio and May Ling fell in love. May Ling is nineteen, a slender, beautiful young woman. Rubio was a few years older, a student at Berkeley. In the normal course of things, college students have been exempted from the draft, but nothing is normal when rules are applied to Chicanos, and two years ago, Rubio Truaz was drafted. Three months ago, his unit was shipped to Vietnam, and after that, each evening, May Ling watched her television set, hoping for some sight of Rubio Truaz. A few nights ago, her watch was rewarded. She saw him. He was in the cameraman's lens when a bullet struck a grenade attached to his belt. The grenade exploded, and he was enveloped in fire, and he died this awful, terrible death while the young girl who loved him watched.

"Today, my brother's wife, Sally, May Ling's mother, telephoned me and told me what had happened. Whether the damage done to this child is as permanent as the damage done to the man she loved, I don't know. But after I spoke to my sister-in-law, I realized that whatever I had written to say here tonight was without importance. All the importance in the world was with that child, my niece, and all the symbols which adhere to the state of being a woman were bound up in her suffering and condition. I don't know what will come of this meeting here tonight, and I truly do not know whether there can ever be a women's movement powerful enough to undo what the men in this world have done. Yet they are the victims—more

280

the victims than we have ever been. When they put us in bondage, they encased themselves in their own madness, and there, in Vietnam, we are witnessing the ultimate maniacal result of male chauvinism.

"So I am thankful, deeply thankful for this opportunity to talk to you. I said that I don't know whether we can have a great women's movement. Now I say that we must have it, because everything else has failed. We inherit that failure. We inherit all the agony and all the madness, and somehow we must put it right. There is no mankind without us. It comes out of our loins. We must free ourselves from this age-old bondage, and in so doing there is at least the slim hope that we can free all humankind. Women have always prayed that the war would be the last war. It is time we stopped praying and made certain that it *is* the last war!"

An early morning plane out of New York brought Barbara to San Francisco Airport an hour before noon. Back in her house, she skimmed through her pile of mail, found a letter from Sam, put the rest aside, and opened it eagerly. "Dear mom," he wrote. "The semester ended today—just in time to secure what remains of an overworked brain, not the best to begin with. How often I reflected on my four years of French in high school, and our hours of bright conversation in said language. Only natural that I should end up in the Hebrew University in Jerusalem. Hebrew, dear mother, is not a language, it's a form of Jewish torture, and two years of premed in the Hebrew tongue only proves that I should have opted for dedicated Episcopalianism. But you've heard all this before, and to be quite truthful, my Hebrew is not bad. I read easily, and when I listen carefully, I can understand most of what an Israeli says. They speak in sentences, having never heard of the theory that there should be spaces between words. Enough of that. My marks are pretty good, and I have come to believe that this place provides the best medical training in the world. Well, we shall see.

"But more than that, I'm concerned with your advice that I remain is Israel through the summer. I know how you feel about the draft, but since I registered before I left, I'm on legal grounds there, and from all I hear, they are not drafting college students. In any case, I would stand my ground as a conscientious objector—and if you think it is any easier to be a pacifist here than in the States, you're wrong. I've had more damn wild arguments on that score than you can shake a stick at. There are a lot of great things here, but pacifism is not one of them. I'm homesick for the smell of the bay, for the hills, for our house on Green Street, for you. It's a year since I was home. I know how you feel about the war and I know what war has done to your life, but aren't you a bit unreal about it?

"All right, I've had my say, and it's not as bad as it sounds. Freddie's mother feels the way you do, and like me, he's consigned to exile. He's coming over from Paris next month, and we're going to cover this place on foot, every inch of it. I'm really excited about that, because for two years, except for my trip home last year, I haven't taken my nose out of the books and the frogs, toads, and rabbits I've been dissecting. Two years, and I really haven't seen the place. Freddie will look into Israeli wine, which he says stinks and I agree with him, and we'll both do a bit of leering at Israeli womanhood. And remember—you promised to come over to see me in September, and I'm holding you to that. I love you very much. SAM."

Being alone, Barbara permitted herself a good cry, and then she felt better. An hour later, she was in her car and on her way to Napa. She had only just stepped out of her car in front of her brother's house when the door opened and May Ling ran out and embraced her.

"Darling Aunt Barbara! I'm so glad you're back. I've just finished reading your new book. It's great. I loved it. And now you're here in the flesh. Will you autograph it? Just to me?"

Smiling, bubbling with pleasure, May Ling put her arm through Barbara's and led her into the house. "You will stay for dinner, won't you? You won't run away?"

"No, of course not. I won't run away."

Sally was inside, waiting, as they entered. She shook her head slightly and put a finger to her lips. "If you do want Barbara to stay for dinner, May Ling, we'll have to feed her. So be an angel and go into town and pick up a fresh pork shoulder at Schultz's. Medium size. Just tell him to put it on our bill."

"Now, mother?" Aunt Barbara's just arrived."

"She'll be here."

When May Ling had left, Sally took Barbara into Joe's office. He smiled wanly as he kissed her. "Welcome back, sister. It's a great big beautiful world, isn't it?"

"I don't understand. She's so happy."

Joe looked at Sally and shook his head hopelessly. "Sit down," Sally said to Barbara. "You might as well hear the whole thing."

"You mean it was a mistake?" said Barbara. "It was someone else?"

"It was Ruby Truaz. Let me tell you what happened that night. We were all sitting in the living room—all except Danny. He was in bed, thank heavens. May Ling had been watching the ten o'clock news religiously, always hoping to catch sight of Ruby. It's war in the living room, you know. Joe was reading. I was sort of watching, not very intently. I hate those war shots, but I did glance up when it came on the screen. I can't describe it to you. It was too horrible, too hideous. Those cameras they have now can leap in for a close-up without the cameraman moving at all, and how he could stand there and keep his camera going, I don't know, but I guess that's what they're paid for. It

283

was Ruby, unmistakably. Of course, I looked at May Ling——"

"The thing is," Joe said, "that neither of them said a word. Sally gasped, and I looked up at her. Then I looked at May Ling. Her face was white, her fists clenched, her body rigid. The first thing I thought of was an attack of some kind. The notion of an epileptic seizure flashed through my mind, one of those instant reactions you get, but it didn't match. But I never looked at the screen, never saw the damn thing."

"For which you can be grateful," Sally said. "Joe said something—I don't remember what—and I just sat paralyzed, staring at May Ling. Then May Ling leaped to her feet and ran into the bathroom. I ran after her, of course, and Joe followed me. He still didn't know what it was all about. May Ling was bent over the toilet bowl, vomiting convulsively. I put my arms around her, and the vomiting went on. Then she stood up, holding her hands to her stomach. Joe still didn't know what was playing, and he got a glass of water from the sink and told May Ling to rinse her mouth. She did that. Then Joe told her to drink some water, and she did so, very obediently. Then she said, in that plaintive tone a sick child uses, 'Thank you, daddy. It must be one of those funny viruses of yours. All of a sudden I felt so sick.' "

"I was still in the dark," Joe said, "thinking it could be something she ate, and I wanted to get her into the office and look at her. But Sally said no, all she needed was to lie down and rest, and when Sally gets that tone in her voice, I don't argue."

"I went upstairs with her," Sally said, "and she undressed and crawled into bed, and she put her arms around me and kissed me, and then she said something about poor daddy, he looked so worried, and I must tell him that she'll be fine in the morning, and she couldn't really be sick because she had promised Ruby that she would remain healthy and exactly as she was until he got back from Vietnam. Spooky—oh, believe me, very spooky. I stayed there, and five minutes later, she was sound asleep. So there it is."

"Poor baby," Barbara said. "But what does it all mean?"

Joe shook his head.

"You're a doctor, Joe."

"Oh, I know what it is, and I've discussed it with the people in psychiatric at the hospital. It's not a very common reaction in kids her age. She is almost nineteen. It's more frequent in the prepuberty stage, a kind of infantile amnesia. The mind receives a shattering blow, and as a defense, the mind blocks it. It never happened. The only trouble is that another part of the mind knows that it happened, and the defense May Ling used will crumble."

"When?"

"Today, tomorrow. It's five days, and that should be about the limit. Ruby's body arrived in San Francisco yesterday. I think we'll tell her today."

"I'm so afraid of that," Sally said.

"I'm glad you're here, Bobby. It will help stabilize things."

"I think Bobby might tell her, I'm such a coward," Sally said.

"But then what happens?" Barbara asked. "Will she remember?"

"The strange thing is that she does remember," Joe said. "The mind isn't one whole thing. It would be good if you told her, Bobby. She'll be back in a few minutes. Only if you want to."

"Where's Danny?"

"He'll be hanging around school, so he won't be back until after four."

Sally took the roast into the kitchen when May Ling returned.

"Do you need help, mom?"

"I'll just put it in the oven and be with you."

285

Watching her, Barbara was baffled. How could she remember yet not remember, know and yet not know? "Come, sit here with me," Barbara said, dropping down on the couch. May Ling sat beside her, and Barbara smoothed her soft black hair.

"I'm so glad you're here. You can't imagine how strange it is to read a book and then have the writer right in front of your eyes, especially when she's your aunt. I have a hundred questions for you—but of course you're not going to tell who the President's wife is."

"Because she's a figment of my imagination, darling."

Joe came into the room, stood watching them.

"But before we get into that, darling, I have something very important to tell you———"

Now Sally appeared and slowly sat down in a chair facing them.

"—something very sad."

May Ling turned to face Barbara, all the pleasure fading, her dark eyes misting over with tears, and Barbara realized that it was done, that her mind had come together and accepted the memory. She rose, stood still for a long moment, and then went to Sally, dropped on her knees in front of her and put her head in her mother's lap and stayed like that, sobbing.

At dinner that same evening, in their home at Higate, Adam Levy saw another side of his wife's character. Eloise was a gentle woman. It was not a pose she assumed; she had been that way since childhood, living what appeared to many as a continuing apology for her existence. Unfeeling people described her appearance and her manner as a cliché, the clear pink skin of a child, the small retroussé nose, the Cupid's bow of a mouth and the blond curls that required neither tinting nor permanents. Her first husband, Tom Lavette, had despised her and mistreated her. Adam adored her and in twenty years of married life had hardly once raised his voice to her. Eloise, on the other hand, remained what she was, a kind and gentle woman whose only weapons were defenselessness and vulnerability. But tonight, at the dinner table, she said to her husband, with unexpected firmness, "Adam, I must discuss something of great importance."

"Now or later?"

"Now, I think, because I want Joshua to hear what I have to say."

"O.K. Shoot."

"Joshua registered for the draft today."

"Oh? Well, it had to come. He's eighteen."

"Is that all you have to say?" she asked him coldly. "Cándido brought Ruby's body back today. The coffin is sitting there in his living room."

"Baby, I know that. I was with Cándido all afternoon. Don't think I'm callous to what happened. But what has that got to do with the fact that Joshua registered? Every kid has to. Freddie registered."

"I don't believe what I'm hearing!"

"Mom, hold on," Joshua said. "All pop means is that registering doesn't put me in the army."

"I'm quite aware of what registration means. I'd like both of you to be aware of something else. No force on earth is going to take my son into the army."

"Eloise, we're a long way from that."

"Are we? Let me remind both of you of something. Your grandfather—Grandma Clair's father," she said, looking pointedly at her son, "died in the First World War. He was captain of a munitions ship, blown to pieces in the North Sea. Grandpa Jake was in that war and he survived by a miracle. Yes, I got it from him," she said when Adam looked incredulous. "Steve Cassala was wounded and almost died. In World War Two, your father's brother died, and my own brother died in Korea, and the two men your aunt Barbara loved and who could have given her a rich and wonderful life, the kind of life I've had—both of them dead in these insane wars. It's enough. Our family has paid a high enough price, and I will not send a son of mine into that crazy slaughter. I know I sound angry and a little hysterical, and that's because I am very angry and hysterical, and what makes me most angry is the way the two of you sit there and indulge me! I don't want you to indulge me! Ruby Truaz was one of the sweetest, nicest boys I ever knew. Why did he have to die? What sense does it make?"

There was a stretch of silence then. Neither Adam nor Joshua had ever experienced anything like this from Eloise. It was too incredible for anything but Joshua's somewhat inane comment: "But, mom, Ruby was in the army. It happens."

"Oh!" she exploded. "Oh, you are both so impossibly stupid!"

That too was incredible. They stared at Eloise in silence. She took a deep breath and said quietly, "I want your promise. I am very serious and very determined. Either you will give me your word that Joshua never goes into the army, or I will leave this house tonight."

Father and son looked at each other hopelessly. "What can we do?" Adam finally asked her.

"Any number of things. We can send Joshua to Canada. We can hide him if we have to. We can do things if we make up our minds to do them. I want you to promise me."

Again the silence. Then Joshua said, "All right, mom, we'll promise."

She turned to Adam.

"Yes—if you feel so deeply about it."

"I do!" Then suddenly, she burst into tears, left the table and ran into the kitchen. Joshua said to his father, softly, "I never heard mom talk like that before. She was really upset."

Adam nodded.

"You think she really would have left us?"

"I don't know," Adam replied. "I just don't know."

"Mother," Barbara said to Jean, "will you please stand still for a moment, or sit down."

Pacing back and forth in her living room, Jean replied, "I need a drink."

"Then have one. Shall I make it for you?"

"No." She turned to Barbara. "Do you know, ever since Danny died, your Dr. Milt Kellman assumes that I am his personal property, to be kept alive at any cost. I don't want to be kept alive. I am seventy-six years old. If I only knew some truly stylish way to end it all, I wouldn't hesitate."

"What nonsense! Will you please sit down. What happened? Did Milt tell you no more drinking?"

"Exactly. Not that I would pay any attention to him, but I can't drink. It does something awful to me. I'm going to sell this house. It's absolutely insane, one old woman living alone in this great barn of a place. And it reminds me. Oh, I hate memories! It's more than half a century since Danny built this place."

"Perhaps you ought to travel again—for a while."

"It bores me. I've been everywhere I want to go. I couldn't bear to go alone, and I think poor Stephan's traveling days are over." She sat down now, staring at Barbara. "He has cancer of the bowel."

"Oh, no!"

"Bobby, being an old lady is a wretched business—like being at a party and overstaying your time, and then just staying on and on and your hosts are dying for you to leave——"

"This is your day, isn't it? That's awful about Stephan, but you are very much alive and still attractive."

"I will have a drink. All this nonsense about an ulcer. Will you join me?"

"Certainly."

"Just wine. If I told Milton I had a cocktail, he'd be enraged."

"Shall I get it?"

"I'm quite capable." She went to get the wine. "White? Yes, I think so. Don't let on if you see Stephan. He wants no one to know, poor dear. They'll have to operate in a few weeks." She handed Barbara her glass. "Cheers and things. It's Higate's best, and quite good. Adam sends me a case each month. He's eternally grateful that it was through me he met Eloise. They say marriage is impossible, but that one does break the rule, doesn't it?"

"It certainly does."

"Oh, I do miss the kids. Will Freddie and Sam ever come back?"

"I hope not until this wretched war is over. Why don't you go to Israel? They're spending the summer there, both of them."

"That is a thought. Oh, I don't know, Bobby. But tell me, how is May Ling taking the death of that boy she was so enamored of—what was his name?"

"Rubio Truaz."

"Oh, yes—a Mexican, wasn't he?"

"A Chicano. She took it very hard, but I suppose in time she'll get over it."

"Well, perhaps it's for the best."

"Mother," Barbara exclaimed, "there are times when you astonish me!"

"Bobby, I don't mean the boy's death. It's just that they were wrong for each other."

"How do you know?"

"Bobby, do you know you bully me? I said nothing so terrible. I just don't see a match between that child and a Chicano, as you call him."

"Any more than you could see a match between yourself and the son of an Italian fisherman."

"That's not fair. You're determined to strip me of all my prejudice. I don't have much else left."

Barbara couldn't stay angry at her mother. Jean was of a time and of a place. The time was gone forever, and if she sold the house on Russian Hill, one of the last of the old mansions, then the place too would vanish.

Barbara went to her and kissed her. "I do love you."

"That's very rewarding. Now tell me, how was New York?"

"Exciting and wonderful. And I want to tell you about it."

When Barbara had finished her account of what had taken place in New York, Jean shook her head hopelessly. "Dear Barbara, you are precious. You never change. You are still going to feed the hungry and change the world."

"Nothing so exalted. Only whatever little bit I can do."

"And you actually believe that women will find some kind of equality?"

"If they fight for it. We're half the human race."

"The poor, as you sometimes remind me, are most of the human race, and I haven't noticed that they can do much about it."

"This is different."

"Yes, it always is." She was smiling now, watching her daughter. "I was talking with Grace Pettyborn the other day—you know, she does an occasional review for *The New York Times,* which puts her among the very intellectual elite—and she referred to you as Miss Goody Two-Shoes. Of course, she's right, and you do exist with both feet firmly planted in midair, but in this worst of all possible worlds, thank God for the few mad ones like you. You know, when I'm so absolutely down that nothing appears to help, I remind myself that you're my daughter and that I did at least one thing right. Now what is it this time, Bobby?"

"I'm going to stop this filthy war, which will be my small contribution to the women's movement."

"Oh? All by yourself?"

"No, I'll have some help."

"I shall miss you terribly if you end up in jail again. You are also totally mad."

"I've thought of that. But I wonder whether I'm any crazier than the next person. It may be the change of life, or perhaps living alone."

Jean shook her head. "No, you've always been this way."

"Mother," Barbara said, "what's the state of your finances?"

"That's an odd question. I have all the money I shall ever require. Why? Do you need money?"

"Not right at this moment. Perhaps later."

"When you set about stopping the war?"

"Something like that."

"Barbara," Jean said, "I don't like this. You appear to be reasonably sane, but appearances can be deceiving. You are fifty years old——"

"Fifty-two, mother."

"Fifty-two then, and it's unseemly that I should be lecturing you as your mother. Twenty years ago, I would have told you to find an eligible man, marry him, have children, and live the way most people do."

"You did, mother."

"Yes. Today, it would not address the problem. My dear, wars cannot be stopped. They are a part of our way of life, like death and taxes. None of it can be stopped, altered, or bettered. I don't know what you are thinking or planning, but why can't you be satisfied just to live and be reasonably miserable? The rest of us exist that way. Why can't you write another book? Or teach somewhere? Or lecture? Or ride? Suppose I were to make you a gift of a horse. You always loved horses."

"Mother, I haven't been on a horse for thirty-five years."

"You don't forget."

"You're a dear," Barbara said, "and I do love you."

"Which is condescending and changes nothing. Well,

I've said all that I can say. How much money do you want for this idiotic scheme of yours?"

"I have no idea—yet."

"Of course, your mother is absolutely right," Boyd Kimmelman said to her. "It's not that you're insane in the legal or medical sense of the word. If you were to kill someone, I'd have the devil's own time pleading you a loony."

"Thank you. I have no intention of killing anyone, so you can put your mind to rest."

"On the other hand, you're completely out of touch with reality. As I understand it, you are going to start some kind of women's movement to end this thing in Vietnam. It just happens that there are at least two hundred organizations in existence right now with the same purpose and goal. All you have to do is to pick up the morning paper to see how successful they are."

"I know," Barbara agreed. "I know what you're saying, and so often I wonder why I do what I do. Why can't I live with it? My own son is safe for the moment. After we finish lunch, if I can get you to take a few hours off, we can have a walk in the park. We're fond of each other, and we have enough money to live pleasantly. And as far as the human condition goes, it's always been this way, hasn't it, and I suppose it always will be this way. Back in January, President Johnson told us that for a year, we had only thirteen hundred dead kids in Vietnam. God knows how many maimed, crippled. But they're not my children. They're always someone else's kids, aren't they? He said the enemy had thirty-five thousand dead, but they're not our kids either, and why should it disturb my sleep? I don't know. I honestly don't know. I'm sure that if Mr. McNamara were here, he could argue very brilliantly why this horror must go on. Of course, I can't stop it. I'm not a total idiot and I don't have any delusions of grandeur. And I don't want to go to jail again. I can't tell you how much the thought of prison terrifies me."

"No," Boyd said slowly. "You're just the way you are. If you were any other way, you wouldn't be Barbara, would you?"

"You can't imagine how tiresome it becomes— being Barbara."

"I don't find it so. Now let's be very practical. Whatever you're going to do—well, I imagine you'll do it. This is not fifteen years ago. McCarthyism is over. You will not go to jail. On the other hand, whatever you do must be done openly, and the people who do it with you must understand that. There's an interesting legal footnote to all this. We're not at war. Congress has never voted a declaration of war against Vietnam. This is a presidential action, which is pretty damn weird, but there it is, so you will not be breaking any law. I still think that whatever you do will make absolutely no difference, but that is because I am a cynical and tired middle-aged lawyer."

"You're probably right."

"And I'll be delighted to take the afternoon off and walk in the park with you."

They went to the Japanese Tea Garden and sat on a bench, looking at the wonderful red five-storied pagoda. Barbara had never been to Japan. "I'd like to make the trip someday—Japan, China."

"I'll take you," Boyd said.

"It can wait. We'll save it for the declining years, if you haven't found a wife by then."

"I don't look forward to the declining years."

"Mother and Stephan Cassala wandered through Italy, two very distinguished older citizens. I think they enjoyed it. Now Stephan is dying of cancer."

"I'm sorry to hear that."

"Yes, I suppose there's nothing else to say. I've heard that if a soldier dies in battle, another who survives is gratified because he's spared, and out of that

294

comes the guilt. You were wondering before why I do what I do. I live with my own guilt."

He didn't pursue that. He knew about her guilts. There was no point in trying to talk about it.

Stephan Cassala was alone when Barbara entered his hospital room. A thin wraith of a man, he smiled with pleasure. "How good of you to come, Barbara. Please, sit down." She had brought a pot of African violets. There were flowers in the room, but no other African violets. "I do love them. My mother used to raise them," Stephan said. "You know, my son, Ralph, was here. He left just a few minutes ago. I would have liked for you to see him."

I will see him at the funeral; the thought entered her mind without her willing it, making her think then how rotten a thought can be, how heartless. Was she really unfeeling, manufacturing thoughts and emotions? Did nothing come as a natural response from her innermost being? She put down the violets and went to the bed and kissed him on his cheek.

"Why, that's the nicest thing," he said. "Thank you, Barbara."

"How do you feel?"

He shrugged. "They keep the pain down. I'm no good at pretense, Barbara, even to myself. It's metastasized, as they say. I lie here thinking that I'll be dead very soon—well, it's not too terrible. It is, yes, terrible, but then again it isn't. I don't know whether that makes much sense. Your mother's been here every day. The three months we spent together in Europe were the happiest time of my life. That's no disloyalty to Danny, is it?"

"Oh, no. No."

"You know, long ago, back in nineteen thirty, pop had a bank. I think you heard about it, the Bank of Sonoma—just a small bank, not like the Seldons' bank. Well, we had a run, and that destroyed us, but during the run, I was going crazy trying to cover. Danny and his partner, Mark Levy, had the big department store down on Market Street then, and I came to them, and they emptied their cash drawers for me, over thirty thousand dollars. We could never pay it back and they never asked for it——"

It was difficult for him to talk. "Don't strain yourself," Barbara told him.

"I mean, to make Jean a little happier—that's not disloyalty to Danny—I love her so much, but God Almighty, that's not a sin."

"Steve, just for that I'm more grateful to you than I can tell you. Please rest now. Don't try to talk anymore."

Stephan Cassala died nine days later. He was buried in the Catholic cemetery in San Mateo. Barbara drove Jean to the funeral and sat beside her in the church. "Dear man," Jean said, when it was over. "Dear, sweet man. Now they're all gone, all of them."

Sam met Fred at the airport in Tel Aviv—and at first meeting, each stared at the other in amazement. They had filled out. Both were bearded, Fred's beard of tight strawberry-blond curls, his sandy hair shoulder-length, Sam's beard and hair sun-bleached, his skin bronzed, his pale blue eyes seemingly paler than ever. They embraced, pummeled each other, and then stood back to regard each other again.

"By God, I'm glad to see you, cousin!" Sam exclaimed. "Two years of exile in the land of the Jews! What a treat to meet a bona fide American white Protestant *goy*!"

"You've survived very nicely, cousin. What's all this crap about breaking your ass studying? You didn't get that coat of tan sitting with the books."

"School's been out for a month. I've been wasting my life at the beach here, being a bum."

"And that's how you live—in shorts and a shirt and sandals?"

"That's how I live, cousin. I've redeemed myself sufficiently, enrolled at Hebrew University, two years of trying to master premed with this incredible language, and now I'm young Sammy Cohen, on the town. I have a little room in Frishman Street, ten bucks a week, easy walk to the beach, and I've been unwinding. Don't look at me like that. I deserve it. And I've fixed it for you to bunk with me—just a few days, and then we'll take off. Is that all you've got?" pointing to the single bag Fred was carrying.

"You said it was all I needed."

"It is, no doubt. This is no place for formal attire. We'll get a cab, and then we'll get you into some proper clothes and feed you"

To Fred, everything was new, strange, and amazing, but nothing so amazing as the sprawling, exuberant city. He had heard of Tel Aviv in terms of a spread of sand dunes upon which some Jewish settlers had put down the beginnings of a village in 1909. Nothing had prepared him for the miles of streets, the thousands of people who thronged the sidewalks, the buses, the bumper-to-bumper traffic, the noise and smell and confusion, the haphazard stucco houses interspersed with towering skyscrapers. It was neither beautiful nor inspiring; but it was marvelously alive. The room Sam had rented in a Mrs. Segal's house, rooms to let, was small, reasonably clean, and cool, something to be valued in the shimmering heat of the city. She had improvised a cot, squeezed in alongside of Sam's bed. Sam told his cousin, in a fit of generosity: "The bed is yours."

"You're all heart," Fred told him, "but I'll take it. You're the host, boy."

Mrs. Segal hovered over them, looking suspiciously at the tall, blond-bearded young man who had been introduced as Sam Cohen's cousin. After Fred had changed into blue jeans and a sport shirt, they walked to Dizengoff Street. At one of the outdoor cafés, Sam ordered pita stuffed with various exotic fillings and beer for both of them.

"Good beer," he told Fred, "and good food, too, if you stick to his kind of thing and don't look for any haute cuisine, which is usually lousy. Well, what do you think?"

"It's one hell of a jumping place." He bit into the overstuffed pita. "This is good. What about wine?"

"Forget it. Too sweet for the most part, but if you're that hooked on wine, you can buy French or Italian—at a price. I watch my money, sort of. I haven't taken a nickel from mom since I'm over here. It's my madness, and I figure I should pay for it."

"How did you manage that?"

"I sold the boat before I left."

"Oh, no. You sold it. You dumb kid. Why?"

"Makes me feel better—or something. Anyway, it kills me to take money from my mother. This way, I have enough to take me through another year, and then it'll be either medical school here or in the States. The truth is, I'd just as soon go back now, but mom gets crazy at the thought of me being drafted. O.K., I can understand that, after what she's been through, and I suppose that if you grow up as the son of Barbara Lavette, you're a pacifist. I don't quarrel with that. But try being a pacifist in Israel." He pointed to boys sitting around with their dates, boys in uniform, their guns across their knees. "Just look around you."

"I wondered about that."

"*Zahel.* That's the army. It's a tiny country, so mobilization has to be instantaneous. They get a day's leave, they have to take their weapons with them. A great place to be a pacifist. Somehow, they got onto the fact that Bernie Cohen was my father, and they ran a big story about him in the Jerusalem *Post* and about me being a student here."

"Still, as an American cititzen, you're exempt, aren't you?"

"I am. And I suppose as premed, I'd stay in school no matter what. But here, no one is exempt, When it happens, it's everywhere. Well, I don't worry about that, and I'm still exempt at home, and if it gives mom peace, O.K."

"And the rest of it—how's it been?"

"Interesting. The truth is, I like it. I'm all in one piece. Oh, I get homesick, so damn homesick I could cry, and then I'd give anything, anything to be back in San Francisco. I couldn't live here. I don't think I could live anywhere I couldn't see the bay, but I've been able to work out some things. I have a history professor who calls me Shmuel ha Cohen—which roughly translated means Samuel the priest. And damn it, I learned the language. It's a mean language to learn, but beautiful, simple, logical. And talking of language, we have a date tonight. Mine is an Israeli, a Sabra, which means she's native-born. Miriam by name. She works at the museum. Her friend is an archaeological student from Pittsburgh who's one of the volunteers at a dig up north in Megiddo and is down here for a few days to do research at the museum."

"You've left no stone unturned, have you?"

"Ah, well, Freddie, I do my best. We have three days here before we take off to see the country, and I don't want you bored. Now tell me about yourself."

"What's to tell? French food and French wine. My French is probably no better than your Hebrew, but I have taken a course in wine. You name it, I've been there—Corbières, Minervois, Languedoc, Gaillac, Bordeaux, Armagnac, Cahors; you might say I'm the world's greatest smart-ass walking encyclopedia on the subject; Médocs, Graves, Champagnes, Sauternes, Chablis, Nuits—I could go on and on, which only means that when I get home, I'll be more intolerable than ever. I've been in love three times. One I almost married, and thank God her father hated me. There are parts of France where they still obey their fathers. A lot of guilt. I enjoyed it too much. My mother is as crazy as yours on this Vietnam business. But enough is enough. Come September, I'm going home."

"And the draft?"

"The hell with it. I'll take my chances."

"You heard about Ruby Truaz?"

"I heard. More guilt. It stinks, Sammy, it stinks to high heaven. This is a war being fought by the poor and the dispossessed. Kids who can hide in the universities or abroad—you and me as explicit examples— get out of it. Those who can't, go."

"Which doesn't make this Vietnam obscenity any less obscene. Anyway, we still haven't been called."

"And when you are?"

"God knows. In any case, Freddie my lad, we're not going to settle the problems of the world. We have our own. We're going to walk and hitch our way from here to Galilee, and tonight, we have a date with two very cute chicks."

They had dinner that night in a Yemeni restaurant in old Jaffa, which adjoins Tel Aviv to the south. Miriam was a tiny, dark-haired, pretty young woman of twenty. Her friend was Rita Hogan, a tall, slender, freckled Irish Catholic archaeologist with red hair and unlimited enthusiasm about everything Israeli. Before the evening was over, Fred was in love again.

The women filled Barbara's living room, which was both small and narrow, the complaint lodged most often against the old wooden house that survived on the San Francisco hills. There were Sally, May Ling, Eloise, Clair Levy, Jean Lavette, Carla Truaz, Ruth Adams, and Shela Abramson. Ruth Adams was a professor of economics at Berkeley and Shela Abramson was the wife of a manufacturer of plumbing supplies. Both of these women were old friends of Barbara's;

years before, they had given her money for the hospital in Toulouse which she had helped support. Now, on this evening late in June of 1966, they drank coffee, sipped brandy, and listened.

"I'm embarrassed," Barbara told them. "I am not even the victim of a legitimate delusion. The truth is that for more nights than I care to remember, I talked myself to sleep with a fantasy about how a group of determined women could help put a stop to this war. None of my thinking has been very logical lately, which I put down to a change of life or something of that sort. I tell my son to stay on in Israel with some rationale about keeping him out of Vietnam, which is an indication of how logically I've been thinking. Anyway, I began to believe my fantasy, but if most of you think I'm crazy, we can just spend a pleasant evening and go home."

"I think you're a bit crazy," Clair said, "but why not give it a try?"

"The thing is," Sally said, "that when you start working out these fantasies, you don't leave any loose ends hanging. I know. I'm a specialist in the field, and if my daughter wasn't here, I could really spin out one or two. But between a mother and a daughter—oh, the hell with that! Let's hear it, Bobby."

"It's very simple. Just something about mothers, there are so many of us."

"I love you," Ruth Adams said, "but that doesn't make much sense. Motherhood is as old as apple pie. Just as fattening, too."

"Not clever," said Shela Abramson. "Give the girl a chance."

"What I meant before," Sally told them, "is that if Bobby's been walking around with this fantasy and going to sleep with it instead of some good-looking young buck, she probably has the damn thing worked out. So let's listen."

"The trouble is, I don't have anything very much

301

worked out. I just had the feeling that no one has ever gone to mothers, there are so many of us. It's your son getting chopped up or blown to bits. How do you feel about it? I have a very strong feeling that it's always someone else's son. I've been reading and talking to people about this new women's movement, and a lot of them don't agree with me, but I have the conviction that the crux of it is war—the absolute definition of a man's world. They make us pregnant and there's the nine months of vomiting and trying to sleep with a belly that doesn't belong to you and screaming your guts out while you try to bring a new bit of life into this sorry world, and then these lunatics work out a solution for the whole thing in a place called Vietnam. Do I make any sense?"

"I have four sons," Shela Abramson said.

"But how do we make any difference?" Sally asked. "We live in a world where no one matters except the curious swine who run countries. None of us run countries. None of us matters a damn, and that's the plain truth. So we bewail the fact that we're mothers with sons. Who listens? Who cares?"

"Maybe no one cares," Eloise said. "The girls I know don't even talk about it. They talk about how rotten their marriages are and their shrinks and the new car and the pill. And the men are worse. I thought I knew Adam. He goes to pieces if one of the kids cuts himself or has to have a tonsillectomy or something like that, but when it comes to a war, he just shrugs it off. I care. If Bobby wants to scream, I'll scream with her. Even if no one listens."

"Can the old lady say something?" Jean asked.

Barbara looked at her mother with interest. When she first proposed that Jean join them, she was met with a stubborn refusal. "Do whatever you have to do, Bobby. But leave me out. I told you that if you needed money, I'd help. That's as far as I go. I am an enlightened reactionary, and I intend to remain so for the rest of my life." Finally, she gave in to Barbara's plea that she come and listen. No one should buy a pig in a poke, Barbara insisted. Now what? Barbara had ceased to anticipate her mother's actions years ago.

"In the first place," Jean said, "I have always voted Republican. I shall continue to do so, and my ideological position rests on my total distaste for Mr. Johnson and that dreadful little bald-headed Dean Rusk, who speaks for him. I also have two grandchildren of draft age. Very well. My husband, Dan Lavette, divided the population into two sorts. I must say that he enjoyed simplification more than I do, but nevertheless, in his case it worked. There were the movers and there were those who were moved. Danny used to get very impatient about the dreams everyone in town dreamed about the Golden Gate Bridge, which did not exist at that time. Talk, talk, talk. God damn it, he said once, if I wanted to do it, I'd do it. How would he do it? In his terms, he'd bull it through. Talk a group of engineers into laying it out on spec, and then take the specifications and raise the money. And if he had wanted to, he would have done it. A thing in motion, he always insisted, gathers accretion. Now don't you think that the things you are saying are being said in a million homes around the country? I assure you. But it's talk, talk, talk. This country is full of mothers. If you think it's going to make an iota of difference in this wretched war, then reach out to them."

"And what do we tell them?" Ruth Adams asked.

Barbara was asking herself, once again, how it was that one has a mother for half a century and more and knows almost nothing about her. Was the reverse also true? Were they all strangers to each other?"

"Barbara?"

"Do you know," she said slowly. "I'm not sure that we have to tell them anything—I mean at this moment. They know it," thinking that if her mother knew it so clearly, it was hardly a secret. "I think that if we make them aware of each other, that would be a beginning. Afterwards, there will be other things."

"But what are we? Are we an organization?"

"If we are," Shela Abramson said, "and if Barbara goes to jail again, we all go. No more fancy quixotic nobility."

"No one will go to jail," Barbara said. "I've discussed it thoroughly with my lawyers. We will not go to jail. I assure you."

"Famous last words."

"I still want to know what we are."

"We're women. Isn't that enough?"

"Not quite," Clair said. "We have to declare ourselves, and that means a place, an address, a telephone number, and of course a name."

"This can be the place," Barbara answered, "and the telephone is here. As for a name—" She turned to Carla Truaz. "You and May Ling haven't said a word all evening. Do you like the idea?"

"Yes, I do," Carla said softly.

"What would you name it?"

Carla hesitated, uneasy in front of the faces turned toward her, staring at her hands. "I couldn't—I can't think of a name."

"Try," Barbara said gently. "You've been listening to all of us talking our heads off."

"Well—I think—well, just Mothers for Peace."

"That's lovely," someone said. "Mothers for Peace."

"And if you had to have a slogan?" Barbara urged her.

"Oh—I couldn't think of a slogan, Miss Lavette." Suddenly, she was at the point of tears, "I don't really know what a slogan is, I mean what you mean by a slogan."

"It's very simple, my dear. In just a few words, it's what we want to tell people. It's something we want to tell everyone. If you could, Carla, if you could talk to everyone in the world—" Now they were silent and attentive, watching the Mexican girl. She closed her eyes to stop the tears. "If you could, what would you say?"

In just a whisper, "War is bad."

May Ling, sitting beside her, put her arm around Carla and wiped away the tears. "She's right," May Ling said. "War is bad—for children and all living creatures."

In four days of leisurely walking, Sam and Fred covered the distance between Tel Aviv and Megiddo. They carried knapsacks, wore shorts and sneakers, and cheated on their determination to see the land on foot only once, when they accepted a ride from a truckload of boys and girls returning to a kibbutz. Most of the ride was occupied with an attempt to find an appropriate Hebrew translation of the name Frederick. It failed, but they did ride for eighteen kilometers. They were fed at the kibbutz and afterwards there was a dance. The next morning, they were off again, turning inland from the seacoast at Hadera. "I've found it," Fred said. "This is it. I marry Rita Hogan and turn Jewish. This place needs me. I can teach them how to make drinkable wine."

"You and Moses. He found water, you give them wine. Rita Hogan is a Catholic and you're some kind of WASP."

"Circumcised."

"You're not serious?"

"Who knows?" Fred said. "I haven't had this much fun in years. I like it. It's my kind of place. You know that girl last night that I was having the heavy discussion with?"

"The one with the big boobs?"

"That's all you ever think about. Well, what do you think we were arguing about?"

"Sex."

"Not at all, sonny. These kibbutz chicks are not pushovers. We were discussing Graves's translation of

Suetonius, which she had just read—in English, cousin. Just imagine a farm girl at home reading Suetonius in Hebrew."

"Why on God's earth would a farm girl in California read Suetonius in Hebrew? If she could find one in Hebrew."

"You don't read me at all."

"Only too well. Did you make out?"

"I told you. You don't make out with these chicks."

"I do."

"Big talk. Did you ever try on a kibbutz?"

"I don't go for country lasses. You figure Rita Hogan to turn Jewish and live on a kibbutz with you?"

"Who knows?"

"How many times have you been in love, Freddie?"

"I don't count. I enjoy being in love."

They walked on. Sam became silent, looking about him curiously as they walked, his face tight. When Fred asked him what was on his mind, he shook his head, almost in anger.

"What is it, kid? Something I said? You know the way I talk."

Sam shook his head. Then, after a moment or two, "Somewhere—probably in sight of where we are—" He waved at the rock-strewn hills. "Here's where my father was killed, back in 'forty-eight. Probably no more than a mile or two from where we are."

"You don't know exactly?"

"No way to know." He pointed to a kibbutz in the distance, the green rows of tillage, the buildings, and the orchards. "There—and there," pointing to another block of fields and groves. "None of it was here in 'forty-eight. I don't know why I should want to know where it happened, but somehow I do. They were four of them, my father, an American, name of Brodsky, who was with him in the Spanish war, and two Israelis. All of them killed by the Arabs. A senseless, tiny piece of war, as senseless as most war. Not even recorded anywhere. I tried to track it down. No way. He fought through the Spanish war and then six years in the British army in World War Two, and then to die here. Why? Who was he? I've lived my whole life with all the heavy shit of being a hero's son. Heroes. I could have had a father."

"I can see why you had to come here," Fred said.

"I dream about him. I've seen pictures of him, but in the dreams, he has no face."

At the Megiddo dig, Rita Hogan found them a supply tent where they could bed down for the night, and informed them, with great excitement, that she had managed a day off to show them around the ruins. "I don't truly have it coming. I've used up all my off days. But Bert Meadows—he's the boss here—is a good guy and let himself be talked into it. You can also eat at the mess tonight."

"What do they pay you here?" Sam asked.

"Pay me? I'm a volunteer. They only charge me three dollars a day for food."

"They're all heart, aren't they?"

"You're not an archaeologist."

"Just a confused premedical student."

"If you were," Rita said, "You'd know what a privilege it is just to be allowed to work here."

"Don't mind Sammy," Fred said. "No romance and no higher thoughts. Here we are at the navel of civilization, and all he can think of is money. He's a barbarian."

The barbarian walked behind, watching them with interest as Rita guided them through the dig. It was a beautiful day, hot, clear, the sky overhead like a burnished blue steel plate, the wide plain of Megiddo shimmering in the summer heat. Here was the ultimate symbol of war, the battlefield of the ages—*Har Megiddo* in Hebrew, which St. John transliterated as Armageddon—where the final combat would be fought. As always, day in and day out, as in all his days in Israel, Sam asked himself what he was, Jew or Gentile. Barbara's son or the son of the man who had died here. Not too far from this place, his father had paid the endless price of blood and still more blood. Did California exist? What did the fierce warriors who once long ago stood on this plain have to do with California—or with him? He was a tourist, the visitor, the observer, watching, noting, observing, here as on the streets of San Francisco or in the ivy-decked halls of Roxten Academy, belonging nowhere, trying to be a Jew and finding it the hardest thing he had ever attempted, watching Fred and Rita walking ahead of him, tall, slender, narrow-hipped, manufacturing in his mind a Jewish reaction, as he saw it, "A fine, blond *goyish* couple." Yet in twenty-four hours, Freddie had become more Jewish than he had managed in two years. Freddie threw himself into the place. He loved it, the food, the people, the deliberate lack of courtesy, the arrogant self-sufficiency. Yet Freddie had fought no such inner battles as his own. Freddie had a Jewish stepfather whom he adored; his life was programmed precisely in the vine-covered slopes of Napa; Freddie was Jew or Gentile without pain or discomfort. Freddie fell in love as easily as one put on a pair of shoes, and where, Sam asked himself, was his own love? Why had he found no one to love in two years? "This one is it," Freddie had informed him. "She is a great girl. I am absolutely going to marry her. Rita—that is a beautiful name. How do you translate it into Hebrew?"

"You don't," Sam replied sourly. "It's a damn *goyish* name, like yours."

Now the girl with the "damn *goyish* name" and the freckled arms and the flaming red hair was showing them the stables that had been excavated. "Solomon's stables," she said. "Room for nine hundred chariot horses. Can you imagine—nine hundred horses."

"They weren't built by Solomon," Sam said. "They were built by King Ahab, who was Jezebel's husband."

"I know that," Rita said. "But they're called Solomon's stables."

Fred was looking at him curiously. He felt foolish and abashed. "I'm sorry," he said. "I didn't mean to put you down, Rita."

"I know. Come on, I want to show you the Canaanite temple."

"I've been here before," Sam said. "You two go ahead. I'll catch up with you."

He sat on a stone, running his fingers over the carving on its surface. The stone was warm to his touch. "Damn you," he said softly, "you should have been here with me. God, I need you so much." But his father had no answer for him.

Phil Baker, who was executive editor of the Los Angeles *Morning World,* opened the door to Carson Devron's office, and asked him whether he had a few minutes to spare.

"All the time you need. What is it, Phil?"

"This came up from advertising. Kelly thought I should look at it. I think you should." He spread out on Carson's desk a proof of a full-page advertisement. "For tomorrow's edition."

The advertisement had a single picture; the rest was type. Carson recognized the picture. It had been taken years ago, during World War Two, perhaps before then, during Japan's invasion of China. It showed a naked infant, lying on a ruined street in a ruined city. The picture had become very well known during that time, printed and reprinted, and had become a staple in photography exhibitions. Across the top of the page, in large type:

MOTHERS FOR PEACE

And beneath: "We are a group of women who have come together to do our utmost to bring an end to the war in Vietnam and hopefully to all war. Our purpose is to make American mothers aware of the feelings of each other. In so doing, we propose to make our government aware of the fact that millions of women in this land oppose the war and cry out for peace. To this end, we offer a simple statement. If it appears to be a child's voice crying out in a dark wilderness, then we can only say that 'a child must lead them.' This is our statement:

'War is bad for children and other living creatures.' "

Beneath this was the picture of the infant, and beneath the photograph: "Can so quiet and gentle a statement become the loudest voice in the land? We think so, and we ask you to join with us in spreading our statement and our name across every state in this land. Write to us. We will supply you with lapel buttons, bumper stickers, posters, and banners. If you wish to help financially, send us whatever you can. If you cannot afford to send a contribution, we will send whatever material you need free of charge."

It was signed with Barbara's name, and with the names of five other women. Carson recognized the name of Sally Lavette, Barbara's sister-in-law. The other names were strange to him. The address was Barbara's address on Green Street.

Carson turned to Baker. "I've looked at it. Well?"

"Do we run it?"

"Is their credit in question?"

"It came with a check."

"Then why the devil are you asking me whether we run it? Since when do we turn away business?" Carson asked harshly.

"Come on, Carson, don't chop my head off. You know that editorially we've been careful as hell about this lousy war."

"This isn't editorial. This is advertising. We've run antiwar advertisements."

"Little ones. This is a full page."

"Well, what in hell difference does that make?"

"The old man——"

Carson cut him off sharply. "My father doesn't run this paper. I do!"

Baker nodded, turned on his heel, and left the office. Carson sat at his desk, staring at the proof sheet in front of him. For perhaps ten minutes, he sat there, and then he got up and left his office. On his way out, he said to his secretary, "Call my wife and tell her that I had to go up to San Francisco. I'll be back tonight. I don't know what time."

"Where can you be reached, Mr. Devron?"

"I can't be reached. The paper will survive."

He got to the airport in time for the ten-thirty plane, and then, once on the plane, began to regret the impetuosity of his action. What did it mean? Had he been waiting all these months for an excuse to see Barbara? Could he be indulging in anything so childish? Why had Phil Baker brought the proof sheet to him? Was it because anything that had to do with Barbara Lavette was still recognized as his province, his interest? He solved none of his inner problems by the time the plane landed, whereupon he relaxed and decided to let the day play itself out. He knew what he intended to do, even if he did not know why he proposed to do it.

Like so many men, Carson created illusionary islands of changelessness. Certain things must remain as they are, one of them being the house on Green Street. Let him be divorced from his wife and married to another woman, yet a pocket of memory would remain untouched, and in that mood he left the taxi that had brought him from the airport and walked up the old wooden steps of Barbara's house and reached out to press the bell button. A printed card stopped him. "The door is open. Please enter." While he stood reading this, two women pushed by him and went into the house. He followed them into a bedlam of women, noise, and activity. The furniture in the small living

311

room had been pushed back against the wall, and a long board table on trestles had been set up for the length of the room. Eight women sat at this table, four on either side, with piles of papers, envelopes, cards, and stamps. In the breakfast room, three young women were operating a mimeograph machine. Over the entrance to the dining room, a large card announced: "Information here." In what he could see of the dining room, there were two women typing and at least half a dozen others milling around. At his right, as he stood in the tiny hallway, were two open cartons of lapel buttons, the boxes further decreasing the size of the entranceway and forcing him to press back against the wall to allow another woman to pass by him. From the kitchen, someone was shouting, "Coffee! Who's for coffee?" While from upstairs, high-pitched to be heard above the bedlam, a voice called: "Alice! Will you get up here! We need help!"

He stepped into the living room and stood tentatively, conscious of more and more eyes turning to him, increasingly uneasy in the crowded room, grateful for Barbara's appearance at that moment, coming down the staircase and noticing him. She went to him and took his hand and kissed his cheek, "How very nice to see you. What brings you to our madhouse?"

"I had to be in town," he lied, and then retracted the lie. "No, I didn't have to be here. I came to talk to you. Can we have lunch?"

She hesitated for just a moment, then nodded and said, "Of course, Carson. Talking anywhere in this shambles would be impossible. Give me just a moment to tie up a few loose ends and get my jacket, and I'll be with you."

Barbara felt a need to stretch her legs, so they walked down the hill to the Embarcadero, and then to Gino's on Jones Street. It was a fine, cool day, windy enough to raise little whitecaps across the bay yet pleasant enough to fill the Embarcadero with tourists.

Walking with Barbara, Carson felt a sudden and elated sense of freedom, like a small boy indulging in truancy, freedom laced with just enough guilt to give it added zest. The clean, sweet Pacific air, the great, wide vista of the bay, the colors of the summer dresses of the tourists and the white houses climbing the marvelous hills—all of it filled him with exuberance. "Why don't I live here?" he asked Barbara. "Why do I live in that smog-filled city in the south?"

"Rhetorical questions never call for an answer, do they? I imagine every tourist on the Embarcadero asks the same thing. Our population doesn't increase."

"You don't want it to. You're the most clannish people in the country with the loveliest city in the country, and you want to keep it just as it is."

In the restaurant, studying Carson's tanned, youthful face, Barbara asked him, "Why did you come here, Carson?"

"To give you this." He took a check out of his pocket and handed it to her.

"What is this?"

"The price of your advertisement."

"You mean you're not going to run it?"

"Of course we're going to run it. You'll see it in tomorrow's paper."

"Then this," she said, staring at the check. "I don't understand this at all. Why are you giving it to me?"

"Because I don't want you to pay for an ad in my paper."

"Why not? You run a business, not a charity."

"Let's just say it's my contribution. You do take contributions. Your advertisement asks for them."

"Yes, we do take contributions," Barbara said slowly. "From people who sympathize with what we are trying to do."

"I didn't know you had conditions."

"I am only trying to understand why you are giving me a very large amount of money. Your paper has

313

fudged on this filthy war. You've found all sorts of reasons to not denounce it. You use that unspeakable phrase 'the body count' every day, as if we were killing flies, not people."

"Yes, that's true."

"Then why?"

"Couldn't you put it down to the fact that I loathe Lyndon Baines Johnson and that stable of male whores who work for him?"

"Because he's a Democrat and the Devrons are true dyed-in-the-wool Republicans."

"Is that really what you think of me?"

"No. No, I'm sorry I said that. It was rude and undeserved."

"Will you take the check?"

"Of course I will," Barbara said, smiling. "You're a dear, Carson." She put the check in her purse. "This and anything else you want to add to it. I have no scruples about that. In spite of that beehive of activity you just saw, we are poverty-stricken. We spend money much faster than it comes in. We're running that ad in the New York *Times* and in the Washington *Post*. We've taken a hundred radio spots, and we've printed a hundred thousand bumper stickers and two hundred thousand leaflets. We have a volunteer office in New York and another in Chicago, and we're going to open branches in Los Angeles and in Washington. We supply them all with material. Last week, we spent eighteen hundred dollars on postage alone. My sister-in-law Sally, who was once a film star and who has dreamed for years of some way to get out of being a Napa housewife, is traveling around the country, doing TV interviews and talking about what we are trying to do. That meant hiring a public relations outfit to arrange the interviews and paying her way as well. That's only the flashy stuff. The real thing is our correspondence, and I haven't even touched on that. We are getting five hundred letters a day, and we think that in another month it may be a thousand."

"And you did that all yourself?"

"Never, never, Carson." She shook her head with annoyance. "What you saw in my house was a light day. When the weather's as good as this, most volunteers don't come in. But we have volunteers, dozens of them, and they're wonderful, simply wonderful."

"I've never seen you like this. I've never seen you so excited about anything."

"I am excited about it. When we started, it was only a sop to my conscience. In my wildest dreams, I never thought it could work like this."

"But where does the money come from? It must be costing you a fortune?"

"It is. My mother gave me fifty thousand dollars."

"Your mother? You're telling me that the dowager queen of Russian Hill gave fifty thousand dollars to an antiwar organization?"

"That's exactly what I am telling you. And it's not tax-deductible. Those rats at the Internal Revenue Service will not give us a tax-deductible status, so raising money is like pulling teeth. I've never been in anything like this before, and believe me, it's a total education."

"But your mother?"

"I know. I put up twenty thousand dollars of my own money, and I think that shamed her into it."

"Where the devil did you get twenty thousand dollars?"

"My book is selling like mad. I don't need the money. Other friends of mine put up almost a hundred thousand more, and some money comes in every day, dollar bills, five-dollar bills. A woman in Kansas whose son died in Vietnam sent us his back pay, which she received from the army, over a thousand dollars. And a young woman who works with us—her name is Carla

Truaz, she's a Chicana—put in her savings, four hundred and twelve dollars. I call that blessed money."

The food came; Carson sat staring at Barbara in amazement. "Please eat," she told him. "You've just enriched me, so my afternoon is well spent. And we've talked enough about me. I haven't seen you since your marriage."

"No, you haven't."

"I'm sure she's a wonderful person."

"That's specious, Barbara. You've never met her."

"Are you unhappy, Carson?"

"I'm dutifully married, and I have a nine-month-old son, so I've paid my dues to the Devrons," he said bitterly. "If you feel that I've been disloyal by using your advertisement as an excuse to come up here, you're probably right. In what remains of our ethics, disloyalty is less frowned upon than infidelity. I wanted to see you. I desperately wanted to see you."

"I'm sorry, Carson. I'm so damned sorry."

"The thing is," he said hopelessly, "that I'm fond of her. She's a decent person."

"And very beautiful," Barbara said. "I saw her picture in the paper."

"Yes, she's good-looking."

"And if she could see us here, Carson, she would be very rightfully puzzled by your attraction to a scrawny middle-aged woman, whose hair is rapidly turning gray."

"You're not scrawny."

"Bless your heart, Carson, dear man. I love you very much. I always will. That doesn't change. Only fools and egotists believe that love must be reserved to one person."

"Thank you, Barbara," he said quietly.

"And now, will you eat your lunch?"

"Absolutely. One thing, I'd like to send someone up to do a story on your organization."

"Sure. Why not? We want all the publicity we can get, good or bad."

"It will be good."

Austin Campbell was a Texan, of whom it was said that he had no other ambition than to serve the President. In his prior life as a private citizen, he had amassed many millions of dollars in the oil business, and being an old and trusted friend of the President, he was in a unique position to aid him. He had a small office in the White House, ready access to the President, and to use the newspaper cliché, he maintained a very low profile. He was a stout, jolly man with many chins and a small pug nose, given to wide-brimmed Stetsons and expensive high-heeled boots. Tom Lavette's knowledge of Campbell was limited. He had never met him, but from all he had heard of the man, he had reason to respect him. When Campbell's secretary called from Washington and suggested that Campbell, who would be on the West Coast, would like to meet with Mr. Lavette, Tom readily agreed.

Campbell came into Tom's office with a country boy's expression of respect and admiration. He shook hands with Tom warmly and then looked around the oversized, expensively furnished office. "Well, this is something," he said approvingly. "Down there in Washington, they give me a little cubbyhole a man can't properly blow his nose in. I like that Jackson Pollock you got over there," pointing to an enormous canvas on one wall. "It is a Pollock?"

"It is, yes," telling himself, "Careful. Don't be taken in by the cowboy boots."

Campbell walked to the big picture windows that opened to a view of the bay, the Golden Gate Bridge, and the Marin County hills. "Well now, this is something. This is one damn fine little city you got here, Tom. You don't mind my calling you Tom?"

Tom shook his head, controlling his annoyance. The

first-name gambit was a ploy he despised. It was a cop trick. Call a man by his first name and you break down the first barrier to a stranger.

"Would you like a drink?" Tom asked him.

"Well, just a touch of bourbon, a little branch water. No ice."

Tom pressed a button that brought a bar out of the wall, made Campbell the drink, took nothing for himself, with the explanation that it was too early in the day, and then sat on the edge of his desk, while Campbell made himself comfortable in a black leather Eames chair.

"Thomas," Campbell said, "the President thought we might have a little chat. We both know you're a strong man in the opposition party, but then the President met your daddy some years back and he has fond memories of Big Dan Lavette, so just let's put the party thing aside for one minute. The President's carrying a big burden, a mighty big burden. No one wants to end this Vietnam business more than he does, but God Almighty, it has to be ended leaving us with a passel of honor and dignity and without handing Southeast Asia over lock, stock, and barrel to those slant-eyed bastards in China. So how do you suppose he feels with our best and finest over there, laying down their lives and being knifed in the back on the home front?"

"It's a difficult situation," Tom agreed.

"Damn difficult, with those college kids going crazy all over the country and with Fulbright putting a knife in his back and twisting it. Well, that comes with the job, but now there's a new boy in town. Or should I say a new girl? How do you deal with motherhood? It's like apple pie or Coca-Cola. But this time, it's like a damn plague." He paused and looked at Tom questioningly, inviting a response.

"I don't quite follow you," Tom said deliberately.

"I'm talking about your sister's organization, since

318

you want me to spell it out. It's called Mothers for Peace."

"Yes, I've heard of it. I can't imagine it's large enough to be bothersome. There are other antiwar organizations."

"Tom, it is bothersome. More than that, it's a goddamn pain in the ass. It may have started out as some kind of chickenshit quilting party here in your town, but now it's sure as hell all over the country and spreading like the measles. They've even opened an office just a hoot and holler away from the White House. Now—"

Tom started to interrupt him, but Campbell brushed his words aside. "Now you just listen a moment, Tom. These biddies are putting a rod right up our ass. We can deal with the kids and we can deal with the commies, but this mother thing hurts. We want it stopped. You've been in the game, and I don't have to hand you any bullshit."

"And just how do you expect me to stop it?"

"It's your sister."

Tom smiled for the first time since Campbell had entered his office. "Do you know my sister?"

"I have not had that pleasure."

"If you had, you would understand that she's not amenable to pressure. I have no influence over her, none whatsoever."

"Well then, I would respectfully suggest that you change that situation."

"How?"

"That, son, is your problem."

"Mr. Campbell, I'm fifty-four. How old are you?"

"Oh, I got five or six years on you."

"Not enough to be my father," Tom said coldly. "I resent being called son, by you or anyone. I resent first names, used by people I have never met before."

Campbell studied him thoughtfully, then nodded. "All right, Mr. Lavette. I must have considered I was down home. I guess you got your own ways here, and since we are going to be cold and snotty, just let me say my piece and go. You run a considerable fleet of tankers." He reached into his jacket pocket and took out a small notebook. "In the past twelve months," he said, leafing through the pages, "you have delivered to Vietnam, under army contract, some three hundred and eighty million dollars of petroleum, fuel oil, and gasoline. There is also a cargo item, apart from the petroleum—runs to sixty-two million. That's a nice piece of business, Mr. Lavette. Just think about it." And with that, he got up, smiled, and walked out of Tom's office.

That evening, at dinner, Tom related the incident to his wife, Lucy. The years had not dealt too well with Lucy; she was four years older than Tom, a tall, dry, thin-lipped woman. Their marriage was strangely loveless, each grudgingly giving the other something deeply felt and needed. She was his mother, and with her he was no longer the firm tycoon, the mover of mountains, the cold and unapproachable Thomas Lavette, but very often a suppliant child, wavering between dependence and hatred; and she was his unhappily tolerated rock and support. She comforted him now, regarding him with a mixture of affection and contempt.

"But what do I do? That fat, oily bastard put his finger where it hurts most. But what do I do?"

"Let me think about it. I'll find a way."

"To influence Barbara? I doubt it."

"Don't doubt me, Thomas," she said gently, smiling at what was as close to humor as she ever came. "Things can be made difficult for her."

"She is my sister."

"We don't kill people. We're not the Mafia. There are more civilized ways."

"I hope so. I do hope so."

It was not until late in October that Carson called

Barbara from Los Angeles and informed her that he was sending a feature writer to San Francisco to do the story on Mothers for Peace. Barbara had just returned to San Francisco. She had been scheduled to meet Sam in Israel in September, but then he changed his plans and decided to spend the last week in August in Paris with Fred. Barbara flew to Paris with Eloise, her first visit to the city since the years she had spent there prior to World War Two. It was a very different place, and Barbara found that instead of the emotional turbulence she had half anticipated, she was strangely unmoved, as if she were visiting a place she had never been to before. Except for her pleasure at seeing her son, she reacted with the detachment of a tourist; or perhaps Sam's reaction to her obscured everything else. It was a year since she had last seen him. He had broadened, filled out; and with his face burned deep brown by the sun, his blue eyes appeared lighter than ever, the blue of winter ice. The eyes more than anything else brought back the image of his father, and as with his father, they appeared to be clouded with doubt, with some deep inner uncertainty. She could detect no happiness in his decision to finish his premedical training in Israel, nor could she get him to explain what unanswered questions still haunted him. Afterwards, she felt that the time with him could have been better but modified that feeling with an acknowledgment that it could have been worse. She could remember quite clearly her own emotions when she was his age.

Eloise, on the other hand, found her world shaking violently. First, she was introduced by Fred to a long-limbed, red-headed archaeologist named Rita Hogan who, as he informed her, had consented to be his wife. On top of that, Fred announced that war or no war, they were both returning to the States. Eloise, who had experienced a few weeks of grateful respite from her merciless headaches, now fell prey to them again. Barbara was relieved when the two of them were on the plane and homeward bound. Fred and Rita were to follow a week or so later.

"It's not simply that she's a Catholic and her father's a steelworker," Eloise complained. "I could live with that. But she's dragging him back to the States, and he could be drafted."

"Eloise, my dear, he could be drafted in Europe, if it comes to that, and it may well be that she's pregnant, which means that as a father, he won't be drafted."

"He only met her two months ago," Eloise wailed.

"That's time enough, if I know Freddie," wondering why it couldn't have been that simple with Sam. Her son was haunted by ghosts, and her heart ached with her inability to reach him, to touch him, to convince him that it was all right, that he was what he was.

They parted in New York, Eloise to go on to San Francisco, while Barbara began a round of lecture dates, New York, Boston, and then a long seminar in Chicago. Wherever she went, there were women reaching out to her and to each other. And then, finally back in San Francisco, she found the center of it, the volunteers in her house on Green Street, totally out of funds, broke and in a near panic. That was when Carson called to tell her that their best lady feature writer, Gertrude Simpson, would be in San Francisco the following day. "Barbara," he assured her, "it can be one hell of a story. We'll run it page one, column one, in the Sunday edition. And Gert's a doll. She's all with you."

"Carson," Barbara said, determined to be shameless, "you're a sweet dear man. We need the story. But more than that, we need money. We are absolutely broke and absolutely desperate. You have so many friends down there who are richer than God, and I've learned how to beg, believe me. If you could get a few of them together in a room and let me talk to them, women if possible, but men if there's nothing else? Could you?"

"Give me a week. I'll see what's possible."

Her next move was to Boyd Kimmelman's office. His face lit up when he saw her. "Bobby! My God, I've missed you!" It was good to be held in a man's arms, to be crushed in an embrace, to be kissed, to feel at least for a moment like a woman treasured, coveted and protected, to have a fleeting fantasy of being a wife with no more obligations than the life of a middle-aged housewife entailed. "When did you get back?"

"Last night. Do you know, I almost went to your apartment. I went home and opened the door and pushed my way in through the cartons, the desks and tables and smell of stale cigarette smoke—and would you believe it, they were collating papers all over my bed, and I was almost ready to turn around and march over to your place."

"Why didn't you?"

"How did I know you'd be alone?"

"I don't believe you. You couldn't think of anything that rotten."

"Don't you believe it. I've been neck-deep in the women's movement for three weeks."

"And what about Paris?"

"Would you believe it, Boyd—it left me cold. Even the ghosts die in thirty years. I thought the memory of Marcel would tear my heart to shreds, but the memory was no different there than here. Oh, it was good to hear French again, to speak French, and to see Sammy. But the wall was there between us. I couldn't climb over it."

"Give it time."

"How long? I feel so old and tired."

"You don't look old and you don't look tired. Let's have dinner tonight with the tourists at the Top of the Mark, and we'll look at the city and remember the old things and pretend that we're exactly as young as we feel—if you can bear to part with the stale cigarette smoke?"

"I can bear it. But right now, old friend, I need help

323

desperately. We are broke. We owe the printers and we owe our paper people and we even owe the people we rent the typewriters and copying machines from. Can we get a loan? Do you know some friendly, open-hearted banker?"

Boyd began to laugh.

"Don't laugh at me. I want help."

"Dear Barbara, you're an impossible risk. You spend money but you don't earn any. An outfit like yours is always in the red. The kindest, most incompetent banker in the world would not lend you twenty cents."

"Thank you."

Boyd went to his desk, opened his checkbook, scribbled in it, and then handed Barbara a check.

"What's this?"

"Five thousand dollars."

"Absolutely not!" she exclaimed. "I didn't come to you for money. I came for advice, for guidance, and like all men in this wretched society, you buy out." She threw the check down on his desk. "And you don't even agree with me. I've argued myself hoarse on this question—with you."

"That's not so," he said quietly. "Give me credit for having enough intelligence to learn. I've learned more from you than from anyone I know. You have no right to say what you did."

After a long moment or two, Barbara nodded.

He picked up the check. "Will you take it?"

She reached out and took it.

"Dinner tonight?"

"Yes." She came around the desk, bent, kissed his cheek, and then left.

Back at the house on Green Street, Gertrude Simpson was waiting for Barbara. She was a small, thin woman, with bright eyes and a tangle of gray hair. She was a chain-smoker, her fingers yellow with nicotine stain, and she took her notes in shorthand, never asking the speaker to pause. She greeted Barbara enthusiastically. "I know you. I mean, I've read your books. That's the way to know someone. Still, I'll bug you to death with questions. Can we find somewhere quiet in this madhouse?"

Barbara led her upstairs to Sam's bedroom, the only room that remained sacrosanct. "My son's room," she explained. "He's in Israel at Hebrew University, trying to find himself or his soul or just being his twenty years. His father was Jewish," she added.

"I have the background. We have a file of clips and I studied them. Call me Gert—everyone else does. I'll call you Barbara—you don't mind? This is one lovely operation you got going. On the plane up here, I was trying to remember what Abe Lincoln said when he met Harriet Beecher Stowe—'So you're the little lady who split a nation and started this war' or something like that. I was going to reverse it for a lead, but it wouldn't work."

"It certainly wouldn't," Barbara agreed. "*Uncle Tom's Cabin* may have started the Civil War, but we'd be fools to imagine that our little pinpricks could end this one."

"It's helping, it's certainly helping. Now, for a couple of hours before you came in, I was talking to your volunteers. Nice ladies. But what surprised me is that most of them said more or less the same thing. Sure, they're interested in your project. They hate the war and they hate the thought of their kids being maimed or killed. But more than that, they expressed a real sense of release. They talked about their frustration at being housewives, at being turned into college-educated zombies, at being locked out of life, because they don't see waxing floors and doing the kids' laundry and cooking their husbands' dinner as any valid expression of existence. Not all of them, but a good many. This way, even if they're only stuffing envelopes, they have a feeling that they are part of something broader. Four of them feel that their husbands are total idiots who don't have the vaguest notion of what goes on, in Vietnam or anywhere else. A lot of anger. A lot of it directed against their husbands. Even when they didn't come right out with it, I could sense it. One of them has two sons, sixteen and eighteen. She talked about her life, bringing them up." She referred to her notes. " 'I'd wake them up, dress them, feed them breakfast, wash the dishes, clean the house, start dinner. When they got older, they were off to school. Nothing changed. I never talked to them about real life or war or this lousy mess all around us because I never knew anything. And my husband didn't talk, not to them, not to me. I became a glazed, functioning moron, informed by TV commercials that I was the most fortunate woman on earth.' Now that's damned interesting, isn't it?"

"You haven't wasted any time," Barbara acknowledged.

"You're not upset about this line I'm taking?"

"Good God, no! It's all the same thing."

"I was hoping you'd say that. Now, your own case is different. You're a very important, successful, well-known, and occasionally notorious woman. From what I've researched, you've never been a part of this burgeoning feminist movement—until you addressed that meeting in New York last spring. Is that what converted you?"

"I haven't been converted, by which I mean that I've never had an opportunity to accept my role as housewife. I did for a while, in the two years between my marriage to my husband and his death—that is, my first husband. I'm not sure that was a very happy time, and I suppose you know enough about my marriage to your boss to know that was not a very happy time either. That's one part of it. The war is something else. I was born in nineteen fourteen, the year the First World

War began. I've lived my whole life with war. I was in Paris during the Spanish war, and the man I loved died as a result of that war. I saw Nazi Germany from the inside, and I was a war correspondent in World War Two. My husband died in the Israeli war in nineteen forty-eight. So you might say that my loathing of this practice of mutual mass murder that men have developed has become something of an obsession with me. I say men advisedly, because as I see it, the practice of warfare has been an integral part of the crazy macho ideology that men live by."

"And you tie this into the oppression of women?"

"Of course I do. The woman bears the child, nurses it, feeds it, raises it, and then the man feeds the child into his death machine and kills it."

"Isn't that somewhat simplistic?"

"It is. If you try to take the complexity of human history and squeeze it into a sentence or two, it becomes very simplistic."

"All right. That makes you a feminist. How do you feel about men?"

"Compared to what? It's all we have, isn't it? I couldn't live without loving a man or being loved by a man."

"And you see no contradiction there?"

"No. The feminist movement is not anti-male. It's a struggle against a very ancient oppression."

"With no necessity to hate the oppressor?"

"No, because the oppression destroys more men than it does women. One can't be free without the other. In any case, we can never do it alone, only with the help of the men."

"O.K., Barbara," she said. "Lets switch tracks. Enough of feminism. Let's talk about Mothers for Peace. How did it begin?"

At the Top of the Mark that evening, with the lights of the city below them like a gargantuan jewel in a setting of limitless, inky darkness, Barbara confessed to Boyd that she was indecently content. "Which has been my curse all along, low-priced contentment. Gert Simpson, who is much brighter than I ever could hope to be, sees me as angry and discontented. She's wrong, of course."

"Of course."

"You agree with her."

"No," Boyd said, "I don't agree with her, but I also don't see you as any angel of contentment. At this moment, you're full of clam chowder and scallops and white wine—all of which help toward contentment. From where I sit, you're a very complex lady who mostly baffles me. You tell this Gertrude Simpson that you can't get along without loving a man or being loved by a man. When it comes to being loved by a man—well I can work that out. But loving a man? Are you sleeping with anyone else?"

"That's a very personal question."

"I'll rephrase it, as the gentlemen in the profession say. Do you love me?"

"At times."

"I'll settle for that. Why won't you marry me?"

"You haven't asked me in months now. Are you asking me now because I've been away?"

"Partly. I get lonely as hell when you're away. And partly to underline certain complexities of your character."

"It's not that complex, Boyd. I'm a year older than you. I've experienced my change of life, and in a few more years I'll be entirely gray. You'd want me to dye my hair."

"Never."

"Anyway," Barbara said, "I hope to pay you back that five thousand dollars next week."

"I don't want it."

"Let's say you'll take it and keep it until the next time I ask for money."

"And where is all this money coming from?"

"I'm going down to Los Angeles to talk to some people."

"Just like that?"

"No. Carson is setting it up for me."

"Carson?"

"Yes, we're still very good friends," And then, after a few minutes of silence, Barbara said, "Boyd, you're sulking. You're jealous."

"You're damn right I am!"

"He's comfortably married."

"Ha! Why not happily married?"

"Very few are."

"And just like that, the publisher of that rotten, warmongering jingoistic rag becomes a supporter of a women's peace movement."

"Perhaps he doesn't sleep well. He's doing a story on us."

"I'll suspend judgment until I see it."

Later that evening, in Boyd's apartment, lying in bed in his arms, Barbara said dreamily. "You know, it's not very complimentary to suggest that just because I happen to be in Los Angeles, I'd leap into bed with my ex-husband."

"I don't know. It's sort of complimentary to suggest that an old girl who'll be gray in a few years is so desirable that a handsome sonofabitch like Carson can't keep his hands off her."

"Go to hell," Barbara told him lazily.

In the morning, making breakfast in Boyd's kitchen, Barbara heard the telephone. "I'll get it," Boyd yelled, and then he called out to her that it was her mother. Barbara cut the flame under the pan, picked up the telephone, and wondered how on earth her mother had found her at eight o'clock in the morning.

"Sin in San Francisco is a public secret. But I am not afflicted with voyeurism, only in need of help. Sally

329

is here. She's been here all night. She has left your brother. It appears to be a family failing."

"That sounds crazy."

"Perhaps it is."

"Why did she come to you?"

"It's a safe, snug harbor. I suppose she had nowhere else to go."

"I'll be there in an hour. Tell her to wait for me."

"The trouble is that I understand it only too well," she told Boyd over a hurried breakfast. "She did it once before, when they had been married only a few years. My brother Joe is a good, kind, gentle person, but as dull as dishwater."

"Most men are," Boyd said, his mouth full of food.

"Don't be so damned complacent and superior, and don't talk with your mouth full. My sister-in-law is a bit insane."

"That's not uncommon."

"Thank you. She's been his nurse—he practices at home—and housekeeper, mother, and cook. When we started this Mothers for Peace thing, she told Joe that he could hire a nurse, that he was making enough money, which was true, and that he treated every Chicano in the valley for nothing, which was about half true, and she took off up and down the West Coast, talking at every little meeting we could pull together. She was quite a film star in her day, and that helped. I feel rotten, and I feel responsible."

"That's nonsense. You're not responsible. And if she wanted to do something she felt mattered——"

"Oh no, hold on. Do you remember what William Blake said? 'He who would do good to another must do it in minute particulars. General Good is the plea of the scoundrel, hypocrite, and flatterer.' I don't hold with those who love mankind and despise people."

"Now you're being judge and jury. Why don't you hear her side?"

"I know, I know." She pushed back her chair. "Be a dear and finish alone. I must run."

Barbara arrived at her mother's house with no set plan or position. Divorce frightened her. It had begun when her mother and father divorced, tearing the world of her girlhood into fragments, and her own divorce from Carson Devron had left her depressed, unable to work. Her brother Joe had always called forth a sense of guilt and protectiveness. Joe was totally vulnerable. He was one of those rare men who could not kill a mosquito without hesitation and remorse. He had no defenses. He was a compassionate and skilled physician, in a world where medicine was practiced only too often with little compassion and less skill. Barbara had watched Sally execute her decision to marry Joe—a decision that had depended very little on Joe's desire. The Sally of twenty years ago had been a wild, lovely, and exciting young woman. She was still beautiful, still exciting, still endowed with the same explosive quality as she paced back and forth in the living room of the Lavette house on Russian Hill. Jean, who could not bear scenes of any kind, had disappeared upstairs.

"No," she said emphatically. "No, Bobby, you don't understand, because you're the way he is, a goddamn saint! And the only thing worse than being a bloody saint is being married to one." And then she was pleading with Barbara that she didn't mean it at all. "You know I love you, Bobby. I admire you. I always have. You were my Joan of Arc."

"Will you stop talking nonsense!" Barbara snapped. "Will you for once in your life look at people the way they are! I am no saint, and neither is Joe. I'm a troubled, confused divorced woman, no different from ten million others. I spent months with a kind shrink, trying to get my head screwed on right, and my son is seven thousand miles away trying to find out who he is because I failed him as much as I failed both my husbands. So just stop this silly fantasy and then perhaps we can talk to each other like two civilized people. Now, what happened between you and Joe?"

"Nothing happened. That's it, Bobby."

"You'll have to make it clearer than that," Barbara told her. "And for heaven's sake, stop moving. Sit down!"

She dropped onto the couch. "O.K., O.K., I'm sitting."

Barbara took a chair facing her. "Now make sense."

"All right. I'm bored."

"Just that? It's not new, Sally. They say most men live lives of quiet desperation. Most women live lives of quiet boredom."

"I am not most women. Do you know what happened when I went out on that tour, talking to groups of women? I became alive. I'm not pretending it's the cause I spoke for. I do hate this crazy war. My Danny's only eleven, but this bastard Johnson can keep his war going forever. But it wasn't that. It was getting away from Napa, from that awful small-town life, from Joe—yes, from Joe—and feeling that I had been dead and some miracle had revived me. And then in Hollywood, I went onto the Paramount lot. Believe it or not, Mike, the guard at the gate, recognized me, and then in a little restaurant right outside the gate, I got together with a whole bunch of the kids, young actors who weren't stars and some old-timers I had known, and we held a meeting right there in the restaurant, and they put up almost eight hundred dollars—I have almost four thousand dollars in cashier's checks in my purse to give you—and it was just—I don't know how to put it, but it was wonderful. And then I was invited to a party that night and I went to bed with someone I had known in the old days, and it didn't mean one goddamn thing except that I felt alive and young—and do you know how long it is since I felt that way?"

Then they sat silently, facing each other, minute after minute, until Sally burst out, "Aren't you going to say anything?"

"Did you tell Joe—about the man at the party?"

"I told him. I told him I had to leave him."

"What did he say?"

"What do you think he said, Bobby?" Her voice was woeful, pleading. "He said he understood what had happened to me. Jesus God, he understood it! Only he didn't. He said he loved me."

"He does."

"It's not enough."

"What do you feel for him? Do you love him?"

"Is love feeling dead? I don't know what love is. I don't want the damn thing! I want to be alive. I'm forty years old. My life has escaped me. I want to find it. I was a star. I wrote poetry and published it. And then I stopped existing."

The trouble was that Barbara understood her and had no argument. None. She could only think what a rotten mess things were.

"And you hate me for it," Sally said.

"Oh, stop that. You'll do what you must do. I'm no judge. What about May Ling and Danny?"

"May Ling spends her days at your house. It's become her whole life. She'll help Joe with Danny. He's old enough to understand."

"No one is," Barbara thought. "You don't want Danny with you?" she asked.

"I can't. I'm doing enough to Joe. I can't do that. I'm going back to films. Oh, I'll never be a star again. I don't have any such dreams. But I'll find work. It's no life for Danny, and May Ling wouldn't leave Joe."

"Did you tell her?"

"Yes—both of them." She began to cry. "Oh, Bobby, I feel so rotten, so guilty."

Not quite as guilty as I do, Barbara thought, and then she went to Sally and drew her to her feet. "Come on, baby, we'll find my mother and have some coffee and talk about your future."

"You don't hate me?"

"Not this morning. We'll see how I feel next month"

A week later Barbara took the eleven o'clock plane out of Los Angeles to return to San Francisco. The previous evening had been successful, and she had over nine thousand dollars in cash and checks stuffed into her purse—most of it from an old lady of eighty-two years, who was some sort of second cousin to Carson's grandmother, lived in Pasadena, and possessed, as Carson put it, more millions than she could count. She had given Barbara a check for six thousand dollars, explaining, "This is not for your organization, child. I lost all taste for organizations when they found our pastor in bed with my niece, Agnes—who was certainly not his wife. This is because you had enough grit to go to jail when everyone else turned chicken and ran. And why Carson ever let go of you, I'll never know." The rest of the money came from a director, a producer, and three actresses who had joined her and Carson for dinner. Late that evening, back at her hotel room, she felt the need to talk to someone about her triumph, and she called Boyd, waking him. He listened sleepily, congratulated her, and told her he would be waiting for her at the airport.

"You don't have to."

"I want to. You need a bodyguard."

"All right. You're a dear. Now go back to sleep."

Still high and excited as she strode through the gate to where Boyd stood waiting, Barbara demanded, "Well, now what do you think of my talents as a fundraiser? A whole new profession, and enough to pay off almost all our debts." It was only then that she noticed his face. "What happened, Boyd?"

"No one hurt, no one dead, but still very bad."

"Will you please tell me!"

"Your house burned down last night."

"Oh, no." She stared at him, shock, disbelief—her eyes filling with tears, her face pleading with him to tell her it was some grotesque joke. "All of it?" she asked hoarsely. "Is anything left?"

He shook his head. "Those old wooden houses, Bobby. It went up like tinder."

"When?" she managed to ask. "When did it happen?"

"About four o'clock this morning."

Everything, she was thinking, a whole life, my books, my pictures, my memories, all of it gone. I'm naked. What do I do now?

"I spoke to Harvey," Boyd was saying. "He says your insurance was in order. So that's some consolation."

"It can't be, it just can't be," she whispered, crying now.

"Don't cry, darling, please."

"No. I'm all grown up. Why should I cry? I had almost a hundred pages of my new book written and sitting in my study. Why should I cry? I can't do it again. I can't live my life over again. I can't write those hundred pages again."

Boyd steered her to his car. She dried her eyes, trying to think, to remember everything that had been there, Bernie's record collection, the photo albums, a seascape that Dan had loved and that her mother had given to her after her father's death, the black-horse-hair-covered Victorian furniture that had belonged to Sam Goldberg, all her books, current and back to her early childhood, her collection of the *Oz* books of L. Frank Baum, which she had loved so and passed on to Sam, the dishes she had collected, the articles she had written for *Manhattan Magazine* when she was a correspondent in Paris, foreign translations of her own books. She had never been capable of throwing away a book. And there was one ancient doll she had preserved, and she had not thought about it or looked at it in years. And of course the manuscript she had been working on. Conceivably, other things could be replaced, but not the manuscript. That was gone. How could she reclaim it or rewrite it? And then, suddenly projected into her thinking, heart-chilling and agonizing, the material of Mothers for Peace, thousands of leaflets, bumper stickers, stationery, envelopes, a Xerox machine that they had just rented, typewriters, lapel buttons, voice tapes, banners, thousands of address plates that linked their organization together, and rolls of motion picture film for a documentary they had been planning—all of it gone.

Until they were in Boyd's car and driving into San Francisco, Barbara was silent, nor did Boyd interrupt her thoughts. When at last she spoke, it was with a kind of hopeless despair. "Boyd, what will I do? How can I ever replace it?"

"I know there are things you can never replace. But you're well insured, and the house can be rebuilt."

"We're not insured for the organization's things. There must have been fifty or sixty thousand dollars' worth of material in the house. You saw it. You know. And the basement was packed with cartons. What I have in my purse won't even pay for the machines we rented. How can we ever work our way out of this?"

"Not all at once, Barbara. You have to get over the shock, and then we'll sit down and talk and do some planning. After all, the organization exists in the people who were working with you, and they're still here, and you'll be surprised at how helpful they'll be."

"I don't know. I just don't know. You're sure no one was in the house, no one was hurt?"

"Absolutely."

"I want to go there now."

"Now? You're sure?"

"Yes, please." Then a while later, she said to him, "How did the fire start? Do you know?"

336

"Not for certain."

"What does that mean?"

"It might have been arson, but the police and the firemen are not sure. It's very hard to tell with the old wooden houses. The heat is very intense. You mustn't expect to recover anything."

"But they suspect arson?"

"They're not sure, Barbara. Someone could have dropped a cigarette into a wastebasket and it might have smoldered for hours. Ruth Adams was the last one to leave last night. She locked up. Also, she doesn't smoke, and she swears that everything was in order when she left."

"It would be. Ruth wouldn't leave it any other way. It's strange, Boyd, I always told myself that material things meant nothing to me. Mother was always in despair with the way I dressed. I hate to buy clothes—and now—now I have a dress and a sweater in my bag and I'm wailing over everything the old house contained. But I did love that house so. Did you talk to mother?"

"This morning. She wants me to bring you there."

"All right. But I want to see the house first."

She stood on the sidewalk on Green Street, looking at the pile of charred wood that had been her home. Ruth Adams, Shela Abramson, Eloise, and several others of the volunteers were there, waiting for her, along with a crowd of onlookers and a policeman. Her house was totally destroyed. There was nothing to be salvaged.

Lucy Lavette sat opposite her husband at breakfast the following morning, observing him carefully as he read the account of the fire that had destroyed Barbara's house. They were breakfasting, as always, in the solarium of the house on Pacific Heights. Lucy enjoyed the environment of flowers and palms. The house had been built by her father, and she had always been very close

337

to her father; after her father's death, she had insisted that Tom take over the house and make it his home. On his part, Tom admired the antique magnificence of the old mansion, a quality that simply could not be built into a modern house, regardless of the money one spent, and he was not at all reluctant to make her childhood home his own. On this morning, he was far from happy; however cool his relations with Barbara, he had always maintained, somewhere deep in his mind, a flicker of pride in the fact that she was his sister.

"You read this?" he asked Lucy.

"Oh, yes."

"Poor Barbara. She loved that ridiculous house. To my way of thinking, it's absolutely insane the way we cling to those old wooden houses on the hills. One day, we'll have a fire as bad as nineteen six."

Lucy reached across the table and took the paper. "You saw this?" And she read from the story, "In addition to being Miss Lavette's residence, the building was used as the working headquarters of the antiwar organization which calls itself Mothers for Peace. According to Ruth Adams, one of the founders of the organization, the loss to Mothers for Peace in material and equipment amounts to seventy-five thousand dollars. While unable to confirm this figure, Barbara Lavette, reached later at her mother's house, where she is staying, said that it sounded like a reasonable estimate of their losses. When asked whether the organization could continue its work, Miss Lavette said that she hoped it could, but that the financial blow was shattering."

Tom listened in silence, watching his wife. She smiled slightly. "You see, my dear," she said to him, "there are more ways than one to skin a cat."

He continued to stare at her.

"I'll send this clipping to Austin Campbell. I think he'll appreciate its significance."

"You consider this a fortunate accident," Tom said coldly.

"There are no fortunate accidents. Only fools depend on accidents. I am not a fool."

"What are you trying to tell me?"

"Only that Campbell will respond to this."

"Lucy, did you have her house torched?"

"And if I did, would you blame me? Or pretend to? Come off it, Tom. You were in deeper trouble than you knew. Mr. Johnson is a vindictive man, and while your sister may have been only a gadfly, he doesn't tolerate such things easily. Now you're off the hook, and how has Barbara been hurt? The house was insured. I made certain of that, and we made certain that no one was in it. What must be done must be done."

"How could you?" Tom said hoarsely. "She's my sister. And without asking me. What am I? This puts me on a level with the Mafia."

"Don't take that tone with me, Thomas. Things far worse than this are done every day—yes, by respectable business organizations."

"Not by me! We could have survived anything that loathsome Texas baboon threw at us. If he wanted a fight, I would have given him one. Where the hell would he get tankers if he put mine out of the picture? And I'm not one damn bit sure that he could. But to engage in anything as low as this—to burn down a woman's home——"

"Thomas! Just cool down and think about it. We knew she was in Los Angeles and we knew the house was empty. She may be very happy to be rid of that miserable shack!"

"It stinks to hell!" Tom shouted, rising and stalking out of the room. Lucy sat at the table and finished her breakfast. She had witnessed these bouts of anger on her husband's part in the past. Left alone for a few hours, he would come to his senses. He always did.

FIVE

It hadn't been until Sam was on his way to Israel, actually in the plane between London and Tel Aviv, late in the summer of 1964, that he had made up his mind about his future. He had with him almost seven thousand dollars in travelers' checks, the proceeds of the sale of his treasured boat, his inheritance from his grandfather. When he told his mother what he intended, the sale of the boat, her first reaction was disbelief and resistance. Finally, Barbara gave in to his decision, recognizing in her son a stubborn will and independence that would not be thwarted. At that time, almost three years ago, Sam had only the vaguest notion of what he intended to do in Israel, or indeed what Israel was like. He projected himself into many roles, a tourist wandering through the land and seeing every corner of it, a member of a kibbutz, toiling uncomplainingly in the soil of the ancient land, a sophisticate spending his days in cafés—although he had no idea whether there were cafés—and his evenings in romantic encounters, a lonely researcher trying to discover his own past and origins; and having projected and imagined each of these various styles of living, he had enough common sense to reject all of them and to consider realistically only two alternatives, either to find a job or to continue his schooling. And since he was not equipped for any job he could regard with any sense of satisfaction, he decided to go to school, and once he reached Israel, he went on to Jerusalem and set about the process of enrolling in Hebrew University.

It was not easy; indeed, it was the most difficult thing he had ever attempted, and his decision to enroll as a premedical student made his life even more difficult. For the three weeks before school term began, he hired a tutor and embarked on an intensive study of Hebrew. He found a room in a house on Bezalel Street, within walking distance of the university, and for three weeks he lived there, emerged only for food, worked fourteen hours a day, and achieved at least a primitive mastery of a language he had never before encountered. Now, somewhat less than three years later, early in June of 1967, he was only days away from his departure. His money had run out, and still unwilling to ask his mother for support, he had received a loan from Jean, his grandmother, enough to purchase his ticket home, nonstop from Tel Aviv to New York via El Al, and from there to San Francisco. There remained some forty dollars, which would see him through the next week and pay for a bus ticket from Jerusalem to Tel Aviv. Today, in the quiet of the afternoon, he sat in the almost deserted library, composing a letter to his mother, which he began with a sort of apology:

"It may well be," he wrote, "that I will return before this letter, the mail here being a bit uncertain at times, but I decided to write this letter in any case. I remember you telling me about your last night in prison and your unreasonable fear that you would die before you were released. It's not a very apt comparison, yet I am so desperately eager to return home that I've been sleeping poorly, afraid that something will intervene to prevent it. Of course nothing will, and even if the mails provide an unexpected agility in this case, I'll be only a day or two behind. Yet strangely, I have come to love this place, and I am torn between that love and my desperate need to go home. When I try to analyze that need and ask myself what it is specifically, I can put aside the place and the landscape, as dear as they are to me. It's a question of family, and I think that I couldn't face life apart from the people I knew and loved from when I was a child. That's the important thing. I can't tell you how much I miss you and Granny Jean and the people of Higate, and Freddie, more or less underlined. I don't think that if we were brothers we could be any closer, and I wasn't a bit surprised that the marriage between him and Rita Hogan never came off. The trouble with Freddie is not that he falls in love with every beautiful girl he meets, but that he falls out of love so quickly. He lacks staying power, but since he's only twenty-five, that may change. Myself, having yet to reach my twenty-first birthday, well, I can afford to be superior.

"Yesterday, Dr. Reznik called me into his office and talked to me about living here in Israel. 'Shmuel,' he said to me, 'now that we have given you of our blood and substance and elevated you from a *naar* (fool) into a being of some common sense, you propose to leave. You have robbed us, and you run away with your loot.' Of course, this is a rough translation of the Hebrew. Dr. Reznik, who is head of the biology department here, is a wonderful old man. I think I mentioned him in some of my previous letters. He was one of the original founders of the university, which has a very strange history indeed. You know, when I came here, mom, the only thing I knew about Hebrew University was the name, and I expected to find something like Berkeley or Stanford. Well, it ain't. The university was started long before there ever was a Jewish state, sometime around 1924 or so, and Dr. Reznik, who is about seventy-five, was here at the beginning. He was born in Vienna, where he got his M.D., and one day he told me the whole story of the founding of the University, when they had no buildings or books or equipment, just the faculty and about a hundred students, and some of the first buildings were built by the students and faculty. That was on Mt. Scopus, which has been cut off by the Arabs since 1948. The place where I've been studying, as you know, is at Givat Ram.

"Anyway, that's what Dr. Reznik said to me yesterday, and I was kind of snotty and told him that he didn't want me there because I wasn't Jewish. 'Ah ha,' he said, 'so you have been deceiving us and lying to us. And where, tell me, did you get the name Shmuel ha Cohen, which is not only a Jewish name but the most distinguished?' He was not really angry, and he knew well enough where I got my name, which in Hebrew means Samuel the priest. And then we talked for a long time about who I am and what I am, and what it has meant to me not to be Jewish by Jewish law and by the laws of Israel and to go through life with a Jewish name. He's a very wise man, and his position, as I understood it, is that being Jewish is a state of mind. I don't have that state of mind, which is strange, because I love this place and I've had more happiness here than unhappiness, and here is where I came to manhood, whatever that is. But if I am not Jewish, then I am not Christian either, and I must exist like something hanging between two worlds, trapped in a Jewish name which I will never change.

"On the other hand, Dr. Reznik does not consider this to be any kind of a tragedy. On the contrary, he feels that I am lucky and that I can understand things I never would have understood under other circumstances. I am going into all this because when I came

346

here and left you for so long, I insisted that I had to and that I had to find out who I am. I'm not sure that I know, but I am closer to it.

"In the fall, if I can meet the entrance requirements, I would like to go to Stanford Medical School, which would be convenient since it functions in Lane Hospital right there in San Francisco. I think it will be a long time before I have any desire to leave San Francisco. As for the entrance requirements, my three years here, I am told, would be the equivalent of four years of college in the States, maybe more, since for the past year I've been doing hospital work. My grades have been good, which ain't easy with the competition one has in this place. Also, Ralph Cassala is a pretty big wheel at Stanford, and I am shameless about pulling any strings which would allow me to study in town.

"I just can't imagine what you thought about me when we were together last summer in Paris. I behaved like a little swine, and it has taken me all this time to realize how rotten I was. Well, I have done a lot of growing in the past year, and look, mom, the house doesn't have to be finished for my return. There are plenty of rooms in the house on Russian Hill, and Granny Jean won't mind having me around for a week or two. If you see Freddie, tell him to come into town for a few days, so we can bum around in the old places.

"In your last few letters, I could read an underlying fear that I might fall in love with a local girl and decide to stay here. You see, it didn't happen. Maybe I was sort of in love with Rachel, and you can see from the picture I sent you that she is one hell of a girl, but she is a kibbutznik, with all the qualities of a kibbutznik. The kibbutz sent her here to study medicine, and then she goes back to the kibbutz. It was impossible. I admit that I have met all kinds of wonderful kids among the kibbutzim, but after a few weekends at

Rachel's kibbutz, which is not too far from Jerusalem, I realized that if I had to spend my life in such a place, I'd go stark raving mad. For one thing, it's pretty much a closed society. Unless you were born in the place and grew up there, you're never really in. It's a great experiment in communal living, but it's still a farm. The thing that Rachel and I could never work out is the way I feel about war and killing. When I think about it, it's my feeling about life and my abhorrence of pain that turned me to medicine, but I could never make Rachel understand what it means to me to be a philosophical pacifist. She would tell me that they are all pacifists here. Jews are pacifists. But if we don't defend ourselves, we will die. We argued for hours about that but never worked it out. Anyway, I am not a farmer. It's a pity, because she's a wonderful girl, but when I suggested to her that she might return with me to San Francisco, she looked at me as if I had totally taken leave of my senses. The question is not even to be discussed. Anyway, our decision to end our relationship was mutual but it was a bad scene while it lasted because we really care for each other.

"You can see now that your fears about war over here were unfounded. You know, mom, you can't go on trying to protect me, no matter how deeply you feel about the war in Vietnam. Anyway, if someday I have to be involved, it will be as a doctor, and the only positive thing I see about war is the physician, who tries to put some of it back together again. Now, if this letter should reach you before I do, I'm taking the early plane out of New York on June 14th, and we'll be landing at San Francisco International just about noon. I'm not standing on ceremony. I want you to be there, just you, with open arms for the returning prodigal. And will I ever be glad to see you!"

He was sealing the letter in its envelope when he heard his name called. "Shmuel!"

Sam looked up and saw Dr. Reznik walking toward him, between the tables of the deserted library. The old man walked slowly, wiping his glasses, and then replacing them carefully as he sat down across the table from Sam. "So here you are," he said. "I looked everywhere, even in your room. It's a lot of walking for an old man." He glanced around him. "Sitting here in this deserted place."

"It *is* empty, isn't it?" Sam said. "I've never seen it this way before, but I guess I didn't think about it."

"You don't know why?"

"I've been here for hours, writing a long letter to my mother."

"You don't know why the library is empty?" Dr. Reznik asked him again, a note of sadness in his voice.

"No. What has happened?"

"We're at war again."

"Oh, no. No."

"Yes, we're at war."

"With whom?"

"Everyone," he said, shaking his head, "everyone, Shmuel, Egypt, Iraq, Syria, Jordan—already you can hear the sounds of war. Not in here." He glanced around the empty library again. "A few kilometers away, and here it's quiet. Here the wisdom of all the ages rests quietly, while men kill each other again."

"I just wrote my mother that I was coming home next week. I have the tickets," Sam said dully.

The old man nodded. "Well, we'll see. Meanwhile, I need you."

"Why?"

"The Jordanians are attacking already. Our forces are going up against them in East Jerusalem, and the war will be on the other side of Samuel Street."

"It's insane. When did this happen?"

"Today, while you were sitting in here." He took off his glasses and wiped them again. "Now listen to me,

349

Shmuel!" the old man said sharply. "The university is empty. Everyone's been called up. We gathered together a handful of the premedical students, along with those of us on staff who are too old, and we're setting up emergency first aid stations in the Guela section, on Yoel Street and Guela Street. One of them will be mine. Rachel is there already and Ari, who is exempted for his clubfoot. We have an older woman, a nurse from the hospital. That's all they could spare. I want you with me."

"I'm not a doctor," Sam protested.

"Am I a doctor? It's twenty years since I practiced medicine. You're the best student I have. You've learned something. You can put on a dressing. You can tie up an artery. You can bandage a wound. You can set a broken bone. It's keeping the boys alive until the ambulances can take them to the hospital. I say boys, but they've started shelling. It will be everyone, women, children."

"I didn't want to see Rachel again. We said goodby."

"What is it?" Dr. Reznik asked harshly. "Isn't half of you Jewish? You will say goodby again."

"Let's go," Sam answered angrily. "You don't have to bait me."

"All right, all right. Now come along, my boy. We'll stop at Hubber's pharmacy on Ben Yehuda Street and pick up some supplies."

"You mean there are no supplies there?"

"Not yet. The war has just begun." Then he added, "Because we are an afterthought. They have the hospitals and the ambulances and the teams of medics, everything waiting and ready except the afterthought. But you will be surprised, Shmuel, at how important the afterthought will be."

It was not until noon of that day that Barbara heard about the war. She was awakened early in the morning by a phone call from Sally, who had just won a major supporting role in a film. After informing Barbara that she had not slept all night because she was more miserable than delighted, she explained that if this job had washed out, as so many others had, she would have gone back to Napa. She had been speaking to Joe on the telephone almost every day for a month now. "And now I don't know what to do," she told Barbara. "I don't even know if I want the job, and it's a wonderful part, but if I take it I have the feeling that I'll never be able to go back to Joe, and he's been such an angel about this, and this is the second time we've separated, and do you think I'm actually pathological, Barbara? Please don't spare me."

"Yes, I think you're crazy," Barbara answered sleepily.

"I know, I know. In this world, who isn't? Bobby, I know I talk my head off and that makes me sound glib, but I'm just about the most miserable woman in the world. Well, not the most, but up there with the top ten, and one day I hate myself for doing anything so stupid as to walk out on Joe, and then the next day I get the shakes at the thought of going back to Napa. You have to help me."

"I can't help you," Barbara said angrily. "For once in your life, you're going to have to decide whether to be married or not to be married. Joe is my brother. You can't keep putting me in the middle of this."

"I know. I'm so thoughtless. Basically, I'm rotten, but I can't turn down the part. It's the first decent thing in months, and now you hate me too, along with May Ling and Danny."

"They don't hate you." It was impossible for her to be angry with Sally. "If you take the part, why don't you ask Joe to come down for a while?"

"He wouldn't."

"Did you ever ask him? Did you ever try? This

351

whole damn women's thing makes no sense if a man and a woman can't live their lives as they feel they must and still be married."

"Would you talk to him?" she pleaded.

"I damn well will not. He's your husband."

The conversation left her more provoked with herself than with Sally, her patience worn thin. Why, she asked herself, was she in the middle of this, in the middle of so many things? Where was Barbara Lavette or Barbara Devron or Barbara Cohen? Why couldn't she pull herself together? It had been a hard, confusing eight months since her house had burned, finding a loft where the organization could continue to work, finding enough money to pay their debts, to start all over again, persuading the women involved that it could still work, still make a difference in the scheme of things. She had not dreamed that they would be so eager to accept defeat, but then they had spent most of their lives accepting defeat, which she understood only too well. There was a strong urge inside of her to acquiesce; they had done something, they had tried and it was over. But once again, she was in the middle. No one of some twenty other women who were active in the organization could have made the decision or wanted to or felt pressed to; it had to be herself. Find things, do things, make something that is dead viable. She never got back to the book she had started, the manuscript of which had been destroyed in the fire. Why, she asked herself over and over, does one person and not another find the state of things untenable? No one saved the world and no one changed the world; it was only an inner pleading that had to be answered, and one's own soul that had to be saved.

At the same time, she had been living for the past eight months in her mother's house, a house she had left as a schoolgirl. She got along with her mother. Jean was amiable enough, but the thought occurred to her after the fire that Jean could have said, "Here is this big, ridiculous mansion on Russian Hill. Bring your Mothers for Peace in here. If they could work in your home, they can work in mine." But Jean never said that, and Barbara would never suggest it. When she mentioned it to Boyd, he suggested that the house on Russian Hill was all that remained for Jean. With so little future, she could only reach back in time to moments half a century ago. Barbara tried to understand; wasn't she herself the same way? Otherwise, why was she driving a contractor out of his mind, rebuilding the house on Greet Street to be precisely the way it was before it had burned? Jean had said to her, "This has always been your home, Barbara, and heaven knows, there is plenty of room." And yet Jean had protested only halfheartedly when Barbara explained that she must rebuild. Mr. Kurtz, the contractor, had protested more violently. "You are asking me for something impossible," Mr. Kurtz had said. "You had a wooden Victorian house, Miss Lavette. Who can build such a house today? You think because you show me pictures of your house, I can build it? Never. Curved dentils. Who can make such a thing today? And the lintels over the windows? Hand-carved they have to be, and nobody does such hand-carving, not for any price. You have engaged pilasters all over the front, Corinthian crowns, broken pediments—am I a magician?"

"You'll find them in the junkyards," Barbara had told him soothingly. "They're always tearing down one of these houses somewhere in town. On Jones Street, they're tearing down four of them, and they're tearing down others over in North Beach. You'll find the carvings you need, I'm sure you will, someone as skilled and inventive as you are."

Yet the project would have been impossible, had not Tom telephoned with offers of assistance, her brother strangely sympathetic, assuring her that the bank, the Seldon Bank, her grandfather's bank which was now Tom's bank, would extend any mortgage loan she required without interest for any term of years she desired. His thoughtfulness and concern moved her, as did the sympathy and concern of so many others. A feature story about the burning of her home appeared in the *Chicago Tribune,* hardly known as a liberal newspaper, yet it brought in a flood of contributions to the cause of Mothers for Peace.

So it might well be, Barbara reasoned, that she was not so different from her mother, treasuring the old house which was the only focus of stability and continuity in her life, driving Mr. Kurtz out of his mind in her effort to reproduce it, haunting antique shops to find furniture like the old pieces Sam Goldberg's wife had bought for the house three quarters of a century before.

These and other thoughts filled Barbara's mind as she showered and dressed after receiving Sally's telephone call. She had driven Mr. Kurtz into a race against time, hoping to complete the rebuilding of the house before Sam's return, and now all that remained was the painting of the exterior and some finishing of the rooms inside. Not that she expected Sam to live with her for any length of time, but even as it was the focus of her security, she felt that it must have some of the same meaning for him.

Jean was already at the breakfast table, complaining to Mrs. Bendler that the coffee was too weak. Barbara joined her. The housekeeper reminded Jean that Dr. Kellman had forbidden coffee entirely, which led Jean to remark that Kellman was an old fool.

"He also forbids me to drink or keep late hours. I was up until two o'clock reading Massie's *Nicholas and Alexandra* and I had three sherries, and I feel perfectly fine. Have you read it, Barbara?"

"No, mother."

"You should. Liberals never read anything that might upset them. Take the coffee back, please, it's undrinkable."

"Leave a cup for me, please," Barbara said. "I can't spend the morning over breakfast."

"Who called at such an unearthly hour?" Jean asked her.

"Sally. She has been talking things out with Joe and half decided to go back to him, and now she's got herself a part in some new film, and she's filled with guilts and all kinds of ambivalence."

"She's quite mad," Jean observed, buttering a slice of toast.

"Yes, I suppose so. But we all are, more or less. Mr. Kurtz is convinced that I am totally insane."

"With reason. To rebuild that strange Victorian house to a facsimile of what it was is just beyond me. I suppose you're on your way there now."

"We have an appointment at ten. And then I'm meeting Boyd at his office and he's taking me to lunch, and after that I'm joining the ladies at the loft. We have a new bumper sticker that's coming in from the printer. I've decided that in our car culture, the bumper sticker is number one in getting your message across."

"You're very fond of Boyd, aren't you?"

"Quite fond, yes."

"Has he asked to marry you?"

"On various occasions."

"Why not?"

"I'm fifty-three, for one thing. For another, marriage doesn't seem to suit me very well. I've known Boyd for twenty years and he's very dear and thoughtful. But he goes his way and I go mine. When we need each other, we find each other."

"Yes, that's very much the order of the day, and I

355

can't say I approve. I do hope it hasn't affected my grandchildren. It would be very nice to see a great-grandchild before I die. And speaking of that, when is our Sam returning?"

"On the fourteenth, which is hardly more than a week away."

"I'm very excited about it, truly, Barbara. I'm very fond of our Samuel. And it's been so long. I do love that child, which is something I must handle very carefully. He's not a child anymore, is he?"

"I'm afraid not, mother."

"I do love Freddie, but Freddie's such a flibbertigibbet and that beard of his. I'll never be reconciled to men with beards. Well, thank heavens he didn't marry that girl."

"Why? She's a lovely girl."

"She's Catholic and Irish."

"Good God, mother, you married a Catholic who was Italian."

"Danny," Jean said calmly, "as I've told you before, had ceased to be a Catholic before we were married, and as for his being Italian, well, San Francisco Italians are different. I mean, you can't think of Stephan Cassala as an Italian, can you?"

"Why not?" Barbara demanded, wondering why, after a lifetime of knowing her mother, she was still unable to anticipate her train of thought.

"He was a distinguished and courtly gentleman," Jean replied.

"Mother, I don't know what to say. You leave me speechless. Your prejudices baffle me."

"Prejudices?" Jean smiled comfortably. "I think I've overcome all my prejudices."

"Of course you have," Barbara agreed. She kissed her mother and left the house. Afterwards, she would recall how very good she had felt on this morning. The house was almost completed; Sam was due home in a few days; the sky was blue and the wind from the Pacific was as sweet as honey. She walked briskly, covering the few blocks between her mother's home and her own house on Green Street in a matter of minutes. Mr. Kurtz was waiting for her, his crew of painters sitting on the steps of the rebuilt house.

"Every minute you're late," he informed her, "costs me money. You think when painters sit and wait for you, they don't get paid?"

"I thought they'd be at it all morning."

"Before you seen the color? God forbid. I got too much experience with you, Miss Lavette."

"But I said white. You know that."

"There is white and white, plaster-white, oyster-white, antique white, gray-white, blue-white, yellow-white."

"Just white."

"There is no such thing as just white. Come and look."

When Barbara had agreed that the white paint he had mixed would be satisfactory, Mr. Kurtz breathed a sigh of relief, instructed his painters to begin, and told Barbara that if she planned any future reconstruction, he would rather not be involved.

"But, Mr. Kurtz, the *Chronicle* ran a long piece about my house, and the writer praised you to the skies and pointed out that your work was superb."

"That's the trouble," Mr. Kurtz agreed.

Barbara left him, her mood still untroubled, and since it was still early, she decided to walk down the hill to Market Street, observing to herself, as she had so often in the past, that here was a place where many walked downhill but only a few walked uphill, and wondering how it had been before there were cable cars, buses, and automobiles. What had Sam written about that—something about horses dragging wagons up the hills, a school composition or was it in one of his letters? She loved the letters in which he took off and let his fancy or memory run freely. There was one letter in which he had described a whole day, in minute detail, of his experiences at that silly school in Connecticut to which she had sent him—and now she couldn't even recall the name of the place. She was trying to remember it when she walked into Boyd's office, and then Boyd told her that Israel was at war.

Barbara stared at him in silence for a moment or two, and then she dropped into a chair. Boyd would have been reassured if she had cried out or broken into tears, but she said nothing, and the moments went by.

"Are you all right?"

She nodded. He poured a glass of water from a jug on his desk and handed it to her, and she drank it, and then asked quietly, "What kind of a war?"

She would know sooner or later. "The worst kind," Boyd said. "Egypt, Syria, and Jordan, all at once."

"Which means they're fighting in Jerusalem."

"Yes, I'm afraid so. I've been on the telephone the past two hours. I had the crazy notion that if I could get through to Hebrew University, I might reach Sam. Out of the question. There is no way to get through to Jerusalem or even to Israel. The international operator said I could be put on a hold list, which might be three hours or tomorrow or never. Then I called an old schoolmate of mine in the State Department, which was not easy because there too it's murder to get through, and he told me that the news out of Jerusalem is very sparse and for the most part contradictory." He hesitated.

"Please tell me whatever you heard," Barbara said.

"You know how the city is divided. The line runs north and south, along the west wall of the old city. Well, according to what they've been able to find out, there's fighting all along the line of the division, and they think the Israelis are more than holding their own,

358

but they're not sure at this itme. In any case, the fighting is at least a mile from Hebrew University."

"At least a mile. My God."

"Barbara," Boyd said, "I know how you feel, and it's not going to get any better for at least a day. I mean there's no way Sam can get through to you or you to him for at least a day—and possibly for much longer. He has no telephone of his own, and my friend says they have no communication at all with the university. You just have to believe that he's self-reliant enough to survive. After all, he's not in the army."

"If Jordan takes Jerusalem," Barbara said dully, "they will slaughter every living soul in the city."

"No! Absolutely not. What makes you think that?"

"The Israelis believe it."

"Barbara, they couldn't take it in nineteen forty-eight. What makes you think they can now, almost twenty years later?"

"Boyd, it's too terrible," she whispered, the tears beginning now. "He would have come home if I had insisted. It's my fault. I can't bear it. First his father, and now my son. It's too much."

Hubber's pharmacy on Ben Yehuda Street was one of the first casualties of the war. "I've been picked clean already," he told Dr. Reznik. "Why didn't you come earlier?"

"Because I was trying to find my young assistant here, who is a philosophical pacifist and was sitting in the library writing a letter to his mother."

"At least he's a good son," Mr. Hubber said. "My son is in the Sinai, and the world would come to an end if he should think of writing a letter to his mother. I'll tell you what, I put aside some stuff, and I'll let you have part of it." He reached under the counter and came up with a liter of iodine, two liters of peroxide, and four liters of alcohol.

"That's not very much."

"No, but it's the bottom of the barrel." He paused to listen to distant explosions. "Larger guns, and closer. I have some American Mercurochrome that nobody wanted."

"We'll take it."

He brought out a case of a dozen small bottles.

"Bandages, dressings?" Dr. Reznik asked.

"I'll give you what I have left, not much but it will help." He piled rolls of bandages, boxes of dressings, and spools of adhesive tape on the counter. "A moment," he said, and then went to the back of the store and returned with a small carton. "More American ingenuity. They're called Band-Aids, small dressings with tape."

"I know," Reznik said. "I've used them. But for our need—" He shrugged. "We'll take them."

Hubber produced two corrugated cartons. "Pack it," he instructed Sam. "I'll make out the bill. You'll sign it, doctor, and I'll argue later with the War Ministry."

Each of them carrying a box of supplies, Sam and Dr. Reznik set out again. The streets they passed through were crowded with soldiers, civilians, men, women, children, all of them strangely calm, as if nothing out of the ordinary was happening, no one running, no one screaming except the driver of a huge half-track who was cursing a cab driver who blocked his way.

"Don't mumble," Dr. Reznik said to Sam. "If you speak to me, speak up."

"I was talking to myself. I was asking myself what kind of a crazy war this is where you go to a drugstore for medical supplies."

"Where else should we go? I told Rachel to bring all my instruments from the laboratory."

"Dissecting tools?"

"We'll make do. I have a few other things. Why do you worry so much?"

"Because I have nothing to worry about," Sam said sourly. "I have my tickets home for next week, and by now my mother knows about this and she's going out of her mind and remembering how my father died here in 'forty-eight—could I reach her? Is there any way?"

"Impossible. I'm sorry," Reznik said sadly. "Your father died here? I didn't know that. In the war?"

"In the war." He didn't want to talk about it. At this moment, he didn't want to talk about anything, telling himself that tomorrow, if it was humanly possible, he'd get to Tel Aviv, even if he had to walk; get to the airport; and sleep in the airport waiting room, if he had to, until the day came to leave. It was not his war. No war was his war, and no war contained one shred of sanity or decency. Several times, as they walked to Bezalel Street, Dr. Reznik glanced at him, but his set face and his tight, thinly compressed lips did not invite conversation.

Dr. Reznik's first aid station, one of many hurriedly improvised, had been set up in the ground-floor apartment of a family by the name of Lieberman. They were Polish in origin, and they had left Poland for Palestine shortly before the Nazi invasion. Rose and Aaron Lieberman were in their fifties; they had one son who was away in the army, leaving his wife and baby with his parents. It was a small two-bedroom apartment, the living room of which had been turned into an emergency first aid station. The fact that their apartment was less than half a mile from the front line did not appear to trouble the Liebermans inordinately. They were both stout, good-natured people. When Reznik and Sam arrived, Rose Lieberman was in the kitchen, cooking. War or no war, nobody in her house would go hungry. Her daughter-in-law, Shela, was nursing her baby in the bedroom, and Aaron Lieberman was sitting in the other bedroom, cleaning his rifle. Too old for the army, he was in the reserve, and now that the apartment had been turned into a first aid station, he felt free to leave his family and walk over to the front and see if he could help.

It served to increase Sam's impression of a world gone mad. Sarah, the nurse the hospital had sent, was spreading a sheet over the couch, so that it might be used as a bed. Ari, Dr. Reznik's assistant, was reading a newspaper. Rachel had opened the door for them, and now she took the heavy box from Dr. Reznik, just glancing at Sam, asking Ari to help her. Ari limped over and took the box from her arms. Sam set his box down on the floor, and now he and Rachel stood facing each other.

"I thought you had gone," she said. She was a tall, well-built, dark girl, small, regular features, dark eyes, and black hair tied tightly in a ponytail.

Sam shrugged and shook his head.

"Since the war is still a few blocks away," Dr. Reznik said, "why don't you two go outside and talk while we arrange things here."

"Do we have anything to talk about?" Sam wondered.

"I think so."

"All right. We'll talk."

She led the way through the front door and they sat down on the outside steps of the house. It was on toward twilight now, and from the direction of East Jerusalem came the constant snapping crackle of small-arms fire, punctuated now and again by the crash of an artillery shell. A woman came out on the street and shouted for her children. Three of them appeared, and she ordered them into the house. A bus packed with soldiers rolled by, and then incongruously a young girl on a bicycle. A company of paratroopers came along the street, marching two by two, their Uzi guns slung over their shoulders, their gait cocky and easy. One of them whistled at Rachel, and she waved at him.

362

Rachel pinned an armband onto Sam's sleeve. It had a Star of David sewn onto it. "Now you're a medic," Rachel said. "You're a very quiet, angry, sullen medic, but you're a medic nevertheless."

"I'm overwhelmed," he said in English.

"Talk Hebrew. You're still in Israel. As a matter of fact, your Hebrew is very good, hardly any accent."

"You said you wanted to talk to me."

"I am talking to you, my dear beloved friend."

"Damn you!" he snapped at her. "Do you think I'm made of iron? We said goodby once. How do you think I feel?"

"Possibly the way I feel, possibly not. All afternoon I've been in that room, waiting, praying that Dr. Reznik would find you and bring you back with him."

"Why? Why?"

"I'm not sure. I love you, Sam, but not only for that. We said our farewells, I accepted it. But now it's either the end of something or the beginning of something. Either our country will die or Jerusalem will be free. I wanted you with me. When we each had a whole life ahead of us, it was different. I would make my life. You would make yours. That's what we decided and we were right. But now——"

"Rachel," he said, taking her hand, "I don't want to be cruel or unfeeling. You're the only girl I ever loved. But this isn't my country and this isn't my war. No war is my war. No war, no cause is worth the murder it entails——"

"Murder! Is it murder to defend ourselves? Should we die the way we died in the Holocaust? Don't we have the right to live?"

"Rachel, we've been through this. I won't argue it."

"Then why did you come back?" she demanded angrily. "We don't need you. Why did you come back?"

"Because I thought I could help." She didn't pull her hand away. It remained there, warm and alive under his own hand. She shifted slightly toward him, so that her thigh pressed against his.

"I make no claim on you," she said softly. "You think I want to make a prisoner of you and keep you here. I don't. I only want you next to me now. Don't fight with me now. Don't argue with me. Just for a little while stay next to me. We'll both be quiet."

"All right," he agreed. "All right, my dear one."

They sat silently as darkness fell. In the east, star shells began to explode, lighting up the sky like a fireworks display. Then there was a high-pitched shrieking sound, and at the end of the street, fifty yards from them, a shell exploded. The concussion flung Rachel against him. It was the first time Sam had ever been close to an exploding artillery shell, and the blow of the compressed air, the air sucking at his breath and ripping at his clothes like something palpable, was new and terrifying. Rachel recovered first and ran down the street toward the place where the shell had exploded. After a moment, Sam leaped to his feet and raced after her.

The shell had exploded against a house, crushing a wall and shattering the windows. A man lay bleeding in the street, and from inside the house, Sam heard cries of pain. "See to him," he told Rachel, pointing to the man on the street. The door of the house had been torn from its hinges. Sam rushed inside, pushing through people coming from the other apartments. The door to the ground-floor apartment was open. A girl of ten years or so lay on the floor, bleeding profusely from a bad gash in her arm, crying in pain, two women echoing her cries and trying vainly to stop the blood. "Let me!" he said sharply, pulling one woman away from the child. He took his handkerchief, made a tourniquet for the arm, and drew it tightly.

"All right, darling, all right, now."

And to the women, "Get me a bandage, a clean napkin, anything. And antiseptic, whatever you have, peroxide, alcohol. Anyone else hurt?"

Apparently not. They ran to do his bidding, and he stroked the child's hair, soothing her.

"It hurts," she whimpered.

The whole length of her forearm was gashed and there were small glass cuts on her face and throat. Someone handed him a bottle of peroxide, and he poured it over the wound. The child screamed in pain. He heard Dr. Reznik's voice: "Bring the flesh together and hold it." The old man bent over him, laying a dressing on the wound and binding it. "We suture it back at the station. Clean out the cuts on her face," handing Sam a wad of gauze.

"She should go to a hospital."

"I know, I know. The ambulances are all at the front. We do what we can. She'll be all right," he told the women. The child was screaming again from the pain of the antiseptic in her cuts. Sam lifted her in his arms.

"Where are you taking her?" one of the women cried.

"To our first aid station. Right down the street at the Liebermans'."

As they came outside, Rachel and Ari were covering the man on the street with a sheet someone had given them. Bystanders helped them move the body to the sidewalk, where a woman kneeled beside it, weeping and striking her face with her hands. Sam carried the child to the station and laid her on the couch. Sarah had the instruments ready, and Reznik went to the bathroom to scrub his hands. The two women had followed them, and with the two women other neighbors.

"Please," Sam told them, "it's a small room. Please wait outside. Your daughter will be all right."

"Why is she crying like that?"

"Because it hurts." He went to the bathroom.

"Wash your hands," Reznik said. "Tell Mrs. Lieber-

365

man we need more towels. No anesthesia. I feel helpless. I haven't sutured a wound in twenty years."

Mrs. Bergan, the child's mother, owned a car and said she could drive the child to the hospital. With a sigh of relief, Reznik closed the wound with adhesive butterfly strips, and Sam carried the little girl to where the car was parked. When he returned, there were two women and a man in the Liebermans' living room, all of them with superficial fragment wounds from a shell that had landed in Mussaief Street, two blocks away. Ari and Sarah attended to them. Rachel was sitting on the front steps and Sam joined her.

"I saw a man die," Rachel said bleakly. "His whole belly was torn open. He was an old man. He looked at me and smiled, and then he died. How could he smile with his whole belly torn open? It was terrible."

The old man's family had carried the body away, and the street was empty, except for two policemen with flashlights who were looking at the shell damage. The streetlight had been shattered by the explosion, and the street was dark except for flickers of light from windows in the houses. One of the policemen shouted for them to black out the windows, and the lights began to disappear.

"How do you feel?" Rachel asked Sam.

"I don't know yet."

"Are you afraid?"

"No. Not yet."

"I was never afraid at the kibbutz. We were attacked once, and I wasn't afraid. But here in the city——"

"I know. It's being home, and being away from home."

"I'm lonely."

"We're both of us far from home, aren't we?"

"I never thought of it that way," Rachel said.

The two policemen walked back toward them. They carried Uzi guns.

"What's going on?" Sam asked them.

They paused, glad to have someone to talk to. One of them lit a cigarette. The other said, "Fine. You yell for them to black out, and you light a cigarette."

"Who sees a cigarette?"

"Are you kids medics?"

"We're medical students from Hebrew University," Rachel told them. "He's an American. I'm a kibbutznik. We have a first aid station inside the house. Dr. Isador Reznik is in charge. We took care of the little girl who was wounded when the shell struck and we tried to help the old man who was killed."

One of the policemen took out a small notebook. "Did you get his name?"

"No. But his people took his body into that house, four houses up the street."

"Can you tell us what's going on?" Sam asked them. "There's a war going on a kilometer away, and no one seems to know what's happening. Are the Jordanians attacking?"

"Not yet—not our boys, not the Jordanians. Just the shooting and a few shells."

"We're cops. We don't know any more than you do."

They moved off into the darkness. Dr. Reznik came out of the house, stuffed his pipe, lit it, and sat down beside Sam and Rachel. "Well, children," he said, "we're at war again."

"There's always been war," Rachel said sadly.

"The existence of our people is a historical affront," Reznik said. "No one is willing to tolerate it. Yet with God's help——"

"He hasn't been too helpful," Sam said with annoyance. "Here we are within shouting distance of the Jordanian side of the city, and these houses are filled with women and children. Why don't we do something to evacuate them?"

"To where?" Dr. Reznik asked softly. "Where can we go, Shmuel? We live in a country the size of a

367

postage stamp. Half of our holy city is held by our enemies. Wherever we go is the front. For my part, I welcome a danger that is not reserved to the young men.
If we must have war, the old should fight it, not the
young."

Rachel touched Sam's hand and smiled wanly. Dr.
Reznik puffed on his pipe. To the east and the north,
intermittent explosions, star shells in the sky, and the
chatter of small-arms fire. A jeep turned into the street,
driving slowly with dimmed headlights. It pulled up in
front of them, and the driver, a soldier, asked them,
"Where's the aid station?"

"Right here. I'm Dr. Reznik."

Two bespectacled young men sat in the back of the
jeep, each with a medic armband. "We're picking up
medics—whatever the first aid stations can spare," the
driver said. "We had a lousy break at the casualty
clearing station. A shell hit an ambulance. We lost three
medics and we were short already."

"Where?" Reznik asked him.

"Between Sanhedria and Fago. Dr. Leventhal and
Dr. Kahanski are running it."

"Let me go," Rachel said.

"No women."

"I'll get Ari," Reznik said.

"What in hell good is Ari?" Sam demanded. "He's
crippled." He went around the jeep and climbed in
next to the driver.

Dr. Reznik made no move to stop him. Rachel was
staring at him. What a bastard I am, Sam thought.
What an unmitigated bastard. Her face, as it was at
that moment, would stay with him.

The driver took the wrong turning. He was from Tel
Aviv and was new to the twisting Jerusalem streets.
"Beautiful fucked-up war," Sam muttered in English,
and in Hebrew, aloud, "Turn right here on Fischel to
the end and then left on Samuel." The screaming

368

sound, and a shell exploded against a house in front of them.

"Isn't there some other way?" the driver asked. "They're shelling up ahead."

"You can get lost in these streets. All I know is that if we stay on Fischel we hit Samuel and if we turn left, it leads to Sanhedria. What's the difference? We don't know where they're shelling."

The driver increased his speed, and a minute or two later, they were at Samuel the Prophet Street, facing the barrier of wire, pillboxes, and trenches that divided Israeli Jerusalem from Jordanian Jerusalem. In the darkness, the barrier was invisible, but the street itself was crowded with military vehicles and troops on foot. The driver edged his way into the road and turned left. The shelling from the Jordanian side was intermittent, the shells screaming overhead to land in the Jewish area. In the distance, suddenly there was a rumbling roar of artillery, the shells exploding in the darkness on the Jordanian side.

"Ours," the driver said.

"Wonderful," Sam said bitterly, in English.

They were stopped by a military policeman, who was informed by the driver that they were looking for Dr. Leventhal's casualty clearing station.

"They've moved to the Dushinski Yeshiva. Do you know how to get there?"

"I think so," Sam said.

A few minutes later, they reached the Yeshiva, which appeared to be ringed in with exploding shells. In the street in front of it were the burned-out shells of an ambulance and two cars. An ambulance had just pulled up, and they were moving the casualties into the Yeshiva building. "That means the attack has started," the driver told Sam. A medic came out of the Yeshiva and asked the driver what he had.

"Three medics."

"Follow me," the medic said. He led them into the

369

building and downstairs. The basement was crowded with pale, bearded rabbinical students, intimidated by the chaos around them. Through an open door to another part of the basement, Sam could see an improvised operating room, blazing lights over the tables and doctors and nurses at work. The three medical students stood there for a minute or so, watching, fascinated. Then a man in a bloodstained white gown approached them, and the medic who had guided them there explained that they were volunteers from the aid stations.

"What are you—medical students?"

They nodded.

"Can you treat superficial wounds, flesh wounds, burns, cuts?

They nodded again.

"All right. Wash your hands. There's a bathroom at the end of the hall. Supplies are in that small room down there. They do triage at the entrance, and they put the ambulatories in that big room over there. Deal only with what you can handle. Anything else send to one of the physicians."

A hand shaking him awakened him. He looked at his watch. It was a few minutes after four—in the morning or in the afternoon. He was confused, and here in the basement there was no way to tell. Then, bit by bit, the events of the previous night slid into position in his memory. He had been asleep only for an hour, and until then it had been the endless line of wounded. Now he looked up into the face of an old, bearded Orthodox Jew, who was offering him a cup of tea and a piece of coffee cake.

"Eat, sonny. It gives you strength."

He stared dumbly for a moment, then took the tea and cake. With the first bite of the cake, he was ravenously hungry and he wolfed the rest of it down.

"There's more outside," the old man told him. "Now Dr. Leventhal wants to see you."

There were six of them gathered in the hallway with Leventhal and a dirt-grimed, weary Israeli soldier. Leventhal himself appeared ready to drop from fatigue, his gown soaked with blood. He wasted no time. "You're all foreign students," he said, "and you're all volunteers. We have enough nurses here now and we don't need you, but over on the Jordan side, where our troops have been fighting, the casualties among the medics are very heavy. We need medics. No pressure. Will any of you go?"

A moment's hesitation, then one by one, they nodded.

"Good. Your kits are made up. Pick them up on the way out. Don't be heroes and don't push. You follow the fighting, behind it. You have morphine and dressings. Deal with pain and bleeding. God bless you."

Then he left them, and the soldier motioned for them to follow him. Sam was still confused; he felt that his mind was not keeping pace with his actions. He had volunteered for something for which he had no training and no inclination, and when he asked himself for an explanation there was none forthcoming. Two of the old men appeared with trays of cake, and he found himself stuffing sweet pastry into his mouth. He had to urinate desperately. "How about the bathroom?" he asked the soldier. The others joined in his request.

"Go ahead, kids. You'll wet your pants anyway, but go ahead."

Afterwards, outside, they were given their kits and steel helmets with medic markings. Sam's was too tight. Then they climbed into an ambulance. As the ambulance pulled away, a shell exploded on the spot where it had stood. The ambulance drove slowly, without lights, for about ten minutes, and then it stopped, and they were told to get out. Even as they left the ambulance, wounded were moved into it. There was a curtain of sound all around them now, shells exploding, heavy machine-gun and small-arms fire.

"Follow me and stay close," the soldier told them.

He led them into the darkness. Vaguely, Sam could make out the gap in the barrier that had separated the two sections of Jerusalem, the piles of barbed wire, the earth churned by the explosion of the bangalores that had been used to break the barrier, pieces of concrete tossed here and there. The soldier who led them carried a flashlight that he used occasionally, and they could see other flashlights. Stretcher-bearers passed them in the opposite direction. "Trench!" the soldier called out, lighting it for them to leap across. There were two bodies at the bottom of the trench. "Jordanians," the soldier said. There was a high-pitched scream, familiar now. "Hit the dirt!" the soldier shouted. They flung themselves down and the shell passed overhead and exploded behind them. Sam's helmet fell off and rolled away. He tried to find it. "Keep going!" the soldier snapped.

Ahead of them, half a dozen flashlights and electric lanterns wove a crazy pattern, and as they approached, Sam realized that this was the casualty clearing station, a flat piece of ground where perhaps forty men lay, a few on stretchers, most of them on the bare ground. From the sound of gunfire, he guessed that the fighting was not much more than a few hundred yards away. A bloodstained man approached them, a doctor. Not even the wounded were that bloody.

"Medics," the soldier told him. "Foreign students."

"Thank you." The soldier disappeared, and the doctor said to them, "We triage in three ways, superficial there"—pointing to one cluster of the men on the ground—"serious there, and damned serious over there." He spoke quickly. "We make mistakes. Look for vital signs and bleeding. Most of them have battlefield dressings. Check the dressings. Bandage. If they're in pain, use morphine. Do you have morphine and dressings?"

They nodded.

"There's a pile of flashlights over there with the supplies. There's no time to brief you. Just get going."

The casualties were coming in as he spoke, men staggering, still ambulatory, clutching their wounds, men carrying others, stretcher-bearers. The three doctors and the handful of medics worked with desperate speed. Afterwards, Sam asked himself whether he had been afraid, and to that question there was no answer that made sense to him. Everything that happened was like an unending dream or nightmare, yet everything that happened was illuminated with a wild reality. He had passed into a state of euphoria. Finally and for the first time in his life, he was functioning without question or doubt or anger. It had all passed away. What made these wounds, what tore and lacerated the flesh no longer concerned him; all moral judgments, all intellectual arguments had disappeared. He was saving life; he was stopping blood; he was conquering pain. The wounded men were a part of him, as young as he was and younger, pink-cheeked, round Jewish faces, brown Jordanian faces, pain-racked, weeping, screaming in agony.

In a strangely controlled manner, Sam related; he was connected; he was untroubled by the blood, the open guts, the feces expelled from tortured bowels.

A doctor paused for a moment to watch him, praised him. "Good. You're doing well."

"The hell with that," he said to himself. "You don't know one damn bit what I'm feeling."

He saw lying on the ground one of the young men who had sat in the jeep with him; the boy had a bullethole in his forehead. The boy's name was Ernesto, a Brazilian. Sam did not know how he could accept it without shouting in rage at the senselessness and stupidity of such death; yet accept it he did.

Dawn was beginning, the sky graying, a faint tint of pink in the east. There was a lull in the parade of wounded, a momentary hush in the firing, and then in the distance someone began to shout, "Medic! Medic! Medic!" The landscape changed as the light increased. Buildings became visible in the fighting area, to the north the Police School, to the south the cluster of buildings in the American colony, and still the agonizing cry, "Medic! Medic!"

A doctor touched Sam's shoulder. "We need someone out there," pointing toward the sound. "Will you go?"

Sam checked his kit, adding supplies from the stores, morphine, bandages, antiseptic, and then he took off. He ran down a narrow road, crouching behind a broken wall as the firing suddenly picked up. The place was furrowed with trenches. He took shelter in one of them. The plea for a medic, weaker now, seemed to come from down the trench, echoing strangely from the trench walls. Sam started down the trench. He stepped over a dead Israeli paratrooper; then there were two dead Jordanians, then an Israeli with his head blown away, then another Israeli curled into a ball, clutching his stomach. Sam stopped, bent over him, and sought for vital signs. The boy was cold and dead. The plea for a medic had faded away. The trench curved, and Sam came across a Jordanian and an Israeli locked in a deadly embrace, both of them kneeling, clutching each other in death.

Then a faint cry for help came from close by, directly in front of him, and he found the wounded man he was looking for.

Half the man's leg was blown away, and somehow he had made himself a tourniquet and fastened it around his leg. Where had he found the strength to shout?

"All right now," Sam told him. "Easy. We'll fix you up."

The Israeli soldier, who couldn't have been much more than eighteen years old, suddenly began to scream hysterically. Sam gave him a shot of morphine, and the boy became quiet, tears replacing the screams of pain. Sam loosened the tourniquet and let the blood flow a moment, then reset the tourniquet. The boy screamed again as Sam applied antiseptic to the wound.

"Where are you?" a voice called.

Sam looked up and saw two stretcher-bearers peering over the edge of the trench. He managed somehow to lift the boy and with the help of the stretcher-bearers got him out of the trench and onto the stretcher. Then Sam stood leaning on the side of the trench as the stretcher-bearers disappeared in the morning mist. He lacked the strength or will to move.

Then he heard the crunch of a step and turned. Two Israeli soldiers were covering him with their Uzi guns.

"Medic!" he yelled. "I'm a medic!"

"Where's Zvi?"

"Who's Zvi?"

"The boy with the leg wound."

"I gave him morphine. The stretcher-bearers took him away."

"Was he all right?"

"He was alive."

"Where's your unit?"

"God knows."

"Stay with us. We need medics. Our medics are dead."

Sam stared at them blankly.

"Wake up, *chevra*. You'll sleep later."

They started down the trench, and after a moment, Sam followed them. What difference did it make? He had lost all sense of direction, and actually he had no unit. One place was no worse than another. They passed two dead Jordanian soldiers, and then the trench came to an end in a bunker. The bunker was a charnel house. They climbed out of the trench into the blazing light of the morning sun. The chatter of gunfire sounded from the distance. They walked down a street, a wall on one side, houses on the other. Suddenly chips flew from the wall in front of Sam, and both soldiers opened up with their Uzis. The firing from the house stopped; they ran down the street, which joined a larger road, and there they found a tank and a dozen more Israeli soldiers. The tank commander was leaning out of his hatch, and the two soldiers who had come with Sam told him about the firing from the house. The tank turned and lumbered up the street they had just left. The soldiers moved on, and Sam moved with them.

"What's this?" one of the soldiers who had joined them asked, pointing to Sam. It was a reasonable question. His clothes, his blue jeans and sneakers and sport shirt, were covered with dried blood, as were his hands and his face.

"Medic. He took care of Zvi."

"Zvi is alive?"

"He says so."

A soldier held out his arm. An ugly gash had been bound over with strips of his shirt. Sam removed the blood-soaked bandage, applied antiseptic, and bandaged it. Another soldier had a bullethole through his hand. They watched approvingly as Sam treated it.

An older man, apparently their commander, asked him who he was.

"Shmuel Cohen. I'm an American student."

"Been at it all night?"

Sam nodded.

"Come with us. We're going to the museum. You can rest there."

"What museum?"

"The Rockefeller Museum. This whole sector's cleared, right up to the wall of the old city."

Sam began to laugh, almost hysterically.

"What's the joke?"

"The Rockefeller Museum," Sam said. "The whole world's a joke."

He opened his eyes, warm and snug in the blanket wrapped around him, a roof only two feet over his head, and from his point of view, the feet and legs of men. It took a moment to remember that he had crawled away to sleep under one of the specimen cases in the museum. Not that there had been too many places to choose from, with all the soldiers bedding down in the museum. Someone had given him a blanket. He was grateful for the blanket. Bit by bit, the parade of events fell in order in his sleep-drugged mind, being put to work in a room of the museum that had been turned into a first aid station—he existed in a world where everything and anything became an aid station—and then at last eating. What a luxury that had been, what an incredible feast! Groggy, barely able to remain on his feet, he had been steered into an improvised dining room, where the menu consisted of canned tuna fish, pita bread, and champagne. He had no idea where the food or the champagne had come from. The room was packed with dirty, unshaven Israeli soldiers who had fought through the night in the wild, bloody battle for East Jerusalem and who were exuberant in the realization that they were still alive and not only alive but victorious. Nothing Sam remembered eating had ever tasted so good. He ate and ate, washing the food down with tumblers of champagne that he learned had been liberated from one of the Jordanian hotels during the night, and then, quite drunk, stumbling through the place, he saw a pile of blankets. One was offered to him. He found his spot under the specimen case, and he fell asleep instantly.

He had no idea how long he had slept. Somewhere, he had lost a day, lost the sequence of events. He lay beneath the specimen case, listening to the voices of the men whose feet he saw, gathering from their conversation that they were Israeli archaeologists, checking and cataloguing the contents of the museum. Outside, the war must still be going on. Here, inside, it was quiet, even the voices of the archaeologists strangely muted.

He waited until they had moved on, and then he crawled out, stretched, folded his blanket, and walked through the museum until he found a heap of blankets, knapsacks, and guns. He added his blanket to the lot, convinced by now that he had been asleep for fourteen or fifteen hours. It was the morning of the following day; the museum was crowded with civilians as well as troops. Somewhere, he had lost his medical kit. Possibly he had lost his profession as well. He made his way out of the museum. Outside, in the street between the Rockefeller Museum and the walls of the Old City, Israeli troops were moving past in the direction of Herod's Gate. There was no sound of war, no gunfire, no explosion of shells.

"We've taken the Old City," he said to himself. "We've taken all of Jerusalem."

Even in his thoughts, it was the first time he had linked himself to what had happened here or accepted, as part of his hopes, the hopes of the people around him.

There were women in the street, serving hot coffee and pita sandwiches. "They're for the *chevra*," a woman said.

"I'm a medic," he told her. He still did not realize what he looked like, his clothes stiff with dried blood, his face and hands still unwashed.

The woman stared at him, then gave him coffee and a pita. Chewing the bread, drinking from the paper cup, he walked with the flow of people to Herod's Gate, through the gate, and down the narrow street that led to the Temple Mount. He had no idea where he was going, but they were all going this way, soldiers, civilians, old Orthodox Jews in their long caftans, women, Jewish kids, Arab kids. He had never been in the Old City of Jerusalem before, the ancient city, locked away behind its high walls, forbidden to Jews on the pain of death. He stared with a tourist's curiosity at the narrow, filth-laden cross streets, the old, decaying houses, the Arab inhabitants of the Old City who watched silently as the Jewish throng poured toward the Temple Mount.

And then he walked on to the Temple Mount, facing the golden dome of the Mosque of Omar. The Mount was crowded with people, cheering, shouting, singing, soldiers embracing each other, other soldiers standing in silent prayer, their lips moving, women weeping, old bearded Jews swaying in prayer, children screaming. Sam stood in silence. After a while he realized that he was crying, the tears running freely over the caked blood on his face.

Sam walked from the Old City to his lodgings on Bezalel Street, passing through a city in tears and ecstasy, a city whose population flowed in the other direction, toward the Old City and the Temple Mount. For them it was a beginning; for him it was the end of a part of his life. In the years to come, he would live over the past forty-eight hours, in his dreams and in his waking moments; but now he was strangely quiet within himself, very much at peace with himself. The rooming house he lived in was deserted, a condition he welcomed. That meant the bathroom would be his. He stripped off his pants, shirt, socks, and sneakers, put on a robe, and stuffed the clothes into a paper bag and deposited them in the communal garbage can. Then, with a prayer that the boiler would be working, he filled the tub with hot water, scrubbed himself, saw the water turn rust color from the blood, let it out, filled the tub once more, and soaked himself again. He put on fresh clothes and set out for the Liebermans' home.

Mrs. Lieberman was in the apartment, minding the baby; someone had to stay with the baby; the others had gone to the Old City. How different everything looked today, the street, the house, the living room which was no longer a first aid station!

"Rachel too?" he asked.

"Yes, Rachel too. You're hungry, Shmuel? You'll have something to eat?"

"If you don't mind. I'm starved. I tried to buy some food, but all the shops are closed."

She fried eggs for him and cut thick slices of bread. As he ate, she sat opposite him, the baby in her arms.

"So we've taken the whole city. Here the war is over, thank God."

"Yes, the whole city."

"You were on the Temple Mount?"

"Yes."

"I'll go later, when they come back. It doesn't seem possible. It's like a dream. How was it? Did many of our boys die?"

"I don't know. I hope not." Watching her, he thought of the stout Jewish woman on the plane when he was returning to San Francisco for his grandfather's funeral. He tried to remember her name, but he could not. How alike she was to this Mrs. Lieberman, whom he had met two nights ago, and who was now treating him like her own son!

"Did Rachel say where she was going?"

"I suppose to the Temple Mount. She was your sweetheart?"

"We're very fond of each other."

"But now you're going away, back to America?"

"Yes."

"It's not my business to ask, but how can you do that? How can you go away now? This is your place. Your Hebrew is better than mine. As hard as I try, I can't speak good Hebrew, but yours is like a Sabra's, and if that lovely girl is your sweetheart—" Embarrassed, she stopped suddenly. The baby in her arms began to cry.

Sam stood up. "I have to go now. Thank you for the lunch. It was very kind of you."

"I shouldn't have said what I said. It's not my business."

"You're very kind." He walked over and kissed her cheek. "Thank you again." Then he left.

Barbara did a great deal of thinking on her way to the airport to meet Sam. While the war—which would be known as the Six Day War—was still going on, Sam had managed to get through to her on the telephone, easing her worst fears, and then a call from New York told her that he had managed to catch his scheduled flight. She still had no inkling of what he had been through during the Battle of Jerusalem; he had simply told her that he was well and safe, and that the rest of it would have to wait until he returned to San Francisco. Meanwhile, during the first days of the war, when she had no news at all from her son, Barbara had lived through her own time of fear. She had faced the possibility that her son, her only child, might be killed, that the tiny state of Israel might be overrun and destroyed and that the Holocaust might once more repeat itself; and since she had suggested that he remain there to finish his premedical training, her guilts were painful. For all of her tolerance and compassion, Barbara was a white Protestant in the ethnic classification so deeply ingrained in American society. She had been raised in the shadow of Grace Cathedral, in the building of which her family had been deeply involved; and howsoever she struggled with herself, she had never been able to accept a Jew without some small voice within her reminding her that Jews were different. Even her first husband was not simply a man; he was a man who happened to be Jewish, and like so many American intellectuals, she lived and moved and worked in a world where there were a great many Jews. When she was provoked by a Christian, she was only annoyed; when she was provoked by Boyd Kimmelman, there was a small voice easing the word *Jew* into her mind. Years ago, when Sam Goldberg had been her father's lawyer, she had turned to him again and again in her moments of distress. He was a small, overweight man with a thin circlet of white hair around his bald head; he had comforted her and reassured her and helped her; but always, somewhere in her mind, he was classified separately as that lovely, dear little Jewish man.

These thoughts went through her mind as she drove to the airport. She was Barbara Lavette and her son was Samuel Cohen. Had this always been a wedge driven between them? When her house burned down, she had the feeling that she stood naked and utterly bereft in a world that never made much sense. She had been filled with self-pity, telling herself that she lost her son, lost her home, lost the manuscript on which she had labored so tediously. She was a woman of fifty-three years who had nothing, who had lived a life of romantic illusions, who had bloodied herself battering against the walls of prejudice and inhumanity. Seeing herself this way, she had to fight an urge to return to Dr. Albright, yet when Dr. Albright telephoned her to ask what she could do to help, Barbara said flatly, "We need money for our organization. Otherwise, I am fine." A check arrived a few days later. She had leaped that hurdle, and from that moment, things within herself improved. And in the time of silence during the Six Day War, when there was no news and she had no way of knowing whether her son was alive or dead, she managed once again to come to terms with herself. Even if she never saw her son again, she would go on living; but if she did see him, she would make a new attempt to understand him.

"I suppose," she told herself on this day, "that I

share with most of the human race the need to be of some importance and the suspicion that I am absolutely of no importance. I wanted desperately to be of great importance to one person at least—I suppose because he is of such importance to me. But all that really matters is that he is of importance to me. The rest of it he'll either work out or not." While this conclusion was not terribly profound, it comforted her.

And then, at long last, she was at the gate and he came off the plane and she saw him. She had not remembered him as being so tall. He was wearing blue jeans, a blue work shirt, and a corduroy jacket, with his bag slung over his shoulder. He was burned brown, his sandy hair bleached by the sun, and Barbara thought to herself, How beautiful he is, how absolutely beautiful! Then she was in his arms, and he was telling her that he was all right, that she should not cry, and that he was back to stay.

She didn't confront him with questions. The important things are not easily revealed. All in due time. And he was pleased and delighted with everything he saw, the bay, the dry hills on the way into town, the sailboats scudding before the breeze, the traffic on the highway. He had changed. Something had crumbled his protective walls, and he opened himself to her. At first, it was nothing of consequence. On the plane he had been sitting next to a French girl who spoke no English. "So I began with the French you had taught me when I was a little kid, baby French. It made a great hit with her. No," in answer to her expression, "I didn't try to date her. I'm taking you to dinner tonight—if I can get into my old city clothes."

"Sam, your clothes went in the fire."

"They wouldn't fit me anyway. Then we'll go to Gino's. He'll feed me no matter how I'm dressed."

"Of course."

"And you rebuilt the house?"

"Every bit of it. I drove the contractor out of his

mind because I insisted that it had to be the same funny Victorian house that had burned down. Sam," she said, "I am dying to ask you a hundred questions. I don't know where to begin."

"Then let me begin and we'll get to everything. How's Granny Jean?"

"Seventy-seven, and she's simply beautiful. I don't know how she does it."

"She's a classy lady. It tells."

"It broke her heart that I wouldn't let her come to the airport. I wanted you to myself."

"Absolutely. And you, mom?"

"Up and down. Today's great."

"You look wonderful."

"Thank you." If he had only known that she had spent most of the morning changing clothes, out of one thing and into another, pleading with Jean, "Tell me what to wear. I want to look my best."

"By the way, where are we staying? Can we sleep in the new house?"

"Darling, the furniture hasn't been delivered. We're staying with mother."

"In the mansion? Good. I can stand a few days of posh living."

"I think the house on Green Street was quite posh."

"Absolutely," he agreed. "What do you hear from the Napa folk? How's Freddie?"

"I haven't seen him lately, but he had a long article on wine-making in the Sunday *Chronicle*. Very erudite."

"I can imagine. Freddie's heavy with erudition. We went into a winery in Israel, and Freddie began to lecture them on what they were doing wrong and why their wine was too sweet. I thought they'd throw him out of the place, but Freddie's such an ultimate, self-confident character that they just listened and agreed. Can you imagine?"

"I'm trying to."

"And May Ling? Has she gotten over Ruby's death?"

"I think so. She practically runs our Mothers for Peace. You know, her mother and father separated."

"Oh, no!"

"Yes. I suppose it's a part of our times. They may get together again, but I haven't much hope."

They went on talking, and Barbara was amazed at how easily it flowed, but it was not until later that evening, sitting in front of the fire in his grandfather's study in the house on Russian Hill, that Sam told them what had happened during the battle. He left nothing out, but related it simply and directly in what appeared to Barbara to be a sort of catharsis. They didn't interrupt him. Both Barbara and Jean sat transfixed, watching the firelight play over Sam as he told them the story of the forty-eight hours. When he had finished, they sat in silence for a while, and then Jean asked him whether he had been afraid.

"Only once, I think, when this Brazilian kid, who was a student too, was killed."

"How awful!"

"No—well, yes and no. I had always heard that if you save someone's life, you go into a kind of a high. One of the regular army medics told me it was like the feeling a doper has with a shot of heroin. Maybe yes, maybe no, and I don't really know how many lives I saved. If I saved any. I hope I did, but I don't know for sure. But I do know one thing, that suddenly it all came together. I was right. I had never been right before, not this way, but that night I had the feeling that I knew why I had been put on earth, in all that madness and hate and killing, I still knew that it was right for me, and that night—God, how I loved those people who were working around me, because it made no difference who the man was, a Jordanian or an Israeli, it made no difference in the way we cared for them."

"And the girl, Rachel?" Jean asked him.

"When I went back to the Liebermans', I was hoping she'd be there. But she had gone. The next day I went to her kibbutz. It was only about fifteen miles from Jerusalem. The funny thing is, I don't really know why I went there. Nothing could have changed. But I felt that I couldn't leave without saying goodby. Well, it was no good. There were only women and children and old men left at the kibbutz. All the others had gone off into the army, and I felt very strange being there. She was kind of cold and aloof, and I could understand that. We didn't even kiss. We shook hands, passed a few words, and then I left. Afterwards, I wondered whether it would have made any difference if I were all Jewish, instead of something that isn't a Jew or a Christian. But that's all right. There has to be an end someday to this dividing the world up into racès and religions and nations, all of them with a license to murder anyone who is different, and I guess that I'm sort of thankful that I'm caught somewhere in the middle."

Fighting to keep back her tears, Barbara said, "It's very late, and you've had a long day, so I think we all ought to go to bed, and tomorrow we can get you some clothes."

"I'm broke, mom. Dead broke."

"Do you suppose you could let me worry about that?"

He went to her and kissed her. "All right—for the time being."

Sally came back to Napa late one afternoon, carrying a small Gucci suitcase and wearing a suit of fawn-colored natural silk. She looked marvelous; indeed, she looked like a movie star. When a movie star enters a room or an airplane or a drugstore, people's attention is focused, possibly because on television the face has been so widely seen, but also because stars walk and move

386

in a way that distinguishes them from everyone else, that tells the watcher that this is a member of the only royalty we have. The star can be stupid, egotistical, frightened, arrogant, schizophrenic, alcoholic, idiotic, even decently bewildered by the fate that has befallen him or her; the star will still have that unique way and manner. Sally had this quality, in spite of the years that had passed since she had been a star. When she walked onto the shuttle plane in Los Angeles that took her to San Francisco, the stewardess recognized it, even though she did not know who Sally was, and gave her the front seat on the right. People pointed to her and whispered. Sally was forty-one, but with stars the passage of years comes easier than with mortal folk. At the Hertz agency, they presumed that she would want a Thunderbird, and while Sally knew exactly how the game was played, she never interfered with it.

Alexander Hargasey, the film producer who had given Sally her first starring role back in 1948, always spoke of her with a kind of awe. "She's got brains," he would say, "more in her little finger than all the rest of them on this lot put together." He had not been exposed to very much intelligence in the people he dealt with, and he had never been exposed to anyone like Sally. Yet her intelligence had been of no help; she always felt moved, used, and frustrated by forces beyond her control, and so often, after she had embarked on some course, she wondered what had pressed her to do what she did. She felt that way today, this afternoon, pulling up in her rented Thunderbird in front of the house she had left almost a year before.

The house in Napa was an old country house that had been built in the nineteen twenties. It had a wide porch that extended around three sides, roses and honeysuckle climbing over trellises, two stories of clapboard with paint peeling. Joe always intended to have the exterior painted, but when he had to face the reality of pulling down the vines that clothed so much of it, he backed away. The front door was never locked, indeed they had no key for it, and Sally entered uncertainly, her heart beating rapidly. The front room was empty. Sally paused there, and then May Ling, who had been upstairs, home today and laboring over applications for college, heard the door open and came down the stairs and saw her mother. She ran to Sally and they embraced, and for a few minutes they simply remained that way, hugging each other.

"You're as tall as I am," Sally said. "You must have grown. Let me look at you."

"Mom, that's silly. I'm almost twenty years old and I've given up growing."

"You're beautiful."

"No, I'm not. Freddie says I look like one of those attenuated Japanese dolls, and he's right. You're the only beauty in this family. You look wonderful."

"Do I? I don't feel wonderful. Where's Danny?"

"Hanging out somewhere. He'll be in soon. You know, we had a housekeeper, but she left. I've been doing the cooking and cleaning. And I am a very good cook. Don't you think that's wonderful? Of course, I had to stop working with Aunt Barbara, but daddy's going to interview housekeepers as soon as he gets around to it."

"Where is he?"

"At the hospital. He'll be back for dinner. He has a new nurse, who's old and cranky. She's very disapproving. She's off today, thank heavens. You know how awful disapproving people can be. I was upstairs with catalogues, because daddy says I must go to college and not waste the rest of my life. You know how he is."

"I know," Sally agreed. Then she heard the door open, and turned around, and there was her son, Danny, breathing hard. He had seen the car pull up in front of the house and had come running, and now he stood staring at her, a sunburned, freckled boy of

388

twelve years, just staring at her with his mouth open. Then he said, "Is that your car, the yellow T-Bird?"

"I rented it," she whispered, pleading that he would come to her. But he didn't move, just stood and stared at her.

She felt very tired and walked to a chair and dropped into it. May Ling watched her, silently, woefully. Sally's eyes filled with tears, and she thought, Your whole world turns to shit, and all you can think of is that your makeup will run.

Danny came over to her and touched her cheek and said, "Don't cry, mom, please."

Sally and her husband, Joe Lavette, differed from each other in many ways. One saw the world symbolically, while the other approached it pragmatically. In Sally's world of symbols, stupidity and injustice lurked everywhere; they were her personal enemies, and in this she was not unlike Barbara, whom she had adored as her heroine since childhood. Joe, on the other hand, regarded Barbara with compassion, and with regret that, in his terms, so much of life had passed her by. Raised by a Chinese mother and Chinese grandparents, Joe had the quality of acceptance. What was could not be changed; it could be sutured, bandaged, helped—but call of that within the framework of what was. Serving as a young army doctor in the South Pacific in World War Two, he healed as best he could; he did not question the war—even as he accepted the war in Vietnam. His role was to heal what could be healed, whereas Sally saw the war as a symbol of man's inhumanity to man. Joe's imperfect world was to Sally a lunatic cage, wherein the stupidity of men brought agony to practically everyone.

This difference between the two of them was strikingly evident today in the manner of Joe's acceptance of her appearance. He had no previous knowledge of her coming; he walked into the house, and there she was, and he smiled with pleasure. Anything else, Sally thought. If he had only been cold and distant at first, or accusing, or deeply troubled—but to smile and accept her presence was simply too much, and she said to herself, "The trouble with the goddamn saints is that they live in the same world we do."

"You look wonderful," he said. "You look absolutely beautiful."

"I don't feel beautiful."

"I'm glad you came. What a wonderful surprise!"

May Ling was in the kitchen preparing dinner. Danny was upstairs. "I'll tell you why I came," Sally said. "I came because you and I are going to talk tonight, and I mean talk."

"Yes, sure, we should."

"I mean talk. You don't know what I mean, because we've never talked to each other."

After a moment, Joe shook his head. "No, I don't know what you mean by that."

"Of course you don't. If you did, we wouldn't be standing here, facing each other like a couple of strangers. Well, I won't go into it now. If you will sit down and try to talk with me tonight, I'll stay. Otherwise, I'll go."

"I want you to stay. I'll try."

May Ling had stuffed and roasted a turkey. It was good, and Sally insisted that May Ling was a better cook than she. Danny, more relaxed now, but still bewildered and confused about the situation between his mother and father, pressed Sally with questions about Hollywood, and she told him and May Ling the story of her first encounter with films, going to see Alexander Hargasey—an old friend of Dan Lavette's—with a script she had written and ending up with a major part in his film.

"Was it good?" May Ling asked. "Why didn't we ever see it?"

"It was terrible, and you were much too young to

390

see films. If it ever turns up on TV, we'll watch it. To my shame."

They went on talking about the film world. Joe was silent for the most part, watching his wife. After dinner, Sally said, "You'll both have to clean up tonight. Daddy and I are going into his office and talk. We have very important things to discuss."

Her two children looked at each other, and then they nodded silently. In Joe's office, Sally seated herself on his old leather couch. Joe sat behind his desk.

Wondering how they had come by two such offspring, Sally said, "They're such damn good kids, it just breaks my heart."

"Maybe we did something right," Joe said.

"Maybe, and maybe I did everything wrong. I don't know. Joe, last week I gave up one of the best parts ever offered to a woman my age. It might have put me up for best supporting actress in the Academy Awards, and I turned it down."

"Why?" Joe asked her.

"You don't know? You can't imagine why?"

"Well, if you mean you didn't want to stay there——"

"Oh, Jesus! Joe, why do you think I married you?"

"I used to think you loved me."

"Why? Why? Why?"

"I never knew. I just never knew. You were the most wonderful girl I ever knew, so beautiful and a lot smarter than I am. I never knew why you married me, Sally. I was just lucky."

"You think you were lucky? You really think you were lucky?"

"Yes."

"Your worst enemy should have such luck! Now, Joe, you listen to me. I'll tell you why I married you. I married you because you are everything I'm not. You're honest and decent and honorable, and I don't think you ever hurt anyone in your entire life—except me."

"You? For God's sake, Sally, that's as wrong as everything else you're saying. I'd die before I'd hurt you."

"Bullshit! Straight unadulterated bullshit! Nobody dies to keep from hurting someone else. You know what you are, Joe Lavette, you are a fuckin' saint, and God help those of us who are married to saints, it's just so much easier to be married to a sonofabitch. Because with a sonofabitch you have it straight on, so when you step in the shit you can pull your foot out. I know I'm talking dirty. I learned to talk dirty when I was ten years old because I heard what other people said. You never hear what anyone says, but when I talk dirty you're shocked into listening."

"Sally, you're getting overexcited———"

"Like hell I am. I said that tonight we're going to talk, and if you don't want to talk, say so, and I'll pick up my lousy three-hundred-dollar Gucci suitcase and head back to that shithole called Hollywood, where I can deal with assholes instead of saints. It's up to you. Either we talk, or else."

"You mean that, don't you?"

"You're damn right I mean it," Sally said.

"All right, we'll talk. I'm listening. You don't have to talk dirty. I'm listening."

"Good. Let me ask you something. When you save a life, whose life are you saving?"

"I don't understand. If it's a patient, I save the patient's life."

"No, my dear. You're saving your own life. You're making it possible for you to exist on this stinking planet, and when I walked out of here, I was saving my own life, and when some poor driven dame finally picks up a gun and shoots the bastard who has been beating up on her, she's saving her own life too. It's all the same damn thing. You feel sorry for Barbara. Maybe a hundred times you've told me how sorry you feel for Barbara, but Barbara's alive and I'm not alive.

Barbara made her choices. All her life she made her choices. That's what it means to be free. That's all it means to be free—to be able to make your own choices, and the essence of what it means to be a woman is that most of us can never make a choice. It doesn't matter that we build our own traps, our own cages; they are still traps and cages."

She finished and sat trembling with her own emotion. Joe was silent.

"I'd like a drink," she said after a while.

Joe went to a cabinet and took out a bottle of Scotch. "Do you want it straight or shall I get some ice and water?"

"I'll have it straight."

He poured a shot, and Sally gulped it down, coughing with the strong drink.

"Do you want some water?"

"No, I'm all right."

Joe returned to his seat behind the desk, chin on his hands, staring at his wife. "Why didn't you ever say this to me before?" he asked her finally.

"Maybe I never put it together before, or maybe I never knew how to get you to listen, or maybe I thought you wouldn't know what the hell I was talking about. When I was a little kid, growing up at Higate, everything made sense. My whole world was there, my father and my mother and my two wonderful brothers and the dogs—just put together like a proper storybook—and you came to work there every summer and I could be in love with this big, inscrutable young man; and then it all came apart. Josh was killed out in the Pacific and you were away patching up the wounded out in the Solomons or some other crazy place, and it stopped making sense and it hasn't made much sense since then. Maybe to you, but not to me. Do you know what I'm talking about? Do you?"

"I'm trying," Joe said. "It's not easy for me to put myself in your place. I'm trying, but it's not easy.

Think of the way it was for me. My father didn't marry my mother until I was fourteen years old. She was Dan Lavette's mistress. He set her up in that little house on Willow Street, where I was born, Dan Lavette's bastard son. Sure, I worked it out as best I could, and he was always a hero, my hero, your hero. Dan Lavette was everyone's hero. Big Dan Lavette—how could you hate him? You say I don't know what makes you tick, but, Sally, how well do you know what makes me tick? You call me a saint, but if you knew the rage and anger and frustration I've lived with, you'd amend that. Still, I had my mother, May Ling, who was the most beautiful human being I ever knew. Her only child. So in some strange way, everything had to be for her. I had to prove it all for her. I had to be the way she wanted me to be. I had to create what she should have had. She was so damned misused, so heartbreakingly misused that I swore to God that no wife of mine would suffer the way she did—and that's screwed up too. So you see I'm trying to put myself in your place, but it's not easy."

"God help us both," Sally whispered.

"Still, I'm not sure I understand why you gave up the part in the picture."

"Because I love you and I love my kids. It's just not enough."

"Loving us?"

"That's right. It's not enough."

"I want you back so much that when I talk to myself, I say I'll get down on my knees and plead—anything, but that doesn't help, does it?"

"No, not much."

"When you left here, it was like being dead. I did what I had to do, but it was like being dead."

"I know the feeling."

"You mean when you were here?"

"No, you damned fool! I mean when I was away."

"What can I do?" he asked woefully.

394

"Acknowledge that I'm Sally. I'm a human being. Instead of thinking of me as your wife or the mother of your children, try to see me as a human being. If you have to operate in San Francisco or in San Diego, or go to a medical meeting in Denver or Chicago, I wouldn't dream of standing in your way. I recognize the need of what you are doing because the whole world recognizes it. But who recognizes my need? Suppose I want to go to San Diego because I'm out of my mind staying here? Would you accept that? Would you accept my going to Hollywood for some crummy little supporting role in a TV thing? That's my need. Could I say to you, Joe, take over because I have to be in Hollywood tomorrow, and just accept that and not weigh it against your need—not force me to run away as I did when I was all over the country speaking for the mothers, and so filled with guilt and resentment at my own guilt that I had to fall into bed with some stupid slob, and then hate myself and hate you and everything else. Every damned marriage I know about is splitting up because a woman gets the notion that she could be alive and human, and then doesn't know what to do with the notion except run. I don't want that, Joe, I swear I don't."

"But what do you want?"

"I'm trying to tell you. I want to be a person."

"You're asking me to turn everything I ever thought about this upside down," he said slowly, seeking words that would spell out his confusion without driving her away. "I'm trying to understand you, believe me, I am, but I'm so bewildered. I tried to explain to May Ling what had come between us, and God help me, I couldn't make any sense of it."

"And now? Do you make some sense of it now?"

"I'll try. That's all I can say—if it will only keep us together. You asked me to talk. I did talk, and I listened——"

"I think we've talked enough," Sally said, getting up

and going to him. "Come on, put your arms around me. I want to cry. Make me feel that you love me."

Jean Lavette was one of those fortunate women who go through life with no illness more serious than a bad cold or an occasional touch of the flu. In addition to that, at the age of seventy-seven, she had all of her teeth, something she attributed to the excellent Boston Puritan stock she had come from. Like so many of Jean's attributions, Barbara simply accepted it without argument or probing into genetic verities. Thus she was disturbed, coming to Jean's house, to find her mother in bed. "And the second day," Mrs. Bendler informed Barbara. "She refuses to have the doctor."

Jean, propped up on three pillows, wearing a mauve, lace-trimmed bed jacket, was reading Isaac Bashevis Singer's novel *The Manor*. "Have you read it?" she asked Barbara, and when Barbara shook her head, "Well, you should. You have all sorts of Jewish friends. All my Jewish friends are dead."

"Mother, what on earth are you talking about? What Jewish friends are dead?"

"Mark Levy is dead and Sam Goldberg is dead."

"Mother, Sam has been dead for almost twenty years, and as for Mark Levy, he died in nineteen thirty, if I'm not mistaken, and you barely knew him and I heard you were never even polite to him."

"Are you trying to be nasty? I'm lying here ill. You might have a little consideration."

"And Milton Kellman is far from dead. Why won't you call him? Why won't you see a doctor?"

"I can't bear Milton. He drives me mad, telling me what I must eat and what I must drink and how much rest I must have."

"Then call another doctor."

"And hurt Milton? He'd never forgive me. He'd never talk to me again."

"I give up. I do give up. Are you really ill?"

"Oh, darling, I don't know. I feel rotten. I don't have a fever, but I do feel wretched and weak and old. And the other day I was down on Market Street and they're tearing it up to build a subway. What is happening to this city with a subway and all those horrible high-rise buildings?"

"It's called progress, mother. And I shall ask Milton to drop by to see you."

"He bores me. Who told you I was never polite to Mark Levy?"

"I think you did."

"Did I? Yes, I suppose it's true. I have changed, haven't I, Bobby?"

"I always thought you were a very remarkable woman."

"I don't know what that means. Will we ever be rid of that wretched Mr. Johnson? I read somewhere that he has a habit of picking his nose. No breeding, none."

"He has worse habits, mother."

"I'm sure. I'm letting my hair remain completely white. I think to tint it mauve or blue is utterly ridiculous."

"It wouldn't suit you, mother."

"Of course not. However, there's no reason why you shouldn't get rid of those gray streaks. You're a young woman."

"I'll think about it."

"I can't stand it when you agree with every silly remark I make," Jean said testily. "You not only have a mind of your own; you have a most unsettling one. Don't treat me as an old woman."

"I wouldn't dream of it."

"There it is again. How are you getting on with your antiwar agitation? Do you need money?"

"We always need money."

"This town is filled with people who have more money than they know what to do with. My accountant says that if you could get a tax-exempt status, you

397

could raise much more. If you're truly desperate, you'll find my checkbook in my dressing-table drawer."

"You've given us enough. And if I may say so, you're giving Sam too much."

"Only what he needs. It's quite amusing. He very seriously signs a note for everything he's borrowed. He insists on it. I do have a codicil in my will wiping out his debts. Has he found a girl yet?"

"Not that I know of."

"Well, there's no hurry about that. He's young enough. I have two very fine grandsons, and I think Danny would be pleased at the way they've grown up. I never expected very much from Freddie, but he's all right. He's beginning to get his head together, as the kids say, and I suppose Eloise and Adam should be given kudos for that. And I don't want either of them in Vietnam. I wouldn't trade one hair of their heads for all the rice in that place."

"We've been lucky so far, mother."

"Well, don't depend on luck. You're the only one in the family who does anything. The rest of them just sit by and let things happen. And now I'm beginning to tire, so just go about your business and you can drop in tomorrow if you have nothing better to do."

Later, Barbara called Dr. Kellman. "Milton, I'm worried," she said to him. "There's something very wrong."

He promised to stop by and see Jean.

Thomas Lavette's lawyers were Richardson, Merrill and Coleman, a very prestigious firm with which he had done business ever since his break with John Whittier almost twenty years ago. Originally Whittier, now dead, had been Tom's partner; when they broke, Tom transferred his business from Seever, Lang and Murphy, who had been Whittier's attorneys, to Richardson's firm, and in the years since then, he and Seth Richardson had become close friends. On the day Barbara visited her mother, Tom and Richardson lunched together in the private dining room in the towering GCS Building on Montgomery Street. Richardson, fifty-seven, two years Tom's senior, a stout, affable man, well versed in the intricacies of corporate law, had reached a point where most of his time was devoted to the affairs of GCS. Tom had taken him into his confidence at the time Barbara's home had burned, and he chided Tom for not coming to him first. "I had intended to," Tom explained. "But when Lucy goes off on one of her direct-action forays, she doesn't give advance notice."

"You should have spoken to me. We do have strings that reach to Washington, even with that oversized Texas dunderhead in the White House."

Now Tom spoke to him, and Richardson listened and then sighed and shook his head hopelessly.

"What are you telling me?" Tom demanded.

"That it won't work. Don't you think I know what you've been living with? But, Thomas, the rich are unique and the very rich are very unique. There are two categories in the United States for whom divorce is most difficult and frequently impossible, the very poor and the very rich. I suspected it might come to this, and I've looked into it. I'm afraid you have to live with it."

"What the devil are you telling me—that the condemned man should eat a hearty meal? I don't need a lecture on social inequalities. The only damned virtue in money is that it will buy anything, and while you're smart as hell, Seth, I refuse to abandon the only faith I have. If Nelson Rockefeller could divorce his wife and marry his light of love, then I can divorce mine."

"The circumstances are different. Oh, it's not a matter of wealth. I admit we're not as big as the Rockefellers, but being in the top twenty-five of the list of *Fortune*'s Five Hundred entitles you to parity. It's just that the circumstances are entirely different. Sure,

399

Tom, you could quote me examples like Tommy Manville and others of his ilk who tossed wives around as if they were poker chips, but these were for the most part legatees who squandered inherited wealth. To put it bluntly, they were in the market for women, and they bought them and sold them. Your own case is very different indeed."

"Suppose you spell it out for me," Tom said.

"All right. When you and John Whittier merged his Great Cal Shipping with the Seldon Bank, you arrived at a financial balance. When you split with Whittier, it was the twelve thousand shares of Seldon stock, originally owned by Alvin Sommers and willed to your wife, that enabled you to force Whittier out of the picture. Lucy voted her stock, but she retained ownership. Today, GCS is a holding company, publicly owned, with three million shares of stock. Lucy owns twenty-five percent of that stock. But that's only the nub of the iceberg. We're a community property state, and that entitles Lucy to half of your acquisitions subsequent to your marriage—which embraces your period of greatest growth. And still we're only at the beginning of the entanglement. It would take the rest of the afternoon to spell it all out. The point is that if you were to undertake divorce proceedings—providing she consented to such proceedings and you did not have to fight and connive for it—she could destroy you. Well, you know your wife better than I do. What would she do?"

A few long moments passed before Tom answered. "Just what you suggest. She'd destroy me."

"There's nothing left between you?"

"Oh, yes. Mistrust and hate."

"That doesn't make it very comfortable."

"To put it mildly. What do you suggest?"

"Somehow, Tom, you have to live with it. Unless she sues for divorce, which might put another face on

400

the matter. It would still be as destructive as hell, but we might have a fighting chance."

"She won't. Why should she?"

"Then you have to live with it. See her as little as you can, put as much distance between you as possible, and live with it. I wish to God I could offer you something better, but I can't."

After the fire, Barbara had found a second-floor loft on Larkin Street which she could rent for a hundred and fifty dollars a month. The place lacked all the conveniences that would make it comfortable, no running water and only primitive toilet facilities on the floor below, but it did have five hundred square feet of floor space in one large room. The women bought sawhorses and planks from Mr. Kurtz, Barbara's contractor. They rented typewriters and pooled their money for stamps, and a boxed editorial, written by Carson Devron and appearing on page two of the Los Angeles *Morning World,* brought in a flood of contributions, over nine thousand dollars, including a three-thousand-dollar check from Carson himself. By the beginning of that year, 1967, Mothers for Peace was back in business, and by the late summer of 1967, the San Francisco *Chronicle* pointed out, with noteworthy objectivity, that "Mothers for Peace, perhaps the least strident of all the national peace movements, has nevertheless become on of the most influential."

Today was Frederick Lavette's first visit to the place. He had been in San Francisco early that day as an invited speaker at a luncheon given by the winemakers association, where he had made a number of friends and a number of enemies.

Tact was not one of Fred's conspicuous qualities. He had taken the opportunity to denounce the California practice of giving their wines French names. "For how long," he had demanded, "must we engage in this deceitful and misleading practice? How long must we crawl to Europe's envy and New York's arrogant claim to taste? Their so-called taste is compounded out of ignorance and insularity. I had the misfortune to be present at a New York dinner party, where certain gourmets —one of whom writes for the New York *Times*— turned up their noses at a bottle of Higate Mountain Red nineteen sixty-four, which I had presented to my hostess, a wine as good as any table wine in the world. They refused to taste it. Not that they could have commented properly had they tasted it, for the gourmets above all others are the victims of the ignorance they berate. But who is to blame? We are. Cabernet Sauvignon is not a California wine. It never can be. It is a wine of Bordeaux, just as Pinot Noir and Chardonnay are wines of Burgundy. The grapes of Médoc and Graves cannot be grown in the Napa Valley without changing their character, and no matter how hard we try, we cannot produce French wine. Why should we? Our wine is superb. I spent two years working and studying in the wine country of France and Italy and Spain. There are great French wines, and there are unworthy French wines. There are great California wines and there are unworthy California wines. We have Napa, Sonoma, the North Coast, Santa Rosa, Shenandoah, Chiles, to name only a few of the places here that produce splendid wine. Isn't it time we stopped lying to the public, catering to this gourmet-inspired worship of everything French, and named our wines for what they are?"

He went on for another ten minutes, and finished to the applause of some of the fifty or so people present and to the angry silence of others who wanted to know who this arrogant young man was and where he had come from. His stepfather, Adam, and Adam's father, Jake Levy, were both present, and Jake stared at Freddie moodily when the meeting was over and wondered whether he had considered the fact that Higate produced both a Pinot Noir and a Chardonnay that they were justly proud of.

"You're absolutely right, gramps. We produce the best red and white wine in California. What we name it is something else."

There were others who confronted him and argued with him, but finally Fred pulled away, and by three o'clock he was at the loft on Larkin Street, where he had promised to meet May Ling and join her in a peace march down Market Street to the Federal Building. He was still euphoric from what he regarded as a well-deserved attack upon the California winegrowers' feeling of inferiority, and coming into the crowded, bustling loft, with its two dozen women, its noise and confusion and sense of urgency, did nothing to lessen his mood.

"What a place!" he said to May Ling. "I never knew you had anything like this going. And you run it?"

"Never. We all run it. Oh, maybe Aunt Barbara mostly, and those two ladies over there, Shela Abramson and Ruth Adams, and I try to be here as much as I can, but with college next semester, I don't know."

"Where are the men and boys? Or don't you allow it?"

"Crying in their beer, I suppose. We allow it. Absolutely. Oh, one or two showed up, but they don't have staying power. Sammy was here for a few days, but this is the first time I've seen you around."

"I'm a working man. Higate Winery pays me ten thousand a year, except that the take-home is a lot less, and for that they get a pint of blood and eight hours a day. Old Jake is a tough coot, and either you produce or you're out on your can."

"Not so. Grandpa is an old darling. Let's get out of here or we'll be late."

"I left my car in the garage. We'll take a bus." Fred studied her as they waited for the bus. Somehow, where May Ling was concerned, he had retained the

403

image of a skinny, attenuated, flat-chested adolescent. The reality—although this was not the first time he had seen her in recent months—startled him, perhaps because this was the first time he had actually looked at her as a woman. She was by no means flat-chested, and hardly skinny. Not an ordinary-looking girl; he had never met anyone who looked quite like May Ling, with her height, her straight shoulders, her tiny features and her black hair, banged and cut square to frame her face. He couldn't decide whether she was very beautiful or very odd-looking. "Somewhere between the two," he told himself.

When they reached Market Street, the parade was already in progress and May Ling and Fred fell into line between two marchers who made room and linked arms with them. The demonstration was not as large as some had been and others would be, but they filled a whole lane of Market Street, stopping the traffic and shouting through at least a thousand throats, "Hey, hey, L.B.J., how many kids did you kill today?" and again, "Hell, no, we won't go! Do you hear us, L.B.J.? Stop the killing, now, today!" At the Federal Building, the crowd was larger, more disorganized. The police had set up barricades and there was some scuffling, and then a woman's voice from the speaker's stand begged for order. "We are a demonstration against violence," the voice told them. "Let's keep it that way."

"Hey, it's Aunt Barbara," Fred said. "What do you know about that?"

"She's great."

Shouting their names, Sam pushed through to join them, explaining that he had been trying to catch up with them since he spotted them at 5th Street.

"That's your mother," Fred said.

"Damn right. Look, children, I'm distributing leaflets and looking for mothers. See you later."

Barbara was saying, from the platform, "We'll sing now."

The voices swelled up, brokenly at first, and then merging into a wave of sound: "How many roads must a man walk down before you call him a man? Yes, and how many seas must a white dove sail before she sleeps in the sand? Yes, and how many times must the cannonballs fly before they're forever banned . . ."

When the demonstration broke up, Fred and May Ling walked back down Market Street toward the garage where he had left his car. Fred had his arm around May Ling's waist. They were both euphoric, feeling the excitement of the demonstration and full of a sense of having been a part of something meaningful. The evening chill was just taking hold, the afternoon fading benignly and gently. They moved down Market Street, through the crowds hurrying home from work, almost absently, both of them unwilling to arrive anywhere specific, content to drift along. Close to the garage, unwilling to let the moment or mood end, Fred said, "I have a great idea. We're both all dressed up, me with this suit and white shirt and tie, no less, all in honor of the winegrowers, and you——"

"Oh, Freddie," May Ling protested, "this is mom's old gray flannel suit. Just a hand-me-down. I look dreadful."

"You look great. Will you listen to me? Let's stay in town and have dinner here in some real stodgy posh place, like the Top of the Mark or the Fairmont."

"Freddie, that's a bundle. You're out of your mind."

"Come on. I can afford it. I'm not dating anyone these days. I'm filthy rich."

"Pop was supposed to pick me up at Larkin Street at six, on his way home from the hospital."

"Then we'll call Larkin Street and leave a message."

"If anyone's there."

"And if no one's there, we'll get there and wait for him."

They were standing on the sidewalk, facing each other. Suddenly May Ling grinned, her whole face

405

lighting up. "Yes, absolutely. I haven't had any real fun in ages. And I'm going to be merciless. I'm going to have oysters and steak and floating island for dessert—the whole, entire bundle, which you have now let yourself in for."

"Right on, and champagne with the oysters, and French Cabernet with the steak, which is treason on my part, but who's going to know, and if that silly restaurant has it, we'll have an Imperial Tokay with our dessert. And I shall buy a fifty-cent cigar, if you can stand the smoke."

"Freddie, it's elegant and we'll be as drunk as lords, but what are we celebrating?"

"Us, you and me, the last of the Lavettes."

"Heaven forbid. You forget my brother, Danny. But it's good enough. Let's find a telephone."

The Top of the Mark was booked full, since it was a tourist month, but they found a table at the Fairmont and everything else appeared as projected except the Imperial Tokay, and they had to make do with a very ordinary Tokay, a single glass of it being all that either of them could manage. "Of course, I knew that," Freddie assured her. "There is no Imperial Tokay in San Francisco, or in most other places either. When Grandpa Jake and Grandma Clair were in Paris, before World War Two, they managed to sell a few cases of our wine to a French wine firm called Lebouche and Dume. A very big deal then. In return Monsieur Lebouche gave Jake four bottles of Imperial Tokay, the real thing from the vineyards of the Emperor Franz Josef. I was just being a smart-ass and trying to impress you by ordering it here."

"You did impress me. You always have."

"You're laughing at me."

"Just a little. I love you, so it doesn't matter."

"What kind of love?"

"Did you ever taste it?"

"Love?"

"No, you dumbbell, the Imperial Tokay."

"Absolutely. When I returned from Europe, Jake opened the last bottle. Liquid sunshine. You know, it's almost impossible to make a good sweet wine. In the whole world, there are only four that are really good, a couple of sherries, the best Hungarian Tokay, and a Chinese wine that I've read about but never tasted—and why are you laughing at me?"

"Because I'm just a little tight."

"I'm a little tight, and I'm not laughing at you."

"That's what mother calls the male infirmity."

"What?"

"Not having eyes in the back of your head."

"You're putting me on."

"Yes."

Driving back to Napa, May Ling said dreamily, "I do wish we weren't cousins."

"I've had the same thought. But then we're not—I mean not entirely."

"How do you take that?"

"We only share a grandfather. It's true that old Dan Lavette was our grandfather, but your father's mother was May Ling and my father's mother was Grandma Jean."

"But Adam is my mother's brother."

"He's my stepfather. Tom Lavette's my biological father, as they put it. So we're not exactly first cousins. You might say semi-first cousins."

"Why are you fussing so about it?"

"Because tonight has been so damn wonderful. I'd like to do it again. And again."

"You can, even if we're cousins."

"I'd also like to go to bed with you."

"Sammy says you've been to bed with half the pretty girls in France."

"Sammy has a big mouth."

"He also says you fall in and out of love as easy as taking off your shoes."

"That's why I didn't tell you I think I'm falling in love with you."

"Nobody falls in love with me, Freddie. I'm too tall and too weird-looking."

"Good God, I'm six one. You're not that tall."

"Not quite."

"And I don't mind you being weird-looking. It's very refreshing."

"Thank you."

"I also think you're beautiful."

"Why didn't you say that first?"

"The real question is, what kind of kids would we have? I wouldn't mind them being Chinese, but genetic freaks are something else."

"Freddie, you're dreadful and you're crazy. What makes you think I'd ever marry you?"

"I'm twenty-five. It's time I got married."

She was silent for the rest of the ride, sitting with her head against his shoulder. When they reached her home in Napa, she reached up, turned his face to her, and kissed him gently on the lips.

"I thought you were asleep," he said.

"Just thinking."

"About what?"

"About what you said. And the next time we talk about it, Frederick Thomas Lavette, you are to be serious or leave the subject alone."

"What are you doing tomorrow night?"

"Nothing. Reading a book. Watching television."

"I'll be here around eight."

"You can come for dinner if you wish. I won't tell mother I have a new boyfriend. I'll just say that my silliest cousin wants to dine with us."

"Your mother's no fool."

"Oh, I know that. And neither am I, Freddie, as you'll learn."

"What the hell! I'll be there. What time?"

"Seven," she said as she got out of the car. "And tonight was just too special. You're a dear."

"I'll be there."

Brooding over his books after dinner, trying to rearrange a pattern of thinking in Hebrew into the chemical, biological, and medical terms necessary to the examinations he would soon be taking, Sam reached out for the telephone, listened, and then said, "Sure. In a moment." Rather than shout, he went down the stairs to where his mother was reading. "It's your brother on the phone."

"Joe?"

"No." He hesitated. "Thomas Lavette." He couldn't say Uncle Thomas. He had met his uncle only once in his life, at his grandfather's funeral.

"Tom?"

He nodded, and then went upstairs and returned the phone to its cradle, dwelling only moments on the oddity of this singular telephone call from a man almost as remote and mysterious in his world as Howard Hughes. He was concerned with no thoughts of anger, like or dislike. Thomas Lavette was simply a shadow at the edge of his vision.

Tom was a good deal more than that to Barbara. They were only twenty-one months apart in age. They had grown up in the same house on Russian Hill, plotted to outwit the same governess, made their first childish sexual explorations together, belonged, as adolescents, to the same riding club in Menlo Park, eaten at the same table for years. The first years are never erased, and even though for twenty years they had only the most formal and intermittent contact, Barbara could never erase the picture of the slender, handsome young man in blue blazer and white flannels who, as she thought of him, appeared to have stepped directly out of the pages of F. Scott Fitzgerald. She had never been capable of hating him, and tonight, hearing his voice, she found herself responding with pleasure. It was not until after she had spoken to him that she considered the fact that the last time they had seen each other was three years ago.

"I want to see you and talk to you," Tom said.

"Yes, of course."

"Tonight? Or would that be imposing?"

"No, not at all. Has something happened?"

"Can I see you alone?"

"Certainly. I'm just sitting here reading. Sam's here, but he'll be in his room. Are you all right, Tom?"

"I suppose so. I'll be there in half an hour."

Barbara put down the phone. "Well, I'll be something or other," she said softly, and then she sat and stared at the past. Sam came down the stairs.

"Everything all right?"

"That was my brother."

"I know."

"Sammy, stay in your room. I don't think he wants to see anyone but me."

"I can live without seeing him."

"I don't want to have that kind of talk," Barbara said sharply. "This man is suffering."

"I'm sorry, mom. I really don't know him."

The man who came into Barbara's living room half an hour later was hardly the young aristocrat out of the pages of F. Scott Fitzgerald. At fifty-five, Tom Lavette looked ten years older, and the change from the last time they had met took Barbara aback. He had gained weight; there were bags under his eyes and folds on his cheeks; his thinning blond hair had turned white and it was carefully combed sideways across his skull. Entering the room, he looked about him in astonishment.

"It's incredible."

"Thanks to Mr. Kurtz."

"Charley Kurtz, the contractor?" He was nervous, standing tightly, clenching and unclenching his fists. Barbara made an effort to keep it light; be amusing;

relax him. Here was a man ready to explode or disintegrate.

"You sent him to me, Tom, for which I can thank you and he will probably hate you to his dying day. He says I took ten years off his life. I made him put it back the way it was. It took him eight months, but here it is."

"Can I have a drink?" Tom asked.

"Sure. Bourbon—if I remember?"

"Just straight with some ice."

She went into the kitchen for the ice. When she returned, he was staring at the wallpaper, touching it.

"I found it in an old hardware store in North Beach. It had been lying on their shelves for years, and I bought their whole stock for twenty dollars. Valid Victorian. It must have been printed before the earthquake. The black horsehair stuff came from a little shop in Napa. I must admit it became an obsession with me. I don't know why I had to put the whole thing together again, it's such a funny old house, but it's my cave and my refuge. A psychiatrist I know says it's my permanent reaction to the mansion on Russian Hill. Be that as it may. If it weren't for the heartbreak and shock and the loss of my books and pictures and letters, which I can never replace, I'd say it was all to the good. At least the plumbing is new. The old plumbing was always coming apart at the seams."

Tom gulped his drink, looking around him and then sat down on the horsehair sofa, staring at his sister. "I burned it down," he said slowly and distinctly.

Barbara had no response to this, wondering whether he was drunk or whether this was some kind of symbolic apology.

"I said I burned it down. Didn't you hear me?"

She sat facing him. "I heard you, Tom. I haven't the faintest idea what you mean."

"A sonofabitch was sent here from Washington by

411

our President, and he informed me that either I closed you down or they'd cut GCS out of the war boodle. I told Lucy, and she hired a torch to burn your house."

For a few moments, Barbara did not react, and then she said, quite calmly, "That makes no sense, Tom. It sounds like something out of a bad film."

"My whole life is something out of a bad film."

"Are you telling me that Lucy hired someone to burn down my house?"

"Yes."

"Did you know about it?"

"Only after it happened."

The whole notion was preposterous; it made no sense. This was her brother; he was overwrought, harassed, troubled, but he was not a monster. His wife was an obsessive, angry woman, but Barbara had known her all her life. They had gone to the same private school; as young girls, they had met at dances and parties. Such people don't burn down houses—or do they? There was a war going on in Vietnam; whose war was it? Who made it, serviced it, continued it? Who was guilty and who was guiltless? She had to see this thing through, calmly, quietly. Her brother had come to her. The house had burned and been rebuilt. Other things had burned and would never be rebuilt. The dead were dead; there was no Mr. Kurtz to reproduce them from photographs. Her mind was wandering. If her house had not been photographed and included in a book of old San Francisco frame houses, it could never have been rebuilt. And suppose May Ling had been sleeping in the house when it burned down? She had frequently stayed there overnight.

"Say something. Don't just sit there."

Yes, she had to say something, make some observation. You are a total bastard, my brother. Emphatic, but incorrect. He was not a total bastard. It was just possible that no member of the human race was a total bastard. They were all trapped in the same agony.

412

What should she say to him? We are all part of the same agony, my brother? She was apart from herself, seeing herself as a character in something she was writing, contriving, and stopped, blocked, because no words could satisfy the moment.

"You said before," speaking slowly, quietly, carefully, "that this man from Washington threatened to cut GCS out of the war boodle. What did you mean?"

"I meant that our profits from this stinking war are enormous. We sell oil and ship it to the services in Vietnam. We ship food and we ship munitions."

"Why do you call it a stinking war, Tom? It's a good war. It's making you richer."

"Don't go pious on me, Barbara. Our father, the great Dan Lavette, made his millions out of two wars. In World War One he did the same damn thing I'm doing, and in World War Two, he built the ships."

"Then why call it a stinking war?"

"What do you want me to say, that I love this war, that I'm up to my elbows in blood and getting my jollies out of that? I didn't make this war."

"Who made it, Tom? You burned my house. Tell me how many houses were burned in Vietnam, with no insurance and with no Charley Kurtz to rebuild them."

"Is that all you've got to say to me?"

"What can I say to you, Tom? You come here after nine years to tell me that Lucy had my house burned. I'm trying to be sensible, not judgmental, but for God's sake, I'm a human being. I feel, I hurt. I've tried to forget other things that happened, and I suppose in time I'll be able to look at this dispassionately. Now I can't. I'm trying to sit here and convince myself that my brother is not a complete bastard, but it's not easy."

"I'm trying to face up to things, for once in my life."

"Admirable," Barbara said coldly. "Do you love her, adore her?"

"Lucy? I hate her guts!"

"Why don't you divorce her?"

"I can't. Don't look at me like that. I can't. I'm trapped. If I divorce her, she can tear GCS to shreds. Don't ask me to explain that. It's a fact, as my attorney demonstrated to me at great length. If you want revenge, don't look any further. It's right here."

"I don't want revenge."

"It's free for the asking. I had to talk to someone or go out of my mind. Yesterday, I hired someone to kill her. It's what they call putting out a contract."

"Oh, no! No!"

"You can rest easy. I had a failure of nerve and rescinded the whole thing."

"God Almighty," Barbara whispered, "what kind of a world do we live in where you can hire people to burn houses and murder wives?"

"The same lousy world we've always lived in."

"What do you do? Do you look in the Yellow Pages under killers?"

"There are services. Damn it, Barbara, don't play the innocent. You've been around. You know what goes on."

"I don't want to know what goes on. Why did you tell me this?"

"So I wouldn't be tempted."

"Ah, yes. So you wouldn't be tempted to have your wife killed. God help us both, Tommy."

He stood up. "Thanks for the drink."

"I'm sorry. I'm so sorry," Barbara said.

"About the house—" He shook his head hopelessly. "We all lose things we love. I lost Freddie. I lost Eloise, and tonight I lost you. That makes me quite a loser, doesn't it, Bobby?"

After he had left, Barbara could only think that at the end, each of them had used the childhood name of the other. She thought she knew why, but that was not helpful.

*　　*　　*

Dr. Milton Kellman always felt impressed when he entered the old Lavette mansion on Russian Hill, and this feeling annoyed him. He was impressed, not with the fact that the Lavette house was one of a half dozen of the great old houses left on the hill, but because it was the home of Jean Seldon, who long ago had married Dan Lavette and become Jean Lavette. And Jean Seldon was the daughter of Thomas Seldon, whose huge brownstone castle was one of a dozen brownstone castles that had crowned Nob Hill in the long ago and were the homes of the nabobs who ruled the city and plundered the new land of California. Like a good many San Francisco Jews, he had a special and very un-Jewish feeling of place and identity. He was not an immigrant to a place that was finished. His grandfather had come here at the beginning, when San Francisco was still called Yerba Buena and the town consisted of a few 'dobe buildings and a scattering of lean-tos and tents. Yet in only a few decades, the nabobs and pashas had divided themselves from the rest; they were the hard-bitten, hard-nosed white Protestant Yankees who drove West with a sense of the divine right of conquest, greed, and rule as firmly implanted as the divine right of kings had been in old Europe. Seldon was of this small coterie, and among them, Jean Seldon had been a princess; and Dr. Kellman was old enough to remember, and this memory lingered, so that entering the Lavette house, he was both impressed with his presence there and provoked with himself for being impressed.

And he liked Jean. He liked the game they played, the way they fought each other and sniped at each other and the way Jean hooted at his medical advice. Yet in her eyes he had saved Dan's life when Dan had his first heart attack, and he knew that she was grateful and that she respected him enormously. He was very fond of her, and when Mrs. Bendler opened the door for him, he asked anxiously, "Where is she?"

"In bed."

"Has she been eating?"

"Very little. She says she has no appetite. I've been staying overnight. I don't like to leave her."

"That's good."

He went upstairs. Jean's bedroom door was open. "It's Milton," he said. "Are you decent?"

"I haven't been decent since I was a teenager. Come in, Milton. I suppose my daughter sent you here?"

He drew a chair up to the bed, where Jean lay propped against a mound of pillows, wearing a blue, lace-trimmed bed jacket, and opened his bag, remarking that if he had been invited to her house occasionally, there would be no need for Barbara to send for him.

"Ha! Invite a doctor indeed! You're all so busy making money you have no time for anything else. Anyway, I don't entertain these days."

"More's the shame. It would do you good instead of lounging in bed."

"I'm ill."

"Oh?"

"Not your kind of ill. I just feel rotten. Don't want to do anything or go anywhere."

He shook down his thermometer. "Open your mouth."

"Nonsense. I don't have any fever."

"Either you open your mouth or I'll insert it rectally."

"You wouldn't dare. On the other hand, it would be the closest thing to sex that I've experienced in quite a while. And don't shake your head at me. I can't tolerate prudes."

He held her wrist while the thermometer was in her mouth, and when he removed the thermometer, she said, "I told you. I don't need a doctor to tell me whether I have a fever."

"How do you feel?"

416

"I told you. Rotten."

"What is rotten? Any pains, specifically?"

"No, Milton, not really. I feel weak. No appetite. And when I get out of bed, I tire so quickly. I know I'm an old woman, but that's no reason to feel so weak and depressed. Or is it?"

"You're not an old woman. You're a woman, and still a very lovely one. I'll tell you what I want you to do. I want you to get dressed and I'll drive you to my office."

"Why?"

"I want to give you a thorough examination."

"Well, do it here."

"I can't do it here. I want to go over your breasts and give you a vaginal. I want my nurse present."

"Milton, I'm seventy-seven. In six months, I'll be seventy-eight. Don't be an old biddy."

"I don't trust myself," he said, smiling. "Did you ever read Ben Franklin on the subject of old women?"

"Yes. He was addressing himself to young men, not to silly old fools."

"This old fool will wait outside until you get dressed. And don't be all day about it. I have other patients. And no makeup. You look fine just as you are."

"I don't go outside without makeup."

"I'll wait outside."

Sitting in his car as they drove to Kellman's office, Jean said, "You're really worried about me, aren't you?"

"Just a bit."

"You're a dear man, Milton."

"That doesn't make up for the other things you called me."

"I have no intention of wiping the slate clean. I still think you're a very dear man."

"That doesn't alter my bill. Not one penny."

"Of course not."

The examination went on for over an hour. Kellman

was nothing if not thorough. Then he told Jean to get dressed and instructed his nurse to bring her to his office. There, he asked her, gently, to sit down facing him. He sat behind his desk.

"It's nothing good," Jean said. "You'd make a rotten poker player."

"I'd rather not discuss it just yet, because I want additional tests and some other opinions. I've phoned Mt. Zion Hospital and reserved a room for you. I'm going to take you there now."

"You're quite out of your mind," Jean exclaimed. "If you think I'm going to the hospital without knowing what's wrong with me, you are crazy."

"I told you we'll discuss the whole matter after I get the tests and some other opinions."

"Milton, you just listen to me," Jean said deliberately. "We've known each other more than twenty years. I know something about you. You're the smartest damn doctor in this town, and you know exactly what is wrong with me. Don't give me that nonsense about other opinions and tests. Now let me tell you something about myself, which I would hope you know already. Whatever it is, I want the truth. I don't want to be protected and I don't want to be lied to. And if you can't tell me the truth, I'll find a doctor who will."

He stared at her thoughtfully, his elbows on the desk, his palms together, fingertips pressed against his chin—that way for a long moment, and then he spread his arms, sighed, and said, "All right. If I talk to you, will you promise to go to the hospital?"

"For an operation?"

"No, for tests. I am not lying to you."

"You have a deal, Dr. Kellman. You spell it out for me, and then I'll go to the hospital with you."

"All right. But your conviction that I'm the smartest doctor in town is emotional and has very little basis in fact. I want you to keep that in mind. I can be wrong. Any doctor can be wrong."

"Come on, Milton. I don't want to expect anything but the worst. Then if it turns out to be better, I can be agreeably surprised."

"Very well. This is rotten psychology, but I don't have any other Jean Lavettes among my patients, and we'll break the rules this time. I'm pretty sure you have cancer of the breast, Jean. You want the truth, and I don't know of any other way to put it. If we leave it there, I would raise a very strong possibility of doubt and stress the fact that we have no way of knowing whether what I felt in your breast is a malignancy or benign tumors. Then the biopsy would give us a definite result. But since you want the truth, I can't leave it there. I examined you not too long ago, and the rapid development of your condition appears to indicate something else. You will recall that I spent a good deal of time probing your abdomen, and insofar as I can determine, you have nodules, growths on your liver. That is insofar as I can determine with this kind of examination. That is why we must hospitalize you immediately."

"Then you believe that the cancer has spread to my liver?"

"What I believe is not the point. I don't know. That is why we must get you to the hospital immediately, to discover whether the malignancy has metastasized."

"You're lying to me, Milton," Jean said calmly. "You damn well do know."

"There is no way for me to know. I can only guess."

"And if it has spread to my liver, what then?"

"Why don't we wait until we get to the hospital. We'll know in a few hours."

"Oh no, Milton. We made a deal. You spell it out."

"I have spelled it out."

"No, doctor. I want to know what happens if it has already reached my liver."

"Please don't push me, Jean."

"I am pushing you. I insist."

419

"Very well, my dear. I'm so damn sorry. If it has reached your liver and taken hold, then it's fatal."

Now Jean sat silent for at least a minute, staring at Kellman. Then she asked him, softly, "No chance, no way, no hope?"

"I'm afraid not."

"What does fatal mean? How long will I have?"

"You're presuming on what we don't know."

"Milton, Milton, once you have pronounced the death sentence, you have no right to play games. You're too good a doctor not to know exactly what my condition is. I have said I will go to the hospital. Now please tell me how long I have."

"If it is the liver," his voice dropped, "it could be a month, two months, possibly a year."

"Will I be an invalid until the end?"

"You will gradually lose your vigor."

"And pain?"

"Very little pain."

Jean sat with her eyes closed for a moment or so; then she said, "We'll go to the hospital now." On her way to the hospital, she said to him, "This is between you and me, Milton. No one else is to know, not Barbara, not anyone. The last thing in the world I want is for my friends and family to come around and bite their tongues and mutter platitudes to a dying woman. I have witnessed that scene, and I will have no part of it. I suppose Barbara will discover that I've been to the hospital and she'll be calling you and trying to ferret the truth out of you. We will both tell her that we undertook some tests and the results were negative."

Kellman had never encountered anyone quite like her. He tried to argue, but she cut him short. "No. It has to be this way, Milton."

"You may be bedridden. What then?"

"Let me handle that."

"You don't want Barbara to know you're at the hospital?"

"Not until I've come home."

"Well, I'll try. Barbara's no fool, but perhaps we can work something out that will explain it."

Dressing to leave the hospital the following day, Jean wondered why she had permitted herself to be taken there. She did not require the tests to confirm her condition. From the moment Kellman had finished his examination, she had known what the verdict would be; and from that very moment, she had felt an intense need to be her own woman, to command whatever moments were left and to suffer no needless indignity. Probing her body, poking needles into it, gouging out bits of her flesh, these were indignities. She should have put her foot down firmly and had no part of it. Surprisingly, she found that she felt no real fear, a certain nervousness, one or two moments of intense anxiety, but fear had not taken hold of her, and she wondered whether this was due to her annoyance at Kellman and whether a terrible and morbid fear of death would set in later.

Kellman insisted on taking her home himself, and by then her annoyance with the doctor had dissipated. Kellman, on the other hand, was full of a peculiar guilt, that he should have been the one to tell her, and that he shared a fault of ignorance and helplessness, being one of a profession that had found no alleviation for her illness.

"You've done whatever you could do," Jean said, patting his hand. "Our problem now is to keep this secret, and on that score I'm not so certain of you, Milton."

"Usually, it's the other way round, and the patient's the one who doesn't know. In this case—well, it's hard to be just a physician, Jean. I am very fond of you. I hate myself and I hate what I do, we're so useless, we know so little."

"Milton, don't weep for me. I've had a long and a

421

rich life, and there are worse ways to die. You've been a dear friend and a wonderful mother hen, and shall I tell you something I never told anyone else? Ever since Danny died, almost ten years, I've been fighting my way through a day at a time. I learned to love a man, and it wasn't easy, because in the beginning I couldn't love anything, not myself and not anyone else. But I learned, and in the good years with Danny—there were fifteen of them—I had something that few women have. After he died, I simply stayed on because there was no other place to go. I truly don't care anymore."

"I wish I had your courage," Kellman muttered.

"It's not courage, Milton, it's indifference."

"Well—" There was nothing he could say to that. "Barbara telephoned me. Mrs. Bendler told her you were in the hospital."

"What did you tell her?"

"I told her it was no use to come and see you, since you'd be home this evening. I guess she'll be over to see you."

"And the rest? What else did you tell her?"

"Malnutrition, a general run-down condition. I hate to lie to someone like Barbara."

"Of course you do. You're caught between two strong-minded women, and that's a painful place to be. But thank you."

But Barbara, coming to the house on Russian Hill that evening, was suspicious. "What does malnutrition mean? I'm surprised at Milton."

"It means I've been eating too little and the wrong food. It happens when you get to be my age, my dear. Milton has given me all sorts of pills and tonics, and you are not to worry about me."

"When have you ever allowed anyone to worry about you?" Barbara demanded. "You're the most headstrong and arrogant woman I've ever known. And I do love you," she added.

"That's very nice," Jean said. "Children today are so

preoccupied with hating mothers and fathers that to hear you say you love me is like a breath of fresh air."

"I should think you would have known, even if I hadn't said it."

"I think I would have. Now for the next few weeks I'll be housebound and spending a good deal of time in bed. Milton prescribes rest. So if you can get those two grandchildren of mine to come by and spend a few minutes with an old lady, I would appreciate it."

"They'll come by," Barbara said.

Over the next weeks, Jean's strength decreased rapidly. She did not enjoy entertaining in her bedroom, and each day she dressed carefully and made her way downstairs. If the weather was good, she would sit on the balcony, which was a sort of cantilevered terrace, with a wonderful view of the bay and the Golden Gate Bridge and the hills of Marin County. A thousand times she and Dan had sat there, breakfasted in the morning, dined at night, watched the sun set in its endlessly varied vortex of color, watched the stars blink on in the velvet-black sky. If the weather was cold and damp, as is so often the case in San Francisco, she would sit in the library, which was the room in the house Dan had most preferred, with its overstuffed furniture and the painting of Dan's first ship, the *Oregon Queen*, hanging over the mantel. Mrs. Bendler would start a fire in the grate, and there Jean could sit for hours, watching the flames. She lived a good deal in the past, both in her waking hours and in her nighttime dreams.

Jean had never attempted to work out a philosophy of life. She had learned and grown out of her own suffering and her own inner agony, and like many sensitive people, she had feelings and insights which she could not articulate. Her dissatisfaction with the condition of the world was not ideological; she had no theories or utopian dreams, and unlike her daughter, she had neither the desire to change things nor the confidence to think that she could. She had no explanations to go along with her sense of the disintegration of the society around her, only an awareness of disintegration and change. The cruel war in Vietnam was beyond her comprehension, yet its horror reached her and touched her, and out of her own background and breeding came her contempt for the men who ruled the nation. The city, her beloved San Francisco, where she had lived all her life, was no longer the city of her childhood or youth; now it was bound over with six-lane concrete highways, overburdened with high-rise office buildings and apartment houses, swarming with new people and new trends, sects, and movements which she read about without understanding. The past was better, easier, more comprehensible. In the past she could remember Dan, waiting to pick her up in front of her father's house, sitting in a one-horse chaise, all decked out in white flannels and a blue jacket, twenty years old and ready to conquer the world—and conquer the world they did, the world that had gone away with time.

But her strength waned, and very soon that time came when she couldn't leave her bed. When Dr. Kellman came to see her, she said to him flatly, "Is this it, Milton? Am I dying? How long?"

He would not or could not answer her question as she wished it to be answered.

"How can I keep up this charade of malnutrition? Barbara knows there is something very wrong."

"Perhaps we should tell her."

"I'd rather you didn't."

When the doctor had left, Jean called Boyd Kimmelman and asked him to come to see her, to bring with him her will and all else that pertained to her estate, and to say nothing about it to Barbara. They made an appointment for the following day.

Boyd had not seen Jean for some months. He had been told by Barbara what she knew and what her suspicions were; still, he was taken aback by Jean's appearance. Her face was lean, her cheeks sunken, her arms and hands fleshless. He had never thought of Jean as an old woman before. She was very much a frail old woman now.

"Sit down, Boyd," Jean said, studying him with interest. "Pull a chair up to the bed. My voice is not what it was and neither is my hearing. Don't mind my staring. I look at everything and everyone now as if I am seeing things and people for the first time."

"I should have come by to see you," Boyd said. "Barbara told me you were run-down——"

"Don't apologize, and I'm sure Barbara's suspicions go further than that."

"Yes, I guess so." He drew up a chair and sat down.

"The truth is, Boyd, that I am dying. I have cancer. It's incurable, inoperable, and it's spread through my body. I hate to shock you, but it has to be said."

"But surely——"

"No!" She interrupted. "We'll waste no time with platitudes or sympathetic gestures. What I said is a fact. You are the only one in the family who knows. I say in the family, because while marriage is somewhat out of style these days, you've been going with Barbara and sleeping with her for years now. And today, we have a good deal of work to do, as much as my strength will sustain. So let's get down to it. The will first."

"Yes, I brought the copies of your will."

"Whatever we decide to change, Boyd, I want done here and now, so that I can sign it or initial it or whatever you do about such things. Is that understood?"

"Yes, certainly, Mrs. Lavette. If anything is very extensive, I'm sure you have a typewriter somewhere in the house."

"Nothing so fancy. You do have a fountain pen?"

Boyd was attempting to maintain his equilibrium, but was losing it more quickly than he could reenforce it. He had walked into a room to be told flatly, by the mother of the woman he loved, as she might refer to the weather, that she was dying. He had also been instructed, in the manner in which a schoolboy is instructed, to display no sympathy and to express no regret. On top of that, he had been asked, in a critical manner, whether he had a fountain pen.

"It's all too much, isn't it?" Jean said to him, smiling at last. "Dear boy, there is no way to treat a dying person. We live in a country that never faces the fact of death, even though we have become so competent in inflicting it. Don't be troubled."

"I am troubled. Good heavens, as you yourself pointed out, you're practically my mother-in-law."

"Which should make it easier. Now let's get down to the facts of the will. I understand that my estate, apart from this house and its contents, amounts to about two million dollars."

"That's about correct," Boyd agreed. "Stocks, bonds, and cash in your bank account. But the house, considering your collection of paintings, comes to a good deal more than that."

"All right, we'll discuss the house first. It doesn't belong to our time. I've lived here because it's filled with memories, but it's a relic of another age, and here, on Nob Hill and Russian Hill, such relics are no longer tolerated. Barbara will never use it, and my will already provides for its sale. There is no mortgage, and Harvey Baxter assured me it will bring enough to pay the estate tax."

"Most likely. But I'm surprised you didn't ask Harvey to come here instead of me. He's better acquainted with your affairs."

"Harvey is an old woman, and I couldn't bear to have him weeping over my bedspread. Now about my paintings. Please read me what is specified in my will."

" 'The Piet Mondrian and the Picasso *Blue Woman* I leave to my dear friend Eloise Levy, who has been

426

like a daughter to me—' " He broke off and asked, "Does that identify the Picasso sufficiently? I presume there is only one Mondrian?"

"Oh, yes. I have two Picassos, and each is titled."

" 'To my daughter, Barbara, I leave the painting of the *Oregon Queen*, the Winslow Homer *Fisherman*, and the two paintings by Thomas Eakins.' Are there only two?" he asked.

"Only two? My dear boy."

"Well, my knowledge of art is limited. The rest of your paintings, Mrs. Lavette, are to go to the San Francisco Museum of Art."

"Which, heaven knows, they need desperately, considering what they have there. Well, I'm changing that somewhat. I want to select two for the boys, one each for Freddie and Sam. We can get to that later. The main change has to do with a bequest to Sammy. I was going to leave him a considerable amount of money or stock or whatever, but if I do that, Freddie will be hurt, and to leave money to Freddie is ridiculous. I'm sure Tom will include him, since Barbara tells me Tom and his wife are no longer even on speaking terms, and aside from that, I hear that Higate is on the way to becoming one of the most important wineries in the state. So I want Sam's bequest eliminated. It is all to go to Barbara, with the exception of ten thousand dollars to Mrs. Bendler, who has been very good to me, and Barbara can decide what Sam should have. But—" She paused, observing Boyd thoughtfully. "Do you influence her?"

"Barbara?"

"Yes."

"Not if she has her mind set on something. No one does."

"I commend your honesty. My daughter is a most peculiar woman, to put it mildly. My father left her fifteen million dollars, which she gave away, and since she is a product of a Seldon and a Lavette, it proves that common sense is not hereditary. Can you make it impossible for her to give away the money I leave her?"

"Yes, that can be done. We can put it into a lifetime trust. But," Boyd said, after a moment's pause, "that will give her only the income."

"I'm sure that will be ample. It has been for me, and my tastes are more expensive than hers."

"You will need executors for the trust."

"I think you and Harvey are adequate."

They continued to discuss the will and its details for another half hour, at which point Jean was completely exhausted. Boyd sat down at her dressing table to write in the changes, and Jean watched him, wondering idly what kind of a man he was, not his surface or his manner or his mind, but deep down underneath, where a human being may have an essence unknown even to himself. Not that it was too important to her at this moment; she had cast loose already. She had brought something into this world, not too much, but something that could be measured in the scale of mankind. Barbara would discover what kind of a man Boyd was, for better or for worse. To have a daughter like Barbara was not a small thing, not an inconsequential thing; it was the spinning of a thread that would go on, and even Tom was a thread that would go on, spinning through Freddie, as Barbara's did through Sam. It was all right; as Dan had once said to her, speaking of Barbara, "We must have done something right." There was no happiness in the legacy of the rich, but that was a secret. Life was filled with secrets; death has only one secret.

She was dozing off, slipping into that warm space between sleep and waking, where flashes of the past assume a reality not totally dreamlike, when Boyd finished.

"Mrs. Lavette?" he asked softly. "You must sign this. Your housekeeper and I can witness it."

"Oh, yes. I was dozing. I tire easily." She managed to sit up, so that she could initial and sign her name. "My condition," she said to Boyd, speaking slowly and painfully now, "is a confidence between myself and my attorney. You will respect it as such. I don't want Barbara to know—not yet."

"Can I tell her I was here?"

"Not yet. No. And Boyd?"

"Yes, Mrs. Lavette?"

"My daughter is a remarkable woman. I think you are a fortunate man."

"I know I am." He bent over and kissed her, feeling her hand tighten on his with unexpected strength.

After he had left, she said to herself, "Let go. There's no reason to stay anymore." There was pain, not too much, but pain. She took two of the yellow pills Dr. Kellman had left for her. They were very effective and made her drowsy, and she slipped back once more into that warm state between sleep and waking.

When she came to see her mother a few days later, Barbara knew, even though Jean still would admit to nothing more than weariness and weakness. An hour later, Barbara stormed into Kellman's office. "My mother is dying! Do you know that?"

"Sit down, Barbara," he said. "Please, sit down." Something in his voice broke through her anger. "Yes, your mother is dying."

"And you know this?" Milton, how could you?"

"Your mother believes that there are some things a person must do alone. Dying is one of them. Now if you will calm down and sit down, I will break my word to your mother and tell you what the situation is. It hasn't been easy for me." Barbara did as he asked, and then he told her how it had come about. "It wasn't

429

only my opinion, Barbara. I called in two of the best people at Mt. Zion. We had biopsies and X-rays. It is not operable and there is no treatment. Your mother is a very forceful and unusual woman, and she exacted a pledge from me that I would tell no one."

Her face streaked with tears, Barbara nodded.

"When you see her again, please don't let her know that you know. This is something she is deeply sincere about."

Barbara agreed. A week later, Jean died. Barbara was with her. Jean simply closed her eyes and whispered, "I'm very tired. I think I'll nap for a while."

"Why," Joshua wondered, "am I the one who has to build the fire?" He was tolerated. As Fred's younger brother, he had always felt that he was simply tolerated.

"Because it's cold," Fred explained. He was sprawled out with his head on May Ling's lap.

"I'll build the fire," Dan said.

"You will build nothing," Joshua told him. "You are here on sufferance, permitted to be among your elders and listen to them. I build the fire because those two idiots"—nodding at Sam and Fred—"don't know how to build a fire, and if they did, they would be too lazy to do it."

"Is it really an Indian fireplace?"

"Asking questions," Joshua warned him. "You are being tolerated. No questions." Finally Joshua had joined the elders.

"I'm thirteen years old."

"Stop being a bully," Carla told Joshua, and then assured Dan that it was not a real Indian fireplace. "Joshua's father built it when he was a kid, I guess about thirty or thirty-five years ago."

"Do you remember the first time we built a fire here?" Sam asked Carla. "I couldn't have been more than ten years old, and that seems like an eternity ago—and thirty years—"

"A time sense is a highly subjective thing," Fred informed them. "For a child, a day is an eternity. At young Danny's age, a month is still a long, long time. At our age, we're dealing with years, but they still seem to be pretty long. But, you know, when I talked to Grandma Jean before she died, she said that when she looked back in her memory to half a century ago, it was as if only a moment had passed."

"Half a century ago," Sam said. "Nineteen eighteen. That's pretty heavy, to think of nineteen eighteen as only a moment ago."

"It's very upsetting," Carla said, moving closer to Sam. "I hate to think that way. It's frightening."

Sam put his arm around her. "My dear child, fear nothing. You will be young and beautiful forever."

"What is this dear child thing, Sammy? I'm three years older than you."

"I know. That's why I never asked you to marry me."

"You're absolutely an expert in bullshit, aren't you?"

"No, my dear. Freddie's the expert in bullshit."

"Anyway, no marriage for me—ever."

"Why?" asked May Ling.

"I have my reasons."

"When it comes to women, Freddie's the grasshopper type. We're giving it a year. If he still wants it then, well, maybe. Otherwise, we part friends."

The fire was burning brightly now. Fred rolled over, and then let out a yell. "Damn you, Josh, you didn't bring those lousy marshmallows up here again! You're not going to burn them black and pass them around! It's obscene."

"Nostalgia," Joshua said.

"I love roasted marshmallows," Danny said.

"My brother's the only really nice person here,"
431

May Ling said, "and you all treat him rotten. Poor Grandma Jean. What a crew of depraved descendants!"

"Oh, no," Dan protested. "They're cool."

"What did you mean, calling me a grasshopper?"

"I was only alluding to your polygamous tendancies."

"Polygamy, my love, is a state of multiple marriage. I've never even been married once."

"By the grace of God," Sam said.

"You, sir," Fred told him, "are a sanctimonious fraud."

"Among other things."

"Do you want a marshmallow?" Joshua asked, holding out a flaming blob.

"Take it away. The sight of it sickens me."

"Anyway, Carla," May Ling said, "no marriage *ever* is a little extreme. How do you know?"

"If you had seen as many Mexican wives as I have being pushed around and beaten up on and knocked up every nine months, you might feel the way I do. I'm working with the Seaside Repertory Company, and they pay me sixty dollars a week, and I'm doing just fine. And if Hollywood ever decides to employ Mexicans, I might have a shot at that."

"You're really hooked on the self-pity bit," Sam said. "And why the devil do you keep calling yourself a Mexican? Your family's been here in Northern California seven generations. Maybe a Chicana, but you're no more Mexican than I am."

"Chicana! Chicana!" Carla exclaimed. "You Anglos have everything down pat, except a little brains and sensitivity."

Leaning over and kissing her, Sam said, "Forgive me, but I'm no Anglo. I'm a Semite, so how could I be an Anglo?"

"Yes, like I'm Chinese."

432

"I'm Chinese," May Ling said.

"Not me," Dan said. "I got freckles. Chinese don't freckle."

"There speaks a voice of wisdom," Freddie observed. "It's an interesting fact that the older we get up here around this fire, the more idiotic our conversations become. At this rate, in our forties, we'll be slobbering sheer gibberish."

"So be it with the children of the pioneers," Sam agreed. "The Levys and the Lavettes crossed this great continent and planted their seed in the green hills of California. Little did they know what fruit would come forth."

"You two are absolutely absurd," May Ling decided. "Of course it was to be expected. Anyone who would look around at the lot of us, noting our mutual characteristics say ten years ago, and then name us the wolf pack—well, he had to be a total idiot. Can you imagine—wolf pack."

"Is that what you called yourselves?" Dan asked. "Fantastic. The wolf pack."

"Who wants a marshmallow?" Joshua asked.

"Who did invent that name?" Carla wondered. "I don't remember."

"I did," Fred sighed. "I had a spell of reading Jack London then. Well, you live here and you read Jack London, what would you expect?"

"Freddie, that's very noble and honest of you," May Ling said. "If you'll stop falling in love with every cute blonde you see, I'll marry you."

"I haven't been in love with anyone else for six months. I'm becoming as sad and serious as Sammy. Will you stop eating those damn marshmallows," he told Josh. "You'll blow up like a balloon."

The setting sun now touched only the high lip of the hills facing them across the shadowed valley, and the gash of gold and red was so startlingly beautiful that all conversation stopped. The color lasted only moments.

It was like turning off a great light switch that plunged the Napa Valley into darkness. Below them, lights twinkled on in the houses of Higate, and above them the stars began to appear.

"This is the most beautiful place in the world," May Ling said softly.

"It's the only place I've ever been happy," Carla said. "Out there it's them. It's always them. Here it's us, but we're a fraud. We come up here and pretend that out there doesn't exist. We try to pretend we're kids when we come up here, but we're not kids. Ruby stopped being a kid when they murdered him in Vietnam, and Sammy stopped being a kid in Jerusalem, and with Freddie it happened long ago down South. And when did May Ling and I stop? A long, long time ago, and now the three of you are registered for the draft and we count every lousy day before they decide to take you. And I work for that lousy Seaside Repertory Company, and every week it's: "Just be patient, Carla, and we'll be doing a Spanish thing one of these days, just be a good girl and type scripts and prompt actors. Spanish! Seven generations in this country, and I wait for a Spanish part!"

She burst into tears, and Sam drew her closer, stroking her hair. Carla was not articulate. Tonight was the first time he had ever witnessed an outburst of words and emotion on her part. He wiped away her tears, kissed her, and whispered, "Come on, baby. You are loved. You are deeply loved."

"I heard," Joshua said morosely, "that they're going to start calling up college kids."

"Great," Sam said. "That's the kind of thought we need right now."

"Well, you got to think about it." Then they were silent for a time, while the night darkness deepened. Joshua, feeling put upon, built up the fire and stared into it. He had already made up his mind that if he were to be drafted, he would go, but he felt it was no

434

use to tell that to the others or to try to explain to them why he must go. He knew what it would do to his mother, but that couldn't be helped either; and far from being able to explain it to anyone else, he had trouble sorting out in his own mind the threads that might lead him into the army and conceivably to Vietnam. It had something to do with the fact that his father had taken part in the Normandy invasion, had fought his way through France, had been badly wounded, and had finished the war as a major in the United States Army, with all of his promotions field promotions. Adam never spoke of the war, but Joshua knew, just as he knew about Adam's brother, after whom he had been named, and who had died in the Pacific in the same war, just as he knew about his grandfather, Old Jake, who had fought in France in 1917 and 1918. It had nothing to do with any military or aggressive proclivities on his part; he was the most easygoing of all of them; it was simply deep-rooted in his mind as a matter of fate. If it was to be his fate, that was all right. He would follow it through. He didn't disagree with Fred or Sam; he just knew what had to be for him.

Sam reached out and touched his shoulder. "It's all right, kid. We'll ride our luck."

"We're not really frauds," Fred said. He had been thinking about Carla's sudden outburst. "We never made this world. We got born into it, and we do the best we can. All of a sudden, we're people instead of being kids, and if we have any sense, we look around us and we realize that it stinks. From Vietnam to those cretins in Washington, it's all one fucked-up beautiful mess, but I wonder whether it's ever been any different. The other day, I was speaking to some real estate developers before Old Jake chased them off. They've been buying up vineyard land up and down the valley for tract houses, and of course Jake says he'll see them in hell or go broke before he sells an acre of Higate

435

land. Well, there's no danger of us going broke, but there's the handwriting on the wall. Jake and pop and mom want everything to remain just the way it is, but that's real kid thinking, isn't it?"

"That's why they used to get so crazy upset about us smoking pot," May Ling said. "Not wine. We could always have wine. But pot was something new."

"No more. Funny, I haven't even thought about pot in years." Sam shook his head. "On the other hand, this is the valley. You say one word against wine, and you're lynched."

"And rightly so," Fred agreed.

"Back in Prohibition days, when Grandpa Jake bought the place, that was it. No wine, no booze in the whole country," Joshua said. "It's unreal, absolutely unreal."

"You can have the past," Fred said. "Right now is pretty damn good." He squirmed around, so that he could look up at May Ling. In the firelight, her face was like a chiseled ivory cameo. She touched his face and then ran her fingers across his lips.

"Dear boy," she said softly, "you talk too much. If you do find a wife, you'll talk her to death."

"I've found one."

"We'll see."

"Idea," Fred said. "Let's the four of us have dinner in town next week."

"What about me?" Joshua asked.

"Next week, brother, you'll be back in Stanford studying viticulture. However, if you can find a lady acceptable to your elders and you don't mind driving up, we'll be happy to have you join us."

Dan, lying on his stomach, chin propped on his hands, respectfully silent, listened to the two young women and the three young men with awe and admiration. He was grateful that they permitted his presence. Someday—yes, someday. All things were possible someday.

* * *

The world turned, and spring came to the year 1968. In San Francisco, Lynda Johnson Robb, the President's daughter, was ordered off a cable car for eating an ice cream cone. It attracted more attention than an earthquake some months later in Iran that killed twelve thousand people. In Memphis, Tennessee, Martin Luther King said, "I'm happy tonight. I'm not worried about anything. I'm not fearing any man. Mine eyes have seen the glory of the coming of the Lord." The next day he was assassinated by James Earl Ray. It was a time for assassinations. Two months later, Robert F. Kennedy, candidate for President of the United States, was assassinated in Los Angeles by Sirhan B. Sirhan, a Jordanian Arab. Peace talks began in Vietnam, as they had so often before, and on April 27, there was another peace march and rally in San Francisco. In Oakland, a man beat up his wife because she had joined a women's peace organization.

In San Francisco, in Barbara's house on Green Street, Boyd Kimmelman loosened his belt, leaned back, and voiced his satisfaction. "You are one hell of a good cook," he told Barbara. "Where did you learn? Or does it come naturally?"

"Nothing comes naturally. I learned in Paris, painfully for a kid who didn't know how to boil an egg."

"You've found the way to a man's heart. Have you ever been to Malibu?"

"That's almost a non sequitur. Why do you ask?"

"Jim Bernhard, who's an old friend and a client and lately a successful film producer, has a house in the Malibu Colony, which is a very posh part of Malibu Beach. He has to go away for a couple of weeks, and he asked me whether I'd like to come down and use the house for the time he's gone. He has a housekeeper, so there's nothing we'd have to do but eat and sleep and walk on the beach."

"It sounds enticing."

"You're only lukewarm."

"I've been there. I'm not overfond of the people who live there."

"I presume that's when you were working in Hollywood. Ten years ago. The way they roll over the houses down there, there probably won't be a face you recognize."

"It's Sam's spring break, but I imagine he's planning to spend it at Higate in any case. The organization can get on without me for a few weeks. Let's drive down."

"Wonderful. How about we take old Route 1 and stay overnight at Big Sur?"

It was a quiet two weeks that they spent at Malibu. They went to no parties, entertained no one, and had only a nodding acquaintance with other people in the colony. The house was large enough for two people to be comfortable. Bernhard had left a few days before they arrived, and his housekeeper, an elderly Mexican woman, accepted them entirely, due to Boyd's excellent command of Spanish. She took it for granted that they were married, and they did not disabuse her of the notion. They wore jeans, walked on the beach barefoot, and occasionally dared the cold ocean water. Nights, they sat in front of the fireplace, talking sometimes, silent sometimes, occasionally reading or playing backgammon. They made a point of not turning on the television or reading a newspaper.

One evening, sitting in front of the fire, Boyd observed that they got along nicely. "We both have better than half a century behind us, and still we're a pretty well set up pair. We don't seem to get on each other's nerves, and for a couple in their middle fifties, we have a damn good sex life. We respect each other's independence, and on top of that, I'm totally in love with you and can't think of anyone I would rather have around."

"What's all this leading up to?"

438

"I don't know. I was just thinking that we could get married and probably make a go of it."

"Probably."

"I never told you, but your mother asked me to come and see her after Kellman told her the illness was terminal."

"Did she? Why?"

"Some changes in her will. Nothing important. But I spent the afternoon with her, and we talked a good deal. It was the first time I had ever actually talked to her, I mean more than to pass the time of day."

"But why you and not Harvey Baxter?"

"She said that Harvey was an old woman, and she didn't want him crying on the bedspread."

"Yes, that's mother. Did she also pledge you to care for her poor orphaned daughter?"

"Jean Lavette? Come off it, Barbara."

"I wondered, this sudden offer of marriage. It's been months now."

"I thought I'd wait an appropriate length of time after your mother's death. Here and now, it appears to make some sense."

"I suppose so. On the other hand, what difference would it really make? I'm not much good at marriage. One lasted two years, and the other less than a year, but you and I, we've kept our thing going for how long? It must be eight years."

"That's true. I just hate to keep asking, What are you doing tonight?"

"On the other hand, there's an element of uncertainty that conceivably we both need."

"Oh?"

"Ask."

"What do you mean, ask?"

"You're nice and very clever, Boyd, but not very quick-witted. Ask me what I'm doing tonight?"

"All right. What are you doing tonight?"

"Nothing much, but I'm tired of sitting here in front

of the fire like an old lady. Let's take a walk on the beach."

They pulled on their sweaters, and hand in hand they walked along the beach, watching the surf break. The moon was high and full, lighting the night, and out in the surf, a single fisherman was casting.

"Not that the institution won't continue," Barbara said. "It seems that Freddie is going to marry May Ling one of these days, and Sam is hanging out, as they say, with Carla Truaz, a pretty little Chicana girl you may have seen around the loft."

"Very pretty, dark hair, dark eyes, looks like Natalie Wood?"

"You haven't lost your eye."

"Does he want to marry her?"

"I don't think Sam's ready to marry anyone yet. He's just about got his head on straight, and he has to finish medical school, and then the army may grab him if this insane war isn't over. You do worry your head on the subject of marriage."

"That's something you don't understand about me," Boyd said. "Twenty years ago, when I first went down to Washington to defend you in that rotten contempt of Congress case, I fell in love. From that time until now, all I ever wanted was Barbara Lavette. Now I have you, I live from day to day in fear of losing you."

She stopped walking, turned to him and kissed him. "Poor, dear Boyd. We never have anyone. That's the great illusion, isn't it? We don't even have ourselves. We reach out so desperately because we're afraid, and in this lunatic world, how could any sane person live without fear? I don't know about love anymore. It's the most overused, corrupted word in the human lexicon. But to trust someone, to know that he'll be there when you need him, well, that's pretty damn good. I feel that way about you, Boyd, and somehow I don't think the feeling will change."

440

Boyd thought about it for a while. Then he said, "I think I can live with that."

They walked on, each of them thinking that all had been said that had to be said, and then, since it was getting quite cold, they turned around and walked back to the house.

THE LAVETTES

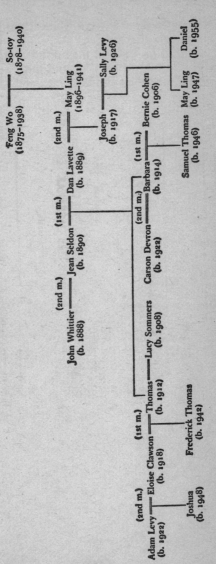

THE LEVYS

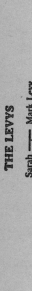
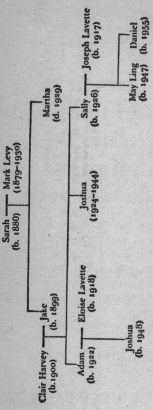

Sarah (b. 1880) — Mark Levy (1879–1930)

Clair Harvey (b. 1900) — Jake (b. 1899)

Eloise Lavette (b. 1918) — Adam (b. 1922)

Joshua (b. 1948)

Martha (d. 1929)

Joshua (1924–1944)

Joseph Lavette (b. 1917) — Sally (b. 1926)

May Ling (b. 1947)

Daniel (b. 1955)

THE CASSALAS

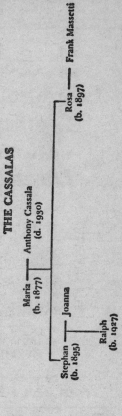

Maria (b. 1877) — Anthony Cassala (d. 1930)

Stephan (b. 1895) — Joanna

Ralph (b. 1927)

Rosa (b. 1897) — Frank Massetti

443

Lose yourself in fabulous, old-fashioned storytelling— the triumphant *Lavette Family Saga*

_____	#1 THE IMMIGRANTS	14175-3	$4.50
_____	#2 SECOND GENERATION	17915-7	4.50
_____	#3 THE ESTABLISHMENT	12393-3	4.50
_____	#4 THE LEGACY	14720-4	4.50
_____	#5 THE IMMIGRANT'S DAUGHTER	13988-0	4.50

from HOWARD FAST

At your local bookstore or use this handy coupon for ordering:

DELL READERS SERVICE—DEPT. B1394A
6 REGENT ST., LIVINGSTON, N.J. 07039

Please send me the above title(s). I am enclosing $ _____ (please add 75¢ per copy to cover postage and handling). Send check or money order—no cash or CODs. Please allow 3-4 weeks for shipment.

Ms./Mrs./Mr. _____

Address _____

City/State _____ Zip _____

See for yourself why

HOWARD FAST is called one of the best novelists this country has produced

Fiction

_____	MAX	16106-1	$3.95
_____	THE OUTSIDER	16778-7	3.95
_____	SPARTACUS	17649-2	4.50

Nonfiction

_____	THE JEWS: Story of a People	34444-1	4.50

 At your local bookstore or use this handy coupon for ordering:

DELL READERS SERVICE—DEPT. B1394B
6 REGENT ST., LIVINGSTON, N.J. 07039

Please send me the above title(s). I am enclosing $ _____ (please add 75¢ per copy to cover postage and handling). Send check or money order—no cash or CODs. Please allow 3-4 weeks for shipment.

Ms./Mrs./Mr. _____

Address _____

City/State _____ Zip _____